Margaret Thornton was born in Blackpool and has lived there all her life. She is a qualified teacher but has retired in order to concentrate on her writing. She has two children and four grandchildren.

Her first novel, *It's A Lovely Day Tomorrow* ('a gentle novel whose lack of noise is a strength' *The Times*), was runner-up for the Netta Muskett Award, and is also available from Headline as is her second novel, *A Pair of Sparkling Eyes.*

Also by Margaret Thornton

It's A Lovely Day Tomorrow
A Pair of Sparkling Eyes

How Happy We Shall Be

Margaret Thornton

KNIGHT

First published in 1994
by HEADLINE BOOK PUBLISHING

First published in paperback in 1995
by HEADLINE BOOK PUBLISHING

This edition published 2002 by
Knight an imprint of The Caxton Publishing Group

10 9 8 7 6 5 4 3 2 1

ISBN 1 84067 412 1

Phototypeset by Intype, London
Printed and bound in Great Britain by
Mackays of Chatham plc, Chatham, Kent

Caxton Publishing Group
20 Bloomsbury Street
London WC1B 3JH

For Barbara and Celia, my college friends, who may detect similarities to a certain training college in West Yorkshire. My thanks to you both for our continuing friendship.

The towns of Leeford and Castleburn and the training college which Patsy attends are fictitious places, although readers may find in them many similarities to existing Yorkshire towns. Blackpool, however, is quite unmistakably Blackpool, as I remember it in the fifties.

Chapter 1

Patsy was relieved when the train finally pulled away from the station. Partings were hell and the sooner you got them over with the better. Besides, she was running out of things to say to her mother. For the last few minutes their conversation had been nothing but inconsequential chit-chat. And Mum did fuss so . . .

'Now, are you sure you've got everything you need, love? You've remembered to pack your ration book? Goodness knows how much longer we're going to need those wretched things. The war's been over for seven years and they still won't let us get rid of them.'

'Yes, Mum. I've got it here.' Patsy smiled as she patted her imitation leather shoulder bag. 'And before you ask, yes, I've got a clean hanky too.'

Jenny Bradshaw smiled as well, but Patsy could see just the trace of a tear glinting in the corner of one of her greenish-brown eyes. 'Yes, love, I know I fuss,' Jenny said, 'but you'll have to forgive me this time. It isn't every day that I have a daughter going to college, and you know you've never been away from home before – for any length of time, that is.'

'Good gracious, Mum! Anyone would think I was travelling to Timbuctoo,' Patsy replied. 'Leeford's only about fifty miles away. Just a hop, skip and a jump. I could be home in a couple of hours.'

'Yes, but they won't let you come home whenever you feel like it, will they? A couple of weekends a term, that's all you're allowed. They want to make sure you get on with your studies. You're a lucky girl, you know, Patsy. I never had the chance to do what you're doing. Not that I was brainy enough, not by a long chalk. But your Auntie Violet was a clever girl all right. She'd have given anything to go to college and be a teacher.'

Patsy nodded, but she didn't answer. She had heard it all before. Violet seemed to be doing very well in Vermont in the USA, with her husband and three children. She was very happy and prosperous, too, it seemed from all her letters. Patsy was quite sure that her aunt no longer had any regrets that she hadn't fulfilled her girlhood ambition to become a teacher.

'And you've put your money away safely, haven't you, love, the pound notes that your dad gave you? You can perhaps get a taxi when you get to Leeford. It'll save you lugging your suitcase on and off those trams.'

'Yes, Mum. I've got it safe.'

'And don't forget to eat the sandwiches I've put up for you. They're salmon paste, your favourite. You'll be feeling peckish before you get there. You didn't eat as much as a sparrow for your breakfast this morning.'

The guard at the far end of the platform waved a green flag and blew a shrill blast on his whistle. Jenny turned and looked apprehensively in his direction, then turned back to her daughter. 'Well, that's it then, love. You're off.' She stood on her tiptoes and Patsy leaned from the window and kissed her mother's cheek.

'Tara, Mum. Don't worry. I'll be all right.'

'Don't forget to write and let us know how you're settling down.'

'No, I won't forget, Mum. I'll write . . .'

The train was moving away now with a hiss of steam and a clatter and clang of iron wheels. Patsy leaned out of the window and waved, watching the lone figure of her mother, still frantically waving, growing smaller and smaller. Then abruptly she pulled her head inside. If you leaned out for too long you were liable to get covered in nasty black smuts and Patsy didn't want to risk getting her new camel-hair coat all dirty. Already the acrid smell was in her nostrils and the taste of the thick grey smoke at the back of her throat. She lifted her suitcase on to the rack above her head and sat down in a corner seat with a sigh of relief. The train seemed to be fairly quiet, thank goodness. There were only two more people in Patsy's compartment, a middle-aged man with his head buried in his newspaper and a woman, probably bound on a shopping trip to Leeford. Neither of them, Patsy was relieved to see, were taking much notice of her. She wanted time to be alone with her thoughts.

What a fuss Mum was making about a separation of just a few miles. Leeford was the nearest big town – city really – to Castleburn where the Bradshaws lived, and Patsy and her mother and sister had often gone there on shopping expeditions. Patsy wasn't altogether sure why she had chosen to go to the City of Leeford Training College. She was wondering now if it might have been better to have decided on one further away, but CLTC, as it was known, had a good reputation. Anyway, Patsy reminded herself ruefully, it was Mum who had chosen the college, wasn't it? Just as it had been Mum's idea that Patsy should train to be a teacher.

The compartment was plunged into blackness as the train entered a tunnel just outside the station, then, emerging into the autumn sunshine again, they were on the outskirts of Castleburn. Patsy glimpsed, in the distance, the cattle market and the square tower of the Norman church, and the castle on the hill which gave the market town its name. Then the familiar greystone houses of Castleburn gave way to wide green fields, divided by the characteristic drystone walls of the West Riding of Yorkshire. In the background was the vast stretch of moorland, brown with bracken and purple with heather, with huge outcrops of rock, largely indistinguishable at this distance from the motionless sheep grazing on the hillside. Patsy loved the wildness of the landscape and knew that this was one of the reasons that she had agreed to go to college in Leeford; she didn't think she could bear to be separated from the hills and valleys of Yorkshire that she had come to love so much during the seven years that she had lived there.

But closer to the carriage window the scenery was largely repetitive, resembling an endless kaleidoscope pattern of fields, trees and cows; fields, trees and cows . . . Patsy stared at it unseeingly, the monotonous clattering of the train wheels making a soporific accompaniment to her thoughts.

As Mum had reminded her, it was the first time in her eighteen years that Patsy had been parted from her parents for any length of time. She had been on occasional visits to her grandmother in Blackpool, sometimes on her own and sometimes with her sister, but never for more than a week or so. She would be sure to miss her family at first until she became acclimatised to college life. And her family would miss her too. Perhaps not so much Victor, her young brother, nearly eleven and interested in very little but football. His farewell this morning as he had departed for school, football boots crammed into his bulging satchel and his school cap perched crookedly on top of his ginger curls, had been brief and casual. 'Tara, our

Patsy. Be seeing you.' His cheerful smile and impudent wave as he went out of the door had shown Patsy that he was fond of her, or, more likely, took her for granted, but he wouldn't miss her. He was an extrovert all right was Victor, more like Mum than Dad in temperament, and more like her sister, Rosie, than like Patsy herself. But then . . . how could he be? Patsy frowned to herself. There was no blood relationship between Rosie and Victor; nevertheless, they were very much alike.

It was probably Dad who would miss her the most. Patsy had seen the concern in his grey eyes this morning and the moistness of an unshed tear as he had kissed her goodbye, something he didn't often do, before departing for work.

'Here you are, lass,' he had whispered, fumbling in his wallet at the last minute and then pushing two pound notes in her hand. 'I reckon you'll be able to use a bit of extra brass.' Patsy had felt the tears pricking her eyelids as she had muttered her thanks. 'And take care of yourself, love. Your mother and I will be thinking of you all the while. You can be sure of that.'

Patsy knew that that was true. Tom Bradshaw didn't say much, but his affection for Patsy, as it was for all his family, was deep and steadfast. Not that he ever told them so; he was a reticent sort of man and the introspective moods that came on him from time to time had increased as he had grown older. It had always been hard to communicate with him, and Patsy had found it more difficult than ever of late to get close to her father. It seemed that there was only Rosie who could get right to the heart of him. Patsy found herself shaking her head impatiently and sighing to herself as a picture came into her mind of Rosie and her father. Irritably she pushed the intrusive thought away.

As the train gathered speed, gobbling up the miles between Castleburn and Leeford, Patsy began, in spite of her misgivings, to experience a heady sense of freedom in the thought of breaking loose from her parents for the first time. Home and family ties were strong in the north of England, and Patsy knew that her own mother and father were inclined to over-protect her. But with a distance of fifty odd miles between them – not all that far, to be sure, but far enough – they would no longer be able to tell her what to do. Mum in particular, of course. A half smile played round Patsy's lips as she thought of the independence that lay ahead. Now she would be able to read in bed late at night without dire warnings of damage to her eyesight. She might still have to resort to a torch beneath the bedclothes – 'lights out at eleven' was a rule at CLTC she had heard, except at weekends – but there would be no fear of an irate Mum storming in and catching her. And she would be able to stop wearing her vest before the proverbial May was out; she might even discard the silly old-fashioned garment altogether. And she would be able to experiment with the odd cigarette or drink as she knew some of her more liberated friends were already doing, but which was frowned upon in the Bradshaw household. Rosie had done it though, without Mum and Dad finding out. Patsy remembered her sister taking a crafty drag with a couple of giggling schoolfriends, behind the bike shed at the Grammar School, when she was only fifteen. And Patsy knew that Rosie had sometimes gone to the pub at lunch-times with the new friends she had made at the local art school, something that was strictly forbidden in the sixth form that Patsy had attended.

Rosie . . . it was strange how Patsy's thoughts kept returning to her. But perhaps not so strange, considering that the two girls had been close friends for so many years. They had been bosom pals before they had been sisters. It was during the war that her mother had made the decision to adopt the little evacuee whom she had been looking after. Patsy recalled how delighted she had been by the stupendous news that Rosie was going to stay with them for ever and ever, was going to be a real sister, in fact. It had been an answer to Patsy's childhood prayers. How often she had asked God to send her a brother or sister or, failing that, a really best friend. And how often Mum had told her that she didn't think God would be able to grant her request; not, at least, as far as the brother or sister was concerned.

But He had. God had surprised them all, not least Jenny, Patsy suspected, when her brother, Victor, had been born in 1941. Patsy knew now, from odd remarks that had been passed over the years, that Victor's birth – or conception, rather – had come as a complete shock to everyone. And her father hadn't seen his son until the end of the war when Tom was released from the prisoner of war camp.

Victor was OK; he was a good sort, but he was only a kid brother when all was said and done. It was Rosie who had always claimed the lion's share of Patsy's affections. The pair of them had been inseparable during their formative years, into their teens, until recently. Patsy wasn't sure how it had happened, how they could possibly have allowed it to happen, but of late the two of them had been gradually, unconsciously at first, drifting apart. And Patsy was aware, though she would hardly admit it, even to herself, of feelings of jealousy towards this girl who had been at the centre of her life for so long.

And perhaps that was the reason for her jealousy, Patsy thought now. Rosie's sparkling personality, her liveliness and quick wit, had made her always the centre of attraction, at school and later at the Youth Club and Saturday night hops at the church hall. Patsy had recently found herself a little weary of trailing along in Rosie's wake, hovering uncertainly on the brink as she knew she was apt to do, while her sister, the gregarious extrovert, very quickly became the focal point of an admiring throng.

Patsy sighed as the train rattled along. She would miss her sister; it was difficult to imagine herself coping on her own without Rosie's ebullience to bolster up her own lack of self-confidence. But Patsy knew, nevertheless, that it was time that she learned to stand on her own two feet. And she was determined that she would do it too. She would make a life of her own; she would learn to fight her own battles, to make her own decisions. Yes, it was just as well that the two of them had parted company for a while. Rosie had also fled the nest for the first time, in fact she had left a couple of months ago to settle into her 'digs' in London before starting her course at the Art School there. She had left home light-heartedly, or so it had seemed, with no qualms about the new life she was planning, so far from her roots in the north of England. But Rosie would survive and make her way in the world, whatever she planned to do. Rosie was a born survivor.

And there was another partially formed thought persistently recurring at the back of Patsy's mind. Rosie was a couple of hundred miles away in London, too far away for Mum and Dad to visit her, or for her to come home for more than the very occasional visit, whereas she, Patsy, was within hailing distance of her parents. Maybe now she would be able to lay claim to a larger share of their affection which was surely due to her as their natural daughter? Patsy hated herself for these disloyal thoughts towards her lifelong friend, but she had noticed, so often,

Mum's eyes light up with fondness as she looked at Rosie, and had recognised, to her surprise, the ease with which Rosie could converse with Dad, something that she, Patsy, seemed unable to do. And it had hurt. But now Rosie was a long way away. Out of sight, out of mind, maybe?

Patsy realised with some surprise that they were only fifteen miles or so from Leeford. She had been day-dreaming and had completely forgotten about the snack that Mum had so painstakingly packed for her. She realised now that she was feeling a little hungry and rooted in her shoulder bag for the packet of salmon paste sand-wiches. 'Feed the inner man,' Mum always said, just as her own mother, Patsy's grandmother, had been in the habit of saying. A good meal inside you was the north-erner's answer to all sorts of problems and Patsy found now that the tasty snack not only filled up an empty corner but helped to bolster her against feelings of appre-hension as the city of Leeford came into sight.

The fields and drystone walls gave way to the red brick semis of suburbia on the outskirts of the city, then to rows of grimier terraced houses, with mill chimneys forming a backdrop at the end of the cobbled streets. In this older part of the town many of the streets still had cobblestones, as they had had since the days when the woollen mills had dominated the lives of all the folks who lived in the area; when the factory hooter, sounding at six o'clock in the morning, had summoned thousands of workers to hasten and obey the demands of their lords and masters, the wealthy mill owners; when the streets had echoed with the sound of metal clogs on cobblestones and the chattering voices of those who were wide-awake enough to chatter. Many of them, young children among them, would still be rubbing the sleep from their eyes and cursing the knocker-up who had woken them from their slumbers at such an unearthly hour.

Now, in the early 1950s, wool was no longer king. The woollen industry had begun to suffer as long as thirty years ago from a combination of increased overseas production, foreign tariffs and currency restrictions. Many of the mills had closed, or were engaged in the production of the new man-made fibres, although a few were still operative. There would always be some demand for good Yorkshire woollens, the worsteds, tweeds and twills which had made the area famous throughout the world.

The train passed the railway sidings and drew up at Leeford station. Patsy humped her suitcase down from the luggage rack and stepped out on to the platform. The case was heavier than she had realised and the weight pulled her slender figure sideways. She was glad that her unaccustomed affluence, thanks to dear old Dad, would enable her to take a taxi instead of heaving her luggage on and off the tram, to say nothing of the walk involved at either end of the journey. Most of her belongings had been transported to the college the previous day, in a massive trunk, by a road haulage firm and should be awaiting her on her arrival. Even so, her hand luggage felt like a ton weight.

She soon found a taxi on the rank outside the station and the taxi driver lifted her case into the boot with a cheerful smile. She leaned back in the hard leather seat feeling somewhat decadent at such self-indulgence – it was only about the third time she had ridden in a taxi in her life – and watched the various aspects of the busy city of Leeford unfolding before her eyes. The city square was crowded; this was the starting point for both the buses and the trams and people were dashing about as though they hadn't a moment to lose, forming queues and boarding the characteristic orange vehicles that would take them to their destinations in all directions from the city centre. Patsy could see, at the far end of the square, the impressive Town Hall, built in the mid-Victorian era from locally quarried stone, an elaborate Gothic structure with towers and turrets and embellishments, and a tall clock tower of Italianate design which could be seen for miles around. Outside the main entrance stood the statue of Richard Oastler, the early-nineteenth-century philanthropist, with two of the children he had fought so hard to free from long working hours and appalling conditions in the local mills.

The taxi followed the tram track out of the square and up an incline, to the outskirts of the city, passing the Wool Exchange, another Victorian edifice of even more fanciful design than the Town Hall. This building had, from 1870 onwards, influenced the world's woollen industry for more than thirty years. Bishop Blaize, the patron saint of woolcombers, stared down from his pedestal over the front entrance; Patsy recalled the ghastly story she had learned at Junior School of how he had been tortured to death by means of iron combs in AD 316, hence his involvement with the woollen industry, poor fellow!

They passed the Market Hall and the Infirmary, and a modern shopping parade at the end of which was the cubist-designed, cream-coloured Odeon, looking incongruous in the midst of so much ornate Victoriana. Then, about a mile from the city centre, the soot-blackened menacing structure of Barraclough's mill, one of the few still engaged in the production of woollen cloth. In the shadow of its tall chimney were row upon row of small terraced houses, many of them of the back to back design, where the mill workers had lived. Indeed, many of the occupants of these houses were still employed at the mill. Across the narrow back alleys were strung washing lines with sheets, shirts and towels flapping in the breeze. Front gardens were non-existent, and the back yards too tiny to allow a large sheet to dry without coming into contact with a grimy wall. In houses such as these had lived the youngsters for whom Richard Oastler, commemorated in the city square, had fought so unflinchingly. Patsy remembered her paternal grandmother, Granny Bradshaw, who had died two years ago, recounting tales of the shocking treatment of children in the weaving sheds, kept awake only by the cruel whip of the overseer. Not that Gran had suffered such persecution, Patsy thought now with a smile, in spite of her inclination to impart such gruesome stories. Granny Bradshaw had started work at the mill in Castleburn when she was only twelve, but the mill owner there had been a humane man who had treated his employees with respect.

After they had passed the University and the football and cricket grounds they entered the suburban area of Leeford, Woodley Bank, where the college was situated. The narrow streets were now replaced by wider, tree-lined avenues of semi-detached residences with large front gardens. The taxi turned left into one of these thoroughfares, Sycamore Avenue, at the top of which were the iron gates, now open, of the City of Leeford Training College. Patsy had arrived.

Chapter 2

Patsy paid the taxi driver, giving him, somewhat embarrassed, a tip of sixpence, and he carried her case up the steps and into the reception area of Calder Hall, the hall of residence to which she had been allocated and which was to be her second home for the next two years. She stared around, a little confused. There was no one else in sight. Gwendoline Travers, the girl who had been assigned to act as Patsy's college 'mother' and whom she had met on a couple of occasions, had half-promised that she would be there to meet her when she arrived. Patsy was not surprised, however, to find that Gwen was not in evidence. She had already formed the opinion, after their two meetings, that the person who was of supreme importance in Gwen's life was Gwen.

Patsy gave an inward shrug and walked to the noticeboard at the back of the entrance hall where she could see that there was a list of names. She drew her finger down the list. There it was, near to the top – there was an advantage in having a surname that began with B – Bradshaw, Patricia, room number 14. Another girl joined her as she stood there staring at the list of unfamiliar names, and they smiled uncertainly at each other.

'Hello,' said the other girl, slightly built with wispy blonde hair, a pale face and anxious-looking, mild blue eyes. 'Are you new as well?'

'Mmm.' Patsy nodded.

'A bit scary, isn't it? Trying to find out where we're supposed to be, and leaving home and all that. Still, I suppose it'll be all right once we've got used to it.'

'I'm sure it will,' said Patsy with far more confidence than she was feeling. This girl looked even more alarmed than Patsy herself. 'Have you looked for your room number? What's your name?'

'Shirley Jenner . . .'

'There you are.' Patsy pointed. 'Room number 18. I should imagine that's quite near to mine. I'm in 14. And I'm Patsy Bradshaw, by the way. Come on, let's see if we can find our way. I should think they'll be on the first floor. I hope so anyway. This case weighs a ton.'

They passed a dining room and a large lounge and a couple of rooms with closed doors which belonged, according to the name plates, to the resident lecturer and matron, and then they went up a flight of stone steps. There was little evidence of comfort so far and it was with some trepidation that Patsy stood outside the brown-painted door of number 14, in the middle of the stone-floored, echoing corridor.

'This is mine,' she said, 'and yours must be just along there. See you later, I expect. Come along and have a chat when you've unpacked, if you feel like it.'

'OK. I might do. See you then.' Shirley smiled nervously and lugged her suitcase to a similar brown-painted door a few yards away.

The key, a huge iron monstrosity that there could be no danger of losing, was in the lock and Patsy turned it and went in. At least her trunk had arrived. It stood in the middle of the floor, seeming to fill more than half of the small space. Patsy took off her coat and flung it on the bed then looked around.

The bare walls of the room, painted in a bilious shade of pea green, closed in on her, serving to exaggerate the faint drumming that was beginning in her temples, the onset of a headache. The room held all the essential furniture and seemed overcrowded. A solid oak wardrobe of massive proportions, with a huge drawer at the bottom; a table-top desk with the polish worn thin, revealing the white wood underneath; an easy chair of faded green moquette with wooden arms, and an empty bookcase. And the bed, of course, looming large in the far corner of the room, walled in on three sides with high wooden panelling. If you were to turn it round the other way, Patsy mused, with the open side facing the wall, it would be for all the world like sleeping in a coffin. She shuddered. It looked as though it would be the very devil to make every morning, let alone to change every fortnight, as she knew the students were required to do. The stark white sheets were tucked in tightly with envelope corners as if daring anyone to disturb their pristine neatness, and the folkweave counterpane covering the bed was predominantly the same sickly shade of green as the walls.

Patsy sighed. Oh well, she would perhaps feel a little better when she had unpacked, and the room would look more habitable when she had spread a few of her own bits and pieces around. She unlocked her trunk and flung back the lid, revealing the contents. It held, in the main, books and clothing, warm garments – which her mother had insisted upon – both for under and outer wear, to combat the severity of a Yorkshire winter. These were soon stored away in the wardrobe and drawer, then Patsy knelt on the wooden floor and started to unpack the books, shoving them into the bookcase near at hand. Books on the practices and principles of teaching; the complete works of Shakespeare; Chaucer's *Canterbury*

Tales; the works of Keats, Tennyson and Shelley, and novels by Hardy, the Brontë sisters and D. H. Lawrence, for Patsy was to study English as her main subject. And these were only a few from the required reading list, to be added to, no doubt, as the course progressed.

When she rose from the floor Patsy became aware of the stiffness in her legs. No wonder. She glanced down and noticed, for the first time, that the floor was uncarpeted except for a narrow strip of worn green Axminster near the bed. She made a mental note to bring her own bedside rug back with her the first time she went home, a cheerful creation of pink and blue flowers that Mum had made from a kit. It would brighten the room up no end. At least there was central heating, Patsy thought, as she walked over to the window, placing her hands on the large, albeit ugly, radiator. This was a luxury known only to the most affluent households in 1952. Her own home in Castleburn didn't have it, and Patsy reflected what a pleasant change it would be not to have to fling on her clothes on a cold winter's morning in an icy bedroom. Perhaps, for the first time, her hands and feet would be free from chilblains.

The view from the window showed a stretch of well-tended lawn on the other side of which were the two stone-built halls of residence where the men students lived, Kirkstall and Fountains, named after two well-known Yorkshire abbeys. The four women's halls were on the near side of the lawn and were named after Yorkshire rivers, Aire, Calder, Derwent and Wharfe. It was a pleasant scene, with a wooded area in the background, all very green and peaceful-looking at the moment. There was not a soul in sight, the students who had already arrived still engaged in the job of unpacking. But it would, no doubt, be a hive of activity by tomorrow when lectures got under way. Apart from Shirley Jenner, Patsy hadn't seen a single person yet, although she could now hear voices in the corridor outside.

'Hi there, Marj. Good holiday?'

'Super, thanks. I'll tell you about it later. Glad to be back, Gwen?'

'Ugh. What do you think?'

There was the sound of laughter, then retreating footsteps. How the place did echo! Gwen . . . That would probably be Gwen Travers, her college 'mother'. Patsy thought she had recognised those cut-glass tones. Perhaps the girl would be coming to seek her out before long. Patsy became aware that her head was positively thumping by now and she must take some aspirins to alleviate it. She unwrapped a newspaper bundle she had placed on the bed and took out two blue and white striped mugs and two matching plates, discarded oddments from her mother's kitchen which would be a constant reminder of home. She picked up one of the mugs and went out into the corridor. There was no wash-basin in the room, but she had an idea that the bathrooms and communal washrooms were at the end of the building. Yes, she was obviously right because ahead of her, at the end of the corridor, were two open doors, proclaiming unashamedly that these were the lavatories, and round the corner were the wash-basins.

'Hi there,' said a familiar voice as she entered the room. 'I was wondering if you'd shown up yet.' The speaker was a tall girl with her long dark hair drawn back in a pony tail with a black velvet ribbon, and an aristocratic-looking face: Gwendoline Travers. Her delicately arched eyebrows were raised questioningly as she greeted Patsy. 'Settling in OK, are you?'

'Yes thanks. I've got a headache though. I've just come

to get some water.' Patsy ran some water into the mug, then swallowed the two tablets. 'Just tension, I daresay. Travelling and unpacking and all that.'

'Oh, poor you! Yes, that's what it'll be. It's a bit traumatic at first, but you'll soon get used to it. And you'll feel better when you've had something to eat. Tea in about half an hour.' Gwen consulted the small gold watch on her wrist. 'At five o'clock in the dining room downstairs. You've seen that, have you?' Patsy nodded. 'The food's nothing to write home about,' Gwen went on. 'A lot of stodge and starch, but at least we don't go hungry.'

Patsy nodded again. 'Perhaps that's what's wrong with me. Come to think of it, I do feel a bit hungry.' She recalled that all she had had to eat since breakfast time was the few sandwiches that her mother had made. Mum had been right after all.

'Sorry I wasn't here to meet you,' said Gwen. 'As a matter of fact I've only just arrived. Daddy was having trouble with the Bentley. It's gone to the garage, so he had to hire a car to bring me. Damn nuisance really. I'd simply loads of stuff to bring back, but we managed.'

Gwen was one of the few girls who didn't have to rely on the services of a road haulage firm to transport her belongings back and forth. Gwen's father was a solicitor in York with a posh car and a detached home on the outskirts of the city. Patsy had visited Gwen and her family there, and Gwen, too, had paid a visit to Patsy's home. The Bradshaw household with its cluttered comfortable informality was a complete contrast to the palatial surroundings in which the Travers family lived. Patsy had been aware of Gwen's somewhat patronising glances towards Jenny, bustling about in her pinny, and Tom, settled by the fireside with his slippers and pipe. Jenny Bradshaw, however, hadn't seemed to notice, and had made the girl welcome as she did all visitors. Patsy thought that Gwen seemed more approachable today and it was good to see a familiar face amongst so much that was strange and unfamiliar.

'I thought we might go to the pictures tonight,' Gwen went on. 'All of us – our family group, I mean. I'll see what the others say. I don't know what's on, but they show quite reasonable films down in the village. It'll take your mind off things for a while; stop you feeling homesick.'

Patsy smiled, feeling more cheerful now. Perhaps Gwen wasn't so bad away from her home surroundings. 'Sounds like a smashing idea. I'd better go and finish sorting out my things now. I'll see you at tea-time then, shall I, Gwen?'

'Yes, I'll give you a shout when I'm going down.'

Back in her room Patsy closed the lid of her now empty trunk and placed the two framed photographs she had brought with her on top of the bookshelf. There was one of herself with Rosie, taken at Blackpool last summer. The two of them were standing with their arms round one another on the promenade with a view of the sea and sand and North Pier in the background. They were both laughing – at Victor in his 'Kiss me Quick' hat, Patsy recalled – but the black and white photo didn't really do justice to either of them. It didn't show the rich auburn of Patsy's curly hair which, to her relief, had darkened considerably since her childhood when her flaming locks had won her the nickname of Carrots. Nor did it show the vivid blue of Rosie's eyes, a startling complement to her glossy black hair which she wore long in a page-boy style. It showed, however, that Rosie was taller than her sister by a few inches and was smiling down at her, as she had always done.

The other photo, of Mum and Dad and Victor, was a holiday snapshot too. They looked happy and relaxed, with Dad smiling broadly for once. He had his arm round Mum's shoulder; they were much of a height, neither of them very tall, with Victor at the side of them, clowning about as usual in his silly hat, already up to their shoulders. Patsy's face grew serious as she studied them. Mum's dark curly hair, she reflected, was now streaked at the front and sides with silver, although Jenny still looked remarkably youthful for her forty years. Dad, Patsy thought, would never look much different; his sandy hair, flopping over his brow, was of the sort that didn't turn grey quickly. But what a contrast he was to Mum. Patsy had always thought so. His reticent manner and his occasional moodiness seemed to be completely at variance with Jenny's liveliness and the bubbling warmth of her personality. But the pair of them seemed to get on well enough; it was said, after all, that opposites attracted one another.

'Hello there. Ready, are you? It's tea-time.'

Patsy rose from her knees with a start as Gwen knocked and poked her head round the door. She had been wool-gathering and had lost track of the time.

'Mmm . . . All ship-shape, I see. You have done well.' Gwen's eyes travelled enquiringly round the room. 'It's more than I can say. My room's still the most awful tip. Of course, I've brought simply loads of stuff . . .'

I don't doubt it, thought Patsy, grinning to herself as she accompanied Gwen along the corridor and down the stairs with dozens of chattering girls, all going the same way.

The solid oak tables in the dining room, each surrounded by eight oak chairs of equally solid proportions, were covered with checked tablecloths and a variety of food deemed suitable for a 'high tea'. Patsy learned that the main meal was served at midday, as was still the custom in the north of England, and that as well as a cooked breakfast and a high tea, supper also was served in the dining room, for those who wished, from nine o'clock. So, as Gwen had told her, she certainly wouldn't go hungry.

The tea, stronger than Patsy was used to, poured from the huge enamel pot into thick white cups with no adornment, was nevertheless welcome, as was the simple serve yourself meal. Thick slices of vivid pink spam, tomatoes, limp lettuce and pickled onions, with doorsteps of bread, spread sparsely with margarine. It was the practice for each girl to look after her own butter ration, taking it down to meals each day, then keeping it in the coolest possible place in the study bedroom. But, as yet, the ration books had not been collected, so it was margarine or nothing for this first meal. And to follow slabs of sponge cake covered with watery icing. Not a patch on Mum's home baking, thought Patsy, but it helped to fill the gnawing emptiness inside her and she found, to her relief, that her headache had quite disappeared.

Her neighbour at the table was Shirley Jenner, the girl she had met in the entrance hall on arrival.

'Sorry I didn't manage to get along for a chat,' said Shirley, nervously blinking her pale blue eyes. 'There was so much to do, and I had this dreadful headache.'

'Same here,' said Patsy, grinning.

'And an awful stomach ache, too,' Shirley went on. 'Of course I always do . . . at the time of the month,' she added in a whisper, leaning closer to Patsy. 'But the doctor doesn't seem to be able to do anything about it. Then, of course, I've been worried about Mummy. She's just come out of hospital after a terribly serious operation – she nearly died – and poor Daddy has had to have time off work to look after her.'

Patsy found herself a captive audience to her new friend, and had little time to take much notice of the other girls in the group. The two who were sitting opposite her, Jocelyn and Kath, seemed like a couple of friendly girls. Kath, an open-faced girl with a dusting of freckles across her nose and the sandy hair that often accompanied such a complexion, caught Patsy's eye on one occasion and gave her a conspiratorial wink. And Jocelyn too, Kath's 'mother', smiled pleasantly as though she would like to get to know Patsy better.

After tea there was a 'welcoming' hour in the lounge, including the introduction of the matron, Miss Macallister, a white-haired, homely-looking woman, and the resident tutor, Miss Pritchard, a small dark-haired woman with tiny hands and feet, dressed entirely in emerald green, down to her pointed-toed shoes, emphasising her pixie-like appearance. Patsy was later to discover that this was her Education lecturer. The students then handed in their ration books and consulted numerous lists to find out to which divisions they had been allocated. Patsy was in Division B, one of the three groups that were training for Infant teaching and, to her delight, so was Kath Merriman, the cheerful girl who had sat opposite her at teatime.

She found herself walking with Kath later that evening as the group of girls, with Gwen in the lead, made their way down Sycamore Avenue to the cinema in Woodley Bank. Patsy discovered, although she had guessed as much from her accent, that Kath was a Geordie from Newcastle – many of the students at CLTL, indeed, came from that area – one of a large family and one of the most amiable girls Patsy had ever met. She felt that she had found a friend.

They sat on the worn red plush seats in the darkened cinema which smelt of floral disinfectant and stale cigarette smoke, handing round popcorn and packets of Rollo. 'Our treat tonight,' Gwen had told them. 'You daughters don't need to pay a penny.' The film was an old Betty Grable movie in which the blonde-haired star, along with a chorus of other long-legged lovelies, fought her way to stardom via London, Paris, San Francisco, New York . . . But Patsy was oblivious to what she was watching, so crowded had the day been with new and unfamiliar impressions.

'Supper party tonight in my room,' Gwen informed them when they returned to Calder Hall. 'Put your dressing-gowns on first, then we'll meet about ten o'clock.'

They sat on the bed as there was only one easy chair, or on cushions on the floor. Gwen had several of these in bright colours and there was a sheepskin rug by the bed, an incongruous touch of luxury in the Spartan surroundings. Gwen and Marjorie, another second-year student, came in carrying tin trays laden with mugs of steaming cocoa.

'We're not allowed to make drinks in our rooms,' Marjorie explained. There was, in fact, no power point in any of the bedrooms. 'It would use too much electricity. But there's the GP room down the corridor.'

'GP?' queried Kath. 'What's that?'

'General Purposes. There's a sink for washing out your undies – all the other stuff goes to the laundry – and an iron and ironing board and a clothes maiden. And a kettle, of course, and an assortment of beakers, though we usually use our own.'

Patsy leaned back against the side of the bed, listening to the conversations going on around her. It seemed to be the second years who were doing most of the talking.

'Yes, it was a super holiday. The first time I've been to Derbyshire. Of course it made all the difference, Trevor being there.'

'Lucky old you, Marj.' This was Gwen speaking. 'You wouldn't catch my mother and father letting me go away with a chap. They'd die at the thought.' Patsy had realised that, for all their affluence, Gwen's parents kept her on a very tight rein. Gwen's holiday to the South of France, wonderful though it sounded, had been strictly chaperoned.

'We were only Youth Hostelling . . .'

'All the same . . .'

'What about you, Brenda? Did Jeremy manage to get leave?'

Brenda, a tall, aloof-looking blonde who was Shirley's 'mother', nodded and gave a little smile. She glanced down at the tiny diamond cluster on her left hand. Although only half-way through her training, Brenda was engaged to a flying officer in the RAF.

'I hope you first years are going to work hard, not spend all your time chasing after the men,' said Gwen in a mock serious tone, wagging her finger at them.

But Shirley answered her solemnly, 'Of course. That's what we've come for, isn't it, to work hard? I'm not interested in men, anyway.'

'I've heard that before,' said Marjorie, laughing. 'Not interested indeed. Pull the other one! Just wait till the Kirkstall men start sniffing round, it'll be a different story then.'

'Not for Jocelyn, though,' whispered Brenda, in an aside to Marjorie. 'She'll be looking for other fish to fry.'

Marjorie laughed and nodded. Jocelyn Reynolds, to whom they were referring, didn't seem to have heard them. Patsy turned to look at her. She was rather an odd-looking girl, with dark hair which curled naturally, but her nose was prominent and her mouth was small. She became aware that Patsy was looking at her and looked back, her dark eyes staring intently into Patsy's. Then Jocelyn smiled, and Patsy thought how much more attractive the girl looked now. Rather self-consciously, Patsy returned her smile.

Then she glanced surreptitiously at the other occupants of the room. Marjorie, the Youth Hosteller, was a robust girl with short curly hair, a determined chin and a somewhat aggressive manner. She reminded Patsy of 'Pansy Potter, the strong man's daughter', from the *Dandy* comic. Or was it the *Beano*? Patsy grinned to herself, then found she was hardly able to restrain her laughter when she realised that Marjorie's daughter, Edna, with her sharp nose and round spectacles, was for all the world like 'Keyhole Kate' from the same comic.

Patsy bit her lip to stop herself from laughing and glanced at Shirley Jenner who had gone very quiet. The girl looked anxious and fit to drop, Patsy thought solicitously. She was sipping furtively at the last drops of her cocoa and it seemed as though she was trying hard to fight back the tears. Poor girl. It had been a long day for all of them and Patsy realised that she, too, was tired out.

'Come on, girls. Time for beddy-bye.' Marjorie got to her feet. 'We'll love you and leave you now, Gwen. Thanks for the cocoa.'

'What about the cups?' asked Patsy. 'Shall we wash up?'

'No, it's all right. Mothers' privilege tonight. You can do them another time.'

'See you in the morning.'

'Sweet dreams.'

As the girls trooped out into the corridor Marjorie put a friendly arm round Patsy's shoulder. 'Don't worry, kid,' she said. 'It'll get better. It'll all seem different when you've had a night's sleep.'

Patsy lay on her back watching the faint moonlight shining in through a chink in the curtains. She had thought she was tired, but now sleep seemed very far away. Then she heard a noise in the corridor outside, shuffling feet and giggling and murmurs of 'Shhh'. Then the singing started:

'We are Doc Pearson's army,
No earthly good are we.
We do no work, we do no swot,
We sometimes do SP.
And when SP is over
Our Doc will surely say:
"Mon Dieu, Mein Gott,
Thank God that lot
Have all gone down today." '

Patsy grinned. She recognised the hymn tune, 'The Church's One Foundation', and guessed that it was the second years serenading their daughters. And though she had only been at CLTL for a day she knew that SP was the dreaded School Practice and that Doctor Pearson was the principal, a shadowy figure who rarely emerged from his room.

Then they started to sing again, this time to the tune of 'What a Friend We Have in Jesus':

'When we leave this blinking college
Oh how happy we shall be;
No more sausages for breakfast;
No more bread and jam for tea.
No more getting up at seven;

No more rising to the bell.
When we leave this blinking college,
It will be like leaving . . . well!'

The voices and footsteps died away and Patsy lay very still in the quiet darkness, exhausted from the day's events and, if she were honest, a tiny bit homesick.

Chapter 3

Patsy found on awakening the next morning that Marjorie's words were true; she felt much better after a night's sleep. But would she ever get used, she wondered, to the clanging bell, rung up and down the corridors by each girl in her turn, to rouse sluggards from their slumbers at 7 am? Patsy hadn't needed its clamorous tones to wake her this morning. She had been wide-awake since six o'clock, but she knew that as the term progressed she might not always be so alert, and could think of no worse way to be roused than by such an ear-piercing din. And would she ever grow accustomed to having her morning wash in company with a crowd of other girls in the communal wash-room? She had met several of them in the corridor as they made their way there, yawning and rubbing the sleep from their eyes, towels slung round their necks and sponge bags over their arms, some with curlers protruding from beneath turbans and sleeping nets.

She was surprised, on entering the dining room, to see a letter on her breakfast plate.

'Mail for you already,' Jocelyn Reynolds remarked. 'Somebody loves you. You're lucky – there weren't many letters this morning.'

'No?' Patsy smiled, looking at her questioningly.

'I'm in charge of the mail, you see,' Jocelyn explained.

'I put it out on the breakfast plates. I don't know everyone's name yet, so I've left most of it in a pile. But I knew you, of course.' She smiled and raised a quizzical eyebrow. 'Boyfriend?'

'No, not a boyfriend. I haven't one . . . at the moment,' Patsy added with a laugh. She looked at the handwriting on the envelope. 'Looks as though it's from my mum.'

Patsy gave a little frown of annoyance. Trust Mum to write so soon, fussing as usual. She couldn't have anything really important to say; Patsy had only said goodbye to her the day before. She tore open the blue envelope and scanned the single sheet of matching notepaper. Yes, as she thought it was: 'Just a little note hoping that you're settling in all right, love, and to let you know that Dad and Victor and I are all thinking about you. The house seems quiet without you . . .'

Patsy smiled to herself and felt a little guilty at her ungracious reaction when she had first caught sight of the letter. It was nice of Mum to write, though totally unnecessary. None of the other girls on the table seemed to have letters, except for Brenda, the tall blonde girl who sported the engagement ring. Her head was buried now over several closely written sheets of tiny black writing.

Jocelyn nodded in Brenda's direction. 'She keeps the postman busy, don't you, Brenda?' The blonde girl looked up and gave an aloof smile, her usual answer to such comments, before turning back to her letter. 'The handsome Jeremy, God's gift to the RAF,' Jocelyn went on, a trifle waspishly, Patsy thought. 'Writes nearly every day he does. The Royal Mail'll never go bust as long as those two are around.'

'Enjoyed our singing, did you?' asked Gwen as she poured out the cups of tea. 'Put your own milk in, will you, girls? It's not correct, of course. It should be milk first, but we have to act like plebs while we're here ... We sang you to sleep all right, did we?'

'Yes, it was super,' Patsy replied, turning to the girl next to her. 'Wasn't it, Shirley?'

'Mmm.' Shirley nodded uncertainly. 'I enjoyed it,' she said, sounding as though she had done anything but.

'Old custom, is it?' asked Edna, the girl who reminded Patsy of Keyhole Kate, from the other end of the table.

'Suppose so.' Edna's 'mother', Marjorie, shrugged. 'All we know is that they did it last year when we arrived, and we're carrying on the tradition. I daresay they've been doing it for donkey's years.'

The 'sausages for breakfast' mentioned in the song proved to be an accurate forecast because that was what the students were eating that morning. Fat, well-browned and crispy, oozing out of their skins, Patsy found them quite delicious, although they would have been more appetising without the juice from the tinned tomatoes running all round the plate, and the fried bread was hard enough to break your teeth. All in all, though, it was a decent meal, substantial enough to fortify them for the new experiences of the day that lay ahead.

They all trooped across to the Main Block about half an hour later in ones and twos and small groups, mostly chattering animatedly. It was amazing how quickly barriers were broken down and friendships formed.

Patsy walked with Kath Merriman and together they managed to find the room where the first lecture of the day was to be held.

This was Nature Study, and after an introductory talk about the necessity of a nature table in each classroom, Mr Bowman suggested that they should take a nature walk in the nearby woods. They were each to gather, in the allotted time, several of the specimens he had suggested, then bring them back to the lecture room and label them.

'We're like a crowd of children let out of school, aren't we?' said Patsy, as they followed Mr Bowman along the gravel paths to the woodland area at the back of the college, all chattering like magpies.

None of the girls had brought coats with them to the Main Block, it being only a couple of minutes' walk from the halls of residence, and they found that neither did they need them now. The autumn sun was strong and bright and there was only the gentlest breeze. The grass, however, was still wet with dew and Patsy was glad of her Hush Puppy shoes to keep her feet dry. The sun, shining through the overhead branches, cast a shimmering dappled light all around them, and Patsy felt a surge of inexplicable happiness. For the first time she felt really glad to be there, though how long the feeling would last she wasn't sure.

'We used to go for nature walks in Castleburn,' she remarked to Kath as the group of students, mostly walking in twos, followed the lecturer along the path through the woods. 'Only in the first form, though, at the Grammar School. It was thought to be too childish after that. There are lots of little woods and coppices all around. It's grand for Nature Study.'

'Yes, Castleburn's a lovely place,' Kath agreed. 'I remember going on a day trip there once with me gran. It was a heck of a long way, come to think of it, and I was sick in the chara.' She laughed. 'I enjoyed it though. There's a castle, isn't there, and an abbey near the river? Have you always lived there, Patsy?'

'No, only about seven years,' she replied. 'I was born in Blackpool. I'm what they call "sand-grown" round there. We had a boarding house, you see . . .' She hesitated. 'No, that's not really true. It was my grandma that had the boarding house – she still has – but it seemed as though it was us that had it. My mother worked there, and my sister and I seemed to spend as much time at Grandma's as we did at home.'

'And then you moved to Yorkshire? You must have missed the seaside?'

'Yes, I suppose I still do,' Patsy replied thoughtfully. 'But Rosie – that's my sister – and I had got a bit too big by then for building sand-castles. I miss Gran but we go over a few times a year to see her.'

'Why did your parents decide to move to Yorkshire? Your mam had got fed up, had she, of working in the boarding house? Whoops! Sorry – I'm being dead nosy, aren't I?' Kath put her hand to her mouth. 'Trust me and my big mouth. I always manage to put my foot in it.'

Patsy laughed. 'Not at all. I don't think you're being nosy. And I think you've just about summed it up. Looking back on it now, I daresay Mum thought she'd worked for her mother for long enough. I didn't realise it when I was a child, but I suppose my mum was little more than a servant really for my gran. She'd worked there ever since she left school. Anyway, when my dad came out of the army – he'd been a prisoner of war – he wanted to go back to Yorkshire. That's where he'd been born, and so for once my mum fell in with his plans.'

'And you've a sister? Rosie, did you call her?'

'Yes . . . Rosie,' Patsy answered softly. 'She's just nineteen, last week in fact. She's started at art school in London.'

'Crikey! Your parents didn't waste much time, did they?' said Kath. 'The two of you in . . . well, it must be a lot less than a year.'

'What?' Patsy looked at her friend in puzzlement, then

she laughed. 'Oh, yes, I see what you mean. No, Rosie's not my real sister. She's adopted. There's only nine months between us actually – I'll be nineteen next June – but people that don't know us tend to think that Rosie's a few years older than me. She was our evacuee,' Patsy went on. 'She'd stayed with us since the beginning of the war and then her mother was killed in an air-raid in Liverpool. So Mum and Dad adopted her. Well, it was Mum really, although she knew Dad would agree – he'd got ever so fond of Rosie. But he was a prisoner of war at the time. We didn't see him again till the war was over. And my little brother, Victor, was born while he was away. Dad didn't see him till he came back from Germany.'

'Mmm.' Kath nodded. 'The same thing happened in our family. Our Len was born while me dad was away in the army. Mam took it all in her stride though. She was quite used to having kids. Len was number four, and there's six of us now.'

'Gosh! That's a big family. And you're the eldest, are you?'

'Yes, that's right.' Kath grinned. 'I keep 'em all in order. I don't know how Mam'll manage without me around.' She paused for a moment then went on, 'No, I don't really mean that. Mam's great with the kids, and Dad an' all. He's got 'em all organised like a regiment. He was a sergeant major, was me dad. And they've both been grand about me coming away to college, though it'll be a bit of a squeeze as far as money's concerned. But it's what I've always wanted to do, you see, so they were determined I should have my chance.'

'Yes . . . I see.' Patsy was thoughtful.

'I worked though, for two years,' Kath went on. 'I didn't go into the Sixth Form like most of my friends did. We needed the money at home, you see. So I worked in a shop, then in a nursery.'

'Growing plants?' asked Patsy.

'No, yer daft thing!' Kath laughed. 'A proper nursery, looking after kids. Getting me hand in. Plants indeed! I can hardly tell a daffodil from a dandelion. Talking of plants, I think we'd better shut up and listen to what Mr Bowman's saying. We'll be getting into trouble, chattering our heads off like this.'

The girls broke off their conversation as did the others near to them, and they stood in a semi-circle round the lecturer as he talked to them about how to identify the various trees, not only by their leaves, but by the bark or by the outline of the tree as a whole. The trunks of trees, he pointed out, were not always brown, as young children painted them, but could be various shades – silver-white, for instance, like the silver birch, or grey like the ash.

'Of course you can all identify the oak leaf,' Mr Bowman went on, 'and the sycamore . . .' Most of the girls nodded in agreement, but Kath whispered to Patsy in an aside, 'Not me! I've told you, I'm hopeless.'

'. . . their leaf shapes are distinctive, but it's not so obvious, to young children that is, when you come to the beech or elm or alder . . .'

'I don't know about young children,' said Kath as they recommenced their walk through the wood. 'It's all Greek to me as well. That's what comes of being brought up in the city. Proper town mouse, I am. I suppose you know all this, Patsy, with you being a country mouse?'

'A lot of it,' she agreed. 'But I didn't before we moved to Castleburn.'

She was silent for a moment, concentrating on the scene around her of bushes and trees just starting to be tinged with the colours of autumn. The sycamore leaves were edged in brown and yellow and some had already fallen, and the winged seeds flushed with red had formed on the branches. The scarlet berries of the rowan tree, one of the loveliest trees of all, made a vivid splash of colour against the blue autumn sky, and at their feet lay pine cones and 'conkers' which had burst from their prickly shells, like miniature hedgehogs, on the chestnut tree. This wood, part of the college grounds, was an idyllic spot and Patsy was glad that they had been introduced to it on their first morning. It was a propitious start to the course, but she knew, too, that a great deal of hard work lay ahead.

She considered what her new friend had just told her about working for two years before coming to college, and thought what a sheltered life she, herself, had led by contrast. Kath seemed to be so much more mature than Patsy was. Obviously two years in the working world had added a great deal to the girl's experience of life. That, and looking after the youngest members of her family.

Patsy returned to this subject now. 'You've some quite young brothers and sisters then, have you, Kath? Two more, besides the one born during the war?'

'Yes, that's right.' She grinned. 'Maureen's eight and our Billy's six. That's why I wanted to be a teacher,' she continued, 'because I'm so used to looking after kids. You'd think I might be fed up with it, but I'm not. Glutton for punishment, I am. And I had a Sunday School class too. I enjoyed that. What made you decide to be a teacher?'

Patsy was silent for a moment. Then, 'I don't really know,' she answered quietly. She realised how foolish that must sound and gave an embarrassed little laugh. 'I'm not at all sure that I do want to be a teacher,' she said slowly, putting into words for the first time the thought that had been plaguing her for ages. And Kath was such a friendly, open sort of girl, Patsy felt that she wanted to confide in her. She saw Kath look at her in surprise, and said, 'I suppose it was my mum's idea really. She's always wanted me to be a teacher.' Oh, how feeble she must seem. She went on speaking hurriedly, trying to justify herself. 'But I'm determined that I'll make a go of it. Now I'm here I'm going to work hard, and I'm going to be a good teacher, I've made up my mind.' Even if it kills me, she added to herself, but didn't say it.

'But what about *you*, Patsy?' Kath's lovely clear grey eyes were clouded with concern. 'Haven't you thought about what *you* want to do? I mean, it's all very well trying to please your parents – I know we all owe them a lot – but was there nothing else that you wanted to do instead of being a teacher?'

'Yes . . . as a matter of fact, there was. There is,' replied Patsy. 'I'd like to work in a shop. An antique shop, I mean, not just an ordinary shop like Woolie's. I've worked in one in Castleburn for quite a while now – just at weekends and during the school holidays sometimes – Mr Fothergill's. I really love it, all those beautiful old things, china and silver and jewellery and old books. I'd have liked to go on working there. I'd like my own shop one day . . .' Her brown eyes shone with enthusiasm and her voice was animated. Then, just as quickly, the sparkle left her eyes and she went on in flat tones, 'But Mum says it's a waste of time just working in a shop. She says there's no future in it and there's no point in wasting my education in a dead-end job.'

'But if it's really what you want to do . . .' Kath protested.

'You try telling Mum that. When she gets a bee in her bonnet there's no shifting her,' said Patsy with more than a touch of asperity. 'She wants me to have the chances she never had, you see,' she went on, more reasonably. 'I suppose you can't blame her. Like I've told you, she worked like a slave for my gran, and she never had the chance to do anything else. I get on famously with Grandma, but I think she could be rather a tartar and she had this thing about it being a waste of time educating a girl. My Aunt Violet wanted to be a teacher, apparently, but her mother thought differently . . . so Mum's decided that's what she wants for me. And what Mum says, goes!' She grinned ruefully. 'We all know that in our household.'

Kath gave a sympathetic smile. 'I hope you're doing the right thing, Patsy. I should imagine teaching can be an awful job if your heart and soul are not in it.'

Patsy raised her shoulders in a shrug. 'Yes, I know I must sound terribly spineless, giving in to my mother like that, but . . .'

'No, I don't think so at all.' Kath shook her head decisively. 'It shows that you're a considerate girl, trying to please her. I just hope you grow to like it, that's all. You've said you're going to try.'

'And so I am. Not that I seem to have done all that well so far.' Patsy gave a wry smile. 'I had a Sunday School class, like you, Kath, but I couldn't make the little blighters pay attention. They spent all their time whispering and giggling and making paper aeroplanes. Goodness knows how I shall go on School Practice.'

'Don't worry. You'll have the backing of the class teacher then, and it's no use meeting trouble till you come to it. That's what I always think. Sufficient unto the day, you know, like they told us in Sunday School. Come on, we'd better stop nattering and get some of these specimens collected.'

'It's all right. There's plenty of time yet.'

The students were left to their own devices for the next quarter of an hour or so to gather suitable exhibits for a proposed nature table. Patsy and Kath rooted about like a couple of squirrels hoarding pine cones, conkers, nuts, berries, and leaves of differing shapes and hues. They talked as they ferreted around, Patsy returning to the subject of her family.

'Rosie's had the guts to stick up for herself, though. She was always determined that she'd go down to London to finish her art course. Mum and Dad wanted her to stay in Yorkshire or go to Blackpool. Art students are supposed to do their training in their own neck of the woods – something to do with their grant – but she managed to pull a few strings and get her own way. Trust her!' Patsy concluded feelingly.

'Quite a character, is she, your sister?' asked Kath.

'You can say that again! Yes . . . she's strong-willed and not frightened of anything. She seems to have taken to London like a duck to water. She's not a bit like me,' Patsy added, a trifle apologetically, 'but then there's no reason why she should be when you come to think of it.'

'Don't run yourself down, Patsy,' said Kath kindly. 'I think you're all right, you know.' She gave an approving nod.

'The funny thing is, though,' Patsy went on as though she hadn't heard, 'our Victor – that's my kid brother – and Rosie are so much alike it's incredible. In disposition I mean, not in looks. And yet they're not really brother and sister.'

'That just shows that environment can be more important than heredity,' said Kath. Then she grinned. 'Just listen to me! Those are high falutin' words, aren't they? And I've not even started my Education course yet. I tell you what though, Patsy, it sounds to me as though it'll do you good to be away from Rosie for a while. Bossed you around, did she?'

Patsy looked at Kath in surprise. It was amazing how accurately her new friend had summed up the situation, almost as though she could read her mind. Kath, she could tell, was a very perceptive girl. Her clear grey eyes were candid and Patsy felt that whatever she said had the ring of sincerity. Her face was pleasing, attractive rather than pretty, with her light sandy hair, more golden than red, curling back gently from a high forehead. Her mouth was wide and was often curved in a smile, as it was now.

'Yes . . . I suppose you could say she bossed me about.' Patsy grinned. 'Rosie was always the leader. Just lately I've been getting a bit fed up with it, always having to fall in with her plans. And I've been feeling a bit jealous, too, I must admit. Everybody seems to take more notice of Rosie than of me, even Mum and Dad. And I hated myself for feeling like that; we'd always been such good friends. She's great really, is Rosie.'

'I shouldn't worry about feeling jealous,' said Kath evenly. 'It happens in all families. There have been times when I could cheerfully have throttled our Maureen, just because she always seemed to be able to get round our mam.'

Patsy smiled warmly at her friend. With just a few words Kath had managed to get the whole thing into perspective and to allay Patsy's fears. She felt tons better already, now she had got it all off her chest, all that business about Rosie and about not really wanting to be a teacher. She stooped down to pick up a pine cone she had dropped on to the gravel path, and a shower of sycamore seeds fell from her other hand, some taking wing in a sudden gust of breeze.

'Damn and blast!' Patsy laughed as she tried to catch them and shove them into a cardigan pocket already bulging with leaves and berries. 'Mr Bowman should have provided us with bags . . .'

After a few weeks had passed Patsy felt as though she had always been at CLTC, but there were still times when she was alone in her little room, especially in the early evening, when she missed the warmth and friendliness of home, and her mum and dad and Victor . . . and Rosie. The study bedrooms were pretty cheerless places, although the students tried to put the stamp of their own individuality upon them by scattering their personal possessions around – pictures and photographs, books and ornaments and knick-knacks, often to remind them of home.

On Patsy's wall there was a framed print of the abbey at Castleburn, a print that was reproduced in thousands for the tourists who now, in the upsurge of prosperity after the war years, were flocking to the little market town. It showed the sun casting dark shadows on the golden-grey walls and Gothic arches, and in the background were the limestone hills and trees in the full green of summertime.

Pinned to the wall, too, though unframed, were two of Rosie's lightning pencil sketches. One was of Victor, his flaming coppery hair only hinted at by the rapid strokes of Rosie's coloured pencil, but she had caught and portrayed so accurately the mischievous glint in his brown eyes and the merry expression of his upturned mouth. The other sketch was of Patsy herself, not that it was vanity that compelled her to pin her picture on the wall, more a pride in her sister's achievement; Rosie certainly was a talented artist. Here again, the dark auburn of Patsy's curly hair was only suggested, and the deep hazel-brown of her eyes. But Rosie had captured her pensive expression, that contemplative look that came into her eyes when she was in a thoughtful mood, which made people think she was unhappy when she was really only thinking. Rosie's talent as an artist had been recognisable when she was only a child, but Patsy didn't think that it was this branch of art – portrait drawing – that particularly interested her sister. She had an idea that Rosie had aspirations to become a designer, a dress designer, maybe. And she'll do it, thought Patsy, as she glanced again at Rosie's drawings. Rosie, she was sure, would achieve whatever she set her mind to.

Every week without fail, in a letter from home in the familiar blue envelope, came a ten shilling note, Patsy's 'allowance'. She had noticed that most of the girls, on her table at any rate, seemed to receive the same amount. She wasn't sure about Gwen who was always very secretive about it. Possibly the girl had her own cheque book? Their needs were very few as their board in the hall of residence, along with their tuition, was paid for by their own local Education Authority, and a small additional grant was often paid to parents to help with such items as clothing and books. The ten shillings went on tram fares into town, cups of coffee, sweets and chocolates – the small amount that could be bought with sweet coupons – occasional visits to the cinema and the odd pair of nylons. At all events it went, and next week's allowance was eagerly awaited.

Patsy was, on the whole, contented. She had made some good friends – Kath, in particular – and was beginning to think that perhaps her mother's idea that she should become a teacher was not such a bad one after all. She didn't think of envying the comparative freedom that her sister, far away in London, was enjoying.

Chapter 4

Rosie sprawled on the divan bed, her hands clasped behind her head, and thankfully closed her eyes. Gosh! She was exhausted, bone weary with all that standing, and her feet and her legs, all of her in fact, were just one dull ache. She hadn't realised how much she was aching till she had flopped down a few minutes ago, but she knew that a short rest would soon revive her. She stretched her long legs and wiggled her toes encased in black woollen stockings. Her flat patent leather shoes had already been kicked to the other side of the room where they had landed next to her duffel-coat and long hand-knitted scarf – a present from Mum – that she had discarded in a heap on the floor.

The tiredness was something she would have to put up with, and Rosie knew that she was well able to cope with it. All art students got tired, because all of them, almost without exception, had to do a part-time job to help with living expenses. And many of them were employed, as Rosie was, at the Lyon's tea shops that were to be found all over the city of London and its environs. Rosie had been fortunate enough to get a job at one on the Cromwell Road, only about five minutes' walk from her flat and about the same distance from the art school. Her hours were flexible, usually a couple of hours at tea-time or early evening and then all day either Saturday or Sunday. She would be able to get the odd weekend off though, if necessary. The management were understanding – they relied heavily on casual labour – and there was never any shortage of students to fill in with extra hours when needed.

She had been working at Lyon's for about two months now, since before the term had started. It seemed to Rosie as though she had already spent a lifetime dishing out beans on toast, toasted tea-cakes, stodgy buns, sausage and mash, poached eggs, scrambled eggs, fried eggs . . . to what seemed like an endless queue of ravenous customers who bolted down the uninspired – but, on the whole, well-cooked – food with cups of dark brown tea or coffee. Rosie had become a seasoned coffee drinker since starting work at Lyon's. At home they had drunk mainly tea, as most northerners did, but now she had come to love the bitter taste and pungent aroma of coffee. She loved the bubble of the machine and the hiss of steam as the boiling liquid was ejected into the huge jugs. The coffee, she thought, was the best part of Lyon's, the characteristic fragrance that greeted you as soon as you opened the door. And when she wasn't serving she was clearing the tables, stacking the wooden trays high with thick white cups and saucers, and scraping away the congealed mess of egg yolk, bacon rind, half-eaten sausages and stub ends of cigarettes left on the plates. It amazed Rosie that folk could be so disgusting in their habits when ash-trays were provided on every table.

It was little wonder then that she was tired, but she knew that ten minutes stretched out flat on the bed was all that was needed to bring her round. Indeed, it was all the time that she could allow herself; she had a design to finish before she went out, and she had promised to meet some friends later on that evening in the pub opposite the college. She found herself wondering, idly, if Jeff would be there . . . No, probably not. The George and Dragon was the stamping ground of the students and Jeff was, after all, a lecturer. Still, you never knew. Rosie had an idea she had seen him there once, at the beginning of term, before she had known who he was.

At any rate she didn't have to waste time cooking herself a meal. She had grabbed a quick snack of baked beans and two cups of coffee before leaving work and that would keep her going till morning. It was rarely, in fact, that Rosie used the grimy little gas stove – 'private facilities for cooking' – which had been a salient advertising feature of the one-roomed flat. She just about managed to toast a piece of bread in the morning, or if she was late, as she frequently was, to eat a chunk straight off the loaf, or sometimes didn't bother with breakfast at all. Mum would be horrified. She had made Rosie promise that she would never go out without a good breakfast inside her, but that was easier said than done. She thought ruefully at times about the 'good breakfast' she had been compelled to eat at home – cereal followed by a boiled or scrambled egg, and bacon and eggs on a Sunday – but Castleburn seemed so far away now. Another world, another time . . .

Rosie had been determined that she would come down to London to complete her art course. The glittering city beckoned with its art galleries and museums and exhibitions, a place that Rosie had seen only once on a weekend visit, but where, she had decided, she would ultimately go to live and study.

Mum, of course, had been dead set against the idea and at first Rosie, too, had been puzzled as to how she might achieve her aim.

'Go down to London!' Jenny Bradshaw had sounded horrified, almost as though Rosie had suggested going to Calcutta or Peking. 'I've never heard of such a thing! Why on earth do you want to go to London? There's a perfectly good art school in Leeford, isn't there? Why don't you go there, Rosie? Our Patsy's going to Leeford, and it would be nice for the two of you to be together, in the same town at any rate. You've always wanted to be together, ever since you were little girls, and besides, I think Patsy could do with you there. Then she won't feel so lonely, like.'

But Rosie knew that she and Patsy were not quite as close as they had been as children, that recently they had been growing apart.

'I think it would be much better if Patsy and I went to different places,' she said. 'We can't stick together all our lives, can we, like Siamese twins? And Patsy won't be lonely, Mum. She'll make lots of new friends, you'll see. Don't worry about her. She'll be all right. At least she's decided to stay quite near home . . .' Or you have decided for her, Rosie added to herself, but refrained from saying. 'You must be pleased about that. She could have decided to go anywhere in England, you know.'

'Yes, I know that, love,' said Jenny. 'But our Patsy's a home bird, always has been. She'll want to feel that her dad and I are quite near if she needs us. Goodness knows why you want to go traipsing off down to London, Rosie. Anyway . . .' Jenny paused for a moment, thoughtfully wiping a breakfast plate till it gleamed before replacing it on the dresser. 'I thought I'd heard somewhere that you have to do your training up here, that they won't pay for you to go gadding off to God knows where?'

'You're supposed to be resident in the area . . . yes,' said Rosie. 'But there are ways of getting round it – I know lots of students do. If you know somebody who lives in the area you can give their address, perhaps even stay with them for a while, then you can say that you're resident . . .

'But they only pay for our training. The money for board has to come out of our own pockets. I'll get a job, Mum, when I get to college. All art students do. I'll be able to pay for my own digs.'

'I don't know about that, Rosie,' said Jenny thoughtfully. 'It doesn't seem fair somehow. You'll have enough to do, surely, with all that drawing and painting?' That was how Mum always referred to the art course, drawing and painting. 'You'll not have time to do a job as well.'

Rosie laughed. 'From what I gather they've got to make time. They do all sorts of jobs, art students. They work in cafes and shops . . .' And pubs, she thought, but didn't say. Mum had a 'thing' about pubs. 'And I know some of the lads do painting and decorating. Don't worry about me, Mum. I shall enjoy it. I'm looking forward to it.'

'I daresay we will be able to help out a bit, dear,' said Jenny slowly. She hung up the pot towel on the back of the door and took off her apron. Then she sat down at the kitchen table and Rosie sat opposite her. 'Your Granny Bradshaw left some money to be set aside for your education, you know. For you and Patsy and Victor. Not a lot, mind.'

Rosie had fond memories of Granny Bradshaw, whom they had all seen a lot of after moving to Castleburn, where she also lived; Rosie, though adopted, had never been treated any differently from the other two children. She appreciated that more than she could say.

'So we could allow you something each month to help with your lodgings,' said Jenny. 'Oh dear! I do worry about you though, Rosie love. Our Patsy'll be all right, I suppose. She'll be in a hall – a hall of residence they call them, don't they, dear? But what will you do? Perhaps you'll be able to get digs with a nice lady who'll give you a good breakfast and an evening meal? I think that would be best. They don't seem to have those halls at art colleges, do they?'

'No, Mum,' said Rosie firmly in answer to both questions. 'I'd really thought of getting . . . a flat.'

'A flat!' Jenny's voice rose an octave.

'Yes,' Rosie went on quickly. 'They all do. You have to have somewhere to do your work. All the . . . drawing and painting.' She smiled at Jenny. Then she leaned forward, cupping her chin in her hands and looking beguilingly at her mother, her blue eyes opening wide. She knew how to get round Mum when necessary. 'Oh, Mum, I really do want to go down to London, if I can.' Her voice was soft and persuasive. 'I want it so badly. It would be such a marvellous experience – to see all those pictures in the National Gallery and the Tate, and the collections at the V and A. All art students ought to be able to do it.'

But Jenny knew nothing of pictures and art galleries. 'The V and A?' she said now, wrinkling her brow. 'What's that?'

'The Victoria and Albert Museum, Mum,' said Rosie, but not impatiently. Though she was bent on getting her own way, Rosie knew only too well that Jenny had never had the chances, either for education or for anything else, that she and Patsy and Victor had had. 'It's a big museum in South Kensington,' Rosie explained, 'where they have exhibitions. Paintings and furniture and tapestries and costumes . . . all kinds of things.'

'It sounds lovely, dear. And I'm sure it would be a great help to you with your drawing and painting.' Jenny's greenish-brown eyes looked thoughtful and her forehead was still wrinkled in a frown. 'I do like you to have these opportunities if you can, all of you, Patsy and Victor as well. And I know you're a sensible girl, Rosie. I know I can trust you to take care of yourself in London . . . I'm just trying to work something out, dear. You remember my friend Joan, don't you, who used to live in Preston?'

'Yes, of course I do, Mum,' said Rosie. Then a delighted expression spread across her face. 'And she's gone to live in . . . Oh, Mum, are you thinking what I'm thinking?' Rosie's bright blue eyes opened even wider, just as though she hadn't already had the selfsame idea herself.

'Yes . . . Joan lives in London now. Finchley. They moved down there for her husband's job; he's in insurance or something. We've always been good friends, Joan and me. And she's never had a family so they've plenty of room. Of course we'd have to pay her, just as though you were in proper lodgings.' Jenny's face grew serious as she looked at the excited gleam in Rosie's eyes. 'Mind you, I'm not promising anything, Rosie.' That was what Mum had always said, Rosie recalled, ever since she and Patsy were children, but she usually managed to turn up trumps. 'Don't build your hopes up. But we'll see what we can do.'

'Thanks, Mum,' said Rosie simply. She leaned forward and took hold of her mother's hand across the kitchen table. 'Thanks for everything. You've done so much for me, ever since I was a little girl, and I really am grateful, you know.' She squeezed her mother's hand and could see the trace of a tear glistening in the corner of Jenny's eye, just as she could feel one pricking at her own.

Jenny hastily brushed away her own tear and patted Rosie's hand. 'Never mind all that silly nonsense. I know you're grateful, love. You don't need to tell me.'

Jenny wasn't a great one for eloquent phrases and for demonstrative shows of affection. Rosie remembered that she had been, more so, when she and Patsy were younger, but Jenny had seemed much more staid of late, influenced more than she realised, maybe, by her taciturn, seemingly unemotional husband.

The family hardly ever referred to the time, before Rosie's adoption, when she had been Jenny's evacuee, but Rosie was thinking about it now. It had seemed almost too wonderful to be true, an answer to the childish prayers she had thought would never be answered, when Rosie had known that she was to stay with Auntie Jenny and Patsy forever, that she was to be a real member of the Bradshaw family. As a child, at that time, she had had to push to the back of her mind the dreadful reason for this happening, the tragic fact that her real mother, Daisy White, had been killed in an air raid. She had loved her mother – of course she had – but memories of her had grown very hazy during the time she had lived in Blackpool, absorbed so happily into her new surroundings.

Now, as an adult, Rosie had vague recollections – very vague, because she didn't often allow her mind to dwell on them – of a pretty woman with red lips and platinum blonde hair, and a succession of . . . friends, 'uncles' Rosie had called them. She pushed the memory of these callers at the terraced house near the Liverpool docks to the back of her mind, as she always did. Auntie Jenny had, unbelievably, become her mum and Patsy, her best friend, had become her sister. To Rosie there was no one in the world like Jenny. She had loved her from the moment she saw her at the reception centre in the Methodist Hall in Blackpool, serving tea in her flowered pinny and taking the frightened Rosie so lovingly under her wing. Rosie remembered how scared she had been at leaving home, though she had always tried to pretend that she was such a tough little customer. No, there was no one in the world like Jenny, her mum, and there never would be. Rosie loved her far more than she could say, far more than she could ever let her know.

It had all happened as Jenny had so unwittingly suggested, as Rosie had so artfully contrived. Soon after the end of her two-year intermediate art course in Castleburn, Rosie had gone to stay with Joan and Bernard Carstairs at their home in Finchley. It had been accepted without any hesitation that Rosie was resident there and she was admitted to the art school in South Kensington in September. By this time she had acquired her own flat, a one-room attic apartment in a square just off the Cromwell Road.

The houses which faced the square on three sides were tall narrow buildings of stucco and red brick, built in the Georgian era for the affluent gentry, but now mainly divided into flats for the shifting cosmopolitan population of post-war London. The stucco facing on the houses was now a dirty yellow-cream colour and the paintwork was cracked and fading, but Rosie loved the feeling of decayed grandeur that still pervaded the area. In the centre of the square was a garden surrounded by iron railings – which had obviously managed to survive the salvage campaign of the war – where nannies used to walk their charges in the Victorian and Edwardian days, and where now an army of cats yowled every midnight. During the daytime though it was a peaceful enough spot surrounded by plane trees, their branches festooned with prickly balls and the foliage of autumn. Each morning as she hurried to her first lecture Rosie noticed that there was a fresh carpet of leaves on the ground, swept away each day by the roadsweeper then just as quickly renewed by Mother Nature. On the fourth side of the square was the main road, busy with traffic both day and night. Rosie had thought at first that she would never get used to the roar of London's traffic. Now, after a few months in the city, she took it for granted. It was just a part of the whole scene which she was growing to love more and more each day.

Her flat was at the top of the four-storey building. It was a large room with two small windows at the front overlooking the square, and at the back a skylight from which she had a splendid view of back gardens and roof-tops and chimneys stretching away in the direction of Hyde Park, a half mile or so distant. This window, letting in the north light, was ideal for an artist and had been the main feature which had made Rosie determined to have this flat. All art students did much of their work at home and Rosie knew that in the spring and early summer, when the daylight lengthened, this place would be a Godsend to her. Now, in these days of early twilight, she was forced to work by the inferior electric light, except for the Saturday or Sunday when she was free from her stint at the teashop. Already the walls of the flat were hung with the results of Rosie's first few weeks at the art school: life drawings and studies of inanimate objects; sketches of evening gowns and casual wear; and, taking up most of the space, brightly coloured designs to be transferred eventually to fabrics. It was this branch of art, textile design, which Rosie was finding the most absorbing. And not only because of Jeff Burroni, the lecturer in this subject . . .

Rosie stared at the ceiling now, thinking about Jeff. Just at the point where the ceiling sloped there was an irregular crack, shaped like the map of Italy. Rosie let her eyes slip out of focus and her mind wander. Jeff was part-Italian, as his name suggested. He had the swarthy looks that betrayed his Latin origins, though there could be no mistaking that he was also a Londoner, born and bred. His accent, with faint Cockney overtones that he didn't try to disguise, gave him away immediately. Rosie knew he was from the East End. Bermondsey, she thought she'd heard someone say.

She had been very much aware of him from the first lecture. Most of the women students were. Rosie had noticed the sidelong glances at him as he leaned casually over some student's easel, his lean brown face alight with enthusiasm and his slender hands gesticulating and pointing out faults and ways of eliminating them. His hands were expressive, like quick brown moths flitting about, and he used them continually to express an idea or an image. Jeff was not very tall, nor conventionally handsome. His dark brown, almost black, hair which he wore rather long, curling untidily over the collar of his tweed jacket, was receding slightly at the temples, though he couldn't be more than thirty. His nose was a shade too long, but it was his eyes, deep brown and luminous, that gave his mobile face its arresting quality, lighting it up with warmth and eagerness. One could not help but be aware of Jeff Burroni, but Rosie had tried at first to stifle the foolish thought that he was equally aware of her. Don't be such an idiot, she told herself. Stop imagining that every man you meet is ready to fall at your feet in admiration. Grow up, Rosie Bradshaw. But by now she felt sure that she was not imagining Jeff's interest in her. Or else why would he have invited her to spend next Sunday afternoon with him, having lunch at a pub and then visiting the Tate Gallery?

He had paused by her side a few weeks ago in the lecture room, commenting on her bold use of colour, vivid splashes of crimson and ochre incorporated into a modernistic design which was to be transferred to a cotton fabric.

'Not bad, not bad at all. Quite pleasing, in fact.' Jeff Burroni was never fulsome in his praise of his students' work. 'A brave use of colour, but a more definite curve is needed here, I think.' He stood back from the easel and narrowed his eyes, making a sweeping curve in the air with his right hand. 'Here, let me show you.' He took the brush from Rosie's hand and dipped it in the splodge of crimson paint on the palette. 'Carry this curve down here . . . so . . . and it continues the pattern into the next sequence. You see?'

Rosie nodded approvingly. 'Yes. I can see that's much better.' With only one brush stroke Jeff had improved the design tremendously, giving it a roundness and completeness that had been lacking. 'Thank you.' She turned to smile at him.

He handed the brush back to her and nodded. 'Good . . . carry on.' She expected him to move away to the next student, but he remained where he was, his fingers drumming lightly on the top of her easel. He smiled at her then, the whole of his face coming alight and his eyebrows raised in a quizzical manner. 'You're enjoying these lectures, aren't you? You're really absorbed in it all.' He nodded at her thoughtfully a few times, his eyes suddenly growing more serious. 'I've noticed you, your complete involvement . . . Margaret Rose, isn't it? Margaret Rose Bradshaw.'

She laughed out loud. 'Yes . . . Yes, it is, but nobody ever calls me that. I've not been called Margaret since I was a little girl at school. Teachers sometimes insist on calling you by your first name, even though you tell them that you're always called something else at home. It's the first name on the register, I suppose. "Me name's Rosie," I used to say to my first teacher – that was when I lived in Liverpool – but she took no notice.'

Rosie stopped abruptly, aware that she was chattering inanely, something that she always tried to avoid doing, but Jeff's sudden interest in her, and the use of her full name, had taken her by surprise. She knew, though, that he was very well aware that she was always called Rosie. There was an air of informality about this place, students and lecturers being on Christian name terms and encouraged to regard one another as equals rather than as teachers and pupils. They had all exchanged first names at the preliminary lectures, though the tutors could hardly be expected to remember all the students' names straightaway. But Rosie was quite sure that Jeff Burroni knew her name. He must have heard her friends using it. Maybe he had just wanted an excuse to linger and chat to her, but she was determined not to behave like a silly moonstruck schoolgirl. A trifle embarrassed now at her loquacity, she looked away from him and turned back to her easel.

But Jeff still stood there. 'You were called after the nation's favourite princess, I suppose?'

There was just the slightest touch of acerbity in his tone, though he was still smiling warmly. Rosie wondered if the red tie he always wore with his checked shirt and somewhat shabby tweed jacket was indicative of his politics. Many lecturers, she knew, were left-wing and not everyone was such a staunch Royalist as her mother, who had been more so than ever since the lovely young Queen came to the throne. Rosie and Patsy, as children during the war years, had been nurtured on tales of 'the nation's little princesses', and Rosie had been very proud to be named after the younger of the two girls. Now she no longer thought about it except when someone commented on it, as they usually did when they found out her full name. She knew that it was no longer so fashionable to be named after Royalty, and that a minority of the population were questioning the relevance of the monarchy in the modern world. Maybe Jeff Burroni was one of them?

'Yes, I was called after Princess Margaret,' she answered him now, with a grimace. 'I think a lot of girls my age were, though most of them were called just Margaret, not Margaret Rose. There were six Margarets in my form at the Grammar School, though by that time I'd managed to convince everyone that I liked to be Rosie.' She gave a little laugh. 'It dates us, doesn't it? I daresay when we get older everyone will be able to guess our age. But I thought it was marvellous when I was a little girl, being called after the princess. I used to swank about it to everyone.'

'Mmm . . .' Jeff nodded. 'I think Rosie suits you better, though you're not unlike the princess, come to think of it. She's the pick of the bunch, in my opinion. Quite a spirited lass. I admire her for not always wanting to conform.'

'Yes, I agree with you,' said Rosie. 'I should imagine it's quite a job trying to make Princess Margaret do as she's told.'

'You have the same colouring too,' Jeff remarked, looking closely at Rosie. 'Dark hair and deep blue eyes. I saw the princess drive past once . . . I was struck by the vivid blue of her eyes. Quite remarkable. Yours are just like them, Rosie.' He was staring at her now, unsmiling, and as Rosie looked back into the depths of his dark brown eyes she found it difficult to look away.

Then Jeff smiled again, quite casually, before moving on to the next student. 'Nice chatting to you, Rosie,' he said. 'We must do it again sometime.'

She had felt deflated for a few moments as she had seen him talking, seemingly in an equally engrossed manner, to the next girl student, but had told herself firmly not to be such a ridiculous fool. Since then, however, he had joined her several times at the coffee break, and now he had asked her to meet him on Sunday. There could be no mistaking now, surely, his obvious interest in her?

Rosie had not yet visited the Tate Gallery, though she had had such good intentions when she first moved down to London. But there never seemed to be time, what with working several hours each day at Lyon's, to say nothing of the lectures and tutorials – the main reason for her being in London, of course, and not to be neglected – and all the work she brought back to her flat to complete in the evenings. She had, however, visited the National Gallery in Trafalgar Square, just once, and had discovered, as the other students had told her, that a day was not enough – indeed, a week would not be enough – to absorb its treasures. The Constables and Turners, the sixteenth-century Italian paintings and the Dutch and Flemish works of the seventeenth century . . . Rosie had wandered round the galleries in a daze, mesmerised.

Likewise at the V and A. That enormous treasure house was not very far from Rosie's flat, nor from the art school, but she had been inside the vast Victorian building only twice since coming to live in South Kensington. And that was certainly not enough time to explore fully its seven miles of galleries and the world's greatest collection of decorative arts. But Rosie's two-year course was only just beginning. There would be time enough, surely, in the two years that lay ahead of her to visit all the places that she wanted to explore, to see all the sights that she had heard so much about.

She had wandered frequently, though, through the environs of South Kensington and Knightsbridge, preferring whenever possible to walk rather than to ride on the bus or tube. She armed herself with a good map as she soon learned how easy it was, in London's vastness, to take a wrong turning and end up walking miles in the wrong direction. She felt that she now knew Kensington Gardens as well as she knew Stanley Park in Blackpool or the riverside gardens in Castleburn. The whimsical statue of Peter Pan; the Round Pond, around which grey-coated nannies, employed by the affluent middle class, still wheeled their young charges; and the brooding, monumental structure of the Albert Memorial. Rosie thought this was an outrageous example of Victorian ugliness and sentimentality, and yet there was an awe-inspiring quality about it too. Always she saw things with the artist's eye, as a subject for a painting. With the purple dusk gathering around its soaring pinnacle and the background of skeletal autumn trees, this monument erected by a great British queen to her beloved German husband made an arresting scene.

The colours of her surroundings fascinated Rosie. She carried them in her mind's eye then tried to transfer them to her paintings and designs. Further along Knightsbridge were the barracks of the Household Cavalry. Rosie loved to watch the riders emerge in their ceremonial blue or scarlet, a startling contrast to the browns and yellows of autumn all around them, their black boots and steel breast-plates gleaming in the pale, watery sunlight. She wandered through the various squares and walks of Knightsbridge, many of them not shabby, like the square where she lived, but with dwellings like dolls' houses, neat and tidy and clean, with wrought-iron balconies and gay window boxes.

Then there were the antique shops and craft shops, auction rooms and shops selling furniture and furs, pictures and prints and jewellery. Rosie loved window shopping, and almost always she ended up at Harrods. Harrods was a dream, a constant delight. Sometimes she wandered inside, not to buy but just to look – or, more accurately, to gawp in wide-eyed wonder – for the prices were far beyond her modest purse. But usually she was content to gaze at the magnificent window displays. She had never seen anything like them, certainly not in Castleburn, or even in Leeford, where dresses and coats tended to be crammed together, higgledy-piggledy, with little thought to coherence or design. Here there was style and grace and elegance, one single garment highlighted by skilful use of background and drapery, or several objects grouped together in co-ordinating shades or vividly contrasting colours. And always it was pleasing to the eye, another impression to be stored away in Rosie's mind for future reference when she returned to her sketch pad or palette.

She met Jeff, as arranged, outside the St James's Park tube station at one o'clock. She was pleased that he was the first to arrive and he greeted her eagerly, taking her hand and tucking it closely under his arm. Rosie was glad of her red woollen mittens and the long matching scarf, wound twice round her neck with the ends dangling to the waist of her duffel-coat. Jeff, she noticed, wore no scarf and did not appear to feel the cold though today, as a concession to the approaching winter, he was wearing not the familiar tweed jacket but a dark coat almost identical to Rosie's. It was the first really chilly day of autumn, late October, and their breath made clouds in the still air as they walked quickly through the quiet London streets. It was the only day of the week when the city was not a maelstrom of madly hurrying traffic and people, and Rosie welcomed its Sunday somnolence.

They ate a simple snack lunch of cheese and pickles with crusty bread, followed by apple pie, at a small pub-cum-eating-house that Jeff knew of, just off Victoria Street. It was a cosy place with a log fire, not brought up-to-date with the introduction of a juke-box, nor made to appear olde-worlde with horse brasses and mock Tudor beams. It was unashamedly Victorian, with oak panelling and red plush seating, etched glass and fly-blown mirrors, and prints of Dickens characters on the walls; a place that Dickens himself might well have frequented, Rosie thought.

'You managed to find your way then, on the tube?' Jeff asked. 'You didn't get lost?'

'Of course not!' she said brightly. 'I'm getting quite used to it now, I can tell you. I'm no longer the country bumpkin I was when I first arrived. I'll be travelling around like a real Londoner soon. I must admit, though, I found it a bit confusing when I first came, especially when I had to change lines. All those different coloured signs and corridors and folk dashing about. And if you're not careful you can get on a train going in the wrong direction. I've done that a couple of times.'

'Yes, it's easily done, I daresay.' Jeff smiled and Rosie was struck again by the liveliness of his face and the warmth in his deep brown eyes. 'Of course the tube's like a second home to me. In fact, that's what it was during the Blitz. We slept down there when I was a lad, you know, away from the bombing raids.'

'Yes, I've heard about that,' said Rosie. 'It must have been terrible down here. We didn't know we were born, up in Blackpool. That was where I lived then . . . I was evacuated there. You didn't serve in the war then, Jeff?' she asked now, not wanting to start talking about herself.

'I should think not, indeed! How old do you think I am, for goodness' sake?' Jeff sounded indignant, but he was still smiling.

'I'm sorry . . . I wasn't meaning to suggest that you're old. Of course not.' Rosie looked at him steadily. 'But I know you must be a few years older than me, and I was twelve when the war finished. So I thought perhaps . . .'

'That I got in for the last part of it?' He nodded. 'You're not so far out, Rosie. I was eighteen just after the end of the war, so I missed it. Worse luck, I thought. I would like to have done my bit, but my ma was relieved, of course. My two brothers had both been in the forces, but luckily they both came back. I know I look older than I really am. Always have done. I'm twenty-five.'

'And you've always lived in London, Jeff? Bermondsey, isn't it?'

'Yes, that's right. Real Cockney, I am, sound of Bow Bells and all that.' Jeff grinned. 'Third-generation we are now, us Burronis. My grandfather was Italian, of course. He came over to work on the docks, and that's where my old man worked as well. He's retired though now.'

'You still live with your parents then?'

'No . . .' He hesitated. 'I have a flat now, not very far away, but I still see my parents as much as I can. I'm the youngest, see, and I feel responsible for them. They did a lot for me, letting me go to college. It's not been easy, but they're getting on their feet now we've all left home and they've only themselves to think about.'

'You come from a big family then?'

'Six of us,' said Jeff shortly. 'Three boys and three girls . . . That's enough about me though.' He shook his head dismissively. 'I don't want to talk about myself. Very boring subject.' He smiled at Rosie then leaned across the table and touched her hand. 'What about you? You were evacuated, you said? On your own or with your sister? I've heard you say before that you have a sister.'

Rosie gave a little sigh before she embarked on the story

that she seemed to have told so many times before, that Patsy was not her real sister, that she, Rosie, had been adopted during the war when her mother died.

'And you and Patsy get on well together, do you?' asked Jeff.

'Yes, fine. We did . . . We do, but it won't do either of us any harm to have a change of scene, Patsy more so than me, possibly.' Rosie paused thoughtfully before going on. She had never confided these thoughts to anyone before. 'To be quite honest, I think Patsy was getting fed up of having me around all the time, a bit jealous, perhaps. You can't blame her. She didn't say anything, of course, but I sort of sensed it.'

Jeff smiled at her, so very understandingly. 'Yes, family relationships are hell at times, aren't they? I know . . . I've had experience of them. And what about your young brother? How does he fit in?'

'Our Victor? Not a care in the world, except for football. He's a happy-go-lucky soul is our kid. You can be sure he won't be worrying his head about things like this, not yet at any rate – he's only eleven – but I doubt he will ever be a worrier.' Rosie picked up her glass of lager and lime, a taste she had acquired since moving south, and took a long drink. Then she replaced it on the beer mat, musingly running her finger down the glass. 'My parents have both been so wonderful, ever since I first went to live in Blackpool. But you can never tell them how much they mean to you, can you?'

'It's almost impossible,' he agreed.

'But, you know, when all's said and done,' Rosie went on thoughtfully, 'Jenny and Tom are not my real parents. I never knew my father at all, and my mother I can remember only very dimly. Sometimes I can't help wondering who I am . . .' She looked across at Jeff and gave a wistful smile.

'You're you, Rosie.' He squeezed her hand and grinned. 'You're Margaret Rose Bradshaw, aren't you? Come on, we'd better be moving if we want to get to the Tate this afternoon.'

He led her through side streets and short cuts, parts of London she had never seen before, past Westminster Cathedral and the Greycoat School on to Millbank. Rosie hadn't been any further south along the river than the Houses of Parliament and she looked around at the new scene with interest. 'You certainly know London, Jeff. It's different, having a native for a guide.'

'I should know it by now. I've lived here all my life, although I doubt that I'll ever know it all, it's so vast. We'll go exploring, Rosie, shall we, another Sunday?'

Her heart leapt and she nodded at him happily. 'Yes, I'd like that.'

'Here we are then. The Tate Gallery. Now, what would you like to see? We can't see it all in one go, of course.'

'You choose.' Rosie smiled at him. 'You've been here before.'

'All right then, I'll try, but I'm spoiled for choice, as I always am. We mustn't miss the Turners, though.'

Rosie found the Tate Gallery, with its displays of more modern paintings, even more fascinating than the National Gallery. She admired the work of the Impressionists, and stood spellbound in front of a painting by Monet in varying shades of blue and greens, depicting the changing light of a summer's day reflected in a lily pond. She felt breathless with admiration of it all, too moved to speak.

'Remarkable, isn't it?' said Jeff, very softly, speaking for her. 'Impressionism . . . the effect of reflected light on an outdoor scene. Just look at the use of colour . . . that subtle turquoise and those touches of pink blossom. Colours fascinate you, don't they, Rosie? I've noticed in class.'

'Yes, I always want to make them live in my designs . . . I can't say I understand these paintings, though,' she commented as she gazed at the examples of twentieth-century art, the works of Picasso and Dali and Matisse. 'But I must admit I find them appealing.'

'Who can understand them fully?' Jeff grinned. 'All these "isms" – Cubism, Expressionism, Surrealism.' He waved his hands expressively in the air. 'It's beginning to have an impact though, Rosie, on modern ideas of design. The Festival of Britain last year was a turning point, all that use of bold colour and exhilarating shapes.' Again he made a sweeping movement in the air with his hands. 'It's finding its way into furniture now, and textiles and wallpaper.'

'Yes, Dad redecorated our bedroom last year,' Rosie told him as they walked back towards the tube station. 'Patsy's and mine – we share a room at home – and Mum was quite shocked at the wallpaper we chose. Well, not shocked exactly – startled would be a better word. It was all rectangles and squares and squiggles – Patsy said it was very Picassoish. I must admit it was my choice really, but Patsy went along with it. Anyway, Mum thought it was most unsuitable, especially in a bedroom. She's still into flowers and leaves.'

'Aren't all mums?' he smiled. 'Give them a few years though, and they'll change their mind.'

'I'll be OK now, Jeff,' said Rosie as they walked into Westminster tube station. 'It's only a few stops on the tube. Thank you so much for today. I've really enjoyed it.'

'No, I'll see you safely home.'

'There's no need, honestly. It's the wrong direction for you.'

But he insisted on accompanying her all the way back to her flat. Dusk was falling as they walked along the quiet streets of South Kensington and stopped outside the tall Georgian house.

''Bye, Rosie.' Jeff put his hands on her shoulders and leaned forward and kissed her cheek. His mouth felt warm against her cold skin, but he made no attempt to kiss her lips, nor to wait for an invitation to enter her flat. It was too soon, the time was not yet ripe, but Rosie could wait. She knew that Jeff would ask her out again, that there would be another chance, plenty of chances . . .

''Bye, Jeff. And thanks again. See you tomorrow.'

'Yes, see you, Rosie.' He lifted his hand in farewell then strode off across the dark square.

The evening air was chilly, but Rosie felt warm, glowing in every part of her.

Chapter 5

'Now, you're sure you'll be all right on your own? I'm sorry to let you down, love, but I really must nurse this cold. I feel pretty grim, I must admit, and I've that essay on Wordsworth to finish before Monday. And my nature notes to do. Oh God! Whyever did I start this wretched course? I'm not going to be able to keep it up. I know I'm not!'

Kath's eyes were streaming and her nose looked red and raw with constant blowing, but Patsy knew that her friend didn't really mean what she said about the course. Kath loved it all, every minute of it, and was an ideal student, conscientious and thorough, with her work always handed in on time. Patsy tried to emulate her, but didn't always succeed. Kath must be feeling wretched to talk like this, even if it was only half in jest.

'Never mind the flippin' essay!' retorted Patsy. 'You're in no fit state to do that now, Kath. Get yourself to bed with a hot water bottle. Look, I'll fill it up for you before I go out. Or would you like me to get Matron? You look as though you should be in the sick bay to me . . .' Kath frowned and shook her head vehemently. 'OK then,' Patsy went on, 'but I'm going to make sure you're comfortable before I go down to Leeford.'

'I feel as though I'm letting you down, Patsy. We always

spend our Saturday afternoons together. It'll be the first one we've missed. Are you sure you'll be all right?' Kath asked again.

'Give over nattering.' Patsy grinned. ''Course I'll be all right. What d'you think's going to happen to me on Saturday afternoon in Leeford? I'm likely to get trampled to death in the shops, but nobody's going to try and run off with me. No such luck! Now, get yourself to bed, there's a good girl, and I'll make you a cup of tea and fill up your hot water bottle. In this cupboard, is it?'

Patsy busied herself in the GP room, boiling the kettle and putting a spoonful of tea into the small brown pot that Kath had brought from home. It made a change for her to be fussing over her friend like this and she was quite enjoying it, though she was sorry that Kath was feeling so rotten. It was a way of repaying her for all the kindness and friendliness the girl had shown her since they started at CLTC about six weeks ago. A friendship that was heartily reciprocated; Kath and Patsy were inseparable now, in the way, Patsy often thought, that she and Rosie had been at one time.

'There you are then. Shove this down by your feet.' She thrust the hot water bottle, shaped like a rabbit with a blue bow round its neck – a reminder of Kath's childhood and a link with home – beneath the chilly white sheet, then handed her the mug of steaming tea. 'I've put plenty of milk and sugar in, the way you like it. Now, you're sure you're warm enough?'

'Yes, I'm fine thanks.' Kath nodded and smiled, but her grey eyes were watering and red-rimmed. 'I tell you what, Patsy. It's a darned sight more comfortable being ill here than at home. I know there's no Mam to fuss round us, but do you remember those freezing cold bedrooms? Ugh! Thank God for central heating, that's what I say. How on earth do they manage with one fire in the living room and the rest of the house like an ice-box?'

Patsy laughed. 'We're getting spoiled. Yes, I've often thought about it myself since coming here. Central heating's the answer, isn't it, for keeping warm? But best not to say anything at home, eh? They'd say we were getting big ideas! Anyway, you'll have to brace yourself for Arctic conditions again. It's half-term next weekend. You've got to get yourself better by then.'

'I'll be OK.' Kath sipped appreciatively at the hot tea. 'Mm . . . This is good. It beats all the medicines. And I've got the Vic to rub on my chest.' She gestured towards the small blue pot on the chair at the side of the bed and grinned. 'Mam's favourite remedy! Now off you go and enjoy yourself. I'll see you later. I'm going to have a sleep if I can when I've drunk this.'

Patsy put on her camel-hair coat and slung her green and white striped scarf round her neck, then walked down Sycamore Avenue to the tram stop. Kath and Patsy's usual Saturday afternoon jaunt was to the city of Leeford to look at the shops, then to treat themselves to coffee and a sticky bun or toasted tea-cake at Gino's coffee bar in the main street. After six weeks at college Patsy now felt as though she had always been part of the place.

She was working hard at the career that she had, if not exactly chosen, drifted into. Every evening between six and eight o'clock was the private study – or PS – period, when the students were supposed to remain in their own rooms, working on essays or projects or reading round a subject. Not that this rule was as strictly adhered to as it should be. Often friends would gather together in one room, talking and laughing and drinking coffee, preferring to leave their work till some other time. When the chatter and hilarity became too loud – the walls, alas, were very thin – there would be an irate shout of 'PS, please!' from further down the corridor, and the miscreants, suitably chastened, would curb their levity.

This private study was part of the day-to-day pattern, as were the other, now familiar, routines that filled the hours, the days, the weeks . . . Waking to the bell at 7 am each morning; eagerly scanning the breakfast table to see if there was a welcome letter from home sitting on your plate; looking forward – or otherwise – to the various dishes on the menu which were repeated with unvarying regularity each week – shepherd's pie, spam and chips, runny scrambled egg, suet pudding, rabbit in a casserole, masquerading as chicken – ugh! Even seven years after the end of the war some restrictions were still in evidence.

Patsy recalled with amusement the 'high tea' the first years had been subjected to on their second day at college, sitting up on the backs of their chairs, endeavouring to eat jelly with a fork! And, the next day, 'low tea', when they were made to grovel on the floor eating corned beef and chips with a spoon. Patsy doubted that Rosie had enjoyed such jocularity – or childishness, depending on how you looked at it – in the sedate surroundings of South Kensington.

Patsy had joined the choir and the country dancing club and the film society. Not for her the debating society or the ramblers' association or the athletic club, but every group had its share of eager followers. And every Saturday evening there was an informal dance in one of the halls of residence, which Patsy had attended a couple of times, when the gramophone blared out old Glenn Miller tunes – 'Moonlight Serenade' or 'American Patrol' – or tunes from the big bands of the era, Joe Loss, Ted Heath, Billy Cotton. Or sometimes, as a change from the gramophone, Neil Emmerson, one of the 'main music' students, played on the piano songs from the shows, *Oklahoma* or *South Pacific*, accompanied by another student on a somewhat squeaky violin. Some danced, while others preferred just to listen or to chat, and at eleven o'clock they all wandered back to their own halls of residence. There was an extension till half-past eleven on a Saturday, and she knew that some of the couples wandered off into the woods.

As for Patsy, she hadn't had any reason to alter her first opinion of the men students. They were friendly and chatty but, on the whole, uninteresting. The piano player, Neil, was a good-looking lad though – you couldn't help noticing him! But Patsy was still heart-whole, although quite a few attachments had been formed already in this first half-term. Or it could be, Patsy sometimes admitted to herself, that she was unused to conversing with men. In their company she seemed to retreat into her shell and to become tongue-tied. The Grammar School she had attended had been an all girls establishment, and at the Youth Club and church socials she had never seemed able to develop the easy camaraderie that Rosie had always shown with the opposite sex. But Patsy was untroubled by her lack of male company. Someone would come along for her one day, she was sure of that – 'Mr Right', as her mother sometimes said – there was plenty of time yet.

The tram clattered and clanged its way down into Leeford, along the now very familiar route, out of Woodley Bank, then past the football ground and the cricket ground and the University, into the city itself. Patsy alighted at the terminus, City Square, where the tram would turn round, and pulled the belt of her camel-hair coat more tightly round her waist and flung her striped scarf round her neck instead of letting it hang loosely, as the students usually did. It was chilly today and she was glad of its warmth and not just its decorative quality. Patsy felt that she really belonged, that she was a true student, now that she had the distinctive scarf of dark green, light green and white stripes; and the blazer too similarly striped, although it would soon be too cold to wear this garment as outdoor apparel.

She went to the bookshop first to purchase a couple of education textbooks she needed in preparation for the dreaded School Practice which would begin soon after half-term. Then she found she was unable to resist the shelves of Penguin books, the orange and white novels and classics, and the green and white mystery series. The latter were more to her taste at the moment as light relief from the serious reading which had to be undertaken for her English course. Margery Allingham, Dorothy Sayers, Agatha Christie . . . her favourite. She ran her finger along the row, reading the titles. *Murder on the Orient Express*, *Peril at End House*, *Death in the Clouds* . . . that was one she hadn't read, and she thought she could just about afford one and sixpence.

She jostled her way along Market Street. Saturday afternoon was always busy in Leeford and it seemed more so than ever today with crowds of people doing early Christmas shopping; there were cards and decorations on sale in the shops already. She pushed her way into Marks and Spencer, admiring the rows of jewel-bright jumpers, ruby and emerald and sapphire blue. She would love a red one, but with her hair colour it was supposed to be taboo. At least that was what Mum had always said. 'You can't wear red with your ginger hair, Patsy. It would look awful.' When she was a little girl Mum had always dressed her in pastel shades, pale blue and green and lemon, but never pink. How she had longed for pink or red! Now it no longer seemed to matter; redheads wore whatever colour they fancied.

Tentatively she picked up a bright red jumper, loving the soft angora feel of it, and held it up against herself, looking into the full-length mirror. Her hair had darkened considerably; it could almost be called chestnut now, and didn't look at all bad against the red. Quite good, in fact. She replaced the garment hurriedly on the rack before a sales girl had a chance to come along saying, 'Can I help you, Madam?' She couldn't afford it today, anyway; she had already bought a book. Perhaps next time, if it was still there. She glanced back at the jumpers longingly, more determined than ever to ask her mother if she could be allowed just a little money of her own.

The skirts were nice, too, especially those pencil slim ones with a long slit at the back – very daring! Black would look fantastic with red, and the style would suit her slender figure. She would present an entirely new image dressed like that . . . Reluctantly she dragged herself out of the shop and back into the main street. Kath wasn't there to keep her company, but Patsy still wanted to leave time for coffee and a bun at Gino's. The atmosphere there was always friendly and even though she was on her own she knew she would feel quite at home.

She paused at the windows of Lewis's and Schofield's. These prices really were out of her range, but it was nice to look. Fashions were still influenced greatly by the 'New Look' of 1947, that revolutionary return to romanticism after the austerity of the war years. Most of the dresses and coats were cut on curving lines, using an extravagant amount of material in the skirt. And costing an extravagant amount of money, too, Patsy thought as she hurried away. Such luxuries were not for her; she would concentrate on her dream of buying the black skirt and red jumper from Marks and Spencer.

She called in at a newsagent's to use her sweet coupons

on her weekly ration. It would just about run to a quarter of pear drops and a block of Cadbury's Dairy Milk to be shared between herself and Kath. She intended to stay in tonight, keeping her friend company, if Kath felt well enough. They could spend a happy evening, chatting and reading and eating sweets, without going to the weekly hop.

Gino's was fairly crowded as it always was on a Saturday afternoon. There was a buzz of conversation and laughter all around, and from the juke-box came the strains of Guy Mitchell, singing of how he loved his 'Truly Fair'. Patsy spotted an unoccupied table in a corner at the back and sat down gratefully; the court shoes that she always wore at weekends were pinching a little by now. She picked up the menu, although she already knew what she would order – a cup of coffee and a toasted tea-cake. She felt, rather than saw, someone looking at her and turned her head and glanced in the direction of the table opposite. Then she looked again and gave a gasp of surprise. Good gracious! Ronnie Sykes – or was it Raymond? She had never been able to tell them apart. And whatever was he doing here in Leeford?

He was grinning widely at her and she noted that he looked just the same; quite a lot older, of course – it must be about seven years since she had seen him and his brother – but so very familiar. Tousled hair of an indeterminate brown, laughing grey eyes, and that fresh-complexioned face, now much more rugged, with the firm, somewhat pugnacious jawline that she remembered so well from her schooldays. But which one of the twins was it?

Patsy rose eagerly to her feet and went towards him. Before she spoke she looked, trying to make her glance casual, at his forehead. One of the twins had had a birthmark, a very faint blemish over his left eyebrow, the only way of distinguishing him from his brother. This young man was without that mark, therefore it must be Ronnie.

'Hello, Ronnie,' she said now. 'How lovely to see you. And what a surprise!'

Ronnie pushed back his chair and stood to greet her. Patsy smiled to herself. His manners had improved; the old Ronnie of a few years back would never have bothered about such refinements of behaviour. 'Patsy Bradshaw! Little Patsy!' He held out his hand, large with squarish finger tips, and took her own hand in a firm grip. 'It certainly is a surprise!'

'What are you doing here?' They both spoke the words together and then burst out laughing.

'You'll join me, of course?' Ronnie Sykes pulled out the chair opposite to where he had been sitting, and Patsy sat down. 'Yes, I'd love to,' she said.

When she looked at him again she realised that it was obvious what he was doing here, in Yorkshire at any rate. He was in the army. He wore the familiar khaki battledress and his greatcoat and forage cap were on a chair beside him. 'You're in the army then,' she said somewhat needlessly. 'Are you stationed near here?'

'Yes – RASC. I'm at Catterick. And I've popped over to Leeford today to see my aunt. You remember Auntie Florrie, my dad's sister? She lives just outside Leeford.' Patsy didn't really remember, but she nodded. 'I've got a weekend pass, so she's asked me to stay the night. I'm going to catch the tram in a little while – she's expecting me for tea – but there's no hurry, no hurry at all.' He grinned at Patsy, showing a row of uneven, but very white, teeth. 'It's marvellous seeing you. I just can't get over it.' He shook his head. 'I said little Patsy, didn't I? But I can see you're not so little now. Grown up, haven't you?'

'I should hope so!' she replied indignantly. 'At least you didn't call me Carrots, did you? Or Titch. I used to hate you and your brother when you did that.'

'I don't think Carrots would apply now, any more than Titch.' Patsy could see that Ronnie was looking approvingly at her auburn hair, which curled on to the collar of her coat, just above her green and white scarf. She felt glad that she had washed it last night and that she was looking her best. 'Your hair's much darker now, isn't it?' he said. 'And you've shot up a lot an' all.'

'I should hope so,' said Patsy again, feelingly. 'I got fed up of being the smallest girl in the class.'

They broke off their conversation as the waitress appeared, her pad and pencil at the ready. 'Here, I'll get this,' said Ronnie. 'No . . . I insist,' as Patsy started to protest. 'What you having? Toasted tea-cake and a coffee? You're sure that's all? OK, then. And another cup of tea for me, luv,' he called after the waitress, 'to keep me girlfriend here company.'

Patsy didn't blush as she might once have done at Ronnie's remark, or as she might have done if any other young man had made it. She had known Ronnie Sykes long enough to take everything he said with a pinch of salt. It was certainly grand to see him again.

'And how long have you been in the army, Ronnie?' she asked now.

'About ten months. I was called up in January,' he replied. 'National Service, of course. I've been at Catterick all the time, but I'll most likely be posted to Germany next year for the last part of my training.'

Patsy recalled now that Ronnie and Raymond, though in the same class as herself at the Junior School, were several months older, their birthday, like Rosie's, being at the beginning of the scholastic year, in September. So Ronnie was now nineteen.

'And you're at college, I see,' he said, nodding towards her scarf. 'You see a lot of them green and white scarves around Leeford, don't you? City of Leeford Training College, isn't it?'

'Yes, that's right,' said Patsy.

'Hmmm . . . Very grand,' said Ronnie, in a droll voice, pulling down the corners of his mouth. 'I didn't know you wanted to be a teacher, Patsy? Of course you were always one of the brainy ones, weren't you, up at the top of the class? Not like me and me brother. Went to the Grammar School, didn't you?'

'Yes,' said Patsy quietly, not wanting to dwell on it. From what she remembered of the Sykes twins they had not been without ability, but had spent a good deal of their time clowning about instead of working. She thought that they had gone on to a Secondary Modern school in Blackpool, but she had lost touch with them since moving to Castleburn. She recalled now that her mother and the twins' mother, Eileen Sykes, had once been firm friends. The Sykes family had lived near them in Green Street, and the two young mothers had spent a lot of time together, but it was a while now since Patsy had heard her mother mention Eileen.

'How is Auntie Eileen?' she asked.

'Me mam's fine, and me dad. He still works for the Electricity Board. I daresay he'll be busy with the Illuminations just now. I think they finish next weekend, so they'll have to take 'em all down again. We moved from North Shore, you know, to a house at Marton.'

'Yes, I remember,' said Patsy. 'That was why we didn't see so much of you when we came over to visit my grandma. And what about your Raymond? He'll be doing National Service, too, I suppose?'

'No, 'fraid not.' Ronnie shook his head, looking serious for a moment. 'He was deferred on medical grounds. We had a bit of a scare a while back, 'cause he contracted TB. It wasn't too serious though, and he seems to be over it now, but the army was out of the question. Lucky so and so!' Ronnie grinned. 'No, I shouldn't say that. I don't mean it, of course, but he seems to be right as rain now.'

'Poor Raymond,' said Patsy. 'Do give him my best wishes, won't you? I remember how alike you were. I used to have such a job telling you apart.'

'We're not so much alike now,' replied Ronnie. 'Our Ray's a lot thinner – with the TB, you know – and he's a lot more serious now. He works in an office – white collar job an' all that. He managed to do quite well in spite of only going to the Secondary Modern, same as me.'

He stopped speaking for a moment as the waitress came to the table with his second cup of tea and Patsy's coffee and tea-cake. Patsy thought to herself that this was the second time that Ronnie had referred to school, to the fact that she had been to a Grammar School and he and his brother to a Secondary Modern. As if these things mattered; it was well known now in educational circles that many children were late developers. She hoped that Ronnie hadn't ended up with an inferiority complex because he hadn't been to a Grammar School. Remembering the Sykes twins, though, she doubted it. They had both been very ebullient characters. Nevertheless, she tried to put him at his ease.

'And what did you do, Ronnie, before you joined up?' she asked now. 'I'm sure you had a good job as well?'

'Not so bad . . . not so bad.' He grinned again. 'I was apprenticed to a joiner and shopfitter. I finished my training and I've a decent job to go back to . . . So you're living in Yorkshire now, when you're not at college, I mean? D'you like it then, as much as Blackpool?'

'Yes, we all like it in Castleburn,' Patsy replied,

'although I still miss the seaside. My father was born in Castleburn, of course. He's a real Yorkshireman and couldn't wait to get back to the other side of the Pennines. And Mum settled down quite well. Rosie's not up here though now. She's at art college in London.'

'That's right! Rosie the evacuee,' said Ronnie, as though he had only just remembered her. But Patsy was quite sure he couldn't have forgotten Rosie. No one ever did. 'She was a rum kid, wasn't she?' Ronnie laughed. 'I remember how she used to look after Ben, that little kid we had staying with us during the war. Proper little mother to him, she was. She gave me such a thump on the jaw once, for teasing him.' He rubbed the side of his face ruefully. 'Aye, she was a character all right . . . Rosie White.'

'Rosie Bradshaw,' Patsy corrected him. 'My parents adopted her, you know.'

'Yes, I did know.' Ronnie nodded. 'She used to stick up for you an' all, didn't she, when us lads used to torment you? Tough little customer, she was. How's she doing then? Is she going to be a teacher too?'

'No, I don't think she'll go in for teaching. I think she'd like to be a dress designer.'

'Mmm . . . Very grand,' said Ronnie again. 'You have come up in the world, you Bradshaws; teaching and dress designing.'

'Not yet, Ronnie. There's quite a while to go yet,' Patsy told him. 'I'm only at the beginning of my two-year course. So's Rosie. We've all sorts of things to get through first – exams and teaching practice and all that.'

'You've done well, all the same,' said Ronnie, looking admiringly at Patsy. 'You sound different as well.'

'What do you mean, I sound different?' She gave a little frown.

'Well . . . sort of posh. Not dead ordinary, like me. You've not got your Lancashire accent any more.'

Patsy laughed out loud. 'Oh, that was my mother's doing. She developed what you might call delusions of grandeur when we moved to Castleburn. Elocution lessons for me and Rosie – I should say Rosie and I, shouldn't I?' she added, grinning. 'She got it into her head that she wanted us to speak nicely, to have all the chances she'd missed as a girl. So it was elocution lessons for the two of us, and piano lessons for me. I didn't get very far with that, though. I just about struggled through Grades 1 and 2, but it'll be quite useful when I get to be an infant teacher . . . if I ever do,' she added quietly. 'Rosie didn't have piano lessons though. She was concentrating on her drawing even then. She's a real talent for it.'

She stopped speaking to find Ronnie regarding her intently, his grey eyes serious now, but alight with a warmth and interest that took her aback for a moment. She smiled uncertainly at him, finding it difficult to look away from his steadfast gaze.

When he spoke again after a few seconds, although it seemed longer, his voice was quieter. 'It's grand seeing you again, Patsy, it really is. I can't get over it, coming into Leeford and meeting you. I'd no idea you were at college here. Would you meet me again?' he asked eagerly, reaching out and taking her hand. 'Next Saturday perhaps?'

'I can't next Saturday,' she said, sounding – and feeling – a little regretful. 'It's half-term and I'll be going home to see my parents. It'll be the first time I've been back since term started. Some other time though. I'd love to see you again, Ronnie.'

'The Saturday after then?' he said quickly. 'A fortnight today. How about that?'

'Yes . . . yes, that would be lovely,' she agreed. 'You

manage to get away from camp all right, do you, Ronnie?'

'Yes, it's not too bad. It's not as if there's a war on. I've got a forty-eight-hour pass this weekend, so I can go and see Auntie Florrie. I could have taken you out tonight, Patsy – to the pictures, or something – except that I've arranged to go to my aunt's. She'll be expecting me, see.'

'That's all right, Ronnie. My friend will be expecting me back at college, anyway. She'd be a bit anxious if I didn't turn up at tea-time. How do you get to Leeford? On the train?'

'Bus. There's a good service from just outside the camp, and it's only about forty miles or so, less than two hours' journey. I haven't been into Leeford all that much, to be honest; there's not been anything to come for, apart from Auntie Florrie . . . There is now, though.' He smiled at her again, creasing the laughter lines around his eyes and mouth. He really was quite a handsome lad, in a craggy kind of way, she thought as she looked at him, though she had never realised it before. 'How about you, Patsy?' he asked. 'You're free on a Saturday, are you?'

'Yes, just one lecture Saturday morning, then we're free for the rest of the weekend. We have to be in by half-past eleven, though.'

'Don't worry. I'll have you back long before that. I have to be back in camp myself by midnight. We could perhaps manage first house pictures, or there's a news theatre, isn't there? How about meeting me outside here – Gino's – the middle of the afternoon, and we'll take it from there?'

'Yes, that sounds fine,' said Patsy happily.

'OK then. Three o'clock suit you?'

Patsy nodded. 'It'll be great, Ronnie.'

'Come on then. We'd best be moving. I'll get this bill paid, then I'll see you to your tram and get meself off to Aunt Florrie's.'

He kissed her gently on the cheek as she boarded the

tram. 'Be seeing you then, Patsy. Fortnight today. Don't forget, now.'

'No, I won't do that, Ronnie,' she said quietly. 'There's no fear of that. It's been lovely meeting you again.'

She waved to him through the window, then watched as he strode across City Square to the tram stop at the other side. Whoever would have thought it? Ronnie Sykes, the terrible torment of her infant schooldays. She grinned contentedly to herself.

'My goodness, you're looking all bright-eyed and bushy-tailed,' Kath remarked as Patsy entered her friend's room. 'Come on. What's the big secret? Tell Auntie Kath.'

'What d'you mean? There isn't any secret.' But Patsy couldn't help the contented little smile that pulled at the corners of her mouth. 'Never mind about me. How are you feeling, Kath? That's what I've come to find out.'

'Much better, thanks, love. I've had a sleep and the Vic and aspirins seem to have done the trick.' The room was redolent with the distinctive vapour and Kath was, indeed, looking much brighter. 'Now come on, tell all. Something's happened, hasn't it?'

Patsy sat down on her friend's bed and grinned. 'I met a lad I used to know, that's all.'

'Some lad, if he can make you look like that!'

'Like what?'

'All glowing . . . Spill the beans then.'

So Patsy told Kath, as briefly and as casually as she could, about Ronnie and how she had arranged to meet him again. 'But I've only just remembered, Kath,' she said in conclusion. 'It's Saturday . . . our day.'

'Now don't you start worrying about that,' Kath told her. 'There are seven days in a week, loads of time for us to see one another. Anyway, you won't be seeing him every Saturday, will you?'

'No, of course not.'

'But you like him?'

'Yes, I like him, or else I wouldn't have said I'd go out with him. I used to hate him when I was a kid, but that's ages ago. He's . . . different now.'

'Mmm . . . He must be,' said Kath, with a shrewd glance at her friend. 'I don't know.' She grinned. 'I let you out of my sight for a couple of hours, and you end up with a fellow. I tell you what, Patsy. I bet you're glad I had this cold, aren't you?'

'Of course I'm not,' she retorted. 'What a thing to say! I'm glad you're feeling so much better, Kath. But I suppose you might say . . . it's an ill wind,' she added slyly.

Patsy couldn't explain the elation she felt at the thought of seeing Ronnie again. After all, it was only Ronnie Sykes. But it had been lovely to see a familiar face from her childhood, someone friendly and kind who took such an obvious interest in her. Patsy wasn't sure whether it was the familiarity that she welcomed or whether she really was attracted to him.

Chapter 6

'Had a good half-term, Patsy?' asked Jocelyn Reynolds as the two girls walked across to Derwent Hall where the weekly country dancing session was held.

'Yes, lovely, thanks,' Patsy replied. 'It was great to see Mum and Dad again, and my kid brother, too. And we went over to Blackpool for a day or two to see my gran. I told you, didn't I? She has a boarding house quite near the promenade.'

'Yes, you've told me – more than once,' said Jocelyn, smiling at her friend. 'I think you miss Blackpool on the quiet, don't you? I can tell by the dreamy look that comes into your eyes when you mention it.'

Patsy laughed. 'Really? I didn't realise I was so transparent. Yes . . . I suppose I do miss it. Rosie and I had some great times there when we were kids. She wasn't there last week – it was too far for her to travel from London – but the rest of us had a smashing couple of days. And we did something we've never done before. We went up the Tower, right to the top.'

Patsy found herself recapturing the excitement as she told Jocelyn about it. 'I thought I would be terrified. I haven't much of a head for heights, but our Victor kept telling me I was a scaredy old thing and I certainly wasn't going to be made to look a fool by a kid of eleven. And I was really glad I'd done it, Jocelyn, when we got to the top. The view was terrific . . .'

It had been the last night of the famous Illuminations and Tom had decided, after they had taken a tram-ride along the promenade to see all the glittering tableaux, that a fitting climax to the evening would be a trip up the Tower. It always amazed Patsy how different her father was when they were away from home. He seemed to cast off his diffidence and occasional moodiness to enter into the holiday spirit. It had been Tom who had wanted, in the first place, to return to his native Yorkshire, but Patsy guessed that at times he missed the seaside just as much as she did.

As the lift climbed steadily between the iron girders Patsy had closed her eyes tightly. 'Cowardy custard!' taunted Victor, digging her in the ribs. 'Just look, Patsy. It's smashing.'

So Patsy, somewhat timorously, looked through the glass window of the lift at the green dome of the Winter Gardens, the square tower of St John's church, the market and the shops and the houses all getting gradually smaller as they climbed higher. Then they were at the top and she stepped out, still a trifle fearful, wondering if she would ever dare to look down. But the whole area at the top of the Tower – a surprisingly large one – was completely glassed in and one got the impression of looking outwards rather than down.

'Gosh!' Patsy exclaimed, as she stood there with her mother, father and Victor, staring at the vast panoramic view. 'It's fantastic!'

It was dark, of course, so it was impossible to pick out landmarks as one could have done during the day – the mountains of North Wales, maybe, or nearer to home, her gran's boarding house – but the spectacle, nonetheless, was breathtaking. All those millions of lights, from the street-lamps, the floodlit buildings, the windows of houses and shops, and, above all, the Illuminations, stretching in a five-mile line along the promenade; multi-coloured lights, some gleaming steadily, others twinkling in and out and all from this distance looking like golden beads and flashing gemstones on a long, long necklace.

Looking inland Patsy could see the Town Hall, the Winter Gardens, North Station, and could make out the long line of Talbot Road and of the railway track leading out of town. And in the other direction the dark fathomless depths of the Irish Sea, the nearer white-capped waves illuminated by the myriad lights, but the farther ones black and forbidding, stretching away to an invisible horizon.

'Oh, I'm so glad we came, aren't you, Patsy?' said her mother. 'Thank you, Tom. It was a lovely idea. Just imagine, all those years we lived in Blackpool and we never went up the Tower.'

Patsy felt quite nostalgic just talking about it now to Jocelyn. 'And I appreciated the home cooking, too,' she went on to say. 'I didn't realise how much I missed my mum's apple pie and hot-pot till I tasted them again.'

Jocelyn nodded. 'Yes, it makes you appreciate home, doesn't it? When you're away from it for a while.'

'Yes . . .' Patsy replied slowly. 'But I wasn't sorry to get back to college. When I walked through the gate and saw Calder Hall again I thought, "Mmm . . . it's nice to be back." '

'College is OK, isn't it? Once you've got over feeling a bit homesick,' Jocelyn commented. 'It's good to get back and see all your friends again.'

Patsy was aware of her significant glance and smiled back at her somewhat warily. Patsy knew that Jocelyn was beginning to look upon her as her own special friend and, although Patsy quite enjoyed dancing with the girl once a week, she didn't really want to get involved with her any further than that. But she didn't quite know how to say so.

The two of them were sitting now at the side of the lounge in Derwent Hall. A space had been cleared in the centre for the country dancing session and they were getting their breath back after a boisterous rendering of 'The Dashing White Sergeant'. Jocelyn and Patsy had partnered one another at the country dancing club, which was attended by far more women than men, since the first week of term.

'I'd better be the man,' Jocelyn had said to Patsy the first evening. 'I'm taller than you.'

'Not all that much!' Patsy had retorted. Ever since she was a little girl at the Infant School she had had to put up with remarks about her height, or lack of it. Now, thank goodness, it was no longer the case. Patsy was pretty much the same height as many of the girls at college, five foot three or so. It was true, though, that Jocelyn was a few inches taller. 'Yes, I suppose you are just a bit taller than me,' Patsy had conceded. 'OK, you be the man, then.'

That was something else that Patsy was quite accustomed to, others taking the lead. First there had been Rosie, then Kath, and now Jocelyn. But Jocelyn was an excellent dancer, light on her feet and sure of her movements, and Patsy had responded well to her guidance.

'We dance well together, don't we?' Jocelyn often said, and Patsy enjoyed this hour of dancing each week tremendously. She did sometimes wish, though, that she could dance with someone else for a change. Jocelyn was an odd sort of girl who didn't seem to make friends very easily. She was Kath's college mother and Patsy knew that

Kath had found her very helpful when they first arrived. There had been no particular rapport between the two of them, though, just as there had not been between Patsy and her own mother, Gwen Travers. By now, of course, the first years were well-used to college life and no longer in need of 'parental' guidance. But that was what Jocelyn still seemed to want to give, not so much to Kath but to Patsy now. Patsy couldn't help feeling rather sorry for Jocelyn. She had an unfortunate manner – very brusque and bullying at times – which made the other girls shy away from her.

'Come on. You've had your rest.' Jocelyn pulled Patsy to her feet. 'It's "Sir Roger de Coverley" now . . .'

There she goes again, thought Patsy. Old bossy boots! She did wish that she could find another dancing partner, but the other students all seemed to assume that she and Jocelyn were bosom pals. Or maybe it was that no one particularly wanted to dance with Jocelyn . . .

'That was great, wasn't it?' she remarked as they walked back towards Calder Hall. 'Good fun and good exercise too. I'm surprised they don't get more there.'

'Each to his own, I suppose,' Patsy replied. 'There are so many activities to choose from, you just have to be selective. You can't possibly join in everything. And there's always work to be done, isn't there?'

'Too true,' said Jocelyn. 'And School Practice looming ahead as well, for you first years.'

'Don't mention it,' said Patsy with a shudder. 'I'm dreading it, I am really, though I feel a little bit better about it since we went on our first visit.'

'Don't worry. You'll be all right.' Jocelyn took hold of her arm. 'Listen, Patsy – I've a load of pictures I collected for my first and second SP. They might be useful to you, especially with me doing Infants, like you. I tell you what, why don't you come and have a look through them? You're very welcome to borrow some of them if you can make use of them. And I can perhaps give you a few tips as well.'

'That's very nice of you, Jocelyn,' said Patsy, though somewhat guardedly. 'Yes, I'll do that. I'll pop along to your room and have a look at them . . . sometime.'

'Why don't you come now?' Jocelyn turned and looked at her intently as they walked up the stairs of their own residence, Calder Hall. 'Just go and take your coat off then nip along to my room. I'll have them all ready for you.' Patsy felt herself flinching at Jocelyn's intent gaze and the girl was still holding on to her arm. Somewhat embarrassed, she eased herself away. 'All right then.' She glanced at her watch. 'It's nearly nine o'clock. I'll come after supper, shall I?'

'Oh, don't let's bother going down to supper,' said Jocelyn. 'I'll nip along to the GP room and make us some coffee, and I've some chocolate biscuits in my room that Mum insisted I should bring back. We'll have a little party.'

'OK then,' said Patsy with an inward sigh of resignation. But, in all fairness, she knew that Jocelyn had the reputation of being a very good student who had done extremely well on her first two teaching practices. Perhaps she might be able to give her, Patsy, some good advice. And that certainly wasn't to be sneezed at. 'See you in a few minutes then,' she said.

'There you are. Take a look through those,' said Jocelyn a little while later, pointing towards two large cardboard folders on the floor in the centre of her room. 'I'll just go and make us some coffee. Or would you prefer cocoa?'

'Yes, cocoa please,' said Patsy.

'Righto. Make yourself at home then. Won't be long.'

Patsy knelt on the blue woolly bedside rug, obviously an acquisition from Jocelyn's home. It was easier on the knees than the bare floor boards or the strips of worn Axminster which was the standard carpeting in the study bedrooms. She stared around; it was the first time she had been in Jocelyn's room, apart from popping her head round the door occasionally on her way to country dancing. The rooms didn't differ much, except in the colour of the walls and curtains and the individual touches that each student introduced. The walls of Jocelyn's room were an indeterminate fawn, the most boring colour imaginable, Patsy thought, but possibly easier on the eye than the bilious green of her own room, and the curtains and bedspread were mainly brown, a dull dingy brown, the colour of soil that needed digging. The blue rug added a splash of colour, though, as did the beautifully embroidered cushion on the armchair, a design of brilliant flowers and birds of paradise. There was another embroidered picture on the wall, a peacock with its tail outspread, in vivid blues and greens and purples. Patsy went closer to admire it, marvelling at the neatness of the stitches and the quality of the workmanship. It must have taken ages to do. Was it Jocelyn's own handiwork? she wondered. Or maybe her mother's.

Patsy had a great admiration for people who could sew as she herself was hopeless with a needle. As soon as she started to stitch up a hem or sew on a button, the cotton immediately tangled itself into knots, and she remembered getting into trouble at the Grammar School when she attempted to sew with thread a mile long instead of the required few inches. Patsy's mother, Jenny, was very competent with a needle, a gift which had not been passed on to her daughter. In fact, Patsy wondered at times just where her own particular talents lay. She had been taught in Sunday School that everyone had talents and must learn to use them, but Patsy was still searching for hers. She was moderately good at quite a lot of things, but there seemed to be nothing at which she excelled. Perhaps her bent would make itself known during her two years at college. She certainly hoped so; it would be great if it turned out, after all, that she had a gift for teaching, though she often doubted it.

She was still sorting through the pictures when Jocelyn entered the room carrying a tin tray on which were two mugs of steaming cocoa. 'I wouldn't mind borrowing these, Jocelyn,' she said. 'There are some good nature pictures and some of Bible stories. You need such a lot, don't you? And I've only just started making my own collection.'

Patsy got up from her knees and took a mug from the tray and a chocolate biscuit from the packet that Jocelyn was holding out to her. 'Thanks. This is really nice of you.' She sat down on the armchair and looked across at the older girl who was sitting on the bed. 'They're very keen on us having an illustration for every story, aren't they? Quite a job when you consider that we have to tell a story every day on School Practice.'

'Yes,' Jocelyn replied, 'and the operative word is "tell". You know, don't you, that you're expected to tell the stories and not to read them?' Patsy nodded. 'Goodness knows why,' Jocelyn went on. 'Children like to see the book on your knee, but you have to learn the story off by heart. I must admit, though, that I cheat sometimes and read it, especially if I know that there'll be no tutor coming in. But if there is, then you have to stick to the rules, I'm afraid, or you'll be for the high jump.'

'Oh dear,' said Patsy anxiously. 'You're getting me all worked up again, thinking about School Practice. Is it very awful?'

'No, not really,' said Jocelyn. 'Not if you're well prepared, and it's up to you to see that you are. I've not much time for the students who are not prepared to do any work, but I know you're not one of those, Patsy. No, you'll be OK, don't worry. Anyway, never mind about school practice now. Let's just enjoy our little party. It's fun, isn't it? Just you and me. It's the first time you've been in my room, isn't it? I think it's strange when we're such good friends.'

Warning bells began to sound in Patsy's brain, although what they were warning her about she was not altogether sure. She smiled uncertainly, then looked away from Jocelyn's hypnotic stare and took another drink of her cocoa. When she looked up again she was glad to see that Jocelyn was no longer staring at her.

'I've been admiring your embroidery,' Patsy said now. 'The cushion cover and the picture on the wall. They're really beautiful. You haven't done them, have you?'

'Of course I have,' said Jocelyn with some pride, which was entirely justified. 'It's a hobby of mine. And I'm doing main course needlework, you know.'

'Yes,' said Patsy. 'So you are. I'd forgotten for the moment. It won't be a lot of use to you, though, in your teaching career, will it? Not if you're going to teach Infants. That sort of work would be more useful in a senior school, surely?'

'Yes, you're right. But they try to educate you as a whole person here, you know, not just to equip you for teaching. The main course is for your own benefit, to pursue your own particular interest. It's the same with the main course you're doing. English, isn't it? You'll hardly be encouraging your Infants to read Thomas Hardy or study Shakespeare, will you?'

Patsy shook her head. 'No, you're right. I'd no idea you were so talented at embroidery though, Jocelyn.'

'Oh, I'm sure there are a lot of things you don't know about me,' Jocelyn said darkly. And Patsy, not for the first time that evening, began to feel uncomfortable.

She got up quickly from the chair, put her empty mug back on the tray and knelt on the floor again. 'I'll just sort out the pictures I want, Jocelyn, and then I'll be going. Thanks ever so much for these.' She put together in a pile the Old Testament pictures and the ones of birds and trees. She found, to her surprise, that her hands were shaking a little and there was a sick feeling at the pit of her stomach. She wasn't sure why, but she wanted to get out of here, away from Jocelyn Reynolds' room, as soon as possible.

She rose to her feet, the pictures in her hands, and Jocelyn stood up too. They stood facing one another in the centre of the room. 'There's no need for you to dash away, is there? Don't go yet. Come and sit down again. I want to ask you something.'

Patsy's instinct was to run, to bolt through the door and get away as fast as she could, but she was a polite, well-brought up girl and felt that to do so would be very ill-mannered when Jocelyn had been so helpful to her. She sat down again on the chair. Jocelyn sat on the edge of the bed and leaned forward, her hands on her knees, her eyes fixed on Patsy.

'What was it you wanted to ask me?' said Patsy in a quiet voice.

'Oh . . . about us. About you and me,' said Jocelyn, still staring at Patsy in the way that unnerved her so much. 'We've danced together for ages now, but we've never been anywhere else together. I think it's time we did. I'd like to be your friend, Patsy.'

For a moment, in spite of her discomfiture, Patsy felt like laughing. She was reminded of the times at school when little girls had begged of one another, perhaps over the borrowing of a skipping rope or some such item, 'Oh, go on, let me . . . and I'll be your best friend.' But Patsy, at that time, had never been in need of a best friend other than Rosie. And now there was Kath.

'But you are my friend, aren't you?' said Patsy, trying to sound casual about it. 'I've made lots of new friends since I came here. You and Gwen, and Shirley and Kath . . .'

'Oh, yes, I know you and Kath are friends. Thick as thieves, the pair of you, aren't you?' Jocelyn's mouth turned downwards, like a petulant child's. 'Everybody's noticed that!'

Patsy felt blazing mad, but tried not to let it show. 'Yes, we get on very well, Kath and me,' she said. She nodded curtly, as if to say: So there!

'But there's no reason why you shouldn't get on with me just as well, is there?' said Jocelyn, her voice taking on a wheedling tone. 'I tell you what, Patsy. There's a new John Wayne film on in Leeford. Shall we go? Tomorrow, perhaps. I love a good Western.'

Patsy couldn't stand cowboy films, or John Wayne either. She was surprised that Jocelyn did, but didn't like to say so outright. 'I'm . . . not sure,' she faltered. 'I have a lot of work to do . . . with just coming back after half-term, and School Practice coming up and all that. I don't think I can manage it. Listen, Jocelyn – if you badly want to see the film, why not ask one of the other girls off our table? Gwen or Marjorie or Brenda?'

'I don't get on all that well with Gwen and Marjorie,' said Jocelyn stiffly. 'And as for Brenda . . . Huh! You can never prise her away from her Flying Officer Jeremy.'

'Not during the week, surely? She only sees him at weekends.'

'I don't want to go with Brenda,' Jocelyn snapped. 'I'm asking you.'

'I can't go tomorrow . . . I've told you.'

'What about Saturday then? It'll still be on. Perhaps we could go into town in the afternoon and have some tea, then finish up with the pictures. You can't say you've got work to do on Saturday, Patsy. No one works on a Saturday.'

She knows jolly well I usually spend Saturday with Kath, thought Patsy, beginning to feel even more panic-stricken. Oh heck! What a mess she had got herself into. She should have known better than to come into Jocelyn's room in the first place. Anyway, this Saturday she was meeting Ronnie . . .

'I can't,' she blurted out, not even trying to be tactful now. 'I'm . . . I'm meeting someone on Saturday.'

'Mmm. Kath Merriman, I suppose,' Jocelyn muttered, looking down at the floor and not at Patsy. 'It's always Kath, isn't it?'

'No, as a matter of fact, it's not Kath. I'm meeting a boy I used to know. He lived in Blackpool when we did and I met him by chance in Leeford a couple of weeks ago. He's in the army.' Patsy had no idea why she was telling Jocelyn all this. It was really none of her business. 'And I'm seeing him on Saturday.'

Jocelyn looked at her coldly, one eyebrow raised in a cynical manner. 'So you've got a date with him?' Her tone was derisive.

'Yes . . . yes, I have. Why not?' Patsy just managed to bite back the words, 'What the hell has it got to do with you?' She remembered now, with a start, how different Kath's reaction had been to her meeting with Ronnie, how Kath had been thrilled to bits about her friend's encounter with her childhood pal. What the dickens was eating at Jocelyn? Patsy couldn't understand it. She only knew she had to get out of here, and quickly, too.

'I should have thought you'd got enough on your plate with all your work, and School Practice coming up,' said Jocelyn frostily. 'You'll find you're far too busy to go out with . . . with men.'

'Oh, well, you know what they say,' Patsy replied airily. 'All work and no play . . .' She tried to laugh lightly.

'Well, don't blame me when you fail your School Practice. I'm only trying to warn you. There are a lot of girls here who are man-mad – Brenda's one of them – and they all end up the same way, with bad reports!'

Patsy knew that this wasn't true at all and she was quite sure that seeing Ronnie Sykes wouldn't affect her work. Come to think of it, she had never noticed Jocelyn showing any interest in the men at college. Most girls did, even if it was only in a jocular manner. She was an odd one all right, was Jocelyn, but Patsy hadn't realised how odd until tonight.

Patsy stood up again. 'Don't bother your head about me, Jocelyn. I can take care of myself.'

'That's what you think!' Jocelyn's glance was venomous.

'I know I can.' Patsy forced herself to look steadily at Jocelyn, though she was almost afraid to do so. The girl really was giving her the creeps. Her eyes were cold now as she glared back at Patsy, as lifeless and empty as two black cinders.

'I really must be going now,' she said quietly.

'Yes, I think you'd better,' said Jocelyn. 'Don't forget your pictures,' she added as Patsy moved towards the door.

'Oh, yes, the pictures.' Patsy turned back and picked them up from the chair although she was sure she would never use them. She didn't even want to see them again.

'Thanks, Jocelyn,' she murmured.

'Goodnight, Patsy.' Jocelyn's voice was flat, devoid of any feeling. 'See you in the morning.'

'Yes . . . see you, Jocelyn.'

Patsy closed the door quietly behind her and walked along the corridor to her own room at the other end. She felt detached, as though all this was happening to someone else, not to her. She opened her door and flung the wretched pictures on the bed, and stared round at the bilious green walls. She couldn't stay here on her own, not yet. She had to talk to someone. Kath . . .

She knocked on the door opposite and her friend opened it. It was then that Patsy's self-control broke. 'Kath . . . oh, Kath,' she cried.

'Good heavens, Patsy! Whatever's the matter?' Kath took one look at her friend's panic-stricken face and ushered her into the room. 'Come on in. Sit down. Whatever is it?'

Thankfully Patsy collapsed on to Kath's bed and her friend sat down beside her. 'Come on, tell me.' Kath put an arm round her shoulders and Patsy leaned against her.

'Oh, Kath,' she muttered, her breath escaping in a long sigh. 'It was awful. Jocelyn . . . She asked me to go to her room. And she kept pestering me to go out with her. To the pictures. I said I couldn't. And she seemed so . . . so jealous. I can't understand it, Kath. Whatever's the matter with her?'

There was a moment's pause. Then, 'Didn't you realise?' Kath said gently. 'Didn't you know she was . . . like that?'

'No.' Patsy looked at her friend, then shook her head in a puzzled manner. 'Like what? What d'you mean? I don't understand.'

Kath sighed and took hold of her hand. 'I was going to

warn you about her,' said Kath, 'but then I decided not to. I thought you would be able to look after yourself, but I wish now that I'd told you. I thought it was a bit risky, going to country dancing with her every week. I thought she might start to get rather . . . possessive. Do you mean to say you never realised?'

'No,' said Patsy. 'Not really.' But light was just beginning to dawn. Oh crikey! Was Kath implying that Jocelyn was . . . ?

'But you must have read *The Rainbow*.'

'Oh, yes, I read that,' Patsy replied. *The Rainbow* by D. H. Lawrence had been one of the books that the students had been required to read before coming to CLTC. 'But I didn't really understand it. You mean Ursula and the schoolteacher? You mean that they were . . . ? I thought there was something . . . strange, but I've never come across it before, certainly not with anyone I know. I've heard about men. There was Oscar Wilde, wasn't there? I've heard a bit about that, but I didn't realise it could happen with women. Do you mean to say that they . . . ?'

Kath nodded. 'So they say.'

'But that's awful!'

Kath smiled. 'You sound like Queen Victoria. Apparently she refused to let her Parliament ban that sort of thing between women because she couldn't believe it existed.'

'How do you know that?'

'I've read it somewhere.'

'It's against the law, isn't it, between men, I mean? I find it all so odd, so confusing.'

'It's unlawful at the moment,' said Kath, 'but who knows for how long? There are some people who think it should be allowed.'

'And you think that Jocelyn's . . . like that?'

Kath nodded. 'I think she might be that way inclined. I know she hasn't many friends, not in the way we have.' She looked at her friend in some concern. 'Patsy . . . We should try to understand Jocelyn. She's not a bad sort of girl really. I know she's a bit of a bully – trying to make people do what she wants – but that's because she's lonely.'

'She's your college mother, isn't she?'

'Yes, and she's been very helpful to me in a lot of ways. Far more helpful, I would think, than Gwen has been to you.'

'And has she . . . has she tried . . . to get friendly with you?'

Kath smiled. 'Not very much. Jocelyn and I have never really hit it off. But I suspected that she might want to get more friendly with you.'

'How did you know about her, that she was . . . ?'

'Oh, intuition, I suppose, and I think I've been around a bit more than you, Patsy, if you don't mind me saying so. And I've heard some of the girls talking, but I don't like to gossip. That's why I didn't tell you.'

'I wish you had,' said Patsy, reflecting at the same time that her friend, as she had just said, was not one for scandal and tittle-tattle. Kath was a fair-minded girl who always tried to see both sides of a question.

'Kath . . .' said Patsy hesitantly. 'D'you think there might be others? Here?'

'I don't know, but it's possible. It can happen when a lot of women live together in close proximity. And men too, of course. I've heard that it's quite common in women's prisons. Emotion has to have an outlet, you see.'

'But we're not in prison here, are we?' said Patsy. 'We can escape sometimes.' The two girls looked at one another then burst out laughing.

'It's good to see you smiling again,' said Kath. 'You looked so scared when you came in, I was worried sick about you. Now try and put it to the back of your mind, if you can. Think about Saturday. You're meeting Ronnie on Saturday, aren't you? Just think about that.'

'Yes, I will,' said Patsy gratefully. 'That seems so normal to me, looking forward to going out with a lad. Don't you think so, Kath? You've had a few boyfriends, haven't you?'

'One or two,' Kath said, smiling. 'Nobody that I really went overboard for, but I know what you mean. It's nice and . . . normal, like you say, Patsy.'

'Life's odd, isn't it?' said Patsy thoughtfully. 'Friendship and all that. Rosie and I were ever so close, real good friends, and we used to walk arm in arm – like you and I do, Kath – and sometimes we'd get into the same bed at night when we wanted to whisper secrets and we didn't want Mum to hear. But I would never have dreamed of – you know – I never wanted to do anything . . . like that. It's the same with you and me, isn't it? We're good friends, but you can put your arm round me, like you did just now, without there being anything strange about it. Jocelyn got hold of my arm tonight and I felt really peculiar. I suppose I should have realised then. Odd, isn't it?'

Kath nodded. 'What we feel for one another is based on friendship. There are lots of different kinds of love. We love our parents and friends, then there's romantic love for the opposite sex, and hero worship, then there's the sort of love for your own sex that some people call unnatural.'

'But you don't think it is?'

'I'm not sure . . . Yes, I suppose I do think it's unnatural, but perhaps that's because I don't understand it.

Anyway, stop worrying your head about it now, Patsy.' Kath held up her hand in a gesture of finality. 'Forget it.'

'But how shall I behave towards Jocelyn? It's going to be awkward, isn't it, when I see her again? And I'll have to see her in the morning at breakfast. Then there's country dancing . . . oh heck!'

'Just behave normally. Jocelyn'll take the hint that you don't want to be too friendly with her, if she's any sense. And I'm quite sure she'll find herself another dancing partner, so I shouldn't worry about that.'

'I'll try not to worry, Kath,' said Patsy. 'And thanks for listening to me.'

'Jocelyn's not so bad really,' said Kath. 'She's just lonely. We'll have to try and include her more – when there's a crowd of us, I mean. She's been quite a help to me since I came here. Now I think we'd better be moving ourselves. It'll be lights out soon.'

Kath frowned to herself when her friend had gone. What she had said to Patsy was only partly true, but she had wanted to allay her fears and put her mind at rest. Jocelyn Reynolds had been helpful and generous, too, but Kath was fearful that she might be the sort who would not easily forget a slight, and she certainly wouldn't like being made to look a fool, even if it was only in her own eyes. Kath hoped and prayed that there would be no nasty repercussions to this little incident.

Chapter 7

'Rosie . . . Rosie, wait a minute!' She turned at the sound of the familiar voice, and Jeff Burroni fell into step beside her as she walked along the corridor to her next lecture. 'I've been trying to catch you on your own for a day or two.' He sounded a little breathless. 'I wanted to ask you . . . are you free on Saturday, or are you working this weekend?'

'I'm always working at weekends,' Rosie replied, 'or one of the days at any rate.' She was trying to sound nonchalant, but already she could feel the all too familiar excitement gripping her as it always did when she encountered Jeff. 'But, as it happens, I'm doing my stint on Sunday this week. So – yes – I'm free on Saturday. Why?'

The question sounded casual, but it belied the elation she was feeling. It was now mid-November, some three weeks since their visit to the Tate. Rosie had been starting to think, by this time, that that outing had been an isolated incident and that Jeff had no intention of asking her out again, that she had only imagined that he was interested in her as anything but a student. She had seen him at lectures, of course, and he had joined her several times in the canteen, sometimes when she was alone and sometimes when she was with a group of friends. But he had made no further reference to his previous suggestion that they should go sightseeing again. She held her breath, hoping against hope that that was what he was about to ask her now.

'I wondered if you'd care to come out with me again?' he asked. 'I thought it might be a nice idea to act like a tourist, for a change.' He smiled at her. 'It's amazing how Londoners hardly ever avail themselves of all their city has to offer. So how about it? What do you say?'

'Thanks, Jeff. Yes, I'd like that,' Rosie answered evenly, determined still not to sound too keen. 'Saturday, you said?' She looked at him questioningly. 'It was Sunday before . . .'

'Ye-es, it was . . .' His reply sounded somewhat guarded and a flicker of apprehension showed for a moment in his eyes. 'But I can't manage Sunday this time. There's a family occasion. You know how it is in a big family. It's always someone's birthday. Anyway, you're working Sunday, aren't you?' he went on. 'So it's worked out just fine. Now, where do you fancy? Westminster Abbey? St Paul's? A trip on the river?'

Rosie was thoughtful for a moment. Then, 'Do you think we could go to the Tower?' she asked. 'I've wanted to go there ever since I came to London, but I've never got round to it. It's the sort of place you have to make an effort to go to, isn't it, if you see what I mean? You can't just pop in on the way to somewhere else.' In spite of her best intentions she knew that the eagerness showed in her voice; she just couldn't help it.

'I don't see why not,' said Jeff, though he sounded a little unsure. Then, 'Yes,' he said. 'Why not? If you want to go to the Tower, then we'll go.' He stopped outside the door to the pottery room where Rosie's next lecture was to be held. 'D'you know, I haven't been to the Tower since I was a little lad? I lived only a stone's throw away from it, but we hardly ever went. It would have been expensive, of course, with all us kids.'

'Oh, yes, it's in the same area, isn't it?' asked Rosie. 'I'd forgotten. Do you still live near to it?'

'Quite near . . . Yes, I'll look forward to that, Rosie. It might be busy on Saturday, but it's mid-November so perhaps it won't be too bad. We'll be a couple of day trippers, shall we?' He leaned closer to her as a group of students pushed past them into the lecture room. 'See you at the same place then, St James's, at twelve o'clock? OK? We can perhaps have a walk in the park first, if the weather's decent. See you, Rosie. Off you go now and get your pots thrown.'

His brown eyes were warm as he smiled at her and raised his hand in a farewell salute. And Rosie felt warm inside, too, at the thought of being near him again for a whole afternoon. Longer, maybe?

The day was surprisingly mild for late autumn, much more so than it had been three weeks earlier. They walked northwards this time on leaving the tube station, towards St James's Park.

'My favourite view in the whole of London,' said Jeff, as they stood on the suspension bridge that spanned the lake. He waved a hand expansively towards the roofs of Whitehall on the horizon. 'You'd never think that they were really something as prosaic as the War Office and the Admiralty, now would you? I always think it looks more like fairyland.'

'Gosh, yes,' said Rosie in an awed whisper, as she followed the direction of his pointing finger. 'Those cupolas and domes – it's like an enchanted palace, isn't it? The sort of place where you'd expect Sleeping Beauty to live.

And with those willow trees in the foreground, all round the island, it's a lovely picture. Quite magical.' Her voice was hushed and she felt moved by the unexpected beauty that could be found in the heart of London.

'I thought you'd be impressed,' said Jeff. 'I know you always see things as pictures, like I do. Haven't you been here before?'

'Only once,' she said, 'and I just walked straight through along the path. It takes a Londoner to know all the best vantage points. And to think I might have missed it.'

'Oh, you'd have found it sooner or later,' said Jeff. 'Tourists always gravitate to this spot. And office workers as well. It's a favourite place for eating their sandwiches, and they can always give the left-overs to the ducks.'

The park was not crowded today, but neither was it deserted. There were no office workers with it being Saturday, but a fair number of late-season tourists were to be seen walking leisurely along admiring the views and feeding the vast variety of water fowl.

'It's a splendid view in the other direction, too,' remarked Rosie. 'And I see the Queen's at home today.' She pointed to the Royal Standard displayed on the flagpole above Buckingham Palace.

'Why, do you want to call and see her?' Jeff raised his eyebrows teasingly and Rosie noticed a trace of sardonic humour in his glance.

'I wouldn't mind,' she answered, tilting her chin aggressively, 'but then she might not be expecting me. I wouldn't want to catch her unawares. I know how I feel when people catch me in the middle of preparing a meal!' She smiled at him mischievously. 'I take it you're not the nation's most ardent Royalist, Jeff?'

'You could say that. Of course I know you are . . . Margaret Rose.' He nudged her arm affectionately and grinned at her.

'It's just the way I was brought up,' Rosie explained. 'My mother thinks they can do no wrong. And I must admit that I look on the Royal Family as a symbol – they represent stability and security, traditional values and all that. But you don't agree with me?' She looked questioningly at Jeff.

'To a point.' He shrugged. 'I suppose there's a need in some people to have something to look up to, but I wonder if an elected head of state wouldn't do just as well? It may come to that, you know, someday. Perhaps not for the next fifty years or so, but sometime. I daresay that's the Italian in me coming out.' He nodded towards her, his brown eyes serious. 'They seem to be managing very well as a Republic. And what is the function of Royalty, when all's said and done?' He waved his hands expressively, as he always did when arguing a point. 'What does it amount to? They can't be said to govern . . .'

' "The right to be consulted, to encourage and to warn," ' quoted Rosie. 'Isn't that what Bagehot said about the royal prerogative?'

'Clever girl,' said Jeff admiringly. 'You know your history all right. That was in the nineteenth century, wasn't it? In Queen Victoria's reign, and things haven't changed much since then with regard to Royalty. We have a woman on the throne again and she still has to do what her ministers tell her.'

'Don't underestimate women,' said Rosie, giving him a warning look. 'There'll be a woman Prime Minister one day, I'm telling you, as well as a woman on the throne.'

'I wouldn't dream of underestimating women,' said Jeff. He raised his hands in front of him, backing away from her in mock alarm. 'But a woman Prime Minister – that's stretching it a bit far, surely? That'll be the day!'

'Yes, it will,' said Rosie. 'That'll be the day, all right.' She nodded sagely. 'It'll come, you'll see.'

'Well, I daresay she could do as well as old Winnie,' remarked Jeff in a casual tone. 'I can't help thinking he's a bit past it now at seventy-eight.'

'He got us through the war though.'

'Oh, that was ages ago. Another time altogether,' said Jeff dismissively.

'It was only seven years ago,' Rosie reminded him.

'Seems longer though. Things have changed a lot since then. Thanks to a Labour government.'

His last remark confirmed what Rosie had long suspected. 'You vote Labour then, Jeff?' she asked.

'It's supposed to be a secret, isn't it?' He raised his eyebrows eloquently. 'No secret with me though. Yes, I should jolly well say I do vote Labour. I'm certainly not one who put him back in there.' They were walking across Horse Guards Parade now, away from the park, and he waved his hand in the direction of Downing Street. 'And what about you, Rosie, seeing that you've made me confess all? You vote Tory, do you?'

'I don't vote at all, do I?' she said evenly. 'I've another two years to wait yet.'

'Of course. I keep forgetting that you're only a child . . .'

'Watch it!' Rosie dug her elbow in his ribs, none too gently.

Jeff smiled at her, his brown eyes teasing yet full of warmth, then suddenly they grew serious. 'No, honestly, Rosie, I do forget when I'm with you that you're a student and that I'm . . .'

'That you're my tutor?'

'Yes . . . I suppose so.' Jeff turned to look at her and they both stood still, there on Whitehall, near to the motionless figure of the lifeguard on his horse and the group of chattering sightseers. Behind them the red buses and taxis and cars rumbled past, but Rosie and Jeff were oblivious to their surroundings. There was an expression in Jeff's deep brown eyes that Rosie had never seen there before. A yearning look, almost anguished, as though he was being torn apart; to be replaced almost immediately by a look of such warmth and tenderness that she was in no doubt, at that moment, as to how Jeff felt about her. Rosie's heart sang with joy for as she looked at him she knew that she had fallen deeply, irrevocably in love; and Jeff's eyes told her that it was the same with him.

'Rosie . . . Rosie,' he murmured, gently touching her cheek with his finger tip. 'You're so . . . so very lovely. I've never felt like this . . . I don't usually . . .'

'You don't usually go out with students?' She laughed up at him, a little embarrassed, though radiantly happy, at the intensity of his gaze. 'I bet you say that to all the girls.'

'No, Rosie . . . honestly. I do think you're . . . quite a girl.' He smiled then, quite normally, and the magical moment had passed. The middle of Whitehall was no place, after all, for protestations of undying love, but the memory of those brief few minutes, when they had both seemed to be part of another world, stayed with Rosie all day. And for a long time afterwards.

They stood at the corner of Trafalgar Square, waiting for the traffic to stop at the lights. Jeff put an arm round her protectively as they crossed the road. 'We'll go and have some lunch,' he said as they reached the other side. 'Then I thought we'd take a boat trip down the river to the Tower. I think they run all year round.'

'Lovely!' Rosie's blue eyes gleamed with excitement as she smiled at him.

'And what about Lyon's Corner House for lunch? It's just round the corner, on the Strand.'

Rosie laughed. 'Lyon's! I should've thought I'd seen

enough of Lyon's. Have a heart, Jeff.'

'You'll find it's vastly different from the little place where you work,' he assured her. 'You've never been in this one?' Rosie shook her head. 'Then you're in for a treat, I can promise you.'

Rosie soon found that Jeff's words were true. The opulent establishment on the Strand bore no resemblance to the little teashop of her acquaintance. The carpets were thick and luxurious, the walls and ceilings were gilded, and everywhere there were palms and potted plants. They were served by a smart-looking waitress, a 'nippy', dressed in black with a tiny white apron at the front. The food was delicious – gammon and eggs, served with mushrooms and grilled tomatoes and golden brown chips – and coffee to follow with the distinctive flavour and aroma that Rosie already associated with Lyon's.

'That was scrumptious.' She leaned her elbows on the table, cupping her chin in her hands, and looked across at Jeff. 'I can't remember when I enjoyed a meal so much. Thanks for bringing me, Jeff.'

'The pleasure's all mine, I can assure you.' Jeff likewise, elbows on the table, leaned towards Rosie. She had taken up the comfortable position unthinkingly; now she recalled how often her mother had told her that it was ill-mannered to put one's elbows on the table and how often she and Patsy had been rebuked with the sharp reproach: 'Elbows!' Now, glancing round, Rosie noticed other diners in a similar pose and no one seemed to mind. How else were you to converse familiarly? she wondered. You certainly couldn't do so if you sat bolt upright.

Jeff was smiling at her, but it seemed to be only his eyes that were smiling. His mouth was set in a serious line, but his eyes were dancing with warmth and humour. What expressive dark brown eyes he had, Rosie thought again, as she looked at him steadily. 'You didn't answer my question earlier,' he said now. 'You didn't tell me how you would vote . . . if you could. I suspect you're a closet Tory, Rosie Bradshaw.'

'I'm not a closet anything,' she replied, a trifle heatedly. 'I would certainly see nothing to be ashamed of, whatever my views. I wouldn't make a secret of them. But, to be quite honest, I haven't made my mind up yet. I can see good – and bad – in both parties. I always try to consider both sides of a question, you see.'

'Dangerous that, seeing both sides.' Jeff frowned slightly and gave a sibilant whistle, but Rosie could tell that he was half joking. 'You should be decisive.' He banged his fist lightly on the table. 'Make up your mind what you believe in and go for it.'

'That's all very well,' Rosie countered, 'but it's difficult. There are always two sides to a problem, I don't care what you say. And your environment and upbringing have an effect, too, on what you believe. It's when you get older that you have to try to sort things out for yourself.'

'Yes, I agree with you with regard to upbringing,' said Jeff. 'My father was a docker, as I think I told you, and his father before him. I'm unashamedly working-class, so I could hardly be expected to be anything else but a Socialist, could I?'

'Your family must be very proud of you, Jeff, that you've done so well. I expect they think it's quite an achievement, don't they, having a son who's been to college and become a lecturer?'

'Oh, yes, they're proud all right.' Jeff gave a slight frown. 'I only wish my brothers and sisters could all have had the same chances I had . . .'

He went on to explain to Rosie how he had been the only one to go to a grammar school, education not being free to all then, as it was now. Over their coffee they went on to discuss the education system and political principles in general.

'Make no mistake about it, Rosie,' said Jeff with conviction. 'The Labour Party's here to stay.'

'Whatever are you talking about, Jeff?' Rosie laughed. 'They were defeated here in 1951. Have you forgotten?'

'Am I likely to?' He grinned back at her. 'A temporary setback, that's all. There'll be no holding them before long, you'll see . . . Anyway, I think that's enough about politics for one day. We've just about set the world to rights. We'd better be moving if we want to get to the Tower and back before it goes dark.'

Rosie insisted on sitting on the top deck of the river boat from where she had a superb view of the passing scenery. It was the first time she had been on the river and the excitement of it all, combined with the cool breeze, brought a sparkle to her eyes and a pink flush to her cheeks. She leaned against the rail, eagerly craning her neck first to one side, then the other, as the guide gave a running commentary over the loud-speaker about the various landmarks that they passed. The Royal Festival Hall; Cleopatra's Needle; Waterloo and Blackfriars Bridges, and St Paul's Cathedral, rising secure and invincible from the blitzed wasteland surrounding it. She turned to smile companionably from time to time at Jeff who had his arm round her shoulders in a relaxed manner.

And then the Tower of London came into view, gaunt and grey, a mass of turrets and bastions and crenellated towers. Along the wharf Rosie could see the massive guns pointing towards the river, with small boys scrambling over them, and the plane trees, now almost denuded of their late-autumn foliage, forming a pleasant backdrop to an otherwise grim scene. She could hardly wait to disembark and enter the environs of the Tower itself. She felt like a child again, looking forward to the pleasures of a Sunday School outing.

It was a memorable afternoon, a kaleidoscope of scenes and impressions that Rosie stored away in her mind. She felt overawed to be surrounded by so much history; there was a palpable sense of the dark deeds and tragedies and rebellions that had taken place within those walls, an incongruous contrast to the jovial day-trippers, most of them concerned with nothing but the enjoyment of an afternoon out.

They stopped by Tower Green, a picturesque spot flanked by the timber-framed houses where the Yeoman Warders lived, and watched the ravens lurching drunkenly from side to side on the grass, their cruel hooded eyes glinting menacingly at the watching tourists.

'Evil-looking birds, aren't they?' remarked Rosie. 'I must admit I feel wary of getting too close to them.'

'You know the legend about them, don't you?' asked Jeff.

'Yes, I believe I heard it when I was at school,' said Rosie. 'Isn't it said that if they disappear then the Tower will fall, and Great Britain as well?'

'Yes, that's right. Not much chance of that though, seeing that their wings are clipped. Poor birds, you can't help but feel sorry for them. And that's the scaffold in the centre, where Anne Boleyn and Catherine Howard were executed, Henry VIII's wayward wives.'

Rosie shuddered. She didn't like to think of barbarity and bloodthirstiness on such a lovely day. And yet she knew that they were an integral part of this grim place, that the very fabric of the walls was steeped with tragedy. 'I'd like to see the Crown Jewels,' she said now. 'Can we go, please, Jeff? The queue didn't seem to be too enormous. And you can't visit the Tower without seeing them, now can you?'

He grinned. 'Yes, I thought you might. Come on then, Margaret Rose, you fanatical Royalist.'

They had to queue for about twenty minutes but, to Rosie, the time flew, so engrossed was she in watching her fellow tourists and gazing round at the awe-inspiring towers and battlements that had stood on that spot for nine hundred years. And with Jeff so close to her she wouldn't have minded queueing for hours. He seemed preoccupied though, and occasionally she caught him glancing over his shoulder and, once, completely turning his back on her.

'Is anything the matter, Jeff?' she asked when he turned around again.

'No, nothing at all.' His cheerful smile reassured her that there could be nothing amiss. 'I'm just a bit bored, that's all, with standing around. I'm a restless person, you know. I have to be up and doing. Look . . . it's our turn to go in now.'

He seemed relieved to be inside and, with twenty or so other visitors, they shuffled round the glass show-case, at a safe distance, gazing at the unbelievable accumulation of wealth that was displayed before them. Rosie could only gasp, speechless with wonderment, at the glowing gold and glittering jewels, the crowns, orbs and sceptres, swords, rings, bracelets and ceremonial plate. Such riches were more than the eye could take in, more than the mind could comprehend, in a few brief moments.

'Wow!' That was Rosie's pertinent comment when they were outside again. 'Fascinating, wasn't it? Unbelievable.'

'I suppose you could say so,' replied Jeff tersely. 'Quite frankly I found it depressing. But I agree with you that it's unbelievable. Unbelievable that such an abundance of wealth belongs to one family.'

'You can't honestly say that, Jeff,' Rosie argued. 'They don't really belong to the Queen. It isn't as if she could sell them or anything. They belong to the nation; they're part of our heritage.'

'If you say so,' he said, shrugging. 'But I can't pretend that I approve of it all when I don't. Never mind.' He put an arm round her shoulders and pulled her towards him. 'We're not going to fall out about it.' Again his smile dispelled any doubts that Rosie might have and she reflected, not for the first time that day, that he was a man of quickly changing moods. The artistic temperament, she supposed, but she knew that it made no difference what Jeff might say or do or think. Rosie knew that she had fallen in love with him.

'Come on,' he said now. 'We've still a lot to see.'

The Beauchamp Tower, where the Dudley brothers were imprisoned; the Bloody Tower, site of the murder of the little princes and the place where Sir Walter Raleigh spent thirteen years; the White Tower with its hoard of weapons and the gargantuan suit of armour of Henry VIII . . . At the end of the afternoon Rosie was overwhelmed with all that she had seen.

Dusk was falling when they disembarked from the boat at Charing Cross Pier. They walked along the Embankment towards Westminster and stopped to lean against the parapet, watching the lights casting a shimmering reflection in the murky water of the Thames. Jeff put an arm round Rosie, drawing her close, and she snuggled against him, feeling the roughness of his duffel-coat against her cheek and his chin nuzzling into the softness of her hair.

'Happy?' he asked, lifting his hand to fondle her neck and the lobe of her ear.

'Mmm,' she murmured, turning towards him. 'Very . . .'

He kissed her then, just once, the first time he had

done so, apart from that fleeting kiss when he had left her in the square outside her flat, three weeks ago. His lips were soft and warm, gentle at first then more urgent as she found herself responding, pressing her mouth against his, wanting more of him. Then, abruptly, he let go of her and took hold of her shoulders. 'Come on, Rosie,' he said. 'I'll take you home.'

She didn't argue this time about his accompanying her on the tube to South Kensington as she knew he wouldn't dream of letting her go home alone. He was a strange mixture, she thought, as she sat next to him on the rattling westbound train. Usually courteous and gentlemanly, and yet, occasionally, abrupt to the point of rudeness; friendly and warm and kind, and then suddenly morose and petulant. She hadn't known about his changes of mood until today. And they didn't agree about everything, not by a long chalk. Politics, Royalty, the accumulation of wealth . . . they had already had a few arguments, albeit friendly ones. But Rosie was confident that he would ask to see her again.

They stood on the pavement outside the entrance to her flat. She took a deep breath and decided to take the plunge. 'Would you like to come in, Jeff?' she asked, trying to make her voice sound casual. 'I could make some coffee or tea before you go home.'

'Why not?' His glance was half-amused, half-friendly. 'I'd like to see where you hang out.'

The hallway and staircase must have been impressive in Georgian and Victorian times, Rosie always thought. Now the grandeur was faded; the ornate plasterwork of the ceiling was chipped and the wood-panelled walls had lost their sheen. But there was still a sense of timelessness, of what once had been, even though the hall smelt of onions and the carpet was threadbare. They made their way up the three flights of stairs with their carved wooden balustrades to the attic.

Rosie switched on the light and stooped to ignite the gas fire. 'Make yourself comfortable,' she said, pointing to the settee, her bed at night, but now transformed into a sofa with a blanket of Aztec design and a trio of scatter cushions, red, blue and yellow. 'Tea or coffee?'

'Coffee, please . . .' Jeff hesitated. 'But I mustn't be too long, Rosie. I said I wouldn't be late.'

She felt a plummeting of her heart, a lowering of her spirits, although she wasn't sure what she had been expecting. She looked at him enquiringly. 'You said . . . ? But . . . who?'

'My mother.' He grinned cheerfully. 'I usually pop round to see Ma and Pa on a Saturday evening and she likes to make me a meal. I mustn't disappoint her.'

'No, of course not.' Rosie smiled at him and turned back to the small alcove that was her kitchen. She filled the kettle and put it on the gas ring and took two beakers from their hooks on the wall. She knew that she would have to make the most of this next half hour or so, if that was all it was to be. It had been naive of her to suppose that Jeff would stay longer, for the whole evening, for the night . . . She put a liberal spoonful of Nescafe into each beaker then added boiling water and milk.

'There you are, service with a smile, in the best Lyon's tradition.' She handed the mug to Jeff. 'The coffee's not up to Lyon's standard, though. It's only instant.'

'Thanks, Rosie. It'll be fine.'

'Oh . . . I forgot to ask. Do you take sugar, Jeff?' She was realising there were so many things about him, the inconsequential little things, that she didn't know. She hadn't noticed at the Corner House whether he had put sugar in his coffee or not, she had been so enthralled just to be with him, listening to him.

'No, thanks. I don't.'

'That's OK then. Neither do I. I think it spoils the flavour.'

She sat opposite him in the shabby armchair, feeling shy suddenly of sitting next to him on the sofa . . . the bed. There was a moment's silence as they sipped their coffee.

Then Jeff said, 'I've enjoyed today. Seeing London as a tourist; well, part of it, at any rate. And there's lots more of it. It would take years to see it all.' He leaned forward eagerly. 'You will come out with me again, won't you, Rosie? You'll keep on seeing me?'

'I see you every day, Jeff,' she answered light-heartedly, but her heart was turning somersaults.

'You know what I mean. You will, won't you, Rosie?'

'Yes . . . of course I will.' Her voice was quiet and they looked at one another for a few seconds, just as they had done earlier that day in the middle of Whitehall.

'There's a new play just started in the West End,' said Jeff. 'Would you like to go if I can get tickets? It's one of Agatha Christie's, *The Mousetrap*.'

'Yes, that would be terrific,' she replied. 'Funnily enough, I've just had a letter from my sister and she's seen it recently in Yorkshire. It was doing a tour of the provinces before coming to London. She's a keen Agatha Christie fan, is Patsy. She thought it was marvellous – Richard Attenborough and his wife, Sheila Sym. Patsy said she wouldn't be surprised if it ran for a couple of years.'

'We've plenty of time then. But we'll go soon if I can manage it. I know somebody in one of the booking agencies . . . I see you've been hard at work, Rosie.' Jeff glanced round at the works of art – still life paintings, abstract designs and fashion sketches – that adorned the walls. 'Very impressive. I've obviously one student who takes her work seriously.'

'Don't remind me of work, Jeff, not today.' Rosie grimaced. But it wasn't really of the return to her studies that she didn't wish to be reminded – she loved her work – but of her day-to-day relationship with Jeff. Not the friendship and fun that they had enjoyed this afternoon; the blossoming of love, on her part at least – and, unless she was very much mistaken, on Jeff's part, too – but the student and tutor connection between them which, of necessity, formed such a large part of their association. Rosie wished at times that it didn't have to be so, that he was, instead, just a fellow student. Very few of her friends at college knew of her friendship with Jeff. She had sensed that he didn't want it broadcasted and so she had kept it to herself, though she was not sure why there should be the secrecy. It wasn't as if they were doing anything wrong in seeing one another outside of college. There was no law against it.

'I've to return to work too,' Jeff said now. 'Back to reality.' His face held a closed look for a moment as he stared unseeingly into space. Then with a sudden movement he drank the last of his coffee and put the mug down on the floor. 'Thanks, Rosie. I must go now, more's the pity.'

He stood up and Rosie stood, too, facing him. He took a step towards her and, for the second time that day, wrapped his arms around her. Their lips met again, more urgently now, and this time she felt the pressure of his tongue against her teeth. She opened her mouth and responded to him, feeling the sensuous softness, aware of the surrender in her limbs and in her mind that could be the prelude to so much more. Then abruptly, as he had done on the Thames Embankment, he released her.

He rested his hands lightly on her shoulders. 'Thanks for a lovely day, Rosie. I'll see myself out. See you on Monday . . . Bye.'

''Bye, Jeff,' she said softly, then stood motionless in the centre of the room, listening to the door closing and to his footsteps on the stairs until she could hear him no more.

Jeff had spent a sleepless night, falling into a fitful slumber only in the early hours. Now, as the cold dawn light spilled through the cheap pink curtains, he lay on his back on the crumpled sheet contemplating the miseries of another Sunday. And thinking about Rosie Bradshaw . . .

He hadn't intended to fall in love with her, but he knew, after that glorious afternoon with her, that that was what had happened. He had fought against his feelings at first, telling himself that she was just another pretty student and that he would be able to forget her. He had been attracted before to girls in his classes; he had chatted to them, spent longer than he really should with them over their studies, and enjoyed their company and their obvious admiration of him, their tutor. But always he had been able to resist their charms, knowing all too well that such flirtations, however innocent, for him were taboo. He wasn't the sort of fellow to turn his back lightly on a commitment, however unwillingly it had been entered into.

But it was different this time. Rosie wasn't just another pretty student. Indeed, it was an understatement to call her pretty. She was lovely, with those deep blue eyes and shining black hair. It wasn't just her looks, but her personality too. She was vivacious and quick-witted and amusing. When she entered a room it was as though a ray of sunshine had pierced through the dark clouds of winter. At least that was how it was for Jeff. He knew to his joy, and also to his dismay, that he had fallen in love with her. It should be a tremendous feeling, falling in love, and when he was with her, that was what it was. But here, at home in the detested flat in Bermondsey, it was a sick feeling in the pit of his stomach, it was guilt and deception and telling lies.

Oh God! What a muddle it all was. And what a mess he had got himself into three years ago in one stupid, senseless moment of madness. He had met Daphne at a party given by a mutual friend and had been attracted – superficially, he knew now – by her pert manner, platinum blonde hair and doll-like charm. He had been flattered by her attention, the way she had of hanging on his every word, gazing at him with her china-blue eyes. He had taken her out a few times, to the cinema and dancing at the local Palais. And then, one Saturday evening when her parents were out, they had made love on the sofa. He had regretted it immediately, knowing in the cold light of morning that too many whiskies had made him act unwisely, and also that he had been led on by a very provocative and sensuous young woman.

He had not been surprised at the outcome of his indiscretion. The inevitable interview with Daphne's parents, and the meeting, later, with his own, had been bitter but pertinent. Both families had been in agreement about one thing: he had to marry Daphne, and quickly too, before she started to 'show'. Jeff had found himself shouldering all the blame for something which, he thought angrily, had been as much Daphne's doing as his own.

When baby Marilyn was born, six months after their marriage, she was the image of her mother. Frail and doll-like with wispy blonde hair and pale blue eyes. By that time they had moved into their own flat in Bermondsey, not far from his parents, but to Jeff its square box-like rooms and its chilling modernity – an exact carbon copy of all the others in the block – would never feel like home.

His thoughts were in turmoil, but he knew that could not be remedied by lying in bed. He rose, and after a quick wash and shave wandered into the kitchen to make himself some breakfast. Daphne had been up for a while, seeing to little Marilyn. Lying in bed of a morning was not one of his wife's faults – the persistent cries of the child prevented her from doing so – but Jeff found himself irritated by her slovenly habit of trailing around in her dressing-gown until lunchtime.

'See to yourself,' she said now, scarcely looking up as he entered the room. 'There's bacon if you want some, and tea in the pot. That's if I haven't drunk it all.'

'No, thanks. I'll just make some toast,' he said indifferently. 'And I prefer coffee. You should know that by now.'

'All right. Suit yourself.' Daphne disappeared again behind the pages of the *News of the World* and Jeff looked with distaste at the crown of her blonde head where the dark roots were showing.

'Daddy, Daddy. Me want toast. Me want toast.' Two-year-old Marilyn was never afraid of making her presence felt and Jeff, in spite of himself, felt a stab of tenderness as he looked at her now. He went over to her in her high chair and wiped the egg yolk from her chin and a pool of milk from the tray in front of her. Mother and child seemed neither to mind nor to notice the mess.

'All right, sweetheart. I'll make you some toast. Say please.'

'Please, Daddy. Please, please, please . . .'

The child's ear-piercing cries filled the room and Jeff sighed to himself as he refilled the kettle and put the slices of bread under the grill. Dear God, what a mess he had got himself into. And what the hell was he going to do? He hated lying and cheating, but he couldn't tell Rosie, not yet; he might lose her. And he knew that he had to go on seeing her. Daphne, so far, had accepted his half-truths – half-lies – about an outing to the Tate Gallery with a group of students, and a Saturday afternoon excursion to study the architecture of the city. Or it could be that she no longer cared. It had been a nasty moment when he had caught sight of a friend of hers at the Tower with her two children. She hadn't seen him, though, he was sure of that. But deceit and lies brought even greater problems in their wake. Jeff knew that the predicament he was in could not be resolved unless he came clean, and that he couldn't do. Not yet. His mind was going round in circles until he thought he would go mad.

He spread two pieces of toast and gave one to Marilyn, watching absently as she proceeded to smear the butter over her hands and into her hair. He poured the milk into his coffee, wondering, as he did every morning, why it was too much trouble for Daphne to put the milk into a jug instead of putting the bottle on the table.

A few years ago, he reflected, he might have been able to gain some respite from his anguished thoughts by attending Mass. But that was now a thing of the past. Daphne had 'turned' when she married Jeff, but neither of them went to church now. Nor would he be able to do so ever again, should it come to a divorce, Jeff thought. Divorce . . . his Catholic upbringing made the very word anathema to him, but Jeff could see no other solution. He loved Rosie and was determined to have her, but, for the moment, there was so much that he couldn't – that he daren't – tell her.

Chapter 8

School Practice was not so bad once you got used to the routine and Patsy found, to her surprise, that she was enjoying it far more than she had expected. The worst part was making the journey on the cold, dark December mornings. It was dark now when she woke at seven, often from a deep slumber penetrated rudely by the clamorous tones of the bell, and still dark when she set off at eight o'clock. Together with a crowd of other students, laden like pack-mules with bags and boxes and long rolls of paper shoved under their arms, and all with the distinctive green and white scarf slung round their necks, Patsy made her way down Sycamore Avenue to the bus stop. There, at the bottom of the avenue, they went their various ways, some taking the city-bound tram for the schools near the centre of the town and beyond, and others, like Patsy, heading northwards towards the schools on the perimeter of the city.

And it was dark again when they returned in the evening at 4.30, or sometimes later, depending on the amount of work to be done at school in preparation for the next day. Patsy felt that she would never see her little room in the daylight again. Always, now, the curtains were drawn and the light was on, the dim 60-watt bulb in its cheap white Bakelite shade. It was difficult to work without straining her eyes and Patsy decided now, on entering the room, that she must replace the dim light. She wasn't sure whether it was allowed, but what the hell? she thought. There would be no one to notice but the maid who came in once a week to do a quick dust round and a cursory wipe of the floor, and she would be hardly likely to bother. Yes, a 100-watt bulb and a pretty shade – she could buy one in Woolie's the next time she went to Leeford – would cheer the place up no end. Patsy wondered why she hadn't thought of it before.

She flung her bag of books down on the bed and flopped into the armchair. Gosh! She was tired. Would she be more tired, she wondered, or less, when she was a real teacher?

Patsy knew that, so far, she was not faring too badly. She hadn't experienced any riots or out and out rebellions, but that was due mainly, she suspected, to the eagle eye of her class teacher, Miss Umpleby. Some of the teachers, when presented with a student for a few weeks, were only too happy to opt out, leaving the hapless student to the mercies of an unruly class and rejoicing at the hours of free time, a rare occurrence, particularly in an Infant classroom. But Miss Umpleby was not of that ilk. Nearing retirement age, with a lifetime of teaching experience behind her, she was only too glad to be able to help those teachers who were just starting out on their careers. Patsy had been somewhat daunted at first by the presence of the teacher, when she was endeavouring to quieten the class in readiness for a story. Miss Umpleby would hover in the background, quiet and inconspicuous, until such a time as the class was under control, and only then would she leave. And Patsy knew that she was always close at hand, ready to assist if the going got rough which, so far, had not happened.

'Hi there. How's it going?' Kath knocked at the door now and poked her cheerful face round. 'Whatever are you doing, Patsy, still sitting there with your coat on? You're all right, aren't you?'

''Course I'm all right. Just tired, that's all. You know what the teachers say? TGIF – Thank God it's Friday. I know exactly what they mean now.'

'Don't we all!' Kath laughed. 'Never mind, kid. Two down, two to go. We've done a fortnight already and there's only another fortnight left. Then it'll be breaking-up time and home for the holidays.' Kath sat down on the bed. 'What's your day been like? Anything funny happened?'

'I don't know if you'd call it funny. My handwork lesson was a disaster. That wasn't funny to me, I can assure you. Nearly all the damned things ended up in the waste paper basket.'

'Why, what were you doing?'

'Making paper lanterns. At least, that was the intention. Honestly, Kath, all the kids had to do was to fold a piece of gummed paper and make a few cuts with the scissors. I ask you, what could be simpler than that? And more than half of them cut into the edges and not into the fold. I wouldn't care but I'd explained it half a dozen times.'

'You have to tell 'em a hundred times, not half a dozen,' laughed Kath. 'It sounds like my fiasco with the Christmas cards. Half of them managed to get the picture on the back instead of the front. And we had purple Christmas trees and yellow snowmen and robins with only one leg. God! You've never seen such a mess.'

'You've cheered me up no end. I thought it was only me that had a bunch of stupid kids. Or I suppose it's more likely that they've got a stupid teacher.'

'No, I don't think it's entirely our fault,' said Kath.

'They just don't listen half the time, that's the trouble with kids. Any teacher will tell you that. You have to tell them over and over again. But it's wearing, isn't it?'

'I'll say it is! And the waste of paper worries me, Kath. I only hope the caretaker has emptied the basket before Miss Umpleby sees it. She'd have a fit. You know what those older teachers are like about waste. Using both sides of the paper and all that.

'But it's quite good fun being on School Practice near Christmas time, isn't it?' Patsy went on. 'My class were practising their Christmas play today. Miss Umpleby's in charge of that, of course, not me, but I said I'd give her a hand with the costumes and masks for the animals in the stable scene and all that.'

'Keeping well in, eh?' Kath grinned.

'Do you blame me?' Patsy smiled back. 'I want to get a good report, don't I? But I enjoy that sort of thing, always have. Oh, I must tell you, Kath, it was ever so funny. Like I said, the kids were practising their play and they make it up as they go along – they're only six and some of them can't read very well yet. Anyway, the wise men arrived at King Herod's palace and asked if there was a baby there. And the lad who plays Melchior – Kevin, he's called, and he's got the broadest Yorkshire accent you've ever heard – he said, "Eeh, well, I bloomin' well hope there is. We've been on t' go for weeks and we're fair knackered, I can tell yer!" '

Kath gave a shriek of laughter. 'And what did Miss Umpleby say?'

'Well, she explained – in extremely prim tones – that it might be better just to say they were very tired. She didn't seem amused at all and I was killing myself laughing. I had to turn round so the kids didn't see me.'

'I expect she's used to it by now,' said Kath. 'She's near

retiring age, isn't she? I don't suppose there's much she hasn't heard before. Anything else happen?'

'Oh, yes.' Patsy giggled again at the memory. 'The little girl who plays Mary. Emma, she's called, a dear little thing with blonde hair and blue eyes – not a typical Mary, you might say, but I think she's one of Miss Umpleby's favourites – anyway, the wise men presented their gifts and Emma said, ever so precisely, "Thank you very much. Just put them down there, would you? I'm sure they'll come in most useful." ' Patsy burst out laughing again. 'Honestly – gold, frankincense and myrrh – useful presents!'

'You never know,' said Kath drily. 'They might be. And don't you mean gold, frankenstein and myrrh? That's what one of the kids in my class wrote.'

The two friends found themselves rolling backwards and forwards with hilarity, a regular occurrence when they were together; more as a relief from the rigours of School Practice than because what they were saying was so terribly amusing.

'Well, let's forget about them for a while,' said Kath, when they had stopped laughing. 'Come on, take your coat off. It's nearly tea-time. And it's country dancing for you tonight, isn't it?'

'Yes, but I don't think I'll go. I can't spare the time with going out this weekend. I've my lesson notes to do for Monday and a picture to draw and a child study to finish. I'd better get them done then I'll be able to enjoy the weekend without having them on my mind.'

'Don't worry, kid. School'll be the last thing on your mind once you see Ronnie again.' Kath gave a meaningful smile. 'It's this weekend that you're going to stay at his aunt's, isn't it?'

'Yes . . .' Patsy looked doubtfully at her friend. 'I feel a bit worried though, Kath. I'm looking forward to it, and I know Ronnie's aunt will make us welcome, but I haven't told Mum about it yet. She doesn't even know yet that I'm seeing Ronnie.'

'So what? You're a big girl now, Patsy. You surely don't need to give your mother a blow by blow account of your every move, do you? I'm sure your Rosie doesn't tell her everything, does she?'

'No . . . I don't suppose she does. But I hate deceiving Mum. She's always wanted to know what I'm doing. If she knew I'd got a weekend pass she'd no doubt say I should be going home, not to Ronnie's aunt's.'

'I shouldn't worry if I were you. You'll be going home in a fortnight anyway. And I'm sure your mum won't object to your going out with Ronnie. Why should she? I've only met him once, but I thought he was lovely. I wish you'd introduce me to his twin brother! Why haven't you told her though, Patsy? What's the big secret?'

'I'm not sure . . . it's complicated. I'll tell her at Christmas. I'll have to because Ronnie wants me to see him in Blackpool. He'll be home on leave, you see, and we usually go over to see my gran for a few days.'

'Great! The Big Dipper and the Golden Mile, and snogging under the pier. You'll have a smashing time, kid!'

'There's more to Blackpool than candy floss and funny hats,' Patsy retorted. 'And my mother'd kill me if she caught me under the pier,' she added a trifle primly.

'Hey! Come down off your high horse. I was only joking.'

'Sorry, Kath. I know you were.' Patsy smiled at her friend. 'It's just thinking about telling Mum . . .' She shrugged. 'Oh, what the heck! I'll worry about that when the time comes.'

'You've had no more trouble with Jocelyn?' asked Kath.

'You got things sorted out at country dancing, didn't you?'

'Yes . . . She's all right with me, thank goodness. I can't say she behaves as though nothing has happened – she's a bit cool – but I don't suppose anyone else would notice. She's dancing with Shirley Jenner now, and I just dance with anyone that's free to make up the sets. Come on, Kath. Let's go down for tea. I'm famished.'

Patsy and Ronnie had fallen into the habit of seeing one another every weekend, on Sunday if not on Saturday, but both knew by this time that it was more than just a habit. They looked forward to their meetings and Patsy felt now that a weekend without Ronnie would be dismal and empty. It was only about six weeks since they had met for the first time in Leeford, but it seemed much longer. It seemed more like six years, but that was, no doubt, because they had such a wealth of childhood memories to look back on. That was what they talked about in the main, of their mutual friends and acquaintances, and experiences that they had shared in war-time Blackpool. Their conversation was frequently interspersed with, 'Do you remember . . . ? or 'Whatever became of . . . ?' But all the time there was growing between them an awareness of each other that was not based entirely on past friendship.

The first time that they had met by arrangement in Leeford, the Saturday after half-term, they had gone to the pictures to see *An American in Paris*. Ronnie's arm had crept round her in the darkness and the kisses that they had exchanged on the back row of the cinema had been pleasant if a trifle furtive. This was a different Ronnie altogether from the frolicsome clown of Patsy's schooldays, but a Ronnie whom she already felt she wanted to know better. There was no time for him to accompany her all the way back to the college at Woodley Bank as he had to return to camp by midnight. Instead, they had a fish and chip supper at a little cafe and said goodnight at the tram stop. There would have been no point in his going back with her anyway. Students were not allowed to entertain visitors of the opposite sex in their rooms – apart from fathers and brothers, of course – and, strangely enough, this was a rule that no one thought of breaking.

Since then they had sometimes spent their Sundays together, travelling by bus to places which, in summer, were well-known Yorkshire beauty spots frequented by tourists. They climbed on the heather clad moors above the town of Ilkley, near to the Cow and Calf rocks. And another Sunday they wandered through the narrow Georgian streets of Knaresborough, down steep steps and alleyways leading to the River Nidd and then up to the ruined castle on the cliff-top. The little towns were deserted on these chilly winter Sundays, but there was always a small cafe where they could buy a pot of tea and a snack lunch. In the early evenings, though, as dusk fell, they would have to part, making their separate ways back to camp and college. November and December were bleak months for young lovers. They needed a haven, a place where they could be warm and comfortable, away from prying eyes and away from the biting chill of a Yorkshire winter.

Patsy had been dubious at first when Ronnie suggested that they should spend a weekend together at his Aunt Florrie's on the outskirts of Leeford.

'It seems such a cheek,' she protested, 'inviting myself. She doesn't even know me. Oh, I don't know, Ronnie . . .'

'You're not inviting yourself. I'm inviting you. And my aunt does know you – she remembers you from when you were a little girl. Aunt Florrie's grand – the salt of the earth. It's a home from home there and she'll make you real welcome. So stop worriting . . . Carrots!' Playfully Ronnie tweaked an auburn curl and grinned at her.

'Don't you dare!' She grinned back at him. 'Yes, I must admit I would like to go, if you're sure she wouldn't mind? But . . .' She hesitated. 'Will there be room? How many . . . ?' She looked at Ronnie apprehensively.

'How many bedrooms have they got? Three. One for Aunt Florrie and Uncle Bill, one for me and one for you. Don't start jumping to conclusions, Patsy. I'm not trying to seduce you. Aunt Florrie'll keep an eye on us, you can be sure of that. I just want us to be able to have a bit more time together. To say goodnight in comfort . . .' He put his arm round her now as they walked along the dark streets of Leeford towards the tram stop and Patsy felt a tremor of excitement as she saw the ardent look in his grey eyes. Yes, she did want to spend more time with Ronnie.

She felt a slight blush staining her cheeks at the thought of it and at Ronnie's telling her he was not bent on seduction. 'I'd never even thought of such a thing,' she said primly. 'I just thought there might not be room.'

'I'll bet you did,' said Ronnie, giving a sly chuckle. 'But, like I said, love, chance 'ud be a fine thing with Aunt Florrie under the same roof. So I'll fix it up for next weekend, OK? I've got a forty-eight-hour pass then, and you can get a Saturday night pass from college, can't you?'

Patsy nodded. 'Yes, that'll be no problem.' The students were allowed two weekends each term, as well as the half-term break. Some students, she knew, flaunted this rule by getting their friend to 'sign them in' on a Saturday night. No questions were asked, it seemed, provided all the names were in at 11.30 in the signing-in book. But Patsy was afraid that, if she were to try it, something would go wrong and her truancy would be discovered.

This proposed weekend with Ronnie was all above board though. She smiled at him. 'It'll be nice not to have to say goodnight at the tram stop. I'll look forward to it, Ronnie.'

'So will I, love. So will I.' His voice was husky and they stopped then in a doorway for a lingering kiss. Patsy felt a tingling awareness all through her. Yes, she was certainly looking forward to spending a whole weekend with Ronnie.

It was foggy when they met at their usual place, outside Gino's, the following Saturday afternoon. They went inside for coffee and were amazed to find, half an hour later, when they came out into the street again, that the fog had thickened so much they could hardly see across the road.

'Good grief! Look at that,' said Ronnie. 'That's a real pea-souper and no mistake. I've never seen one as bad as that before. We'd best get a move on, Patsy, and get up to Aunt Florrie's before the trams stop running.'

He tucked his hand under her elbow and they made their way towards City Square. They were amused to see, on the forecourt of the Town Hall, a brass band of army cadets playing a rousing march by Sousa, retreating into the swirling yellow mist and then reappearing again like wraiths surrounded by trailing clouds of vapour.

'By heck, they're keen,' remarked Ronnie. 'I'm surprised the fog hasn't bunged up their bugles. I tell you what, Patsy, we didn't get fogs like this in Blackpool. The air's a damn' sight cleaner over there.'

'Yes, they call it smog now, don't they?' said Patsy. 'Smoke and fog. There are so many factories here, that's why it's so much worse in the city.' She could feel it at the back of her throat as she spoke, a bitter, acrid taste like poison which, of course, was what it was. She pulled her green and white scarf over her mouth and nostrils and moved closer to Ronnie as they stood at the tram stop. The clinging dampness was getting into her bones now and she shivered. 'You don't really think they'll stop the trams, do you?' she asked fearfully. 'It would be an awful long way to walk.'

'No . . . Look, there's one coming now. And not before time.' Ronnie was blowing on his ungloved hands and stamping his feet, and Patsy's fingers, even in her woolly gloves, were numb at the tips.

On the outskirts of the city the fog was not quite so dense, but they were both relieved when the fifteen-minute journey came to an end. They hurried through the suburban streets to Ronnie's aunt's, passing just a few other pedestrians, all of them keeping close to garden walls and peering anxiously ahead through the swirling greyness. The sound of the traffic was muted and the car headlights, moving at a snail's pace, gleamed palely through the mist like the eyes of a gigantic tiger. Patsy felt as though they were moving through a dream sequence, mysterious and illusory, and so great was the contrast when they reached the warmth and comfort of Aunt Florrie's home that she found it hard at first to adjust to reality.

The hall light which had been left on to greet them shed a welcoming beam through the frosted glass even before Ronnie's aunt opened the door. She did so immediately at their knock.

'Good gracious! Am I glad to see the pair of you! I was worried sick when I saw all that fog.' She ushered them into the hall and closed the door. 'Ne'er mind, you're here now, safe and sound. Come on in and get yerselves warm. There's a nice fire in t'kitchen. You must be frozen stiff and famished an' all. It won't be long afore I get the kettle on and tea's nearly ready. I said to Bill as I'd get the bread cut and the table laid afore you came, then we could have a nice chat.'

Patsy smiled to herself as they followed the little woman along the short hallway to the room at the back of the house. She guessed it would be Aunt Florrie who would be doing the lion's share of the chatting. So far she and Ronnie hadn't spoken a word. Her immediate impression of Aunt Florrie was that she was very much like her grandma in Blackpool and, she guessed, much nearer to that lady in age, even though she was sister to Ronnie's father. A much older sister, most likely. She was short and plump with iron-grey hair and round spectacles and wore a cross-over apron in a floral design which strained across her bosom. Patsy was reminded of her grandma again when they entered the back room which Aunt Florrie had referred to as the 'kitchen'. It was what her grandma always called this room, which was not really a kitchen at all, but a living room.

'It's lovely to see you again, Patsy.' Aunt Florrie smiled warmly at the girl. 'I've heard such a lot about you from our Ronnie and, do you know, you've hardly changed a bit since the last time I saw you.'

'It's this hair, Aunt Florrie.' Ronnie grinned and tugged at one of her auburn curls. 'Ginger nut. That's what you remember.'

'Take no notice of him, love,' said Aunt Florrie. 'He was always a cheeky monkey as a lad and he's not changed much. I was just thinking how pretty it looks.' She patted Patsy's hair. 'Goodness me, that's damp. You'd best get near the fire and dry out . . . Yes, you were only a little mite when we stayed with our Charlie and Eileen. It was just before the war, but I remember you very well. And your mum and dad. Jenny and Tom they're called, aren't they? Don't suppose you remember me though, do you, love?'

'No . . . I'm sorry. I don't think I do.' Patsy knew that it was not very flattering to admit to someone that you had no recollection of them, but as it was so long ago she did have some excuse. 'It's really kind of you to ask me to stay,' she said. 'Well, I know that it was Ronnie that asked really.' Patsy turned to smile at him. 'But it was nice of you to say yes.'

'There's not much as we won't do for our Ronnie, he knows that.' Aunt Florrie looked at the young man fondly. 'That's right, isn't it, Bill?' She turned to the man who had just entered the room. 'We're real glad to see them, aren't we? This is Patsy, see. Grown up a bit, hasn't she, since we saw her last?'

Uncle Bill was not much taller than Aunt Florrie and of the same stocky build. He was almost bald and wore wire-framed spectacles and a shapeless grey cardigan. Patsy surmised from his mumbled 'Pleased to meet you again', and his shy smile, that he would leave most of the talking to his wife. Rather like her own parents, she thought, wondering idly if this was a northern trait, garrulous wives and silent husbands.

Patsy felt from the moment she entered the house that she was going to enjoy herself, and not entirely because she was with Ronnie. You could not help but be at ease with Ronnie's aunt and uncle and they both did all they could to make the young couple feel at home. The high tea that they enjoyed soon after they arrived, steak and mushroom pie with rich brown gravy, followed by deep custard tart, was again reminiscent of the spread always put on the table by Patsy's grandma.

'And now we'll all have to shut up for half an hour,'

said Aunt Florrie, as they finished eating, 'while Uncle Bill checks his coupon.'

'I'll help you to wash up, shall I?' said Patsy. 'Then he can listen in peace. I know my dad always wants us to be quiet while the results are on.'

'No, it's all right, lass. I can do 'em later. We'll have another cup of tea first. Sit yerself by the fire.'

They sat in a semi-circle round the hearth, cups of tea balanced in their laps and eyes fixed on the large brown box in the corner of the room, as the announcer's voice recited the familiar names. 'Manchester United, Everton, Queen's Park Rangers . . .' Now and again there was an aggravated 'tut' from Uncle Bill and an eloquent sigh as his eyes scanned the crosses in the little black and white squares. Just like Dad, thought Patsy. This same scene must be repeated in thousands of homes up and down the country every Saturday teatime. 'Queen of the South, Heart of Midlothian, Partick Thistle . . .' What grand names those Scottish clubs had and how romantic they sounded when spoken in the cultured tones of the BBC announcer.

'Just one more. That's all I needed. Just one more draw,' Uncle Bill moaned, as Patsy had heard her father moan countless times. 'Leeds United let me down again.'

'That's what he says every Saturday,' Aunt Florrie remarked as they stacked the pots near the sink in the tiny scullery. 'It's always Leeds United or Arsenal or Tranmere Rovers that has let him down. It's never his own fault for being a rotten guesser. I don't know what he'd do without his football pools.'

'My father's just the same,' Patsy remarked, 'and my young brother, too. He's football mad.'

'Aye, I reckon there's not much to choose between them . . . Here, love, if you insist.' Aunt Florrie handed a pot towel to Patsy. 'I'll wash and you dry, not that I expect you to do any work. You've come for a rest. Our Ronnie says you're busy at the moment, doing some teaching, aren't you?'

'Yes, that's right. School Practice.'

'That's where they learn you to be a teacher, isn't it?' Patsy smiled and nodded. 'By heck!' Aunt Florrie went on. 'Your mum and dad must be that proud of you, going to be a schoolteacher an' all. There weren't opportunities like that when I were a lass. Not that I'd have been brainy enough, but chance would've been a fine thing. You make the most of it, Patsy love. It's as well to have a good job, even if you do go and get married . . . I was right pleased to hear that our Ronnie had got friendly with you again. Fancy the pair of you meeting in Leeford like that. It's just like a story in *Woman's Own*. And he's a grand lad, is our Ronnie. You could do a lot worse.'

Patsy felt herself blushing. 'It's not like that, Mrs Royston. I mean, we're not serious or anything.'

Aunt Florrie chuckled. 'Don't you be too sure. I've seen the way that lad looks at you. I've never known him so smitten with a lass before. And don't call me Mrs Royston – call me Aunt Florrie, like Ronnie does. I think we'll have a game of Monopoly tonight. It'll pass the evening on nicely and Bill likes a game whenever we've got company. You know how to play, do you, Patsy?'

'Yes, we often play at home. I'd enjoy that.'

'Good grief! Anybody 'ud think it were real money, our Ronnie,' Aunt Florrie remarked when the game came to an end and Patsy had won. 'All that fuss over a bloomin' game. You fellows are all alike, bad losers the lot of you. There's Bill with his blessed football pools, and now you're going all sulky because you've gone bankrupt in a game of Monopoly.'

'I'm not sulking,' Ronnie retorted. 'It's just like old Clever-clogs here though, to get Mayfair and Park Lane.' He gave Patsy a friendly nudge. 'And what do I get landed with? The Angel Islington and Old Kent Road. It's not fair. Now, if I'd had . . .'

Patsy laughed. 'It's only a game, Ronnie, like your aunt says. D'you know, our Victor's just the same when we play at home. He takes it that seriously.'

'I've told you, Patsy, there's nowt to choose between 'em, young or old. They're spoiled babies, the lot of them, and it's us women that do the spoiling, more fool us.' Aunt Florrie folded up the Monopoly board and put the little silver pieces – the iron, car, ship and boot – back into the box. 'I'll make us all a cup of cocoa, then Uncle Bill and me'll leave you two in peace.' She smiled knowingly at Patsy as she went out into the scullery.

Patsy kicked off her shoes and curled her legs beneath her on the settee when Ronnie's aunt and uncle had gone to bed. It was tactful of the couple to leave them alone and it was lovely to be able to spend some time with Ronnie, all warm and comfortable by the fireside, instead of snatching a few kisses on the back row of the cinema or in shop doorways. His arms went round her and for several moments there was silence, except for the ticking of the clock and the crackling of the fire, as he kissed her in a way he had never been able to do before. When he finally let her go she was breathless. She put her hand up to straighten her hair and then pulled her skirt down over her knees.

'Never mind your hair,' said Ronnie. 'It'll be all messed up again in a minute.' He pulled her close to him again. 'There's no one to see but me, and I like you just the way you are.'

His kisses grew more intense and Patsy leaned back against the cushions of the settee, feeling the weight of him upon her body and the rough serge of his uniform trousers brushing against her thigh. Her skirt had risen up again, but she no longer cared. She returned Ronnie's kisses, running her fingers through the wiry mop of his hair and gently stroking the stubble on his cheeks and chin.

After a few more moments he released her again. 'God, Patsy, you're wonderful,' he muttered, reaching inside his jacket on a nearby chair for a packet of cigarettes. 'I must have one of these and calm down a bit.' She could see that his hands were trembling. He grinned at her. 'I can't tempt you, can I?'

He pushed the packet of Players towards her and she shook her head. 'No, I thought I might when I went to college, but I haven't succumbed so far.'

'And you won't if you've any sense. Runs away with the money, but it certainly soothes your nerves.' He reached for her hand and they sat close together staring into the flickering flames.

'Don't forget you're seeing me in Blackpool,' he said. 'I've a week's leave, so I'll be there till New Year's Day, all being well. You'll be over before then, won't you?'

'Yes, I should think so. We usually have a few days with my gran round New Year.'

'Don't suppose we'll get home comforts there though, like we've got here. It's grand this, isn't it, Patsy? We won't be able to do this at your gran's, will we?'

'I shouldn't imagine so,' she replied, thinking it wouldn't be her gran who might object to her seeing Ronnie, but her mother. Patsy still had that hurdle to face. She rather suspected that her mother might object to her having a steady boyfriend so soon, especially when it was Ronnie Sykes!

'There's always our place, though,' said Ronnie. 'Me

mam and dad'll be pleased to see you, and I can always make my brothers clear out of the way.'

'Yes, it'll be nice to see Auntie Eileen again,' said Patsy. 'It's ages since I saw the rest of your family.'

'And I can't get over how lucky I am, finding you again.' Ronnie flung the stub end of his cigarette in the fire and took Patsy in his arms.

When she felt his hand reaching beneath her jumper she made no protest, nor when he fondled her knee and gently pulled up her skirt. She had never had feelings like this before; she knew that she didn't want him to stop. She wound her arms more tightly round him, enjoying the sensation of his hands stroking her body, sensitive parts that she hadn't been aware of before. It was Ronnie himself who called a halt. Suddenly he let go of her and moved a little distance away.

'My goodness, Patsy Bradshaw, you're hot stuff! I would never have believed it.' He smiled at her, then gently stroked her cheek with his finger tip. 'We mustn't though, love. Not here, under Aunt Florrie's roof. It wouldn't be right. Anyway, I'd never do anything to hurt you, Patsy. I'd never forgive myself if I got you in the club.'

'Ronnie! What a thing to say!' She sounded horrified.

Ronnie laughed. 'Aw, come on, Patsy. You can't fool me. You're just as keen as I am, aren't you? Aren't you?' he said again, when she didn't answer.

'Yes,' she said quietly. 'But we can't. We mustn't. It would be awful if I was to . . . No, we can't.'

'But you'd like to, just as much as I would. I know you would,' Playfully Ronnie touched the tip of her nose. 'Underneath that Goody-Two-Shoes image, you're real hot stuff.'

Patsy looked at him keenly. 'Goody-Two-Shoes?' she said, frowning. 'Why did you call me that?'

'Because that's what you look like. All sweet and innocent. But you're not, are you? Not at all . . .'

'I was till I met you,' she replied, grinning, and he answered her with another kiss.

'We'd better go to bed, Ronnie,' she said a few minutes later. 'Your aunt has left us on our own, but you can bet she won't settle till we're safely upstairs.'

'I'm sure you're right, love.' Ronnie knocked at the dying embers of the fire with the poker and placed the fireguard in front of it, then they crept up the stairs with their arms round one another.

'Night night, sleep tight,' he whispered outside her bedroom door.

'Mind the bugs don't bite,' she whispered back, as she quietly opened the door and stepped into the chilly room.

It was a while before Patsy slept. She lay awake in the darkness of the strange room, very conscious of Ronnie lying just a few feet away from her on the other side of the wall. And she thought how dangerous it would be for them to have too many opportunities of the kind they had had tonight.

Chapter 9

A similar fog to the one that had blanketed Yorkshire also hung over London. When Rosie and Jeff came out of the theatre after seeing *The Mousetrap* they gasped in horror at the thick yellow mist which obscured everything beyond a couple of yards. It was impossible to see to the other side of the road and traffic seemed to have come to a halt, judging by the uncanny silence and stillness that pervaded the streets. Cars were abandoned, nose to tail, by the kerbs, and lamp-posts and bus stops loomed menacingly out of the mist, only visible when you had almost collided with them. It was like being wrapped in a blanket, but not one that was warm and woolly; this one was clammy and cold and oppressive, clogging the throat and nostrils and beading the face and hair with a vile, evil-smelling dampness.

'My God! Just look at that!' exclaimed Jeff. 'It wasn't nearly so bad when we went in. That's the trouble, going to the theatre in December. You never know if you're going to get stranded.'

'I wouldn't have missed it for anything though, Jeff,' Rosie remarked. 'Terrific, wasn't it?'

'Yes . . . terrific,' he replied. He sounded distracted. 'Come on, Rosie. I'd better get you home as fast as I can. Thank God the tubes don't stop running like the buses.'

'No, Jeff,' she protested. 'Don't come to South Ken with me. It would be silly. You get on your train at Leicester Square and I'll get on mine. There's no point in making two journeys.'

'Don't talk nonsense, Rosie,' he said impatiently. 'Do you really think I'd let you find your own way home from the tube station? You've never been in one of these London smogs, have you? I'm telling you, all the streets look alike. You could be wandering round all night. No, I'm coming with you. No arguing now.'

She looked at him anxiously and he smiled, all signs of his irritability vanishing as quickly as they had come. 'Come on, Rosie. Best foot forward. We'll look on it as an adventure, shall we? Pull your hood up or your hair will be soaked. And wrap your scarf round your nose and mouth. This stuff can do a lot of damage if it gets on your lungs.'

'I can't breathe,' she said, her voice muffled by the woollen scarf.

'You'll have to do the best you can. It's not far now.' Jeff put an arm round her and they staggered the rest of the way to the tube station.

The conditions at South Kensington were no better and by the time they had reached Rosie's flat, Jeff, as well as Rosie, was more than a little worried. She was aware of his anxiety as they simultaneously breathed a sigh of relief on closing the front door behind them. Jeff didn't speak as they made their way up the stairs, and inside the room he stood motionless as Rosie drew the curtains and lit the gas-fire. She stood up and they looked steadily at one another.

'Rosie . . .'

'Jeff . . .' They both spoke at the same time.

Rosie gave a little laugh. She looked at the floor, embarrassed, then back at Jeff. 'You know what I'm thinking, don't you?' she said quietly. 'You can't get back to Bermondsey tonight . . .'

'No, I can't, Rosie. It would be foolish even to try.' His brown eyes were serious as he reached out his hand and very gently traced the outline of her face, a feather-light touch of his finger tips on her cheek and nose and the curve of her lips. 'I didn't plan this, Rosie,' he said softly. 'You know that, don't you?'

'Of course I know it,' she replied. 'Even you couldn't contrive a London smog. And who would want to? Honestly, Jeff, I don't think I've ever been so scared in my life. You were right. I'd have been terrified walking back on my own. Thanks for coming with me. Take your coat off and I'll make us some coffee.'

Rosie busied herself near the gas stove, setting out the mugs and putting some biscuits on a plate. Her hands were trembling slightly and there was a nervous fluttering sensation in her stomach. It was partly due to the frightening experience of the last hour. That smog had to be seen to be believed. But she knew that her nervousness was not due entirely to the smog and her feeling of excitement certainly wasn't.

She raised her voice, calling out to Jeff at the other end of the room. 'At least you won't have as far to go to work in the morning. I hope the fog has cleared by then.'

'It should have done, Rosie. It doesn't usually last into the next day.'

'And there'll be no one to worry about you getting home safely. That's the advantage of living alone.'

There was a pause before Jeff answered. 'Yes . . . you could say that.'

They drank their coffee and ate the biscuits. Between them they cleared the plate while they talked about the play they had seen that evening, and about recent films and shows that were on in the West End. It seemed as though they had to go on talking.

'Where's the bathroom, Rosie?'

'Floor below, at the end of the passage. There's a sign on the door.'

'OK.' Jeff nodded. 'I'll go and have a quick wash. Oh, my God! I've only just realised. I won't be able to have a shave in the morning.' He rubbed his chin ruefully. 'You've no idea what I look like with a day's growth. What the devil am I going to do?'

'Don't worry, Jeff,' said Rosie. 'I've a friend on the floor below. He'll lend you a razor.'

Jeff frowned and gave her a hard look. 'A friend?'

'Oh, not that sort of a friend. He's not my type, nor am I his for that matter. He's . . . well, let's just say he'll do me a favour and no questions asked. I've turned a blind eye several times to the company he keeps. Nigel's a good friend. I'll go and ask him now, if you like?'

Jeff nodded. 'I suppose I've no choice,' he said uneasily. 'Rosie, I honestly didn't mean this to happen. Look . . . can you find me a blanket or something and I'll kip down in the armchair? I know you haven't . . . I know there's only the one room.'

'All right,' she said with forced brightness. This wasn't exactly what she had expected. 'There's a couple of army blankets in the cupboard. They belong to the landlord. They might be a bit prickly though, and not over-clean.'

'Don't worry. Beggars can't be choosers.' Jeff still sounded distracted. 'I'll just pop downstairs – let you get yourself sorted out.' He stopped in the doorway and looked back at her, his eyes troubled. 'Thanks, Rosie.'

Quickly she pulled out the bed settee as she did every night and spread it with sheets and blankets. For herself.

Or should she suggest that Jeff had the bed while she slept on the chair? He would no doubt refuse – he was quite gentlemanly most of the time – but perhaps she should at least make the offer. Her former excitement had now vanished and she was beginning to feel flat and dejected. Confused, she rinsed out the two beakers under the tap, then went downstairs to see Nigel. His eyes opened wide at her request, but he complied readily as she knew he would. 'Got a friend here myself, dear,' he added in a confidential voice. 'Stranded in the fog. Dreadful, isn't it?'

Jeff refused the offer of the bed and when Rosie returned from the bathroom, in her pyjamas and dressing gown, he was already sprawled in the chair. His clothes – jacket, trousers, shirt and tie – were in a heap on the floor and the grey army blanket was flung across the lower half of his body. His chest and his arms were bare and Rosie noticed that they were brown and muscular, almost as brown as his face. He was watching her guardedly.

'Goodnight, Jeff. Hope you sleep well.' She switched off the light and walked over to the bed, keeping a fair distance from the chair where he was lying. She felt empty inside. The room was not fully dark as there was no way of blacking out the skylight. Normally, the moonlight shone into the room, but Rosie was used to this and the glow did not disturb her rest; she found it comforting. But tonight there was no moonlight, the fog having obscured all the radiance of the sky. Rosie could still see the thick mass of greyness pressing against the window. She shrugged off her dressing gown and crept beneath the blankets.

Only then did Jeff speak. 'Goodnight, Rosie,' he said gently.

She lay still, staring up at the oblong of murky greyness above her bed, knowing it would be a long time before tiredness overcame her tonight, if at all. She felt physically tired, drained with the traumas of the past couple of hours, and dispirited too, her mind a maelstrom of confused thoughts. She could sense that Jeff was not asleep either, though they had been lying there motionless for the last half hour or more.

Rosie made a sudden movement, irritably grabbing her pillow and turning it over to feel the coolness of the other side – she hated a hot pillow – and pulling the blanket round her shoulders. To hell with Jeff Burroni! She would empty her mind, forget about him and get off to sleep. She closed her eyes tightly, willing sleep to come.

And then he was there, at the side of the bed. She hadn't heard him move across the room, but suddenly he was there, lithe and slender, clad in just a minute pair of briefs. She noticed his well-shaped arms and legs, like the statue she had seen in the British Museum, and the swell of his maleness, before he threw back the blanket and lay down beside her.

'Rosie, my love.' He took her in his arms. 'I didn't plan this. Please believe me, darling. I didn't mean to . . . but I want you so much.'

She thrilled at his use of the endearment; it was the very first time he had called her 'darling'. 'I know you didn't plan it, Jeff,' she said gently. 'You keep telling me so.' She reached up and stroked his dark hair and the angular lines of his face. 'But perhaps something else planned it. Fate . . . whatever it is. Sometimes things aren't planned. They just . . . happen.'

He kissed her then, all the while undoing the buttons of her pyjamas, pushing them away. 'Good grief, Rosie.' He stopped for a moment, laughing quietly. 'You don't intend being cold in bed, do you? I promise you won't be cold tonight.'

She wriggled out of her pyjama trousers herself and Jeff divested himself of his single item of clothing. Then she was in his arms again and for the first time – the first time ever, for Rosie – they made love. She gave a little cry of surprise and pain, just once, then surrendered herself to the rapturous sensation of Jeff around her and inside her, loving her, wanting her, just as she wanted him.

'I'm sorry, Rosie,' he said afterwards. 'I didn't mean to hurt you. I wouldn't want to hurt you . . . not in any way.' His eyes, for a moment, looked pained. 'I didn't realise that I was . . .'

'That it was the first time?' said Rosie. 'Yes, it was. But this time it won't be, will it?' She smiled up at him, putting her arms round his neck and pulling him towards her. And the next time, and the third time, it didn't hurt at all. Then they slept.

Rosie drifted through the next few days in a dream. She hardly recognised herself, not normally being the sort of girl to indulge in fanciful thoughts or to lose touch with reality. But that night with Jeff had been real enough, that was no figment of her imagination; the feeling of his strong arms around her, the way he had looked at her, his dark brown eyes intense with longing, and the things he had whispered as their lovemaking reached a climax. Looking back on it, though, it seemed like a dream. He hadn't said that he loved her; he hadn't, she recalled with a pang of disquiet, actually used those words. But he did love her, she was sure of that. It was apparent in his voice, his touch, his glance, just as she loved him.

He had been concerned about her reputation, insisting that they should leave the flat at separate times. But there had been no embarrassment between them in the cold light of morning. The fog had almost cleared leaving behind a stale smoky smell and a clinging nauseating dampness. But it could not dampen Rosie's spirits and the joy in her heart and mind. Jeff's warm smile and the glow in his eyes, still there in the morning, told her that he was hers now. There could be no turning back. Girls like Rosie – well-brought-up girls, that was – didn't give of themselves lightly. To do so implied a commitment, a promise of a more lasting relationship.

Rosie was uneasy therefore when after a week had gone by, Jeff still hadn't said anything to her. He had spoken to her, of course, in class and at break times, sometimes sitting with her and her friends over coffee or lunch in his usual light-hearted manner. But he hadn't asked if he could see her again, if he could visit her again in her flat. When he did eventually ask her out, it was a couple of days before they were due to break up for the Christmas holidays. They had supper together at a little restaurant on the Cromwell Road, an Italian place where they served a Spaghetti Bolognese that Jeff praised as being 'the real thing', and good red wine. He told Rosie, although she had gathered as much from his casual attire, that he had not been home but had been working late at college on end of term lists and records. She, however, had dressed with care in a new black sweater and long peasant-style skirt and had put on more make-up than usual. It was, after all, their Christmas celebration; she wouldn't see him after tomorrow for about three weeks. But Jeff made no comment about her appearance. He accepted her invitation to come up to her flat for coffee, but apart from kissing her ardently several times he made no further advances.

Rosie felt bemused and disappointed. After he had left she fingered the brightly wrapped parcel he had given her. It was obviously a book, just as it had been a book that she had given him, one of modern paintings. At least they had exchanged gifts and it would be a reminder of him when she opened it at home on Christmas Day. Not that she needed any tangible reminder of Jeff. He was there with her, in her mind and her heart, in her thoughts by day and in her dreams at night. But Rosie was puzzled as she travelled home to Castleburn for the Christmas vacation.

'I do think it's a pity you've had your nice hair cut, Rosie,' Jenny Bradshaw remarked again. It had been one of the first things she had noticed when Rosie had walked through the door, and she returned to the same subject at tea-time as they all sat round the table. Both Patsy and Rosie had returned home that day, just a few days before Christmas. Patsy had arrived first and Rosie, whose journey from London had taken considerably longer, only a couple of hours ago. 'I liked the way you used to have it, in that page-boy style,' Jenny went on. 'It looks – I don't know – all raggy somehow.'

Rosie patted at her recently shorn locks and laughed. 'It's called an urchin cut, Mum. A lot of the students have their hair like this. It's modern.'

'It looks daft,' said Victor. 'Looks as though it's been cut with a knife and fork. An urchin cut, did you say? Yeah . . . that's what you look like. An urchin, like that Tom in *The Water Babies*. You look as though you should be going up a chimney.'

'Less of your cheek, Victor. I see you've not changed much while we've been away.' Rosie smiled good-humouredly at her brother. 'Has he, Patsy? He's as cheeky as ever.' She turned to her sister who gave a quiet smile and nodded in agreement. Rosie thought that Patsy seemed somewhat subdued and wondered if there was anything wrong. No doubt Patsy would tell her later if there was anything worrying her.

Rosie was happy to be at home again with her family, and the niggling little pinprick of anxiety that she had felt about Jeff was temporarily pushed to the back of her mind. It was great to see Patsy again; they would have such a lot to talk about when they were alone together. Rosie had forgotten, for the moment, about the slight coolness that had existed between them before she went to London. There seemed to be no sign of it now. Patsy had greeted her exuberantly and only since they had sat down to tea had Rosie noticed her sister's preoccupation.

Rosie turned to her father now. 'What do you think about it, Dad?' she asked. 'My new hair-do. D'you like it?'

Tom Bradshaw, who had been sitting there quietly as he usually did, listening and not saying very much, looked at her and nodded. 'Yes, I like it well enough. It makes you look older though, Rosie. More sophisticated. Mind you, I liked it the way it was before, but I daresay you wanted a change.'

'Well, I think it's smashing, Rosie,' said Patsy. Her voice was loud and everyone glanced at her in surprise. 'You look just like Lesley Caron in *An American in Paris*. Her hair was just like that.'

'Have you seen that picture, Patsy?' asked her mother. 'It was on at the Regal not long ago. I told your dad I'd like to see it, but he didn't seem interested.'

'Yes . . . I saw it with Ronnie,' said Patsy, still speaking more loudly than usual. 'The first time I went out with him we went to see it.'

'Ronnie?' Jenny's greenish-brown eyes looked questioningly at her daughter and she raised her eyebrows. 'Who's Ronnie, dear? Is it a young man you've met at college? Another teacher?'

'No, Mum.' Patsy hesitated. 'It's someone you know, actually. Someone you used to know very well. It's Ronnie Sykes. I met him in Leeford and I've been going out with him.'

'Ronnie Sykes?' Jenny stared at her daughter for a moment, her mouth slightly open and a tiny frown creasing her forehead. 'I'd no idea you'd been seeing Ronnie Sykes. You didn't tell me.'

'Well, I'm telling you now, Mum.'

Patsy's tone was a little defiant and her mother answered sharply, 'Don't you speak to me like that, young lady! Is that the sort of manners they teach you at college?'

Rosie caught her sister's eye and gave her a sympathetic smile. So that was what had been troubling Patsy. Rosie understood now. Her sister had told her in letters about her developing friendship with Ronnie, adding that she hadn't yet mentioned it to Mum. Rosie realised that Patsy had brought up the subject of the film so that the conversation could be brought round to Ronnie. She knew that her sister had been forcing herself to pluck up courage to do so.

'Don't go on at her, Jenny,' Tom was saying now. 'I'm sure Ronnie Sykes has grown up into a very nice young man. Our Patsy wouldn't want to be friendly with him if he wasn't.'

'Huh!' Jenny stabbed her fork into a piece of meat pie with more force than was necessary. 'From what I remember of Ronnie Sykes – and his brothers – they were a bunch of real scallywags. The terrors of the neighbourhood, they were.'

'Who's Ronnie Sykes?' asked Victor brightly. 'Is he your boyfriend, Patsy? Does he kiss you? Are you going to let us have a look at him? Are you . . .'

'Be quiet, Victor,' snapped his mother. 'Ronnie Sykes

was a rough lad who lived near us in Blackpool, just round the corner from your gran's. He was a twin – Raymond was the other one – and there was a younger boy called Leonard.'

'And their mother was your best friend,' said Tom in a quiet voice, looking pointedly at Jenny.

'Yes . . . I was friendly with Eileen at one time,' said Jenny, staring fixedly at her plate. 'I'm not denying that. But I haven't seen much of her lately. We seem to have lost touch with one another.'

'Why is that, Mum?' asked Rosie. 'I remember Mrs Sykes – Auntie Eileen, we used to call her. She looked after Ben, didn't she, the little lad who came from Liverpool with me? You always used to be in and out of one another's houses. Why have you lost touch with her?'

'Good gracious, Rosie! I don't know. Why do you lose touch with people, for goodness' sake?' Two red spots burned on Jenny's cheeks. 'Because we moved to another town, and because we're not very good at writing letters, neither of us. I had a card from her the other day, as a matter of fact. We always send cards at Christmas.'

Rosie nodded. She knew she had needled Jenny by asking her about her friendship with Eileen Sykes, but she was unrepentant. She had done it on purpose – for the way she had spoken to Patsy. Rosie knew only too well why Jenny had lost touch with Eileen, and why she was now so vexed at the thought of Patsy being friendly with Ronnie. Jenny had come up in the world, in her own eyes if not in anyone else's, since the family moved to Castleburn.

'What was Ronnie doing in Leeford anyway?' said Jenny now. She added, more tolerantly, 'I do think you could have told me, love.'

Patsy explained about him being in the army and about how his twin, Raymond, had been deferred because he had had TB.

'Now I am sorry to hear about that,' said Jenny. 'Poor Raymond . . . and poor Eileen too. She must have been worried sick. I'll drop her a line after Christmas.'

'You could go and see her, Mum, couldn't you?' asked Patsy. 'We'll be going to Blackpool to see Grandma, won't we? When are we going?'

Jenny nodded astutely. 'You're very interested in going to Blackpool all of a sudden. And I don't think it's just because of Grandma, is it? Is he going to be there? Ronnie Sykes?'

'Yes.' Patsy looked squarely at her mother. 'He'll be there till New Year. And I've arranged to see him.' She did not add the words 'So there!' but they were implicit in the tone of her voice.

Her mother looked steadily back at her with narrowed eyes. 'All right. Just remember that you're supposed to be training to be a teacher. You've a lot of studying to do, never mind gadding about with lads like Ronnie Sykes.'

'For heaven's sake, Jenny, let it drop,' said Tom, far more forcefully than he usually spoke. 'I reckon we've heard quite enough about the Sykes family for one day.'

'When are we going to Blackpool then?' asked Victor, leaning eagerly across the table. 'I hope there'll be a match on. Blackpool are great.' His brown eyes, just like Patsy's, shone with excitement. 'Stan Matthews and Stan Mortensen. Will we be able to see them, Dad?'

'I should jolly well think we will,' said Tom, smiling at his son. 'We'll make sure we're there for a football match, I'll promise you that.'

'Good for you, Patsy,' said Rosie a little while later. 'I'm glad you had the guts to stick up for yourself. Don't worry, she'll get over it.'

'She'll flippin' well have to,' said Patsy tersely, 'because I intend to go on seeing him, whatever she says.' The two girls were in their bedroom unpacking their cases, hastily shoving their belongings into the drawers and wardrobes. 'Did you hear her?' Patsy went on. 'She was all sweetness and light at first. "Who's Ronnie, dear? Is it another teacher?" Oh, yes, it would have been all right if it had been somebody from college, but she soon changed her tune when she found out it was only Ronnie Sykes. But it was just what I expected. That's why I was dreading telling her. She thinks he's not good enough for me, I suppose. She's so . . . so snobbish, Rosie!'

'Oh, come on. That's a bit harsh, Patsy.'

'Well, what would you call it then? We're ordinary people, aren't we, just like the Sykeses? Like you were saying, Mum used to be Eileen's best friend. I'm glad you reminded her about that, Rosie. It's only since we moved to Castleburn that she's started having such big ideas. I was telling Ronnie about the elocution lessons and piano lessons and all that.'

'Yes, I must admit I was a bit annoyed with her,' said Rosie. 'But I don't think I'd call her a snob. She just wants the best for all of us – you and me and Victor. She left school when she was fourteen, you know, and had to slave away for her mother in the boarding house whether she liked it or not. She wants us to have all the chances that she never had. I don't suppose you can blame her.'

'No, I suppose not,' said Patsy grudgingly. 'But I do wish she wouldn't treat me like a child. She makes me feel like a kid of ten sometimes.' Patsy banged the dressing-table drawer, setting all the bottles and jars rattling. 'I notice she doesn't do it with you.'

There was a touch of resentment in Patsy's tone and in her glance, the same ill-feeling that Rosie had noticed before the two of them went off to college. She hastily tried to smooth things over. 'I daresay it's because I stand up for myself, like you were trying to do. But I've always done it, ever since I was a little girl.'

'She's different with you, though,' Patsy went on, still sounding somewhat disgruntled. 'She treats you more as a friend – an equal – not just as a daughter. I'm just a little girl to her, that she thinks she can boss around.'

'But then I'm not her daughter, am I?' said Rosie simply.

Patsy stared at her in surprise. 'Of course you are. You have been ever since . . . for about ten years.'

'Ever since I was adopted? That's what you were going to say, isn't it?' said Rosie quietly. She gave a grave little smile. 'I suppose that's why she's different with me, Patsy. It's bound to make a difference, me not being her real daughter. And I've always been independent, you know. I grew up pretty quickly when I was evacuated – even before that – much more quickly than you did. So Mum knows there's no point in treating me like a child now.'

'But I'm grown-up now as well,' said Patsy feelingly. 'Not that anyone seems to have noticed.'

'I bet Ronnie's noticed,' said Rosie, laughing. 'Never mind about Mum. I've told you, she'll get over it. Tell me about Ronnie. What's he like now? Is he handsome?' She moved closer to her sister where they sat on the bed. 'Is he amorous?'

Patsy laughed too. 'Yes, he's a nice-looking lad. He's improved a lot, but in some ways he's the same old Ronnie. Dead cheeky still and full of fun. Anyway, you'll no doubt be seeing him when we go to Blackpool. He remembered you very well.'

'Yes, no doubt he would. I gave him a right sock on the jaw once for teasing you.' Rosie looked at her sister slyly. 'Come on, you didn't tell me the rest of it. I said, is he amorous?'

'Shhh! Mum'll hear you.'

'There you go again. Never mind Mum. Tell me, is he?'

'Yes . . . yes, he is,' said Patsy in a whisper. 'Honestly, Rosie, I don't know what we're going to do . . . And what about you and that Jeff? I notice you haven't told me much about him, but you're being dead nosy about me and Ronnie.'

'Jeff?' Rosie gave a quiet smile. 'Yes, we're getting on very well, Jeff and me.'

'Jeff Burroni. That's what he's called, isn't it? It sounds foreign.'

'Yes, he's part-Italian. His grandfather came over from Italy and settled here.'

'Is he a Catholic?'

Rosie frowned. 'Why do you ask that? I . . . don't know.'

'I just thought he might be. You mentioned in one of your letters that he was the youngest of a large family, the only one who'd been to college. And with him being Italian as well . . .'

'Part-Italian.' Rosie shrugged. 'Yes, I suppose he might be a Catholic. We've never talked about it. But it doesn't matter, does it?' She was reflecting as she spoke that there were several gaps in her knowledge of Jeff Burroni.

'No. It would only matter if you and he got serious. It might matter to Mum. You know what she's like. D'you still go to church, Rosie, in London?'

'No . . . there's never time. I work at the cafe some Sundays, and sometimes I go out with Jeff. Or I get on with my work. I've never got round to going to church.'

'Neither have I,' said Patsy. 'Well, I went once to the C of E near college, but I didn't like it much. Too high for me. But since then, like you, I've been otherwise engaged, going out with Ronnie.'

'I shouldn't worry. I've told you – Mum can't dictate to us about our every move, especially when we're not living at home. I don't think she goes to church as much herself now. Do you remember, we all started going to All Saints when we moved here? I suppose Mum thought that Church of England sounded posher than Methodist.'

Patsy laughed. 'Who's calling her a snob now?'

'Well, it's true. But I think she's got impatient with all the old women in the church. She's still quite young, you know.'

'Have you told her about Jeff?'

'I've mentioned him in letters.'

'What does she say?'

'I think she's impressed because he's a tutor. She probably thinks that's all he is – a tutor taking an interest in one of his pupils.' Rosie grinned. 'But that's most likely the impression I gave her.'

'Well, come on then. Tell me some more about him. You said you were getting on well. How well?'

Rosie smiled and lifted her eyebrows expressively.

'I've heard about these Latin lovers,' Patsy went on. 'Have you been to his house? Have you met his family?'

'No. He doesn't live with them now. He has his own flat. But it's in Bermondsey – I've not been – it's such a long way out.'

'But there's your place, isn't there? You're lucky, having your own flat. D'you know, we're not even allowed to have men in our rooms at Leeford? I bet you've had Jeff up to your flat, haven't you?'

'Yes . . . once or twice.'

'Gosh!' Patsy's eyes were like saucers. 'And . . . did you . . . ?'

Rosie smiled again, secretively. 'I've told you, we get

on very well.' She looked at her sister, her eyes suddenly serious. 'I'm in love with him, Patsy,' she said quietly. More than that she could not tell her sister. What had happened between herself and Jeff was much too wonderful and precious to be shared with anyone.

'Gosh!' said Patsy again.

Patsy was not sure about her feelings for Ronnie. When her sister had said she was in love with Jeff, Patsy could tell she was by the light in her eyes. Rosie had seemed to shine all over. All Patsy knew was that she loved being with Ronnie. She looked forward to their meetings, she enjoyed his company and she longed for the times when they were completely alone. She returned his kisses and embraces with an ardour that matched his own and which surprised and frightened her more than a little. She knew that it was probably just as well that they were not allowed to have men in their bedrooms at CLTC! And she knew that her mother's opposition to the young man had only strengthened her resolve to go on seeing him. But whether she was in love with him or not, Patsy wasn't sure.

The Bradshaw family travelled by train to Blackpool a few days after Christmas and intended to stay till after the New Year. Annie Carter, Jenny's mother, didn't take visitors over the Christmas period as some of the hotels and boarding houses did. She reckoned that she deserved a rest from the time the Illuminations finished at the end of October until the Easter weekend. They took a few visitors at Easter, but it wasn't until Whit weekend, at the end of May, that the season started in earnest.

Annie lived alone and had done since Jenny and her family had moved to Yorkshire, and her younger daughter, Violet, had married a GI and gone to live in America.

'Aye, I'm alone, but I'm not lonely,' Patsy had often heard her gran say. 'You can't be lonely with a houseful of visitors all summer. And in the winter I'm glad of a bit of peace and quiet, I can tell you!'

But Ada Bottomley, Annie's niece, who shared the running of the boarding house with her, and her husband, Fred, kept an eye on Annie through the winter and she always spent Christmas Day with them at their home near the town centre.

'And then we have another Christmas when you lot descend on me,' Annie told the Bradshaw family soon after they arrived, as she did every year. 'Our Ada and Fred are coming round tonight and we'll all have our dinner together. I've got me turkey in the oven already. Can you smell it?'

Patsy sniffed appreciatively. She had already noticed the appetising aroma of roasting turkey, a real Christmassy smell, that was drifting in from the back kitchen, together with the mingled scent of mince pies and sage and onion stuffing. She began to feel happy and warm inside, looking forward immensely to the family gathering that evening. Patsy loved her gran and she knew that the love was returned in abundance; she often suspected that she was Annie's favourite grandchild although it was, of course, never admitted.

Patsy looked round now at the shabby comfort of the living room, which her gran always referred to as the 'kitchen'; it had changed very little from the time when she was a child. There was the same clipped rag rug in front of the fire and the same Axminster carpet square, now very worn in places, on the floor with the brown and orange linoleum, polished to a high gloss, round the sides. The sagging easy chairs and sofa had been rejuvenated with cheerful cretonne covers in a design of pink roses, and curtains of a similar material hung at the windows. Patsy remembered well the maroon chenille cloth that covered the dining table when it was not in use. How she had loved to play with the bobbles that decorated the edge; some of them, indeed, were missing, like gaps in a set of teeth. Paper streamers stretched from the centre light to each corner of the room and on top of the mirror over the fireplace was a red and green tissue paper bell that opened like a concertina.

On a small table in front of the window, covered with a white cloth with a crocheted edge, stood the Christmas tree. Patsy couldn't help smiling as she looked at it. She had always thought that it looked like a collection of bottle brushes, though green, not white. It was stiff and unyielding and most obviously artificial, but it was part of Patsy's childhood and she loved it. Its rigid branches were decorated with silver tinsel, coloured glass baubles, a few of them broken, chocolate novelties – those surely must be new every year, thought Patsy – and at the top was a celluloid fairy doll with a once-white net dress and once-sparkling wings.

'She looks as though she's seen better days,' Jenny whispered to Patsy, nodding at the tarnished fairy. 'Like some of the rest of us!'

She smiled at her daughter, a conspiratorial smile, and Patsy felt gratified at the brief exchange. Things had been a little strained between the two of them after their heated interchange soon after Patsy returned from college, but all that seemed to have been forgotten now. Differences were always buried at Christmastime and now they were going to enjoy, as her gran had said, another Christmas celebration.

The Bradshaw family had already exchanged gifts on Christmas morning. Patsy had been secretly thrilled when she opened the present of perfume and lace handkerchieves that Ronnie had given her, but her mother had said very little apart from 'Very nice, dear.' Which was the comment Jenny also made when she saw Jeff Burroni's gift to Rosie, a book of Impressionist paintings by French artists. But now it was time, after Aunt Ada and Uncle Fred arrived at six o'clock, for another session of present giving.

Soon the floor was knee deep in torn paper and tinselled string as the eight people gathered there ripped open their presents and exclaimed delightedly – whether they were really pleased or not – at the contents. The two girls, Patsy and Rosie, had received almost identical gifts. A pair of fur-backed gloves each from Grandma; gloves, too, from Aunt Ada, but this time fairisle ones that she had knitted herself, with berets to match. Neither of the girls, in reality, wore anything on their heads however inclement the weather. Rosie would turn up the hood of her duffelcoat if the cold was extreme and Patsy draped her college scarf over her head; they both, nevertheless, expressed their appreciation of Aunt Ada's thoughtfulness and said how clever she was to be able to do such complicated knitting.

So Ada was well satisfied, as both she and Annie were at their gifts of bath salts, scented soap, boxes of stationery and pure silk stockings. Annie's meal, as always, was delicious; turkey and stuffing, apple sauce, three kinds of vegetables, followed by Christmas pudding with rum sauce, mince pies, and the habitual cup of tea. Patsy had never known a meal at her gran's that didn't end with a cup of tea.

'Aye, that's how we do things up here,' Annie commented, when Patsy remarked on the fact. 'I reckon nothing to yer fancy coffee-drinking habits, like they do in London. That's right, isn't it, Rosie? They don't know how to make tea down there?'

'If you say so, Gran,' said Rosie, grinning. 'But you're behaving like a real southerner tonight, aren't you? Cooking a dinner in the evening.'

'I haven't heard you lot complaining,' Annie replied tartly, but with a twinkle in her eye. 'Aye, it's all right once in a while, but I prefer me dinner in the middle of the day like all proper-thinking folk do.'

'It was a lovely meal, Mother,' said Jenny sincerely. 'We've all enjoyed it.'

'Yes, we have indeed.'

'Smashing!'

'You've done us proud, Ma.'

Annie nodded, well pleased at the comments of her family, and she said, as she did every year, 'Aye, well, if everyone could have a good dinner like this it would be a much better world, that's all I can say.'

Patsy glanced round at her family, a widely assorted group of people – Mum and Dad, Gran, Rosie and Victor, Aunt Ada and Uncle Fred, all wearing paper hats – and at the debris that littered the table – crêpe paper from the crackers, dirty plates and dishes (though all scraped clean), Woolworth's gold-rimmed glasses, now empty of the yearly drink of sherry – and she felt absurdly happy. And in two days' time she would be seeing Ronnie again.

They had arranged, by letter, to meet on New Year's Eve. He was to call for her in the evening at her grandmother's boarding house and they would see in New Year, 1953, together before he returned to camp the following day.

Jenny made no further mention of the young man although she knew that Patsy had received a letter from him. But the thought of him was still there, creating an occasional feeling of unease between mother and daughter. His name cropped up in conversation at dinnertime the day after the Christmas meal and Patsy could have bitten off her tongue when she realised what she had said.

She was tucking into the roast beef and Yorkshire pudding with relish. 'D'you know, Gran?' she remarked. 'They serve this differently in Yorkshire. They have the Yorkshire pudding first with gravy, then the meat and vegetables afterwards.'

'Aye, I daresay they do,' replied Annie Carter caustically. 'They're stingy in Yorkshire. They reckon that if you fill up with pudding first you won't have any room left to eat much meat.' She sniffed. 'A tight lot they are on t'other side of the Pennines.'

'Steady on, Ma,' said Tom laughing. 'There's a Yorkshireman born and bred here, I'll have you know.'

'Oh, I don't mean you, Tom,' said Annie. 'You're a different kettle of fish altogether. You've lived in Lancashire long enough anyroad, to get out of them stingy Yorkshire habits.'

'And we don't serve Yorkshire pudding that way in our house either,' said Jenny. 'Is that what they do at college? I'm glad to hear you're having such good meals, Patsy.'

'Oh no, it wasn't at college,' said Patsy. 'It was at Ronnie's aunt's. His . . . Aunt Florrie's.' Her voice faltered as she realised what she had said.

'Ronnie Sykes' aunt? Charlie Sykes' sister?' Jenny sounded horrified. 'You mean to tell me you've been there? You've had a meal there? Oh, Patsy . . . really!'

'So what's wrong with that?' said Annie Carter, looking indignantly at her daughter. 'You know she's going out with young Ronnie – she's been telling me about him – so it stands to reason she'd go with him to see his aunt. And it seems as though she gave 'em a good meal an' all, even if it were served all upside-down.'

'She didn't tell me, that's what's wrong, Mother,' Jenny retorted. 'This is the first I've heard of it. She's getting proper deceitful since she started seeing Ronnie Sykes.' She turned to Patsy. 'When was this?' she said in a flat voice.

'A few weeks ago.' Patsy's eyes blazed with a look that was almost hatred as she stared back at her mother. She felt humiliated, and angry too, being treated like a child in front of her grandmother. Might as well be hanged for a sheep as a lamb, she thought. She emphasised the next few words. 'We stayed for the weekend.'

'You did what?' Jenny's voice rose in a shrill crescendo. 'You slept under the same roof as Ronnie Sykes? And his aunt had no more sense than to let you?'

'Yes, Mum.' Patsy's tone was verging on the insolent. 'We slept under the same roof. But not in the same room. Not in the same bed.'

'Patsy! How dare you? I've never heard such talk! And in front of Victor, too. You should be ashamed of yourself.'

Jenny cast an anxious glance at her son, but Victor didn't seem to be at all concerned about the fracas going on around him. He was busy pushing the last morsel of Yorkshire pudding into his mouth, then he looked up for a second to wipe a smear of gravy from his mouth and to grin impudently at Patsy.

'That'll do now, Patsy,' said her father softly. 'There's no need to be cheeky.' He turned to his wife. 'Just leave it, Jenny. D'you hear me?' His voice was quiet, but there was no doubt that he meant what he said. 'We've heard quite enough about it all. Just leave it alone.'

The subject of Ronnie Sykes was dropped for the rest of the meal although the atmosphere remained somewhat strained. Patsy was still determined to have the last word.

'And I'm seeing Ronnie tomorrow,' she called as she piled the pudding plates together. 'New Year's Eve. He's calling for me at half-past six.' And you can like it or lump it, her defiant glance at her mother seemed to say.

Chapter 10

'Oh . . .' Jenny pursed her lips and drew in her breath. 'Red . . . with your hair, Patsy?' She looked critically at her daughter in her new sweater. 'It's a lovely jumper, I must admit, and such a nice bright colour. But I'm not too sure about it, not with your hair.'

'It's OK, Mum,' Rosie intervened. 'All redheads are wearing red now. It doesn't matter any more. And Patsy hasn't got red hair anyway, has she? It's auburn. You look smashing, kid.' Rosie smiled at her sister. 'And it looks great with that skirt.' She looked admiringly at Patsy's pencil slim black skirt with the long slit at the back, revealing more than a glimpse of her slender, nylon-clad legs. 'I've never seen you look so smashing. You look real different tonight.'

'She looks different all right,' said Jenny tersely. 'Isn't it a little bit . . . tight, dear?' She cast an anxious glance at Patsy's small pointed breasts, outlined by the clinging red sweater.

'No, I don't think so, Mum,' said Patsy casually. 'It's the same size as I always wear. It's just slim-fitting, that's all. And the skirt as well. They're all the fashion.'

'If you say so, dear.' Jenny sighed. 'Now, you won't be late back, will you? I know it's New Year's Eve, but you must be in by half-past twelve, no later. Your dad and I won't be able to settle till you come in.'

'No, I won't be late, Mum.' Patsy was trying hard not to clench her teeth. Things had been a little easier since Jenny's outburst at the dinner table and Ronnie had not been mentioned since. It was as though her mother was trying to come to terms with the idea and Patsy was determined not to spoil things; she wanted to get out of the house this evening without a row breaking out.

She was waiting for Ronnie now, in the kitchen at her grandma's boarding house, with Rosie, her mother and grandmother. Tom and Victor had gone for a brisk walk along the promenade to work off the effects of Annie's high tea and to chat together about their favourite subject, football. The red jumper which, as Patsy had feared, had caused a little controversy, was new on that evening. She hadn't wanted to waste it on her family, not even at Christmas, but had saved it for New Year's Eve and her date with Ronnie. She knew she looked nice; striking was a more appropriate word, she had thought, as she surveyed herself in the full-length mirror. She had hardly been able to believe that the image in front of her was timid little Patsy Bradshaw. She had been afraid that Mum might say she looked tarty but, all things considered, Jenny hadn't been too condemning.

'Hang on a minute. You've got a smudge on your cheek.' Rosie came over to her, licking a corner of her handkerchief. She rubbed at the smear of Max Factor pancake make-up which Patsy had put on rather more generously than usual. 'There, that's better. And that lipstick's super. It just matches your sweater.'

'A bit bright,' Jenny added.

Rosie went on as though she hadn't heard. 'And you smell gorgeous. Is that the perfume Ronnie gave you for Christmas?'

'Yes. Goya's Gardenia. Nice, isn't it?'

Jenny's smile was rather forced. 'And what are you doing tonight, Rosie? Why don't you go out with Patsy and Ronnie? I'm sure they wouldn't mind.' Patsy glanced warily at her mother and Annie Carter gave an exasperated 'tut', casting an admonitory glance in her daughter's direction. But Jenny appeared not to notice. 'After all, it's New Year's Eve, dear,' she went on. 'You don't want to stay in on New Year's Eve, do you? And I'm sure Ronnie Sykes'll be ever so pleased to see you again.'

'No, it's all right, Mum,' said Rosie. She glanced at her sister and gave a surreptitious wink. 'I said I'd go round to see Aunt Ada. I thought I'd told you.'

'You surely don't want to spend New Year's Eve with Ada and Fred,' said Jenny. 'You should be with the young ones.'

'I get on well with them,' said Rosie evenly. 'Besides, I've some sketches to finish first. I'll go round later. Aunt Ada said I could stay the night if I wanted to.'

'And Rosie's got her own young man down in London, haven't you, love?' said Annie Carter. 'She doesn't need to go sharing our Patsy's.'

'That's right, Gran,' said Rosie. She smiled and looked gratefully at the older woman.

'He's here now.' Patsy jumped to her feet at the sound of the bell and rushed to the front door. She was excited at the thought of seeing him again, but when Ronnie grabbed her in a bear-like hug, she returned his kiss and then quickly wriggled free. 'Not now! Not here! You'd better come in and meet them.'

All eyes were on Patsy and Ronnie as they stood in the doorway. Annie spoke first. 'Hello, Ronnie love. Come on in and have a quick warm at the fire before you go out again. We don't need to bother with introductions, do we? You remember us all well enough. It's a good few years since I saw you, lad, but you look pretty much the same. Bigger, of course, but not much different.'

'And still as cheeky as ever, Mrs Carter.' Ronnie grinned. 'We were a right bunch of tearaways, weren't we, me and my brothers? I remember our ball coming over into your yard more than once, and the telling-off we got.'

Patsy could see that her grandma's eyes behind the thick lenses were moist as she smiled kindly at the young man. 'Aye, you were a young devil and no mistake, but I can't believe you're still as cheeky as ever. Just you take care of our Patsy, that's all.'

'Nice to see you again, Ronnie.' Jenny's voice sounded strained and her smile was obviously forced, but she held out a hand in greeting. 'How is your mother? It's a long time since I saw her.'

Ronnie shook her hand briefly. 'Hello, Mrs Bradshaw.' Patsy recalled that he always used to call her Auntie Jenny. 'Mum's quite well. She wishes to be remembered to you. She says why don't you call round at our house while you're in Blackpool? She'd be pleased to see you again.'

'Yes.' Jenny's voice came out in a high squeak. 'That would be nice. I might do that.' She sounded rather posher than usual, Patsy thought.

'Hi there, Rosie.' Ronnie smiled at the girl. 'Remember me, do you?'

'I'll say I do. Lovely to see you again, Ronnie.' Rosie's voice was warm and her blue eyes seemed bluer than ever as she smiled at him.

Patsy felt a sudden stab of apprehension. It had always been like this at the Youth Club: Rosie smiling bewitchingly at the boys while she, Patsy, hovered uncertainly in the background. She shuffled her feet nervously, ill at ease at all these greetings. 'Shall we be going now, Ronnie?'

she said quietly. 'We might have to queue for the pictures tonight.'

His smile when he turned to her was wider than ever and she could see from the loving glance he gave her that he had eyes for no one else in the room. 'Yes, you're right,' he said. 'We'd best be off. Get your coat and we'll be on our way.'

He grinned as Patsy slung her scarf round her neck on top of her camel-hair coat. 'Yes, I thought you'd be wearing that. Never seen without it, are you, Patsy?'

'She's proud of it, aren't you, Patsy love?' said Jenny, adding unnecessarily, 'Her college scarf.'

'No different from you wearing your uniform,' countered Patsy, feeling suddenly cross with her mother again. 'You've always got it on.'

'Yeah . . . I feel strange, somehow, in civvies now. Well, cheerio, everyone. See you again, I hope. And we won't be late back, Mrs Bradshaw.' He nodded meaningfully at her. 'I'll have Cinderella home from the ball by half-past twelve.'

'Yes, thank you, Ronnie,' replied Jenny tightly. 'Goodbye, Patsy. Have a nice time.'

'Whew!' Patsy gave an eloquent whistle as they walked down the street. 'That was hard going. Gosh! Was I glad to get out!'

Ronnie seemed unconcerned. 'You worry too much, Patsy,' he said. 'But I see what you mean. Your mother doesn't exactly go a bundle on me, does she? But then she never did. Anyway, let's forget about 'em for a while. Do you really want to go to the pictures, love?'

'I'm not fussy,' said Patsy. 'Anywhere – it's just nice to see you again.'

'And you too.' Ronnie pulled her close and kissed her cheek. 'We could go dancing, to the Winter Gardens or the Tower . . . No?' he said as Patsy seemed unresponsive. 'Well, how does this grab you then? Mum says we can stay in if we like, at our place. She'll put us a fire in the front room and make us some supper. And my two brothers are going to the pictures so we'll have a bit of peace. What d'you think? Then perhaps we could go out later and see the crowds in Talbot Square. See the New Year in.'

'I think that sounds a smashing idea, Ronnie,' said Patsy happily. 'It'll be great to see Auntie Eileen again too.'

'And it'll be great to be alone with you again, love,' said Ronnie. They stopped in a doorway for a quick kiss before entering the bus station to wait for the bus to Marton.

'That wasn't very tactful of you, our Jenny,' said Annie Carter when the young couple had gone and Rosie had disappeared upstairs. 'Suggesting that Rosie should go with 'em. I'm glad the lass took no notice of you. They want some time on their own. Anybody with half an eye can see that.'

'Yes, and that's what's worrying me, Mother,' said Jenny. 'Our Patsy carrying on with lads already, and she's only been at college a term. She's a lot of studying to do.'

'Who says they're carrying on?' retorted Annie. 'And it isn't lads you object to, is it? Not lads in general. It's Ronnie Sykes, isn't it? I can read you like a book, Jenny. Always have been able to. You think he's not good enough for her, don't you? You've got too big for your boots since you moved to Castleburn. All them bloomin' fancy ideas.' Annie gave a loud sniff.

Jenny was silent. She didn't want to get into an argument with her mother. They'd had enough of those when she lived in Blackpool, but since they'd moved to Yorkshire their relationship had been much less strained. And

Mother was getting older now. She must try not to upset her. 'I haven't said that, Mother,' she replied evenly, 'that he's not good enough. I just thought she might meet somebody . . . well, different, when she went to college. But I don't really see why she has to be bothering with lads at all. She's only eighteen, you know.'

'And you were only nineteen when you married Tom,' Annie reminded her. 'You've conveniently forgotten that, haven't you?'

'Nearly twenty, Mother,' said Jenny quietly. She was determined not to raise her voice.

'And you were only seventeen or so when you met him,' Annie went on.

'But I wasn't training to be a schoolteacher, was I?'

'No, I should think you weren't. There was too much work to be done here.'

Yes indeed, Mother, thought Jenny. So much work that she hadn't been allowed, when she married Tom, to go and live in Yorkshire, but Tom had had to come and find a job in Blackpool. Jenny had looked to marriage as an escape from her mother's dominance, instead of which she had found herself still tied to her mother and the boarding house for another thirteen years until, at the end of the war, they had finally gone to live in Castleburn.

A dreadful thought suddenly seized Jenny, something she hadn't, until now, considered. Was history repeating itself? Was she, like Annie Carter, turning into a dominant, overbearing mother, setting her own daughter against her? That really hadn't been her intention. She cared so much for Patsy – for all of them – and only wanted the best for them. And the best didn't seem to be Ronnie Sykes, the niggling little thought persisted. But she didn't want to be at loggerheads with her daughter for the rest of the holiday. It would be time soon enough for Patsy, and Rosie too, to return to college. Jenny made up her mind to try to be more tolerant.

She smiled at her mother now, voicing something of what was going through her mind. 'I only want the very best for her, Mother. And I can't help worrying when she's away from home. It wouldn't be natural if I didn't.'

'And how do you know the best for her isn't Ronnie Sykes?' said Annie more gently. 'She has to make up her own mind, you know. And he seems to have grown up into a grand young man.'

'I daresay he's all right,' said Jenny grudgingly. 'But she's young enough yet. Anyway, time'll tell.'

'You don't seem to worry as much about Rosie,' Annie remarked. 'And she's got a young man an' all, down in London. I should've thought you'd be worried sick about that, her getting friendly with one of them Londoners. They're not like us, you know.'

'He's one of her teachers, Mother. Tutors, they call them. He's helping her with her work, that's all.'

The look that Annie gave her daughter said quite clearly: 'And if you believe that, you'll believe anything.' But Jenny didn't notice. She was staring into the fire, thinking about Rosie.

'No, it's true,' she said thoughtfully. 'I don't worry as much about Rosie. It isn't because I don't care about her. I do . . . but it's always been different with Rosie.'

'Come on in, Rosie love. It's grand to see you.' Ada Bottomley ushered the girl into the small room that adjoined the kitchen at the back of the semi-detached house. It was a room that Rosie remembered well from her childhood and it hadn't changed much now. 'I'm glad you've come,' Ada went on. 'Are you going to stay the night, like I suggested? I've put a bottle in the bed, just in case.'

'Yes thanks, Auntie Ada. I'd like that. I told Mum and Gran that I'd probably stay, so they won't worry. Hello, Uncle Fred. Nice to see you again. Are you well?'

'Not so bad, thanks, Rosie love.' Fred rose from the armchair and shook her hand. 'All the better for seeing you, but goodness knows why you want to be bothered with a couple of old fogies like us on New Year's Eve.' His kind brown eyes glinted with amusement as he smiled at her.

Rosie liked Fred. She had always got on well with him, and with Ada too. Fred hadn't changed much over the years, except that he looked a little older. He still had the small moustache that had reminded her and Patsy of Hitler during the war years – that was when Fred had first come on the scene – and his sleek black hair was now greying at the temples. Ada, if anything, appeared younger rather than older, this metamorphosis having begun when she and Fred started courting and continued throughout the twelve years of their marriage. Her hair was entirely grey now, but she wore it in a soft curly style, not the severe roll, skewered into position with hairpins, that Rosie remembered from the wartime years. She wore make-up too, just powder and lipstick, and the glasses that she now wore had pale pink frames which gave her face a gentler look.

But she answered her husband tartly, in a way that was reminiscent of the old Ada. 'Old fogies be damned, Fred Bottomley! You're as old as you feel, and I certainly don't feel my age, if you do. I'll be fifty-four next birthday, Rosie, and I'm not ashamed to admit it, but I'm not going to start behaving like an old woman yet, by heck, I'm not. Of course, Fred's a few years older than me, poor old soul.' She gave a good-natured laugh before going on, more seriously: 'But I must admit I thought you might have had something else you wanted to do tonight,

Rosie – the pictures or dancing or something. There'll be all sorts going on in Blackpool tonight.'

'No, I'm all right, Aunt Ada. I'd just as soon be here. Patsy's gone out with Ronnie Sykes, and I didn't want to play gooseberry. I had some work I wanted to finish and I'll be glad of a cosy night by the fireside.' She sat down in the comfortable armchair and held out her hands to the blaze. 'This is one thing I miss, being in a flat. I've only a gas-fire. Real antiquated thing it is, too. To tell you the truth, I'm glad of a change of company as well. There was rather an atmosphere at "Pleasant View".'

'Ronnie Sykes?' asked Ada raising her eyebrows.

'Yes, how did you know?'

'Oh, Annie was telling me summat about it the other day. How Patsy has got friendly with him again and Jenny isn't any too keen.'

'Yes . . . I think Mum's being rather intolerant. She even suggested I should go out with them – with Patsy and Ronnie. Did you ever hear such nonsense? As if I would! Anyway, Gran started sticking up for Patsy and I sensed things were rather fraught between Mum and Grandma. So I'm not sorry to be out of the way.'

'That's nothing fresh,' remarked Ada. 'Jenny and her mother were always at it hammer and tongs, though I think it's been a lot better since you all lived in Castleburn. I was real glad for Jenny when she managed to get away to Yorkshire. That was what she needed, a break from her mother.'

'And then you got yourself lumbered with Gran, didn't you?' said Rosie, laughing. 'And the boarding house and everything.'

'Oh, I can cope with Annie,' replied Ada. 'You just have to let her see that she can't have it all her own way. No, it's all worked out splendidly. The best day's work we ever did, wasn't it, Fred, going into the boarding house with Annie?'

'Yes, it was that,' he agreed. ' "Pleasant View's" doing very nicely indeed. We were full up every week, right up to the end of the Illuminations. That's the beauty of Blackpool, of course. It's a much longer season here than it is in the other resorts. And it couldn't fail, could it, with two smashing cooks like Annie and Ada?' He beamed at his wife.

'Oh, be fair now, Fred,' Ada replied. 'It's Annie that does most of the cooking. She always did, and I didn't want to go taking her job off her – not that she'd have let me, mind you. I do most of the shopping and I organise the cleaning an' all that. Of course, we employ a couple of chambermaids now, and a couple of waitresses. We're short of nothing we've got, I can tell you. And we mustn't forget Fred here.' Ada smiled proudly at her husband. 'He's the handyman in chief. Does all the odd jobs around the place, and all the painting and decorating. We wondered how it would work out when he gave up his milkman's job, but it's all turned out for the best. And he does decorating jobs for other folk as well, when he's got time.'

'Aye, that's in the winter, when we've closed down,' Fred added. 'Some of the big hotels stay open all year round, and some open up at Christmas. Some of the little places as well, but Annie thought we'd all be glad of a break in the winter.'

'She's not getting any younger, of course,' Ada remarked, 'although she's still marvellous for her age.'

'How old is Grandma?' asked Rosie. 'I don't think I've ever known. She's always looked the same to me.'

'She must be turned seventy now, though she's always a bit cagey about it. She was no spring chicken when

Jenny was born – she must have been thirty or thereabouts – and even older when Violet came on the scene. Annie was my mother's younger sister, you know. They lived in Wigan originally, then Annie and her family moved here to the boarding house after her husband died. And she made a go of it too, even though she'd just been left a widow. I must give credit where it's due: Annie's always been a worker.'

'And was that why you moved to Blackpool, Aunt Ada? To be near Grandma and her family?'

'Good heavens, no, lass! There was no love lost between Annie and me in them days. I moved here to get away from the muck and smoke in Wigan, get a bit of fresh air into me lungs. And I was lucky an' all. I got this place with the Frobisher ladies, and I was with them till the end, God rest them. And, as you know, Miss Maud left me this house when she died, God bless her.'

'And it was no more than you deserved, Ada love,' said Fred warmly. 'You were as good as any daughter to those two old dears.'

'And you're still here,' Rosie commented, looking round the little room, at the firelight glinting on the brass fender and fireirons, the cheerful red velveteen curtains and cushions and the multi-coloured clipped rug on the hearth. 'I remember coming to this room when I was a little girl and I always thought how lovely and cosy it was.'

'Yes, it was my housekeeper's parlour in them days,' said Ada. 'My own little place, although my ladies always made me welcome in the rest of the house. I used to have my meals with them and sit with them of an evening. I was like one of the family really. We've got used to being in here, haven't we, Fred? We sometimes light a fire in the other rooms to air them. But, like you say, Rosie, it's nice and comfy.'

'There was some talk of you selling the house, wasn't there?' said Rosie. 'When you went into partnership with Grandma.'

'Oh, aye. I think Annie would have liked us all under the same roof, but Fred and me, we wanted our own place. We have a couple of rooms, you know, at "Pleasant View", and we stay there sometimes in the summer when we're extra busy. But most of the time we come back here at night. That was why Fred bought the car, to make things a bit easier. It's only a little Morris Minor, but it goes a treat. We have to leave here soon after seven, and it's about seven at night when we get back home. But neither of us is afraid of hard work. You don't have to be, when you're in the boarding house business, I can tell you.'

'No, I've heard Mum say that, many a time.'

'Yes, and things are a darned sight better now than they were when Jenny was a lass, I must admit,' said Ada. 'Poor Jenny. Annie worked her and Violet like slaves. At least we do have a few helpers now, waitresses and chambermaids and that. Jenny and Violet used to do the lot, with Annie, of course. She was a difficult woman, Rosie.' Ada stared into the fire, nodding thoughtfully. 'We had many a dust-up, her and me; it's amazing that we get on so well now. Jenny used to say that Annie and me were two of a kind. Happen that's why we used to fall out so much.'

'I daresay she's mellowed as she's got older,' Rosie remarked.

'Yes, and happen I have too,' agreed Ada. 'I think the world of Annie, you know, even though I used to call her fit to burn. And I was only too glad to be able to help out when Jenny moved to Yorkshire, and Violet had gone to America not long before. It was a blow to Annie, losing 'em both at the same time.'

'Any talk of Grandma going to America again?' asked Rosie.

'No. She's only been the once, and I think she was glad to get back to England, although she loved seeing Violet and Charles and the family. I think Vi's due for another trip over here soon. I can hardly credit it, Violet with three children. Young Gary'll be ten next year.'

'Yes, and Linda's seven and Donna's four,' said Rosie. 'Nicely spread out, aren't they? Donna was only about a year old the last time they came over here. I'd love to see them all again, and I know Patsy would.'

'You'd best start saving up then,' said Ada, 'and take yourselves over to the States. You'll be rolling in it, won't you, you and Patsy, once you start working?'

'That's a good while off yet, Auntie Ada,' said Rosie. 'Like Gran would say, there's a lot of water to flow under the bridge before then. And it all depends on what sort of a job I get. You can't always walk straight into the job you want, not in the art world.'

'And what is it you want, Rosie love?' Ada leaned forward, her eyes alight with interest.

Rosie knew that Ada was always ready to listen to her. She always had been, ever since Rosie was a little girl. 'I'd like to be a designer,' she told her eagerly.

'Dress designing? Like the pictures you see in them posh magazines at the dentist's?'

'No, not exactly. Textile design, I mean. Designing patterns for materials – to make into curtains and bedspreads and all that sort of thing.' Rosie gave a little laugh. 'I know it's probably a ridiculous dream, but it's what I've set my heart on . . . one day,' she added wistfully.

'And I'm sure you'll do it, too,' said Ada, looking at her affectionately. 'If you've made up your mind, then that's what'll happen. You're that sort of a girl, Rosie.

And I wish you all the luck in the world, I do that.'

Rosie was touched by Ada's interest. 'Thanks, Aunt Ada,' she said quietly.

'And you're always welcome here, any time at all. Fred and I are that pleased you've come to see us. Now . . . tell me about Ronnie Sykes. What's he like now? Has he grown into a nice young man?'

'Yes, he seems very pleasant. And Patsy's quite taken with him. To Mum's dismay. I can't help thinking Mum's being a bit ridiculous about it all.'

'Ah, well, that little lass was surrounded by adults till you came on the scene. Too much so, I always thought. It was you that brought our Patsy out of her shell, you know. And it's hard for Jenny to realise she's a grown-up young woman now.'

'Gran was sticking up for Patsy. I could see that Grandma had taken a liking to Ronnie straightaway.'

'Well, Patsy can do no wrong in Annie's eyes. She's always had a soft spot for the little lass, ever since she was born. She was like a dog with two tails when that little baby came on the scene. You'd've thought nobody had ever had a grandchild before.'

'Yes, Patsy does seem to be the favourite,' Rosie remarked. 'I've always noticed that. Not that it worries me. I can't expect Gran to make as much of me as she does of her own flesh and blood. But I think Victor's noticed it too. He and I don't seem to matter as much as Patsy.'

'Annie loves you all,' replied Ada. 'Make no mistake about that. Her heart's as big as Blackpool Tower underneath all that bluff and bluster. And you're as much a part of the family as anyone, Rosie.' Ada looked at her steadily. 'You must never think otherwise. But Patsy was the first grandchild. It was only natural Annie should make a fuss of her. I used to feel, though, that Annie was giving that little bairn all the love that she should have given to her own two, Jenny and Violet. She never seemed to show much affection to those two lasses when they were little.' Ada stopped speaking abruptly. 'I daresay I'm speaking out of turn. That's the trouble with me. I never know when to stop.'

'It's all right, Aunt Ada,' said Rosie. 'It'll go no further. And it's all very interesting. Families are complicated things, aren't they?'

'They are that. Now, what are we going to do with ourselves? Would you like a game of cards – rummy or beggar-me-neighbour? I know it's not very exciting, but we don't want to listen to the radio all night. See if you can find the cards in the sideboard, Fred.'

'Yes, I'd like a game of rummy,' said Rosie. 'I haven't played for ages. And don't worry about it not being exciting, Aunt Ada.' She suddenly felt like confiding in the older woman. 'I didn't want to go out dancing or anything tonight. I've got a boyfriend, you see, in London.' She smiled, feeling all warm inside just at the thought of him. Thoughts of Jeff were never far away, but talking about him made him feel so much nearer. 'It wouldn't be the same . . . without Jeff.'

'Yes, Annie said something about a young man. She didn't tell me much though, Rosie. I wouldn't want you to think we'd been gossiping.'

'I don't mind,' said Rosie happily. 'He's called Jeff Burroni. He's part-Italian,' she added at Ada's questioning glance. 'He's a tutor at the college. One of the younger ones, of course. He's only a few years older than me.'

'A tutor? My goodness! You're doing well for yourself. And you like him, do you? Well, that's a silly question, but you know what I mean.'

'Yes . . . I like him. I like him a lot. There's never been anyone to compare with him before. I was friendly with a few boys before I went to college, but there's never been anyone like Jeff.' Rosie was suddenly filled with untold happiness at the mere thought of him. She felt like shouting with laughter and could hardly wait till next week when she would see him again.

Ada looked at Rosie's flushed face and shining blue eyes and she felt a stab of fear. The lass appeared grown-up in a lot of ways, but she was terribly vulnerable. She gently reached out and touched the girl's hand. 'Be careful, Rosie,' she said. 'Be careful, love.'

'By heck! That's a smashing sweater, Patsy. And a smashing girl inside it an' all.' Ronnie drew a voluptuous curve in the air with his hands. 'Phew . . . Talk about Marilyn Monroe. She's got nothing on you.'

'Ronnie!' Patsy could feel herself blushing and she hastily crossed her arms across her breasts. 'Give over.' But she couldn't help smiling with delight as well that he had noticed how nice she looked. Perhaps nice was not the right word though . . . Marilyn Monroe was not what Patsy thought of as a nice girl. She wasn't sure that she wanted to be compared with her. 'D'you like Marilyn Monroe?' she asked. 'I've always thought she's a bit common. You know . . . tarty.'

'She's a smasher!' Ronnie rolled his eyes and gave what Patsy thought of as a lascivious smile. 'Lots of the lads have her picture pinned up over their bunks. Her and Jane Russell. Now, she's another smashing dame.'

'What about you? Have you got their pictures up?'

'Ah, that'd be telling!' Ronnie tapped his nose with the tip of his finger. 'Anyway, what do I want with pin-up girls? I've got the real thing, haven't I?' He put his arms round her again and Patsy felt herself yielding to his kiss.

'I'm sorry you don't like Jane and Marilyn though,' he said after a few minutes as he released her and leaned back against the cushions. 'Who do you like?'

'Oh . . . Doris Day,' replied Patsy. 'And Debbie Reynolds.'

'Yes, I thought you might,' said Ronnie, laughing. 'Clean, wholesome girls. That straight from college look.'

'You liked Debbie Reynolds as well,' Patsy retorted. 'It was you that wanted to see *Singing in the Rain*. It was your idea.'

'Only because I knew you'd like it,' replied Ronnie. 'You know me. Anything to please a lady.'

'And what's wrong with being clean and wholesome anyway?' said Patsy. 'It's better than being a . . . a sex symbol.'

'So what's wrong with being sexy?' Ronnie lowered his voice to a seductive growl and leered at her. 'You look pretty sexy yourself tonight. Come here . . .'

Patsy laughed as he grabbed her again and for the next few minutes there was silence.

'Gosh, Patsy! I've told you before, you're hot stuff. If Mum and Dad weren't in, I'd be carrying you off upstairs.' Ronnie sighed. 'Don't know how I'm going to hold out much longer.'

'Ronnie!' said Patsy again. 'You know we can't.'

'I know, love.' He smiled ruefully and patted her hand. 'Don't worry. I know when to stop. But don't wear that jumper again if you want to hang on to your innocence.'

'D'you really think it's too . . . sexy, Ronnie?' asked Patsy seriously.

'No, is it heck. I'm only teasing you. You look great. But I've never seen you in anything so colourful before.'

'No . . . Mum was a bit doubtful about it. I don't really

think she liked it at all, though she didn't actually say so.'

'It's not the only thing she's doubtful about, is it?' Ronnie gave a bitter laugh. 'I don't think she's exactly struck on me, is she?'

'She was all right. She was polite enough to you, wasn't she?' Patsy had no intention of admitting to Ronnie the extent of her mother's displeasure when she had discovered that her daughter was seeing him.

'Yeah . . . polite. That just about sums it up. The look your mother gave me 'ud freeze the . . . nose off a brass monkey. Yes, she was polite all right.'

'Well, what more do you want then? It isn't as if she was rude to you.'

'Look, Patsy – if you like somebody, really like them, then you're not just polite to them. You're friendly and kind and you make them feel welcome. Like your grandma did. I knew as soon as I walked in the room that Mrs Carter was pleased to see me. What a difference, eh?'

'Yes, I do know what you mean,' said Patsy thoughtfully. 'Gran's great. She'd always be on my side. I get on famously with her.'

'And you can't say you've not been made welcome here, can you?' said Ronnie. 'My mother was thrilled to bits to see you again, and she showed it, too.'

'Yes, she did,' agreed Patsy warmly. 'And your dad. And it was nice to see your brothers again.'

Raymond and Leonard Sykes had just been leaving for the pictures when Patsy and Ronnie arrived at the house in Marton. She had found Raymond much more changed in appearance since she had last seen them than his twin brother. He was now much thinner than Ronnie, one of the after effects of his illness, and more serious-looking, the glint in his grey eyes being one of earnestness rather than amusement. Leonard, a couple of years younger than the twins, had already grown into a beanpole of a lad, resembling his father rather than his mother.

Eileen Sykes was just as Patsy remembered her, pleasantly plump with a round face, smiling grey eyes – like Ronnie's – behind round pink-framed lenses, and round sausage curls, now more grey than brown. She flung her arms around Patsy when they met in the hallway and there was no doubt that she was delighted to see the girl again and thrilled that Ronnie had been taking her out.

'Just fancy that,' she said. 'You and our Ronnie meeting after all this time. It's fate, that's what it is. I was that pleased when he told us, and our Florrie took a real shine to you, love. You'll go and see her again, won't you? She'll always make you welcome.'

'Yes, we've promised to go again,' said Patsy. 'We had a lovely weekend. And I'm so pleased to see you again, Auntie Eileen.' It came easily to Patsy to call Ronnie's mother 'aunt', as she had always done. She felt her eyes moistening slightly at the friendliness of the woman's greeting and at the remembrance of happy times they had spent together in Blackpool when she and the boys were small.

'Just come in and say hello to Charlie,' said Eileen, 'and then we'll leave you on your own for a while. I've put a nice fire in the front room.'

Charlie Sykes looked up from his newspaper and nodded. 'How do, Patsy. Grand to see you.'

He was the sort of fellow that you didn't notice much when his wife was around – like her own mother and father, Patsy thought – but there was no doubt that he was pleased to see her again, just as Eileen was.

'Straighten yourself up, love,' said Ronnie now, 'and we'll go and see if Mum's got the supper ready. Then we'll get a bus back into Blackpool. We can mingle with the crowds for a while, if you like, before I take you home.'

'OK, Ronnie. That'll be fine.' Patsy stood up and looked in the mirror above the fireplace. It was in the shape of a flower, with pale pink petals, similar to one that was over the sideboard in her own home. She patted at her hair and wiped a smear of lipstick from the corner of her mouth, then pulled her jumper down over the waistband of her skirt. 'There, I think I'm respectable now.' She looked down at her legs, craning her neck to see if the seams of her nylons were straight, and twisted her black skirt round so that the slit was at the back.

'Give over, will you?' said Ronnie. 'You'll get me going again.' He made a playful grab at her and she grinned and jumped out of the way.

'Stop it, Ronnie . . . Just a minute, though. You've got some lipstick on your chin. You can't go in looking like that.' She rubbed at the smear with her handkerchief. 'There, that's better.'

'As if Mum and Dad don't know what we've been up to.' He smiled at her and kissed the top of her head. 'Come on, love.'

Supper was a knife and fork affair in the Sykes household even though they'd already had a substantial tea. They tucked into cold lamb, cut from a joint Eileen had cooked earlier in the day, with pickles and beetroot, followed by apple tart and custard.

'Now, you'll want to be off,' said Eileen. 'You won't want to miss the fun. There'll be some right goings on in Blackpool tonight. Mind you take care of her, Ronnie. It'll be crowded in Talbot Square.'

'Don't worry, Mum. She'll be safe as houses with me.'

'And remember me to your mother, won't you, Patsy?' said Eileen. 'Tell her I'll be pleased to see her if she feels like calling round.'

'I'll tell her, Auntie Eileen. But we'll be going home the day after tomorrow.'

'Yes, I know there's not much time. Perhaps the next time you come to Blackpool . . .'

But Eileen reflected as she watched the young couple walk down the street, arms entwined round one another, that it was doubtful if Jenny Bradshaw would call to see her. And they had been such good friends at one time. Eileen was thoughtful as she watched her son's retreating back in his khaki uniform. She was thinking of another young man who had worn uniform, but it had been of airforce blue, and of her friend, Jenny, who had fallen hopelessly in love with him. Even though she had had a husband serving in the army . . . Eileen smiled sadly to herself. Yes, it was perhaps not surprising that Jenny was keeping her distance. Eileen knew a few things about her that were best kept hidden, wartime confidences that maybe Jenny now regretted. Not that Eileen would tell a soul; she never had done and she never would. It was a great pity, she thought, that she and Jenny couldn't resume their friendship. But Eileen also knew, without being told, that the blossoming romance between Ronnie and Patsy would not be entirely pleasing to her one-time friend.

The crowds were thick in Talbot Square, the younger residents, mainly, and winter holidaymakers waiting to welcome in the New Year, 1953. The Illuminations proper had finished at the end of October, but strings of multi-coloured fairy lights festooned the buildings round the square and on the forecourt of the Town Hall there was a huge Christmas tree decorated with twinkling lights and stars. Everyone seemed to be in a jolly mood, shouting and laughing and singing, and a few couples were dancing on the pavement outside Jenkinson's cafe. Patsy and

Ronnie watched for a while, not wanting to join in, but happy to feel part of the excited throng. Then, without a word to one another, they wandered to the promenade and across the tramtrack to the iron railings overlooking the sea.

Behind them was the sound of distant laughter and shouting, bright lights and bustle and gaiety, and in front of them was the dark sea, silvered here and there by the faint moonlight, splashing and breaking against the sea wall with a muffled roar. Ronnie turned to Patsy, cupping her face in his cold hands. His eyes were serious for once as he leaned towards her and gently kissed her lips. 'I'm so glad I've found you, Patsy,' he whispered. 'So very, very glad.'

'So am I, Ronnie,' she whispered back. 'We're lucky, aren't we? You're going back to camp, but I'll be back at college soon, and we'll be able to see one another again.'

Ronnie sighed. 'Not for long, love. I'm waiting to hear about my posting to Germany. I know it can't be much longer.'

'Oh no . . .' Patsy leaned her head against his shoulder. 'Oh no, Ronnie. I don't want you to go.'

'But you knew about it, love. I told you.'

'Yes, but I've been trying not to think about it.'

'It won't be for long. I'll be demobbed next January, and then you'll have finished at college the next July, won't you?'

'It's a long time off, Ronnie. And I live in Yorkshire, you know, not in Blackpool.'

'Don't be silly – it's not a million miles away. And you do want to go on seeing me, don't you, Patsy?'

'Of course I do. You know I do. But it seems . . . such a long time . . .' Her voice petered out, then was stopped altogether by Ronnie's kiss.

'One step at a time, darling,' he whispered into the

softness of her hair. 'It won't seem long, I promise. And when I come home, you'll be waiting for me, won't you?'

Patsy nodded and tried to smile, but as Ronnie looked into the depths of her lovely brown eyes he could see the glint of unshed tears. And he knew, suddenly, in an upsurge of happiness, that he loved her. She was such a quiet, diffident girl, so unlike him in temperament and outlook, but so loving once she had overcome her shyness. Passionate, in fact – she had certainly surprised him once or twice. And he knew that he had fallen in love with her. He looked at her shining eyes and the auburn hair curling round the collar of her coat, at her pale delicate face and trembling, slightly parted lips, and he knew that he loved her and wanted her more than anything in the world. But he also knew that he would have a long time to wait for her. Very soon he would be posted to Germany for the best part of a year, and Patsy had completed only one term at college. It was too soon to ask her to make any definite promises.

'Cheer up, love,' he said lightheartedly, revealing nothing of the wealth of feeling inside him. 'You'll make it rain with a glum face like that.'

Patsy smiled then. 'I'll miss you, Ronnie,' she said quietly.

And as they kissed again they heard the sound of the bells of St John's church welcoming in the New Year.

'Happy New Year, darling,' whispered Ronnie.

'Happy New Year,' she whispered back. But the thought of Ronnie leaving her, possibly in just a few weeks, filled her with almost unbearable sadness. She wasn't sure, not as sure as Rosie seemed to be about Jeff, but she thought she had fallen in love with him.

Chapter 11

Jenny stopped at the window of Mr Fothergill's antique shop in the market square one morning in early January, attracted as she always was by the pleasing display. China figurines, silver and brass, cranberry glassware, Victorian jewellery, all tastefully and artistically arranged. It was no wonder that Patsy had enjoyed working there on Saturday mornings and during her school holidays, Jenny thought, as she craned her neck to see the price ticket on a Dresden shepherdess. Yes, the cost of the figure was far beyond anything that she could afford but, all the same, it was nice to look. Looking didn't cost anything.

The shop was well placed for tourist trade, in a prime position near to the castle, at the top end of the market square. Not that there were many tourists now, in the middle of winter, but in the spring and summer they would come flocking back. Castleburn, since the end of the war, had become quite a thriving little town, especially as many more people nowadays had motor cars and went out and about at weekends in search of undiscovered beauty spots. And Eustace Fothergill knew when he was on to a good thing. Sometimes, in the summer, he hired a market stall in addition to the shop, where he sold some of the more inexpensive items. Patsy had loved it, her mother remembered, when she had been asked to help out there.

Jenny peered through the window, her view distorted now and again by the bottle glass in some of the panes. It wasn't authentic, but had been put in fairly recently to add to the 'olde worlde' impression of the shop. It was very pleasing though. There was a notice at the side of the window which she had only just seen, so captivated had she been by the merchandise.

'Wanted, sales assistant,' she read. 'Three afternoons a week. Hours negotiable. Enquire within.' Jenny's green-brown eyes were thoughtful. She stared unseeingly for a moment at the goods in the window, then she read the notice again. Her eyes gleamed resolutely as she opened the door and entered the shop.

The bell gave a gentle ping as Jenny stepped over the threshold and she stood for a moment looking round. The interior of the shop was not quite so tastefully arranged as the window. Here was clutter and confusion, although none of the objects appeared to be shoddy and the smell of the place was merely musty, not unpleasant. It just looked as though it needed a good old sort-out.

Eustace Fothergill appeared after a few seconds from the room at the back. 'Sorry about that,' he said, wiping his hands on the front of his brown overall. 'I was dusting some old books – filthy they are – and I had my arms full when I heard the bell. Why, hello, Mrs Bradshaw. How nice to see you.' His short-sighted eyes beamed delightedly at her from behind his pebble-glass lenses. 'I tell you what, my dear . . .' He put his head on one side, nodding confidently. 'I'm missing your Patsy. I am that. Grand little worker she was. Saturdays haven't been the same since she went off to college. I've tried one or two lasses, but they don't seem to have the same flair for it that Patsy had. A week or two, then they've had enough. I'd be glad to have her back, I can tell you.'

'She's training to be a schoolteacher, Mr Fothergill,' said Jenny, unable to keep a tinge of pride out of her voice. 'Although I daresay she might be able to help out a bit during the holidays. If she wants to,' she added.

'I think she'll want to all right,' replied Mr Fothergill. 'Yes, I think she'll want to. Were you wanting to look at something, my dear? Here I am, chattering away and forgetting to serve you. Do forgive me. What can I do for you?'

'No . . . I didn't want to buy anything,' said Jenny. 'It was that notice in the window. I see you want a sales assistant?'

'Yes, that's right. Why, do you know somebody? Oh, I'd be so grateful if you could recommend somebody reliable. The trouble I've had, you wouldn't believe . . .'

Jenny smiled brightly at him. 'Would I do?' she asked.

'You?' Mr Fothergill's spectacles dropped to the end of his nose as he gave a start of surprise. He pushed them back with his forefinger. 'You, Mrs Bradshaw?' he said again.

'Yes, why not?' said Jenny laughing. She could have been offended at his astonishment, but she knew that he wouldn't mean it unkindly. He was such a courteous, old-fashioned sort of man.

'No reason at all, my dear,' he said now. 'Do forgive me. How rude I must have sounded. It's just that I always think of you as being such a busy person, with your husband and three children to look after, and I know you attend a lot of meetings at the church. I didn't think you would have had the time. But I would be delighted, of course. Delighted, Mrs Bradshaw.'

'Not so busy as I was,' Jenny reminded him. 'Patsy and Rosie are away at college now, as you know. And as for Victor, well, he's more often out than in. Football practices and bike rides with his friends and all that.' She hesitated. 'I wouldn't want to neglect him though,' she added thoughtfully. 'The only thing I was doubtful about was the afternoons – that's what it says on the card. I would want to be there when he comes home from school.'

'And quite right too, Mrs Bradshaw. I don't hold with young women going out to work and neglecting their families. There seem to be quite a few of them doing that these days.'

'Yes, our Patsy has told me about the latch-key children,' said Jenny. 'She said there were half a dozen or more in the class she was teaching with keys hung round their necks on a piece of string. Still, we shouldn't criticise when we don't know the full story. I daresay their mothers need the money. But I wouldn't want our Victor to be like that. Listen to me . . .' Jenny laughed. 'I'm talking as though I've already got the job. Is there anything you want to ask me, Mr Fothergill? And I expect there'll be other people you want to interview.'

'Not at all. Not at all. As far as I'm concerned the job's yours if you want it.' Mr Fothergill rocked backwards and forwards on his feet as he spoke, like one of those wobbly toys that you pushed but would never fall over. 'I need somebody honest and reliable and friendly. And you're all those things, I know.'

'But what about experience? I've never worked in a shop.'

'It doesn't matter. You'll soon pick it up. Your Patsy did, and if you're anything like your daughter you'll be very suitable. Very suitable indeed.' He stopped rocking and leaned on the counter. 'About the hours – you could come mornings if you like, instead of afternoons. Perhaps the odd Saturday afternoon, if you could manage it? I'd be willing to fit in with you. I find I'm needing someone to leave in charge when I go to auction sales. At the moment I have to close the shop and it's not good policy to keep trade away. Not good policy at all.'

Jenny smiled to herself at his habit of repeating things, but she was sure she would get on very well with Eustace Fothergill. She knew he was a lonely man, though always very cheerful and amiable. He had lived alone in the flat above the shop since his wife had died a couple of years before. He must be turned sixty now, and he looked it, too, with his white hair fringing a bald head and lines of age as well as laughter lines on his round face. His manner, though, was that of a much younger person. He was very fit and active and his business was thriving as it had never done before. Jenny remembered how, during the months that his wife was ill, the shop had often been closed. She found she was already looking forward to working here, although it had been just a spur of the moment idea when she saw the notice in the window. And Tom knew nothing about it yet.

'Of course I'll have to talk it over with my husband,' she said now, 'but I can't see that he will mind.'

'You mean you haven't told him? He didn't know you were coming to see me?'

'No.' Jenny laughed. 'I didn't know myself till I saw your advert. But Tom'll be all right about it. I'm sure he will.'

'Oh dear, I hope so. I do hope so. I was so looking forward to having you here. And this place needs a good sort-out, as you can see.' Eustace Fothergill waved his hand in the direction of a pile of boxes stacked higgledy-piggledy in a corner. 'I've bought a lot more stuff, but it all wants organising. That's what it needs, organising. Your Patsy was a grand little organiser, but it's all gone to pot again since she left. It was Patsy that sorted out the window for me. And she had some real good ideas too.'

He pointed to a table with a notice: 'Inexpensive gifts'. Jenny recognised her daughter's printing in Indian ink, neat but distinct, the same printing that she now used on notices for her classroom walls. 'She thought it would be a good idea to have a display of things that youngsters could buy as presents,' Mr Fothergill told Jenny. 'Any amount of them came in during the school holidays choosing presents for their mothers' birthdays. And I carried on with it at Christmas, but it's a little depleted now.'

'How did they know about it?' asked Jenny. 'You don't usually find children going into an antique shop, surely?'

'Oh, word gets round. You'd be surprised. Word gets round. Children notice it when they come in with their parents. And I think Patsy spread the word as well.' Mr Fothergill chuckled. 'We had ever so many of her Sunday School class paying us a visit. Good little advertiser she was, and she'd a way with the kids too.'

Jenny smiled. 'Yes, I'm very proud of Patsy. I'm glad she was such a help to you. I just hope I'll do instead.'

'Of course, of course.' Mr Fothergill beamed and rocked so far forward he nearly overbalanced. 'Just talk things over with your hubby, then let me know what you've decided. I'll look forward to working with you, Mrs Bradshaw . . . look forward to it.'

'I don't see why not,' said Tom, later that evening. 'You can go and work at the antique shop if you've a mind.' He did, however, sound somewhat surprised. 'But I thought you'd enough to do, looking after the home. My mother always used to say it was a full-time job.'

'So it used to be, Tom, and there's nobody knows more about housework than I do. I can remember the time I've cleaned twelve bedrooms at my mother's, and then had to help to cook the dinner. And wash up.'

'Yes, I know she made you work hard.'

'You can say that again! But housework's what you make it these days. You don't have to be a slave to it. There's all sorts of modern gadgets coming in. I can't imagine, now, how I managed without the washing machine. That automatic wringer's grand. When I think how we used to heave at that old wooden mangle of Mother's. Talk about blood, tears, toil and sweat!' Jenny laughed. 'That's what old Winnie said, isn't it?'

Tom nodded and smiled. 'No, I don't really mind you getting a job if you want to. I know quite a lot of women are doing it these days. I suppose time's hanging a bit heavy with our Patsy and Rosie away. I know you miss 'em.'

'I do that. I couldn't get used to how quiet the house was at first, even with our Victor still here. It was grand to see the girls again at Christmas, wasn't it?'

'Aye, it was,' Tom said slowly, giving his wife a meaningful look. 'When you and our Patsy had stopped being at each other's throats.'

Jenny didn't answer at first. She knew that she had been the one chiefly to blame, rather than her daughter, and she was never afraid to admit when she had been in the wrong. 'I know, I know, Tom,' she said after a few moments, 'but I can't help worrying about her. I suppose that's why I go on at her; it isn't because I want to fall out with her.'

'You've got to let her have her head, make her own mistakes if needs be. She's a grown-up lass now.'

'That's what I worry about. Her growing up, going with lads . . .'

'With Ronnie Sykes, you mean. Give her credit for a

bit of sense, Jenny. Our Patsy knows what's right and what's wrong, and she's got her head screwed on the right way.'

'I certainly hope so. But it'll perhaps fizzle out, don't you think so, Tom?'

'I shouldn't bank on it,' he muttered, almost to himself. He stared into the fire and Jenny carried on with her knitting.

'I'll perhaps be able to save up and buy a fridge, Tom,' she said wistfully after a few moments. 'Just think – wouldn't it be grand to know that the milk wasn't going to turn sour in the summer? And we'd be able to get rid of that meat safe outside the back door. Mrs Jones next-door has a fridge and she says she wouldn't be without it.'

'Keeping up with the Joneses, eh?' Tom grinned. 'I like you to have what you want, Jenny, and if you'll be happy having a job then it's all right with me. But I like to think I can provide for my wife, you know, without her working. So long as you don't think you have to go out to work. And so long as you're home in time . . .'

'To get your tea ready.' Jenny laughed. 'Don't worry. I shan't neglect you.'

'It was our Victor I was thinking about really.'

'Nor him neither. I'll be here to see to you both, like I always do.'

'Yes, you're a grand wife, Jenny. I don't suppose there's many fellows as has a better one. And I know I'm not much help round the house. I've always been hopeless in the kitchen.'

'That's the way your mother brought you up.' Jenny smiled warmly at him, gratified by his praise. Tom wasn't one to hand out compliments freely. 'Leave it to the women, that was what your mother believed, wasn't it? Never mind, I'm quite sure I can run a home and work a few mornings a week. It'll be a change for me, a way of meeting a few more people.'

'You used to meet people when you went to the church dos. You don't seem to have been much lately.'

'Oh, Tom, all they talk about is knitting patterns and their grandchildren and whose turn it is to do the church flowers. Perhaps when I'm sixty I might join them. But I'm still young.'

Tom looked at her sharply, surprised by the sudden longing that had crept into her voice. 'I thought you were contented, Jenny,' he said softly.

'Oh, I am, I am. I've told you, it's just since the girls went away that I've begun to feel restless. I miss having them around. That's why I want to take this job, do something different. Don't you understand?'

'Yes . . . I suppose I understand. I reckon I'm a pretty ordinary sort of a chap really,' said Tom reflectively. 'But I'm happy, you see, Jenny. I don't want to dash off and do anything exciting. I've got my nice home and family and football on a Saturday. And when I come home of an evening I've got the radio and newspaper and my library book. What else could I want, eh?'

Tom disappeared behind his newspaper and Jenny saw the smoke rising from his pipe, a recent acquisition replacing the cigarettes. What else indeed, Tom? she thought. She stared musingly at the top of his head for a few moments, then she returned to her knitting.

Jeff Burroni had reached a decision. He would go on seeing Rosie Bradshaw; there was no earthly reason why he shouldn't continue to do so. He loved the girl and he was pretty sure that she loved him. She was the most wonderful thing that had ever happened to him and he was damned if he was going to give her up because of

Daphne and . . . Marilyn. He had a moment's hesitation when he thought of the child, but that could all be sorted out, eventually. He was sorry that he hadn't been honest with Rosie right from the beginning, but he hadn't realised that he was going to fall in love with her. And he couldn't somehow pluck up courage now to confront her with the bald facts: that he was married, and that he had a child. None of the students, he was sure, knew of his circumstances, and the members of staff who did were hardly likely to discuss him with Rosie. Why should they?

He would tell her in the fullness of time, when things reached a head at home, as he was sure they would. He had been suspicious for a while that Daphne was being unfaithful to him. There was the insurance man, for instance. Jeff had noticed the sly glances that passed between them when he called for his money, and he was sure that the fellow called round at other times too, when he, Jeff, was at college. And there was the chap in the flat across the landing, a bachelor, who had been changing a plug for Daphne one afternoon when Jeff had come home unexpectedly. Or so they had said. There had been no sign, though, of the kettle that had so suddenly stopped working, or of the fuse wire or anything else, only Daphne's flushed face and the top button undone on her blouse. Yes, Jeff was quite sure that if she was given enough rope, Daphne would soon, in a manner of speaking, hang herself.

She had been singularly unconcerned when he had failed to return home the night of the fog, and had accepted without demur his story that he had been working late and then had been forced to spend the night at a colleague's home. And she no longer seemed to care now about his absences on Saturdays or Sundays. If she could be the one to walk out, to leave him, it would be so much better. Jeff was hoping against hope that it might be so.

In the meantime he decided not to breathe a word of it to Rosie. He loved her and he was so afraid of losing her. But he knew that they must be careful when they made love. That first time he had been unprepared, but nothing appeared to have gone wrong, thank God. He daren't risk that happening and he knew that it was up to him to take the precautions. He hoped that Rosie wouldn't think it was too sordid, too calculating.

She didn't. She was only too happy to be seeing Jeff on a regular basis and wondered why she had been so apprehensive before Christmas, why she had thought that Jeff was acting cagily with her? She decided that she must have imagined it. They now spent some part of every weekend together, either Saturday or Sunday, depending on which day Rosie was working at Lyon's. The weather was cold, but neither of them was worried; to be together was all that mattered. They usually walked in one of the parks, then after a pub lunch they visited a museum or art gallery. And always, as dusk fell, they returned to Rosie's flat.

He didn't stay for the night again, nor did he suggest it. Rosie was untroubled by this; she knew that he was concerned for the reputation of both of them, though he didn't actually say so. But with his being a tutor and Rosie one of his students, she knew that he had to behave circumspectly, or at least appear to do so. She had been relieved when, a few days after the night of the fog, her period had started. She realised how imprudent she had been – they had both been – and the thought of what might have happened filled her with horror. But it hadn't happened, thank God, and now Jeff was making sure, or as sure as he could, that it never would. To become pregnant, Rosie knew, would be letting her parents down. Jenny would be so dreadfully upset . . .

But when she was with Jeff, thoughts of Jenny and Tom, of everyone from her life in Castleburn, were very distant. Jeff was all that mattered. Rosie lived for the times she could be with him. She was hopelessly in love and if she gave any thought at all to the future she saw it as one she would share with Jeff. The reason he hadn't yet spoken about any lasting commitment, she told herself, was because it was too soon. She had still a year and a half of her training in front of her, but when that was at an end, then they would be able to plan their life together.

Patsy often thought about Rosie's flat in South Kensington, even though she hadn't seen it, and found herself envying her sister. Yorkshire, in January and February, was bleak. Snow lay on the moors, piled in drifts at the side of the road, and although Ronnie had managed the bus journey to Leeford every weekend they were always apprehensive that the weather might prevent him from doing so. It was too cold now to wander far afield in their brief, snatched hours together. The popular tourist haunts of the summer, tolerable in autumn, were desolate places in the winter; neither did the city of Leeford, where they invariably met, offer much of a haven for young lovers, desperate to be on their own.

Patsy and Ronnie huddled together on the back rows of cinemas, often news theatres which provided them with refuge for an hour or two. They held hands over endless cups of coffee and tea in Gino's coffee bar, listening to Jimmy Young telling them that they were '. . . too young to really be in love'. They kissed in shop doorways or secluded dark corners on the way to the tramstop, both of them wishing they could find somewhere to be really alone, then reminding themselves that it was probably just as well that they couldn't.

One weekend, when Ronnie had a precious forty-eight-hour pass, they visited Aunt Florrie and Uncle Bill again. This time Patsy told her mother of it in a letter, but was not surprised when the news failed to provoke a comment. Here they were able, as they had done before, to give almost free rein to their feelings for one another. But Ronnie kept himself in check, and Patsy admired him all the more for doing so. She was realising, more and more, what a sterling character Ronnie was. A trifle rough and ready, maybe, and not as educated as she herself was, certainly as far as book learning was concerned, but honourable and trustworthy. Patsy felt that she could depend on him, that he would never let her down, which was why she was so surprised, heartbroken, in fact, when he did just that.

The news that Ronnie was to be posted to Germany at the end of February, for the remainder of his service, was no surprise to either of them. They had been expecting it and dreading it, but had known that it was inevitable.

'Well, love, next weekend's our last one for a good while,' said Ronnie as they sat, one February Sunday, in Gino's. It was early evening and they were making the last cup of coffee spin out as long as possible. 'What would you like to do? I've got a few days' leave, of course, and I'll have to go to Blackpool to see my folks, but I thought we could go to the pictures on Saturday and then spend the night at Aunt Florrie's, OK?'

'I don't know why you're bothering to ask me what I want to do,' Patsy retorted. 'You seem to have got it all planned already. What's the point of saying what do I want to do when you've already decided?'

She was feeling miserable at the thought of Ronnie going away. She had met him only four months ago and now, very soon, he would be leaving her. They had had some very happy times together despite the fact that they were dissimilar both in tastes and in temperament, and despite her mother's opposition to the friendship. Patsy had begun to care very deeply for Ronnie; she thought she had fallen in love with him and, though he never actually said so, she thought that he felt the same way about her. She didn't want to argue with him, but her acute distress at the thought of parting from him was serving to make her irritable rather than sympathetic. There was another reason, too; she was, at the moment, what her mother would term 'unwell'. It always made her feel this way – wretched in mind as well as in body – and, added to the dull pain in the pit of her stomach and a headache, she was cold. Winter was no time for lovers, as she and Ronnie had already proved until they found the haven of Aunt Florrie's. There had been no time to go there today, however, and they had ended up wandering aimlessly through the streets of Leeford, both of them feeling miserable and frustrated.

'Aw, come on, Patsy love,' said Ronnie coaxingly. 'I haven't decided at all. You know we often go to the pictures, so I just thought we could . . .'

'There you go again! You just thought. We always have to do what you just think, don't we? It doesn't matter what I want to do, does it?' Patsy knew, even as she spoke, that she was being unreasonable. It wasn't strictly true either; Ronnie often consulted her about what they were going to do. But it seemed as though there was a demon inside her today, goading her on to say things she didn't mean at all. To her dismay Patsy could feel her lip trembling and tears pricking her eyelids. She stared down moodily at the Formica-topped table, trying to blink them away.

'Well, what do you want to do then? Was there something else you wanted to do instead of going to the pictures?' Ronnie asked now. She could see he was trying hard to be patient with her although he wasn't smiling.

'Yes, as a matter of fact, there was,' Patsy replied, still rather sullenly. 'There's a concert at the Guild Hall. I'd like to go to that.'

'OK. Suits me.' Ronnie shrugged. 'If you want to go, then we'll go. What is it? One of the big bands? Ted Heath? Joe Loss?'

'No . . . it's the Leeford Symphony Orchestra,' said Patsy. 'They're only there once a month and . . .'

'Symphony Orchestra! All that flippin' highbrow stuff? Oh no, Patsy.' Ronnie shook his head. 'You can count me out.'

'But why, Ronnie?' she protested. 'I've been jolly lucky to get the tickets, I can tell you. They're really scarce, but Neil Emmerson at college managed to get hold of some.'

Ronnie looked at her suspiciously. 'Who's Neil Emmerson when he's at home?'

'He's just a lad at college,' said Patsy testily. 'He runs the gramophone society that I go to.'

'First I've heard of it,' Ronnie mumbled. 'I didn't know you went to any gramophone society. And I've never heard you mention Neil . . . Whatsisname before either.'

'Neil Emmerson. Well, I've mentioned him now,' Patsy snapped back. 'It was very good of him to get the tickets.'

'Oh, so you've already got the tickets, have you? So who's making all the decisions now, eh?' Ronnie glared at her. 'Well, I've told you. It's nothing in my line. I'm not going to listen to rubbish like that.'

'Rubbish! How can you possibly call it rubbish? You've never heard it.'

'Nor do I want to, thank you very much. Now, if it had been one of the dance bands, like I said, or a brass band, something that plays a decent tune . . .'

'But they do play decent tunes,' Patsy protested. 'Lovely tunes. They're playing Mendelssohn's Violin Concerto and . . .'

'Violins! Bloomin' screeching fiddles? Aw, come off it, Patsy. What interest would I have in a la-di-da sort of concert like that? And I didn't know you were interested either. You never used to be.'

'How do you know what I used to be?' she snapped. 'You've only known me five minutes. As a matter of fact, I do like classical music.'

'Well, you can count me out,' said Ronnie again. 'I'm not interested.'

'I might have known,' said Patsy tightly. 'It should have been just what I expected.'

'Because I'm common? That's what you mean, isn't it? Because I talk dead ordinary and I don't wear a college scarf, I'm not good enough for Miss High-and-Mighty Patsy Bradshaw, am I? That's what your mother thinks, and it's what you think an' all, isn't it?' Ronnie's grey eyes were cold with anger in a way she hadn't seen before, but there was a look of hurt and bewilderment there too.

Patsy began to feel guilty. What had started out as a few misconstrued words now seemed to be developing into a first-class row. That wasn't what she had intended at all and she was pretty sure that Ronnie didn't really want to quarrel either. 'I'm sorry, Ronnie,' she said, reaching for his hand. 'I didn't mean it. And I don't think any of those things that you've just said. I don't think that at all.' She took her hand away as Ronnie didn't seem to be responding to her. 'Never mind about the concert. It doesn't matter. We can go to the pictures.'

'Don't strain yourself,' he said grumpily. 'You couldn't try to sound as though you mean it, could you?'

'No, honestly – I do mean it. We'll go to the pictures. Come on, Ronnie, Don't let's quarrel.'

She smiled uncertainly at him and after a few seconds he smiled back, but his eyes were lacking in warmth. She could tell that he was still feeling sore. He looked away from her, staring into his empty cup. 'There was a film I wanted to see,' he said. 'I missed it last time it was round.'

So much for 'What would you like to do, Patsy?' she thought to herself, but she didn't say it. 'What film is that, Ronnie?' she asked, trying to keep calm.

'*A Streetcar named Desire*,' he answered. 'Marlon Brando.' Some enthusiasm crept back into his voice as he looked at her again. 'You'd enjoy it, Patsy. He's a terrific actor.'

She felt her anger rising again in spite of her good intentions, and the throbbing in her temples growing worse. 'Then you don't know very much about me, do you?' she retorted. 'If you think I'd enjoy that. Marlon Brando? He's just a thug. Violent and brutal and . . . anyway, it's an X film,' she finished lamely.

'Oh, dear me! An X film! I was forgetting. It would offend Miss Goody-Two-Shoes to see an X film, wouldn't it? Besides, Mummy might not like it.'

'Shut up, Ronnie.' Patsy stared down at her cup, fighting to keep back the tears. To her dismay she felt a tear trickle down her cheek and plop on to the Formica-topped table.

Immediately he was full of concern. 'Oh, Patsy! Patsy love, I'm sorry. I didn't mean to be so horrible to you. Come on, dry your eyes and we'll get out of here. We've been sitting here long enough.' Solicitously he pulled out a huge khaki handkerchief and dabbed at her cheeks, somewhat embarrassed by the curious glances of the couple at the next table. He picked up her scarf from the back of her chair and placed it gently round her neck, then he took hold of her arm. 'Come on, love. It's time you were getting back to college and I've to catch my bus.'

Out in the street, he glanced at his watch. 'Crikey! I'd no idea it was that time. I've only quarter of an hour to get to the bus stop. We'll have to step on it.'

'Don't come to City Square with me then, Ronnie. I'll be all right.'

'No, I'll see you safely to your tram stop. We'll have to walk fast though.'

Patsy had a stitch in her side and her breath was coming in short gasps when they reached City Square. It had been a lousy day and they still hadn't reached any decision about next weekend.

It was Ronnie who brought up the subject just as the tram came into sight. 'Er . . . about that concert. I might change my mind. I might go . . .'

'Oh, never mind,' said Patsy. 'It doesn't matter. I know you don't really want to.'

'Well, if you're going to be like that about it, I don't see why I should.' Ronnie spoke sharply, then sighed. 'Good God, I don't know what's the matter with us today. Listen . . . I'll write and let you know. I've to arrange things with Aunt Florrie anyway. You want to go there, don't you?'

Patsy nodded silently.

'I'll write and let you know then, about the concert.'

Patsy nodded again. She felt steeped in misery, too wretched even to reply. She stepped on to the tram without a word and Ronnie made no attempt to embrace her. It was the first time they had parted without a kiss.

'Goodbye, Patsy,' he said bleakly.

'Goodbye, Ronnie,' she muttered.

'Oh, Kath, I was horrible to him. Horrible!' Patsy sobbed her heart out in the warmth of her study bedroom, glad of her friend's comforting presence. 'I didn't mean to be, really I didn't, but I couldn't help it. I was feeling so rotten and I was upset at the thought of him leaving. But I didn't tell him. Oh, I wish I'd told him, Kath.' Her tears had brought her some relief and now she felt that she wanted to tell her friend about it, to talk the whole beastly day out of her system.

'You seem to have had a lot of headaches lately,' said Kath in concern. 'Don't you think you should see the doctor?'

'No, I don't.' Patsy sniffed and shook her head. 'It's just tension. And my period always makes it worse. I've had a couple of aspirins. I'll take some more soon . . .'

'Yes, I should. And get into bed with a hot water bottle. You'll feel better in the morning. And your problems'll seem better too, I promise you.' Kath smiled at her and Patsy thought again what a friend in a million the girl was.

'I really was awful,' she said again, when she'd finished telling Kath the sorry tale, 'and I feel ashamed now. The point is, I couldn't care less about the blooming concert. I just want to be with Ronnie.'

'Then why don't you write and tell him so?' said Kath. 'Don't be afraid to say you're sorry. And I expect he's sorry too. It sounds as though he said some pretty nasty things as well.'

'I don't think either of us meant them,' said Patsy. 'I'm

not afraid of saying I'm sorry, but he did say he'd write to me, so I think I'll wait for his letter first.'

'Well, that's all right then, isn't it?' said Kath comfortingly. 'There'll be a letter from him in a day or two, you'll see. And everything'll be as right as rain.'

'Oh, I do hope so, Kath. But I was so awful that I wouldn't be surprised if he didn't ever want to see me again.'

'Don't be silly – of course he will.'

Monday was too soon, of course, but there was no letter on Tuesday or Wednesday either.

Jocelyn Reynolds commented on Patsy's obsessive interest in the mail – or lack of it – on her breakfast plate. 'Expecting a letter, Patsy? From someone special?'

'You could say that.' Patsy smiled wrily. 'My boyfriend, Ronnie – you know, he's at Catterick Camp. But I'm beginning to think I've had it. We had a row, you see.'

'Oh dear. What a shame.' Jocelyn sounded concerned. 'Never mind. I expect there'll be one tomorrow.'

'I hope you're right,' said Patsy mournfully. 'If there isn't a letter tomorrow, then that's it.'

But there was no letter on Thursday or Friday.

'I told you, Kath,' said Patsy sadly, but with an air of resolution. 'I was such a so-and-so to him and now I've got my comeuppance.'

'I don't know . . .' Kath sounded puzzled. 'I can't help thinking there's been some mistake. Look – why don't you try to get in touch with him? Go to Gino's on Saturday and see if he's there. Or go to his Aunt Florrie's?'

'No, why should I? I'm certainly not going to throw myself at him if he doesn't want me. And if he wanted me he'd have written, wouldn't he? And I've still got those two tickets for the concert.'

'Well, I know it won't be the same, but I'll go with you,' said Kath.

'Would you, Kath? That'd be great. I know you'd enjoy it.' Patsy tried to smile at her friend, but though her lips curved her eyes wouldn't respond. She felt all empty inside.

'Never mind, kid. There's more fish in the sea.' Kath smiled at her. 'But I still think you should try and see Ronnie . . .'

'No, Kath, I can't. He's fed up with me.' Patsy gave a deep sigh. 'And I can't say I blame him.'

The haunting music of the second movement of Mendelssohn's Violin Concerto filled the concert hall. The audience was hushed, enthralled by the lyrical beauty of the melody, and Patsy felt tears come into her eyes. It was only recently that she had discovered the joy of music, its power to solace and uplift, to remove one to another plane where sorrows and worries could be, for the moment, set aside. But not forgotten. Patsy knew that her tears had been brought about not only by the beauty of the music but because of her unhappiness. At the heart of her there was bewilderment and misery and, above all, disbelief that Ronnie could have let her down so badly. He had said he would write . . . Why then hadn't he written to her?

Jocelyn had fingered the cheap blue envelope on Thursday morning as she laid out the mail on the breakfast plates before the girls came down. Her eyes narrowed and a cunning smile played round her lips. Yes, this would be the one. Richmond, North Yorkshire – that was only a few miles from Catterick Camp. She shoved it into the deep pocket of her skirt. She looked at Patsy a few moments later and tried to smile sympathetically as, for the fourth time that week, the girl looked anxiously at her plate. But Jocelyn made no comment. After all, what could she say?

In the privacy of her room she tore open the envelope and her eyes rapidly scanned the single page of writing. 'Dearest Patsy . . . So sorry . . . didn't mean to upset you . . . of course I'll go to the concert . . . usual place, 2.30 . . . Aunt Florrie's . . . All my love, Ronnie.'

Jocelyn felt resentment boiling up inside her. She had never forgotten how Patsy Bradshaw had brushed her to one side, had refused to spend any time with her. And after the way they had danced together all those weeks! She had been made to look stupid, a complete fool, and had never forgiven Patsy though she tried to pretend that things were no different between the two of them. It would do the little madam good to have a taste of her own medicine. How would she like to feel rejected and unwanted? No, she didn't like it one little bit. She had seen the bereft look on Patsy's face when, once again, there was no letter for her; and Jocelyn had secretly rejoiced.

Later that evening when the hall was quiet and most of the students were busily working she tore the letter into tiny pieces. She crept along to the incinerator at the end of the corridor, an ugly iron contraption used by every girl, once a month. She lifted the lid and threw the small blue scraps on to the flames. She watched them turn brown and then disappear in a pile of ash. And Jocelyn smiled.

Chapter 12

'Come on, kid, snap out of it,' Kath said to Patsy one Saturday evening towards the end of February. 'There's no point in sitting around with a long face. You'd better start getting yourself out and about. I tell you what – shall we go to the dance tonight? It's at Kirkstall.'

'Oh, I don't know, Kath,' said Patsy gloomily. 'I don't think I feel like dancing. Let's go to the pictures. They're showing *The Blue Lamp* again in the village. And I do like Dirk Bogarde.'

'We went to the pictures last Saturday and it made you more miserable than ever,' Kath replied. 'What's the point of sitting in the dark and mooning over some bloke you know you can never have? Never mind Dirk Bogarde. There's a lot of fellows around much more accessible than him.'

'I'm not interested in fellows,' Patsy snapped. 'Only the one I can't have, and I don't mean Dirk Bogarde either. You go to the dance if you want to. You always seem to enjoy them. I'll stay in and read and wash my hair.'

'Don't talk such rubbish! Stay in and read on a Saturday night, indeed! And your hair doesn't need washing either. You only did it a couple of days ago . . . Oh, come on, love. I know you're still upset about Ronnie, but moping around won't bring him back.'

'I can't understand it, Kath.' Patsy looked appealingly at her friend, as she had done so many times during the past fortnight.

'No, neither can I. But, like I've told you before, I'm sure there's some mistake. And you wouldn't do what I suggested, would you? You wouldn't go to his aunt's?'

'I couldn't. My mum's always said it's cheap to throw yourself at a man. And if he didn't want me . . .'

'Never mind your mum. Sometimes you've got to do what your heart's telling you to do, even if it does seem a bit forward. But you're stubborn, Patsy. Sometimes you're so stubborn I could shake you.'

'Yes, I know I am.' Patsy grinned at her friend, in spite of the unhappiness that was still gnawing at her. 'But it's too late now. He'll be in Germany.'

'You could get his address off his Aunt Florrie. Why don't you?'

'No. He knows my address, and he'll write if he wants to.'

'You're an awkward madam, you are!' Kath took a swipe at her with a rolled up magazine. 'I don't know why I bother with you.'

'But you do, don't you?' Patsy looked gratefully at her friend. Kath had been wonderful these past two weeks, putting up with her tears and moans and mopiness. Patsy decided, suddenly, that Kath was right. It was time she snapped out of it. 'I'll go with you to Kirkstall Hall,' she said now. 'Why not?' She shrugged. 'I've nothing to lose, have I?'

'Good girl. Come on then, get your glad rags on and we'll get moving.'

Patsy put on her black skirt and red sweater that Ronnie had so admired. For the past few weeks, since her quarrel with him, she hadn't cared much how she looked. Now she was beginning to realise what a misery she must have been lately. She outlined her lips with crimson lipstick and pressed them together, then blotted them on a tissue. It was apt to come off, all over cups, and all over Ronnie, she remembered ruefully, but there wouldn't be much likelihood of that tonight. She slung her coat round her shoulders and grabbed her shoulder bag, then went along the corridor to call for Kath. She felt more cheerful than she had for ages, but there was still that fluttery feeling, too, at the pit of her stomach, that was always there when she went somewhere different and met new people.

Patsy hadn't been in the men's hostel, Kirkstall Hall, before, but it was almost identical to Calder Hall, except for the notices on the notice board, of rugby teams and boxing matches, plus one or two 'girly' photos, and a row of mud-caked football boots in the foyer. And that indefinable aura of maleness. Patsy found that she knew most of the girls there, if not the men, and she and Kath stood with a small group of girls from their division, chatting and listening to the records played on the gramophone. 'She wears red feathers and a hula hula skirt . . .' sang Guy Mitchell, and Patsy found herself nodding her head and tapping her foot in time to the music. Several couples were dancing in the space cleared in the centre of the large lounge, but Patsy was happy to listen and watch. She was glad she had come.

'Well, hello there.' She turned at the sound of a soft, low-pitched voice at her side. 'If it isn't my little breakfast companion. I wish I had such pleasant company every morning . . .' It was Neil Emmerson – she had recognised his voice even before she turned round – and she found herself smiling warmly at him.

Neil Emmerson was just about the best-looking fellow in college. Patsy, together with all the first-year students on her dining table, had first met him back in November when they had been at college for a couple of months.

The girls of Calder Hall had been astounded when, on entering the dining room at 7.30, most of them bleary-eyed and feeling far from their best, they had been greeted with a chorus of male voices. 'Good morning, ladies. Good morning, Miss Pritchard.' This to the resident tutor who presided at the 'top' table. It was, so the men informed the surprised girls, a college custom. The second-year men of Kirkstall Hall had come over to Calder, and the second-year women of Calder had gone over to Kirkstall.

Thoughts of School Practice, which they all had to endure later that day, were soon set aside in the face of this welcome diversion. Patsy had found herself seated next to Neil Emmerson, the college 'Romeo'. She knew him vaguely, of course – who didn't? – but had hardly spoken to him, and now, of course, there was Ronnie. Her friendship with him, by mid-November, had been gaining momentum, but that didn't mean that she was oblivious to the charms of Neil Emmerson. He hadn't singled her out particularly after they had introduced themselves, but had had all four of them – herself, Kath, Shirley and Edna – laughing uproariously at his exaggerated tales of his experiences on his last School Practice. He was an Advanced Music student training for Secondary Modern teaching.

'Good-looking fellow, isn't he, that Neil?' Patsy had remarked that evening to Kath as they sat on her bed exchanging news of the day. 'He reminds me of Stewart Granger. Tall, dark and handsome, to coin a phrase.'

'Shifty-looking,' Kath added. 'His eyes are too close together. As you say, Patsy, like Stewart Granger. I don't think I'd trust him very far.'

'Oh, come on, you can't say that, just because of the way his eyes are set. He can't help that. I don't think he's shifty at all. Look at the way he had us all laughing. He couldn't do that unless he was an artless sort of fellow.'

'Yes, he likes to be the centre of attraction,' said Kath. 'But artless? Don't kid yourself. I noticed the way he was looking at you, my sweet and innocent Patsy.'

'What way was he looking?' Patsy's eyes gleamed with interest.

'As though he'd like to undress you.'

'Kath, honestly! I didn't notice. I'm sure he wasn't.'

'It was when you turned away to talk to that intense chap on the other side of you.'

'Oh, yes, Bernard Hargreaves. He is intense, isn't he? Him and Edna'd make a good pair. I noticed they were having a good old chin-wag.'

'Don't change the subject. I'm telling you, beware of Neil Emmerson. He's a wolf. He'd eat you for breakfast, like Red Riding Hood's granny. He was looking at you as though he'd have liked to eat you there and then.'

'Oh, come off it, Kath.' Patsy laughed in confusion and could feel herself going pink. 'I think he's OK.'

'You shouldn't be interested anyway. You've got your Ronnie. Don't be greedy now.'

'I'm not interested.' Patsy was beginning to feel embarrassed. 'I just happen to think he's a good-looking chap . . . and I think he's quite nice,' she added quietly. 'You must admit, Kath, he's not like the usual run-of-the-mill types we have here.'

'No, I'll grant you that.'

'He doesn't look like a teacher at all.'

'What d'you mean?'

'Oh, you know. Baggy grey flannels and scuffed shoes. And shabby sports jackets with leather on the elbows.'

'And fairisle pullovers and tweedy ties,' Kath added. 'And chalk dust under their finger nails.'

'And in their hair.' Kath laughed. 'Yes, I must admit they follow a pattern. The men that taught us at Junior School all seemed to be like that. But we shouldn't make sweeping statements, should we? And teachers can't help getting covered in chalk dust. It's an occupational hazard. That's why a lot of women teachers wear smocks.'

'They look as though they're permanently pregnant.' Patsy giggled. 'But you can't expect men to wear smocks.' The two of them collapsed into gales of laughter, as they frequently did, at the most idiotic remarks. Patsy rocked backwards and forwards on the bed. 'Oh dear! I don't know what I'm laughing at. But I can't see Neil Emmerson covered in chalk dust, can you?'

'Or wearing a smock.' That set the two of them off again. 'Mind you,' Kath went on, wiping the tears of merriment from her cheeks, 'any girl who went out with him might well end up wearing one. I've told you, Patsy, beware!'

Neil certainly didn't look like the average male student at CLTC. He usually wore a smart bottle green blazer with the college crest on the pocket and he never looked less than immaculate. His grey flannel trousers were always neatly pressed and his shoes were of expensive brown suede. Instead of a tie or a crew-necked sweater, favoured by most of the men, he frequently wore a paisley-patterned cravat tucked jauntily into a crisply laundered shirt. Kath had said that he looked like a tailor's dummy that you saw in Burton's window, but Patsy was not amused at this.

Neil was the organiser of the gramophone society which Patsy had joined during her first term, and it was from him that she had later procured the tickets for the concert;

the concert that had been the cause of all the trouble between herself and Ronnie. But after the silly conversation about him with Kath, Patsy had hardly given Neil Emmerson another thought. She was far too involved with Ronnie and Neil was going about with an attractive second-year student called Pauline.

'You're not usually at these shindigs, are you?' Neil asked now, raising one eyebrow. 'I haven't seen you at one before.'

'No . . . I'm not. I don't usually . . .' Patsy started to answer him. She hoped she wasn't stuttering. That sometimes happened when she was nervous. She would begin a sentence, like she had done now, then not know how to finish it, especially when the man was looking at her in the way Neil Emmerson was looking at her now. Patsy took a breath and began again. 'I haven't been to the dances lately,' she said carefully, 'because I've been going out with my boyfriend. He's in the army, and he's just been posted to Germany.' You silly fool, Patsy, she added to herself. Why did you want to go telling him all that? He won't be interested.

But Neil Emmerson seemed very interested. 'Jolly good,' he whispered, taking hold of her arm. 'It's an ill wind, as they say. Out of sight and out of mind, and all that. Come on, let's dance.'

He put his arm round her and she felt his hand pressing firmly into the small of her back as he swept her along expertly in time to the quickstep rhythm. ' "A rose in her hair, a gleam in her eye, and love in her heart for me," ' he sang softly. She could feel his breath tickling her ear and her temple. 'Oh, damn. It's finished. No, no, no . . . don't run away, Patsy.' He held on to her arm as she made to leave the floor. 'Stay here. They'll put another one on.'

And while Dinah Shore sang of 'Buttons and Bows'

Patsy danced with Neil again, her feet following his steps perfectly as he twisted and turned and skilfully guided her. He was a superb dancer. And he knows it, too, a little voice whispered, but Patsy was enjoying herself. ' "And I'm all yours in buttons and bows," ' she sang, all inhibitions fast disappearing, as the record came to an end.

They stayed together for the rest of the evening, dancing and chatting and eating the simple supper – sandwiches, biscuits and cups of tea – that was always laid on at these occasions. There were never any alcoholic beverages available at college dos and there was no bar. Students who wanted to have a drink had to go down to the pubs in the village, something that Patsy and her friends had, so far, not done. She knew that a lot of the male students did so, however, and it was not unknown either for them to have bottles of beer in their rooms. She had an idea that there was a college rule banning this, but it was one that it would be almost impossible to enforce. There was no alcohol tonight though and, certainly, Neil didn't seem to need its stimulus. His arm crept round Patsy on several occasions and she found herself relaxing and enjoying his company more and more as the evening went on.

'What about this boyfriend of yours, then?' he asked teasingly as they sat close together in an alcove at the end of the lounge. His arm was round her shoulders, his fingers playfully twisting one of her curls round and round, tickling her ear and brushing against the soft skin of her neck. She shivered at the pleasurable sensation. 'What would he say about you dancing with other fellows?'

'He wouldn't mind,' said Patsy, feeling that she didn't want to talk about Ronnie. She hadn't, in fact, thought about him all evening, not since Neil had asked her to dance. 'We had a row,' she went on now. She knew that

Ronnie most likely would mind about Neil, if she and Ronnie were still a 'couple', but they weren't any longer. 'I'm not seeing him any more,' she told Neil. 'Like I said, he's in Germany, but we'd fallen out before that.'

'Oh dear, oh dear. How very sad.' Neil's fingers brushed her cheek and gently nipped the lobe of her ear. 'Never mind, there's more fish in the sea, Patsy. Nice fat juicy fish, not just little tiddlers.'

And sharks as well, thought Patsy, but she quickly pushed the thought away. 'What about Pauline?' she asked now.

'Pauline? What about her?' He made an expansive gesture with the hand that was not encircling Patsy. 'I'm a free agent, Patsy. Free as a bird . . . We had a row as well, but never mind about Pauline. Come on, let's go and dance again.'

This was the last waltz and as the dreamy strains of 'Ramona' came to an end he gathered up her coat from the back of a chair and piloted her out of the door. 'Come on, I'll see you home.'

Patsy looked round anxiously. 'I came with Kath. She'll be wondering . . .'

'She won't be wondering anything. Kath's a big girl. She can find her own way home.' He put an arm round Patsy, propelling her quickly away from the precincts of Kirkstall Hall.

She wasn't altogether surprised when he took her, not straight back to Calder Hall, but on a circuitous route that led to the woods at the back of the college. This was where the girls had been for their nature walk on their first day and where she and Kath had sometimes strolled together on autumn afternoons when lectures were finished. But this was the first time Patsy had been there at night. If the woods were supposed to be out of bounds after dark, then it was a rule which, like the one about alcohol, it was impossible to enforce and one which was flagrantly broken, for they were by no means the only people there that night. They passed one or two other couples, arms entwined round one another, as Patsy and Neil's now were, but there was ample room for everyone in the deep, dark seclusion of the coppice.

They stopped by an oak tree. 'I'm glad I've found you again, Patsy,' said Neil, very quietly. 'I've thought about you a lot since we had breakfast together. I've seen you at the gramophone society, of course, but you always seemed so intent on the music . . . or miles away. With the errant boyfriend, perhaps?'

'Perhaps,' she said evasively. She didn't want to think about Ronnie at this moment. She gave a nervous laugh. 'Never mind about him.'

'No, I certainly won't. We don't need to worry about him any more, do we? You're a shy sort of girl, aren't you, Patsy?' Neil's voice was caressing as he gently stroked her hair, then her cheek. 'But you won't be shy of me, will you?'

'No . . . no, I won't be shy, Neil. I was at first, a bit, but then I didn't know you very well.'

'We'll soon remedy that, won't we? I think you're a lovely girl, Patsy, so different from a lot of them here. I've wanted to get to know you for a long time . . .' He stopped speaking then. He just looked at her, his green eyes glowing with ardour, then pressed her back against the thick trunk of the oak tree.

His kisses were as expert as she had anticipated. It was obvious that Neil Emmerson was no novice where girls were concerned and Patsy had known, to a certain extent, what to expect. It soon became apparent to her, however, after a few searching kisses, that whereas Ronnie had been a lad, albeit a lusty one, Neil was a man. She didn't demur when he slipped his hand inside her coat and fondled her breast, but when he lifted her skirt and ran his hands up her nylon-clad legs, then she protested.

'No, Neil . . . Don't!' She seized hold of his hands and pushed them away and pulled her skirt back into position. 'I don't want to.'

Somewhat to her surprise he stopped at once. 'Sorry . . . sorry.' He stood back from her, his eyes, almost a pale silver in the darkness, gleaming tantalisingly into hers. He looked anything but sorry, and the small secret smile playing round his lips seemed to say that he would get his own way in the end. 'Too soon, Patsy. Too soon,' he whispered. 'Come on. I'll take you back to Calder.'

'Oh!' She put a hand to her mouth in dismay. 'We'd better get a move on. We've to be in by half-past eleven. I was forgetting. Oh, come on . . .' She pulled at Neil's arm, eager to be away from the wood which had suddenly taken on a sinister aspect. Everyone else seemed to have gone.

'Don't worry.' He laughed gently. 'They won't lock you out. Besides, have you never thought of climbing through a window?'

'No!' Patsy sounded horrified. 'What do you mean? How could you climb through a window?'

'It has been done, believe me. You mean you didn't know?' Patsy shook her head. 'Then you move in very innocent circles, my love. The dining-room window in Calder is often left open for latecomers. You ask your college mother about it.'

'Gwen Travers? I don't think she would . . .'

'No, probably Gwen wouldn't. But some of them do, and I'm sure Gwen knows about it.'

'But what about the signing-in book? Your name has to be there.'

'They get somebody to sign it for them.' Neil laughed

again. 'Oh dear, you're just a babe-in-arms, aren't you, Patsy? I can see I'll have to take you in hand, teach you a few lessons.'

She felt a shiver of apprehension but, all the same, she knew that if Neil wanted to see her again then she would be willing, more than willing . . . They stopped at the bottom of the steps leading to the door of Calder Hall and Patsy noticed, to her relief, that it was open. A couple of girls were going in and they grinned knowingly at seeing her with Neil.

He wrapped his arms round her again and kissed her on the lips, just a friendly kiss this time, but he was completely unconcerned about the other students passing by. 'See you at the gramophone society on Tuesday,' he said. 'You'll be there, won't you?'

'Oh, yes, I'll be there.' Patsy hoped she didn't sound too eager. It was always so hard for her to behave nonchalantly.

'See you there then. Goodnight, sweetheart.' Neil grinned at her, then suddenly his expression changed to one of alarm. 'Quick, Patsy! They're locking the door.' She gave a little gasp and turned round in a panic, then she heard Neil's laughter as he walked away. The door was still wide open.

Patsy could hardly wait for Tuesday to come, although she had a pretty good idea what would happen. Neil would again steer her towards the college woods and, once there, she knew she would have difficulty in resisting his amorous advances. She also knew, deep down, that she didn't want to resist at all. She wanted him to make love to her as he assuredly would do, given the slightest encouragement. But she knew she should refuse because . . . well, because nice girls didn't do it. Her mother had never said so in so many words, but it had always been implicit in Jenny's warnings and guarded innuendoes.

Neil took very little notice of Patsy for most of Tuesday evening, apart from a friendly wink when she came in through the door. She sat with the rest of the students, about twenty of them, while Neil played the records they had requested on the gramophone. The bubbling elation she had felt at the thought of seeing him again was evaporating in the face of his seeming indifference. She was beginning to feel that she had been mistaken about his interest in her and that she was, after all, a one night stand, and not a very exciting one at that. After all, she had said no, hadn't she? When the 1812 Overture, the last of the chosen records, came to an end, she put on her coat and started to walk towards the door.

'Hold on a minute, Patsy,' Neil called. 'I want to ask you something.'

She turned back at once, but he kept her waiting while he closed up the gramophone and put the records back in the box, then locked the cupboard. Even then he didn't speak, just went on eyeing her teasingly while he put on his coat and carefully adjusted his cravat, tucking it inside his collar.

Patsy was feeling ill at ease. She fiddled with her hair and straightened her scarf. 'You wanted to ask me . . . ?' she began hesitantly.

'Yes, I wanted to ask you . . .' Neil raised his eyebrows quizzically, '. . . would you like to go to the next concert at the Guild Hall? It's a week on Saturday.'

'Would I like . . . ? Of course I'd like to.' Patsy couldn't keep the animation out of her voice. Then, 'D'you mean with you?' she asked, a trifle uncertainly.

'Who else?' Neil spread his hands, then laughed quietly.

'Yes, Patsy, I'm asking you to come with me. Just you and me. No one else.' His voice was a warm caress and his eyes, green as the eyes of a witch's cat – she hadn't noticed before just how green they were – smiled seductively into hers. 'Now, shall we take a walk?' He crooked his elbow and she obediently tucked her hand inside as they walked along the corridor and out of the building. And towards the woods.

As he had done the previous time, Neil stopped when Patsy gave the signal, just giving her a half-rueful, half-mocking smile as she adjusted her skirt and fastened up her coat. He seemed to be possessed of the most remarkable self-control, she thought, much greater than her own. Her legs were trembling and she was all of a flummox at their abortive lovemaking, but Neil seemed totally unmoved at having his advances cut off in mid-stream.

Patsy was confused by her feelings; feelings that she didn't entirely understand, and, if she were honest, a little guilty, too. She had never felt quite this way with Ronnie. She had cared very deeply for him and losing him had been heartbreaking. Patsy knew that she wasn't in love with Neil – how could she be? she hardly knew him – but he disturbed her. Dear God, how he disturbed her, arousing feelings in her that she hadn't realised were possible. She hardly dared to admit it to herself, but she wanted him to make love to her . . . and then, she didn't. If she was to lose her virginity she didn't want it to be leaning up against an oak tree in the middle of the college wood. For a moment she felt ashamed of herself, of her thoughts and of what she had so very nearly allowed to happen.

Patsy knew that Kath was concerned for her.

'I hope you know what you're doing, that's all,' Kath said when she arrived back at Calder Hall that night. Patsy took a quick look at herself in the mirror. Her eyes were overbright and her cheeks flushed, her misgivings and her feelings of ambivalence written all over her. It was quite obvious, to someone who knew her as well as Kath did, that she had been, as her mother would have said, 'up to no good'. 'Don't you realise that Neil Emmerson's the biggest wolf in college?' Kath went on. 'Don't say you haven't been warned, that's all, if something goes wrong.'

'What can go wrong, for heaven's sake? Stop fussing, Kath.' Patsy flopped down on to Kath's bed. 'I can look after myself, don't you realise? I've been fighting off Ronnie Sykes for the last few months. I can't see it's going to be much different coping with Neil. It just proves it though, Kath, that fellows are all alike. They're all after one thing.'

Even as she spoke Patsy knew that what she was saying was not true. Thoughts of Ronnie came back then, with a rush of guilty remembrance. She recalled how it had always been he who had called a halt to their lovemaking, behaving sensibly and exercising the self-control that Patsy, once or twice, would have thrown to the winds, even though it must have been hard for him to do so. And she knew that what she and Ronnie had experienced together had been the product of deep affection and of years of shared memories. Ronnie had never actually said the words 'I love you, Patsy', but she had known that he had a deep regard for her and that he had been sensitive of her feelings. And she had been on the verge of falling in love with him, until things had all gone wrong.

But now there was Neil, amazingly and unexpectedly, to take his place. Patsy knew that all Kath said about him was true. She knew that Neil Emmerson was egotistical and that his feelings towards her, Patsy, if he had any at all, were likely to be shallow and fleeting. And if she ever allowed their lovemaking to reach a conclusion, she knew it would be, to Neil, another conquest, not something that had happened because of his affection for her. Yes, she knew all this, but she couldn't help feeling flattered that he had taken notice of her. Fellows like Neil didn't usually bother with the likes of Patsy Bradshaw. But he had, he had . . . and she was determined to hold on to him. She just hoped, as she had insisted to Kath, that she could cope with him.

'Anyway,' she said now to her friend, 'he's asked me to go to the next concert with him, so he can't just want . . . you know.'

'And you've said you'll go?'

'Of course.'

'OK, love. You're a big girl now. But just remember what I told you . . . Beware!'

Perhaps she had been wrong about Neil, perhaps Kath had been wrong, because after the concert he made no attempt to make love to Patsy. It was barely ten o'clock when the concert finished, and they had a cup of coffee at a snack bar near City Square – not Gino's, and Patsy was glad about that – knowing that they had ample time before catching the tram back to college.

'I think that must be the most beautiful music ever written,' Patsy remarked. She felt as though she were walking on air, transported to another world, after hearing the last movement of Rachmaninoff's second piano concerto. 'That finale . . . La lah . . . la lah, la lah . . .' She sang the tune softly. 'Terrific, isn't it?'

Neil smiled good-humouredly. 'Yes, I agree with you. It's one of my favourites too. I love the Romantic composers. You've been to a lot of concerts, have you, Patsy?'

She laughed then, a little self-consciously, hoping she hadn't sounded too much of a fool, airing her knowledge when she really knew so little about it. 'No . . . I must admit I haven't. I've only started going to concerts – proper ones, I mean – since I came to college. We don't get much of that sort of thing in Castleburn. It's rather an intellectual backwater, and Blackpool, where I lived before, is even worse.'

She stopped speaking suddenly, wondering why she had made such a fatuous and censorious remark. She loved Castleburn, and Blackpool, too. They were great places and she had always been so happy living there. She bit her lip, feeling guilty, as though the loyal citizens of those boroughs were condemning her for being such an insufferable little prig.

But Neil appeared not to have noticed her discomfiture. 'There's no shortage of concerts where I come from,' he said now. 'There's always something going on in the "great metrollops". Sometimes I feel I can't wait to get back.'

'Why did you leave then?' asked Patsy. 'There must be lots of good training colleges down south.'

Neil shrugged nonchalantly. 'A desire to see the industrial north – dark satanic mills and all that.' He grinned, then added, more seriously: 'CLTC has a good reputation and I really did want to see some more of dear old England. You can get frightfully insular, living just in one place.'

'You're not from London itself, are you?' asked Patsy.

'No . . . Watford, just north of London. It's easy to get into the city though. And I'm hoping to get a teaching post in my home town. I've an interview coming up in a few weeks.'

'My sister lives in London,' Patsy remarked casually.

'Your sister? I didn't know you had one.'

'Yes . . . Rosie. She's an art student in Kensington. She's not much like me though.'

'What d'you mean, she's not like you?'

'Well, she doesn't look like me for a start. She's got black hair and blue eyes.'

'She sounds a smasher,' said Neil, rolling his eyes.

'And she's very lively . . . and lots of fun,' Patsy ended lamely, wondering why she had mentioned Rosie in the first place.

'As I'm sure you can be.' Neil leaned across the table, his green eyes staring intently into hers. 'I've had no reason to complain, anyway.' He teasingly tapped the end of her nose. 'Come on, let's go for the tram.'

He kissed her, warmly and confidently, on the steps of Calder Hall, but made no attempt to lead her elsewhere. Patsy was surprised and, she had to admit, a little disappointed.

'So you see, Kath, he can't be all that bad,' Patsy remarked to her friend, a few days later. 'He hardly came near me on Saturday night, and tonight we just walked back together from the gramophone society and chatted. He's really nice when you get to know him. And he's so courteous. He always walks on the outside, near the kerb, like a gentleman's supposed to do. And he opens doors for me and pulls out my chair in cafes and all that. Ronnie 'ud just as soon let the door bang in my face as hold it open for me, and he'd just flop down in a chair and never bother about me. He hadn't the same . . . finesse, Kath.'

'He wasn't as smarmy, you mean,' her friend replied.

'Oh, come on. I wouldn't call Neil smarmy.'

'I would.'

'And we like the same things too,' Patsy went on as though she hadn't heard. 'Music and books and all that. We talk for ages about the books we like.'

'And did you run out of things to say to Ronnie? Walked along in silence, did you?'

'No, of course not. We chatted . . . we never stopped talking. Except when . . .' Patsy grinned.

'All right. You don't need to spell it out. What did you talk about, you and Ronnie?'

'Oh, I don't know.' Patsy was beginning to feel irritated. 'About people we knew and things we'd done.'

'Shared memories?'

'Yes . . . I suppose so. But it was all very trivial. I'm just trying to tell you that Neil's so different.'

'We're all different, love. And it's a good job, too. And you think it's important, do you, liking the same things?'

'Yes . . . don't you?'

'I suppose so,' Kath answered slowly. 'Other things matter as well, though. Affection and trust, not just excitement.'

'I trusted Ronnie, didn't I? And look what happened.'

'Yes, I know. But I still think he was a good sort. And I don't want you to go through it all again if Neil lets you down.'

Patsy was silent for a moment. Then, 'I'll think about that when it happens,' she replied.

It was on the following Saturday afternoon that they met Ronnie's Aunt Florrie in Leeford. Since Ronnie had gone to Germany Patsy and Kath had started their weekend outings again, mooching round the stores, window shopping and then ending up with a coffee in a snack bar.

'Yoo-hoo, yoo-hoo . . . Patsy.' The girl turned round at the sound of a breathless voice behind her on Eastcheap and was delighted, in spite of her rift with Ronnie, to see his aunt.

They greeted one another warmly and Patsy introduced Kath. Aunt Florrie, or Mrs Royston as Patsy had called her to her friend, put down her heavy shopping bag. 'Eeh,

I was that upset about you and our Ronnie,' she said. 'I said to him, "Ne'er mind, lad, it's just a lover's tiff." But he wouldn't have it. "No, Aunt Florrie," he said. "She's finished with me. I know she has. She didn't answer my letter, and I can't say I blame her." He told me he'd been real nasty to you and how sorry he was. But when you didn't reply, and then you didn't turn up on the Saturday . . .'

Patsy was staring at her in astonishment. 'What letter?' she said. 'He didn't write to me.'

'Oh, but he says he did, love, and I believe him an' all. Our Ronnie wouldn't tell fibs.'

'No . . . of course he wouldn't.' Patsy shook her head slowly. 'I didn't receive it . . . But I do believe him. If Ronnie says he wrote, then I'm sure he did.'

'Oh dear, oh dear! What a mess it all is.' Aunt Florrie tutted. 'It must be the bloomin' post. You can't rely on anything, can you? And you'd have met him, would you, dear, if you'd got his letter?'

'Yes. I'd have met him, Aunt Florrie.'

'Well, look, love. I'll give you his address in Germany.' Mrs Royston smiled at Patsy, then rooted in her capacious black handbag. She pulled out a diary and a scrap of paper and carefully copied out the address. 'There you are. Happen you can make it up with him. Proper down in the dumps he was, poor lad.'

'Yes . . . I might do that.'

The three of them exchanged a few pleasantries, Florrie Royston insisting that Patsy should come and see her again, and Kath too, if she wished, in spite of Ronnie no longer being there.

'She's nice, isn't she?' said Patsy, after they had left her. 'What do you think of that though, Kath? Strange, isn't it? And maddening too. I've never known the post to be unreliable before.'

'No, neither have I.'

'But there can't be any other explanation, can there?'

'No, there can't. It must have gone astray.' But Kath sounded doubtful. 'You can get in touch with him though now, kid. Isn't it great?'

'Yes,' said Patsy, but her voice lacked conviction.

That night she went out with Neil again, to the pictures in the village and then for a drink at a pub. They walked back with their arms round one another, stopping frequently to kiss, and his embrace outside her hall of residence was eager and ardent, leaving her gasping and wanting more. Ronnie's address remained in her shoulder bag and she did nothing about it. How could she write to him and say she was sorry when she was seeing another man? But just what Neil was up to she wasn't sure.

It was the week before the Easter holidays when he took Patsy into the woods again. She realised then what his game had been. He had made sure she was so eager for him, after all his holding back, that she would not refuse him. When his hands wandered up her skirt and inside her briefs she didn't resist. Not at first, then she came to her senses. What on earth was she doing? She didn't want it to be this way, not here, in the middle of a wood, where anyone might come along. She told him so.

'My room then,' he whispered. 'Come to my room, Patsy. No one will know.'

She was horrified. 'We can't! We'd be expelled.'

Neil laughed softly. 'Rubbish! We might get a telling-off, but nobody would know, would they? I'll check that the coast is clear, then I'll smuggle you in.'

'I can't . . .'

'Don't be silly, Patsy. How many times do you see people when you go into your hall, especially in the middle of the evening? It's usually dead quiet. Don't worry. I'll make sure nothing goes wrong.'

Patsy had the awful feeling he had done this before. She shook her head. 'I'm sorry, Neil. I daren't.'

'All right then.' He kissed her again, to her surprise quite tenderly. 'But think about it. When you go home for the holidays, think about it. You'll change your mind. I know you will.'

Patsy thought of nothing else for a day or two, and when she went home for the Easter break she told Rosie about it. The two of them were walking along the stretch of Blackpool promenade known as the Golden Mile. They had come to spend a couple of days with Grandma Carter at the boarding house – just Patsy and Rosie – as there was a lull in the rush of visitors after the Easter weekend. It was a part of Blackpool that they didn't visit very often, the noisiest and brashest part, but they were on their way to the Pleasure Beach at South Shore and had decided to walk part of the way.

'We had some great times here when we were kids, didn't we?' Rosie remarked.

'Yes, we did.' Patsy smiled at her sister. 'We didn't come along here much though. Mum used to say the Golden Mile was common.'

'So she did.' Rosie laughed. 'But d'you remember going to Fairyland? That was great.'

Fairyland was at the end of the Golden Mile, an automated ride through fairy dells, goblin glades and pixie glens, which had been a firm favourite with the two little girls.

'Mmm.' Patsy nodded happily. 'And d'you remember going on the sands with the . . . the Sykes twins?' she added, more slowly. She hadn't intended mentioning Ronnie, but thoughts of him were intrinsically bound up with her memories of Blackpool.

'Yes, and little Ben, the evacuee, fell in a rock pool and

Ronnie fished him out. We didn't dare go home till he'd dried out.' Rosie turned to look at her sister. 'It doesn't hurt you to talk about Ronnie, does it?' she asked in concern. 'I was sorry you'd split up. I thought, when I saw him at New Year, what a smashing lad he was.'

Patsy shrugged. 'I don't think about him much now,' she said. It wasn't strictly true, but there was something she wanted to discuss with Rosie, something not connected with Ronnie Sykes at all. 'It was just one of those things,' she added. 'I told you, didn't I, that I'd been seeing someone else?'

'That Neil that you wrote to me about? Are you still seeing him?'

'Yes . . . He's getting quite serious.' There was only Rosie that Patsy could talk to; Kath was so very disapproving. Patsy told her sister about how things were, about how Neil wanted her to go to his room, and how she felt she wanted to, but . . .

She was surprised at her sister's reaction. 'No,' said Rosie emphatically. 'I've never heard anything so ridiculous in my life! Don't be such an idiot, Patsy.'

Jocelyn Reynolds had feigned surprise at Kath's guarded question, and then anger. Whatever was Kath suggesting? How dare she? She, Jocelyn, was in charge of the mail and there had never been any complaints before. Her black eyes blazed resentfully, but Kath noticed a tiny spark of fear there too. The lady doth protest too much, thought Kath, but didn't pursue the enquiry.

'OK, Jocelyn,' she said casually. 'Keep your hair on. I just wondered, that's all. It must have gone astray in the post.'

But Kath knew that Jocelyn would never have the nerve to try that trick again. She hadn't told Patsy of her suspicions. Her friend was such a trusting girl, quite naive at times, and there was no point in making the situation between Patsy and Jocelyn any worse. Kath knew when to keep her own counsel.

Chapter 13

Jubilee Lane School was as different as it could possibly be from Parklands where Patsy had spent her first School Practice. The school she had been allotted for second SP, starting in the middle of May, was a Victorian building, two storeys high. Soot-grimed and forbidding-looking and surrounded by iron railings with lethal spikes, it stood in the centre of rows of terraced houses, right in the shadow of Barraclough's mill. Patsy had been given a class of seven-year-olds, 'top class Infants', for this practice, and found to her surprise on her first visit that the grim exterior of the school belied the atmosphere within.

She noticed it as soon as she entered the building. As well as the indefinable 'school' smell, common to all such buildings – a combination of chalk and powdered ink and disinfectant – there was an aura of happiness and contentment. This seemed to emanate not only from the present occupants of the school; it was as though the generations of children who had been taught there in times past had each left their imprint on the place. It was not, however, an atmosphere of serenity, not by any means, as Patsy and her three fellow students soon discovered as they walked along the corridor to the headmaster's study. They were nearly knocked flying by a group of boys coming in the opposite direction, and if they hadn't stood back, flattening themselves against the wall, there would have been a collision. And it wouldn't have been the boys who'd have come off worst, Patsy thought. She could see already that she would have her work cut out controlling the children here, if this little group was a typical example. But, all the same, she felt that Jubilee Lane was a happy place.

She found her class teacher, Miss Kennedy, quite helpful, but nowhere near as much as dear Miss Umpleby had been at her previous school. Miss Kennedy, an attractive young woman in her mid-twenties, with long dark hair swept into a chignon, had an aloof manner, but was much more friendly once you got to know her. Better to be aloof, though, than downright antagonistic, which was what Patsy soon found Miss Fletcher, the teacher in charge of the Infant Department, to be. Patsy thanked her lucky stars she hadn't been allocated that woman as her class teacher!

Miss Fletcher was the only fly in the ointment at Jubilee Lane School as far as Patsy was concerned. She was fortyish, no more than five feet in height, thin and sharp-featured, with a mass of frizzy auburn hair which stuck out like a furze bush. Patsy guessed that she might well have the temper that frequently accompanied such flaming locks and she was to be proved right. It was said that Miss Fletcher didn't like students and that soon became obvious.

She pointedly ignored the four students in the staff-room, unlike the rest of the teachers who, on the whole, made them welcome. They included them in the conversation and, on the first day, invited them to help themselves to tea or coffee.

'Goodness knows what their homes are like,' Patsy heard Miss Fletcher mutter one lunchtime during the first week of School Practice, to no one in particular. The woman was wiping a grubby dishcloth over the table where the tea and coffee were served. 'I should think they live in pigsties, most of them.'

Patsy was amused to see one of the younger teachers – a girl who looked not much older than herself – put out her tongue behind the older woman's back and make a rude gesture with her thumb on the end of her nose.

'Cleanliness is next to Godliness, I always say,' Miss Fletcher went on as she picked up the dirty beakers, many of them chipped and stained with lipstick, and carried them over to the sink. She made a great to-do running the water and banging about with the pots, while the other teachers cheerfully took no notice. They were either getting on with their task of marking books or – many of them – sprawling back in the sagging easy chairs and taking what ease they could in the short time allowed.

Patsy couldn't help agreeing with Miss Fletcher, to a certain extent, about the state of the tea table, because it really looked a disgusting mess. The Formica top was ringed with brown stains, as was the tin tray where the beakers often stood, and the teaspoons, bent and tarnished, were encrusted with particles of instant coffee and sugar. The tea towels looked as though someone had wiped the floor with them, and the dishcloths were an unsavoury grey and stank of sour milk. But Patsy also knew that teachers were very busy people who couldn't always be bothered with niceties in the staffroom. She was sure that their own homes would be reasonably clean and tidy, not, as Miss Fletcher had implied, little better than slums.

'Yes, we're a filthy lot, aren't we?' said Mr Bateson cheerfully. He was one of the teachers of the fourth-year Juniors. 'I'll organise a rota with some of my girls. I've been meaning to do it for ages. They'll love it, washing up after the teachers. That do for you, Miss Fletcher?'

The woman nodded briefly as she draped the grubby tea-towel over the edge of the sink. 'Perfectly, Mr Bateson. You see to that and I'll take these disgusting articles home and launder them myself. Goodness knows what visitors would say if they saw a filthy set-up like this.'

Patsy knew she didn't mean inferior visitors such as students, but august personages like tutors or HMIs. She watched Mr Bateson return to his perusal of the *Daily Express*.

If playground duty was a nuisance, and most teachers, if they were honest, found it so, then dinner duty was a nightmare. The students were not excused this daily ritual, but had to take their turn at parading the dining hall, with another teacher in overall charge, of course, making sure that the behaviour didn't get out of hand and trying to persuade the often reluctant children to clean their plates. For the dinners were, to say the least, unsavoury. They were not cooked on the premises, but were delivered in hugh metal containers from a central kitchen and lost much of their palatability in the transit. Some days it was not too bad; the children did not seem to object to the thick slices of bright pink spam – they often had this at home – or the overcooked sausages, or the spotted dick with vivid yellow custard, or the red jelly with wafer thin slices of banana. But at other times the fare put before them was enough to turn the stomach of the most hardy eater. Patsy had always been fussy over her food and she was full of sympathy for the children who, like herself, found themselves heaving and unable to swallow when confronted with fatty meat, lumpy blancmange or evil-smelling slabs of grey codfish.

The stew was possibly the worst dish of all; thick gravy,

more grey than brown, containing chunks of stringy carrot and pieces of gristly meat surrounded by fat. This was dished up with mashed potato, grey in colour and containing lumps as big as marbles, but this was the part that was devoured quickly, before it went any colder than it already was, while the meat remained congealing at the side of the plate. This was the unappetising meal that was served on the day that it was Patsy's dinner duty, a Thursday towards the end of May. And, to make matters worse, the teacher in charge that day was Miss Fletcher.

Patsy paraded up and down the aisles between the Formica-topped tables, noting that the noise level was a little lower today than it usually was. This was because Miss Fletcher was on duty; she seemed able to quell the high spirits of even the most indomitable children. Patsy was glad, however, that it was quieter today. She had a headache and it was not an ideal day for dinner duty. Even at the best of times, every sound was magnified in the dining room, which was a prefabricated building, a high-ceilinged barn of a place at the end of the school yard. She passed Peter Fennimore's table a few times, noticing the little boy's eyes were filling up with tears as he stared down at the glutinous mess rapidly congealing at the side of his plate. She knew just how he felt; her own stomach was revolting in sympathy and she knew that when she was eventually allowed to sit down and partake of her own meal she would not even attempt the first course. She would have to survive today on chocolate pudding with its accompanying pale brown sauce.

Peter Fennimore was in Patsy's class – well, Miss Kennedy's class really, but she thought of it as her class – a dear little boy who had very quickly become one of Patsy's favourites. She knew that teachers shouldn't show favouritism and tried to disguise it, but he really was a most lovable child. He was somewhat delicate, asthmatic, small for his age and pale with straight dark hair, very soft and silky, and big brown eyes, limpid and trusting, like a spaniel pup's. He was a plucky little lad in spite of his small stature and tried manfully to join in games with the other boys, though he sometimes found it rather difficult to keep up with them. They didn't tease him or bully him, as one might have expected; Patsy was discovering that children could be, incongruously, very sympathetic when they so wished, and they seemed to regard Peter as a sort of mascot. He had endeared himself to Patsy on her first playground duty, when he had shyly sidled up to her and slipped his hand in hers as she walked round the yard with her beaker of coffee.

'I like that story you're reading to us, Miss Bradshaw,' he confided. 'I think it's dead exciting, all that about the lion and the wicked queen.'

Patsy was gratified. She had wondered if *The Lion, the Witch and the Wardrobe* would prove too difficult for seven-year-olds, but it was obvious from Peter's reaction that this was not the case, although they might not understand all the allegories it contained. She had gone against the college dictum this time that stories should be told and not read. It would be impossible to do so with this story by C. S. Lewis, one of Patsy's own favourites. Not one of her childhood favourites, however; it had been published only a couple of years previously and Patsy, in her mid-teens, had been captivated by it. That was why she had chosen it for her class, knowing that when a teacher is enthusiastic about something, that fervour is often captured by the children.

She smiled at Peter; she had already gathered that he enjoyed the tale from the rapt expression on his face in story lessons, a look echoed on many of the other children's faces. 'Do you like books, Peter?' she asked. 'Do you read a lot at home? I know you read very well at school.'

'Ooh, yes, I love reading. I've got a lot of the Famous Five books. They're by Enid Blyton, you know,' he added seriously. 'And I like Just William and Biggles. I get them from the library. And my dad's given me all his Billy Bunter books.'

Patsy knew that children, even the most timid ones such as Peter, often enjoyed tales of the more daring characters of the fiction world, sharing with vicarious delight in their adventures. It had been so with Patsy herself as she read of *The Naughtiest Girl in the School* or of the exploits of the audacious heroines of Angela Brazil. She felt that to foster a love of literature in a child should be one of the prime aims of a teacher. If she failed in everything else – and Patsy was still unsure at times about her vocation for the teaching profession – she could at least try to do this. Books had always been Patsy's main solace and source of delight and she was always pleased to find this trait in others.

'I'm glad you like the story of Aslan, Peter,' she had said, and they had spent the rest of the playtime discussing some of their favourite stories.

Peter, however, was far from happy as he stared at the nauseating mess on his plate. He turned sad brown eyes up at Patsy as she stopped by his table. 'I can't eat any more, Miss Bradshaw,' he said, his bottom lip quivering. 'I've tried. Honest, I have.'

'All right, Peter,' Patsy replied. 'Just eat a tiny bit more, then you can leave the rest.' She separated a small portion of meat and carrot, as she had seen the more sympathetic teachers do, pushing the rest to the side of the plate. 'There, that's just one more mouthful.'

'Leave this to me, Miss Bradshaw.' Patsy turned at the authoritarian tones and found herself looking into the steely pale blue eyes of Miss Fletcher. The woman poked a bony finger into Peter's back, just between his shoulder blades. 'You'll eat it all, Peter Fennimore, every scrap. I've been watching you for the past quarter of an hour, playing about with it and pushing it round your plate. It's your own fault it's gone cold. If you haven't eaten that meal in five minutes – the next time I come round – then I shall give you a jolly good smacking. You're a very naughty ungrateful boy. Do you know there are little children in Africa who are starving? Now, eat – it – up.' The last three words were delivered with three sharp pokes.

Patsy couldn't help herself. 'He's tried to eat it, Miss Fletcher. He has, really . . .'

'How dare you, Miss Bradshaw!' The woman's voice was more chilling than usual and her eyes, venomous with dislike, bored into Patsy's. 'I'm in charge here, and if I say he's to eat it then he's to eat it. I won't have my authority undermined. Now move away and stop molly-coddling him.'

Miss Fletcher moved away and Patsy stood back, ostensibly supervising the next table, but keeping a watchful eye on Peter. She knew that if the child attempted to eat the revolting mess he would be sick. It wasn't the first time that Patsy had seen the woman pick on diffident, defenceless children who were disinclined to stick up for themselves. It would be a brave child, indeed, who attempted to stand up to Miss Fletcher.

There was only one other boy besides Peter left at the table and he was stuffing pudding into his mouth, anxious to join his pals in the playground; he was taking no notice of Peter. Patsy stared in horror as she saw what Peter was doing now. She didn't know whether to laugh or cry. He took out a handkerchief – a nice clean one – from his pocket and spread it over his knees. Then he lifted up his plate and rapidly scooped the dinner on to the square of cotton. Then, quick as a flash, he bundled it up and shoved it into his trouser pocket. Good for you, thought Patsy. Full marks for initiative!

She took a step towards him. 'Good boy, Peter,' she said. 'I'm glad you've managed to eat it all up. Show your empty plate to Miss Fletcher, then you can go and get your pudding.'

But before Patsy had finished speaking the woman was behind her, standing menacingly over the small boy. Her eyes narrowed suspiciously as she looked at the plate in front of her, now scraped clean, with only a vestige of gravy round the rim, and then at Peter's guilty face.

'What have you done with it? It's barely a minute since I told you to eat it.' Miss Fletcher's voice was quiet – indeed, it was very rarely that she shouted – but her anger showed in the dangerous glint of her pale blue eyes and in the red flush staining her cheeks and creeping down her scrawny neck. 'Where is it?' she said again, looking down suspiciously at the floor under the table. She seized the little boy by the back of his grey pullover and dragged him to his feet. Then she took hold of his shoulders and shook him. 'What have you done with your dinner? Answer me.'

Patsy could see that the child was too terrified to answer, but she saw him glance down fearfully at his trousers where an ominous brown trickle was oozing out from the pocket and down his leg. Miss Fletcher followed the direction of his gaze and this time she did raise her voice. 'You . . . you filthy, disgusting child!' She yanked out the offending handkerchief and its contents and flung it to the floor. Then she lifted up Peter's trouser leg as high as she could and administered several stinging slaps. Patsy watched the white flesh turn pink, then red, as the woman's hard hand came into contact with it time and time again. 'You naughty – deceitful – boy! Never in all my years as a teacher have I known anything like this.' She was panting for breath as she flung the child away from her as though he were a piece of rubbish.

Patsy was beside herself with anger; she knew that, whatever the consequences, she would be unable to hold her tongue and, besides, it wouldn't be right to do so. Poor little Peter had to have someone to stick up for him. 'I think that was uncalled for, Miss Fletcher,' she began bravely, though her voice was trembling, partly with rage, partly with surprise at her own boldness. 'He tried to eat his dinner. I've been watching him . . . and I'd like to see you try to eat muck like that!'

'How dare you, Miss Bradshaw!' said Miss Fletcher, for the second time. 'How dare you – a student of all things – presume to tell me what to do? We've a report to make about you, don't forget, and your tutor's going to hear about this. I've never in my life heard such insolence! Now, take this dreadful child away and clean him up, then he can stand outside Mr Thomson's door for the rest of the dinner time.' She glared threateningly at Peter. 'Oh, yes, Mr Thomson's going to hear about this. And I wouldn't be surprised if he gives you the cane. It's what you deserve, you filthy little creature.' She turned to Patsy. 'And I'll deal with you later. You haven't heard the last of this.'

Patsy's hands were trembling and her legs felt like jelly as she took hold of Peter's hand and led him out of the canteen and across the yard. 'Oh dear, you are a silly chump, aren't you?' She smiled down at him, trying to make light of the matter. 'Now we've both got into trouble. Never mind. Let's go and see if Miss Kennedy's got some clean trousers in her cupboard.'

Peter looked shamefacedly at his legs. 'She'll think that I've . . . you know.'

'No, she won't. I'll explain to her.'

'What about my pudding?' Peter turned tear-filled eyes towards Patsy. 'I never had my pudding.'

Patsy, again, didn't know whether to laugh or cry. 'Never mind the pudding,' she said, only now remembering that she hadn't had any dinner either, nor did she want any. 'It'll be cold by now. Look, I've got two Mars bars in my bag. We'll have one each, shall we, when we've cleaned you up?'

'What about Mr Thomson? I've to go and see him.'

'You can eat your Mars bars first.'

'D'you think he'll cane me?' Peter looked up trustingly at Patsy as he clung tightly to her hand.

'No,' said Patsy confidently. 'I'm sure he won't.' Of that much she was certain.

Miss Kennedy looked up and hastily stubbed out her cigarette on a saucer as Patsy and Peter entered the room. She waved her hand vaguely in front of her in an effort to dispel the tell-tale smoke. Teachers were not supposed to smoke in the classrooms, but this was a rule that Miss Kennedy flagrantly disregarded, when the children were not there, of course. Patsy explained in whispers what had happened and Miss Kennedy opened a cupboard and took out a pair of grey flannel shorts, rather shabby, but fortunately not too long or too short. At least Peter would not be a source of ridicule for the afternoon, which was what sometimes happened when there was a 'little accident'. He went in a corner to change while the women talked in low voices.

'Poor little devil,' said Miss Kennedy. 'It makes me wild

the way she gets her knife into these little kids. It's always the same type she picks on. The woman's a sadist.'

'I've got it in the neck too,' said Patsy. 'I tried to stick up for him.' She confessed that she had been insolent. '. . . And she says it'll go on my report.'

'Don't worry, Patsy.' Miss Kennedy patted her arm consolingly and Patsy was touched by this and also by the teacher's use of her Christian name, the first time she had used it. 'The report's largely up to me, and I think you're doing fine. And I'll pop along and get my two pennorth in with Mr Thomson as well. He won't take sides – I can't expect him to – but I know he'll listen. So don't worry. It's Friday tomorrow, then you'll have a long weekend, won't you? It seems as though it's come just at the right time. Are you going home for the Coronation?'

'No, I'm going down to London,' replied Patsy. 'My sister's at art school down there, so I'm going to stay with her and watch the procession. It's quite exciting really, but I've been so busy I've hardly had time to think about it. And now this . . .'

'Never mind this. It'll soon blow over, you take it from me . . . I say, I'm really envious. Fancy you going to London.' Miss Kennedy's plucked eyebrows rose half an inch. 'I shall be watching it on the television, which is quite something, I suppose. My parents have bought one 'specially. Now, young man. Let's have a look at you.' She smiled at Peter who had sidled up to the teacher's desk with his gravy-stained trousers in his hand. 'Oh, yes, very smart. Now, I'll pop these in a bag till home time, and Miss Bradshaw can take you along and give your legs a wash.' There were still vestiges of the gravy clinging to his knees. She turned to Patsy. 'Take him to the staff washroom. It'll be more private.'

Peter still looked fearful. 'I've to see Mr Thomson. Miss

Fletcher said . . . She'll kill me if I don't go.'

'Don't worry, Peter. I'll come with you to see Mr Thomson.' Miss Kennedy's eyes were full of sympathy.

The staff washroom and toilet was not a place where one would choose to linger. It was a box-like room, badly ventilated and evil-smelling, and not just of the usual lavatorial smell. There was a gap above the skirting board in the toilet cubicle and when Patsy was forced to go in there – as infrequently as she possible could – she was always fearful that a mouse or a gigantic spider would suddenly appear. For the ominous smell, she was quite sure, was that of a dead mouse. There had once been one in the airing cupboard at home and she recognised the unsavoury aroma.

But at least the place, unsatisfactory as it was, was preferable to the toilets that the children used. They were forced to cross the yard to the two blocks, one for the boys and one for the girls, at the far end of the playground. The caretakers fought a losing battle to keep them clean and Patsy was quite sure, after her one brief visit there to quell a minor riot, that they were enough to render a child permanently constipated. New toilets, however, to be built inside the school building – the Victorians had frowned on this as an insanitary idea – were on the agenda, and if Mr Thomson had his way this would be sooner rather than later. He wasn't one to kow-tow to the authorities and there had already been several improvements made since his arrival. Climbing frames and ropes for PE lessons; extra shelves and cupboards in the classrooms; and now sinks were being installed in some of the rooms. Miss Kennedy's room, however, was not yet equipped with one.

'You got into trouble, Miss, because of me, didn't you?' said Peter shyly as Patsy wiped the gravy smears from his legs. 'She shouted at you, didn't she?'

Patsy smiled wrily. 'Yes, she did. But never mind, Peter. I'll survive. Now, are you all right, that's the main thing?' Poor little kid, she thought, as she straightened his jumper and trousers. The red marks were still there on the back of his legs. It was to be hoped they had disappeared by hometime or there might be an irate mother coming to school. On the other hand, it would jolly well serve Miss Fletcher right if she was hauled over the coals for this.

'Yes . . . I'm all right,' said Peter in answer to her question. 'But I'm hungry, Miss. You said . . .'

'Oh, yes, of course.' Patsy smiled at him and put her hand to her mouth. 'The Mars bars. Come on, we'll go back to the classroom and finish our lunch.'

Peter's mother did come into school the next day, but not, as Patsy had expected, to make a complaint. She arrived at the end of the afternoon when the children had been dismissed, pushing a small boy of about eighteen months in a push-chair, with a small girl hanging on to the handle. Patsy knew, from what Miss Kennedy had told her, that Mrs Fennimore had been a teacher before she started her family, and that her husband had a good job in a local government office. They lived about half a mile from school, away from the streets of small terraced houses that surrounded Barraclough's mill, on the fringe of a private housing estate.

She entered the classroom somewhat diffidently, a small, fair-haired woman with delicate features, very much like the little girl at her side. The boy in the push-chair was dark, like Peter, but the whole family seemed small in stature.

'I've come to say thank you,' she began, looking at Miss Kennedy. 'I believe Peter was in trouble yesterday, and he said that you were very kind to him, you and Miss Bradshaw.' She turned to Patsy. 'Are you Miss Bradshaw? I've heard a lot about you.'

'Yes, it's Miss Bradshaw you have to thank, really,' said Miss Kennedy. 'She took Peter under her wing. I did very little.'

'I believe you spoke to Mr Thomson though?' said Mrs Fennimore. 'Defused the situation?' She looked knowingly at Miss Kennedy, as one teacher to another.

'Yes, I suppose so. It was the least I could do.' Miss Kennedy gave an imperceptible shrug. 'Look, I'll leave you to chat with Miss Bradshaw. She's had more to do with Peter recently than I have. Where is Peter, by the way?'

'He's waiting outside the door.'

'Good gracious. Let's bring him in.' Miss Kennedy ushered a bashful Peter inside the room. 'There, you sit and read a book while your mum has a talk with Miss Bradshaw.'

'I really am most grateful,' said Mrs Fennimore, sitting down on the edge of one of the children's tables. 'Peter was so distressed, and he'd have been much worse if you hadn't taken care of him. He's really frightened to death of Miss Fletcher,' she added in a whisper.

'I'm not surprised,' said Patsy, although she knew she shouldn't. It was what Miss Kennedy would call 'unprofessional'. 'A lot of them are. I got into trouble too.' She grinned. 'Did Peter tell you, and about the dinner and everything?'

'Yes, he did.' Mrs Fennimore sighed. 'It's a problem. He hates school dinners, but what can I do? It's too far for me to come for him at dinnertime, with these two as well. He'll just have to learn to put up with it, like the other children do. And with Miss Fletcher, too. At least he was never in her class, that was one blessing. And I believe she keeps applying for Infant headships, so with a bit of luck she may not be here much longer . . . I've been a teacher myself, so I wouldn't dream of complaining about her. She's a bit heavy-handed, I know, but I suppose we all have different ways of keeping order. She's one of the old school. You haven't got into real trouble, have you, because of Peter?'

'No, I don't think so. I must admit I was rude to Miss Fletcher though. I couldn't help it. But she's said no more about it today. She's just ignored me. I expect it'll all blow over.'

'I hope so. I wouldn't want it to spoil things for you, stop you getting a good report. I'm sure you deserve one. Pete's always telling me what a smashing teacher you are. You're enjoying it, are you?'

Patsy hesitated before she answered, looking into the clear blue eyes of this woman whom she had only just met, but who already felt like a friend. 'I'm not sure. Sometimes I enjoy teaching. Other times . . . I'm scared. Scared that I'm not in the right job, or that I'll end up like Miss Fletcher, all bitter and bad-tempered. It was my mum's idea really, you see,' she said on an impulse. 'She wanted me to be a teacher. She wanted it so badly.'

Mrs Fennimore smiled sympathetically. 'Same here. My mother wanted it too. That's why I trained to be a teacher. I wasn't sure that I wanted to do it either, but I sort of . . . grew into it. And I shall go back when this lot are off my hands. I only did four years before I left to have Peter.' Patsy gathered from that that Mrs Fennimore was in her early thirties.

'I'm Barbara,' she said now. 'And you are . . . ?'

'I'm Patsy,' she replied, smiling. 'Miss Bradshaw here though, most of the time. They're very formal.'

'A nice school though. Don't you think so? And a good school too. Peter's very happy here, on the whole, apart from . . . what we've just been talking about. It's a real cross section here. There are some really tough characters from the streets near the mill. And then there are the . . .' Barbara laughed. 'I nearly said, "the people like us", but you know what I mean, don't you?'

Patsy laughed too. 'Yes, I know. It's a real mixed bag. But they all get on well together. Mr Thomson's excellent at fostering good relationships.'

'So you're off for a long weekend now, are you, Patsy?' asked Barbara. 'Peter said you had a day or two off for the Coronation.'

'Yes, the school's closed just for the Tuesday, as you know, but they've been very good to us at college. We've got three days, so that we can get home if we want to.'

'And are you going home?'

'No, I'm going to London on Monday to stay with my sister. We're going to watch the procession.'

'Gosh! I'm really envious,' said Barbara, just as Miss Kennedy had. And Patsy began to feel all excited at the thought of it. There just hadn't been time so far even to think about it. But now . . . now it would soon be happening.

'We've bought a television,' Barbara went on. 'I was going to say you would be very welcome to come and watch with us, if you had no other plans. But to be actually going to London . . . that's terrific!'

The two young women smiled at one another and Patsy felt instinctively that this was the beginning of a new friendship.

'I know how lonely you can feel at college sometimes,' Barbara went on, 'away from your family. Would you like to come and have tea with us one day, when you come back from London? We'd love to have you, and I know Peter would be thrilled to bits.'

Peter, ostensibly reading *The Folk of the Faraway Tree*

from the book corner, but with one ear on the conversation, looked across at them and grinned slyly.

Patsy suddenly felt very happy. 'Yes, thank you. I'd really like that,' she said. She leaned towards her new friend and whispered, 'Miss Fletcher's been good for something after all, hasn't she?'

Chapter 14

The Coronation had crept up on her unawares. Patsy had been so busy with School Practice that she had hardly given a thought to her planned visit to London.

Rosie had mooted the idea when they had met during the Easter break, and Patsy had immediately been enthusiastic. The parents of Julia, one of Rosie's friends at the art school, had a small shop on Oxford Street, a confectioner's and tobacconist's, and as it was on the processional route they had invited a few people to share the viewing facilities. They didn't live on the premises, but the upstairs stock room could accommodate a dozen or more people and they would have a superb view from there of the returning procession.

'Gosh, that's great!' said Patsy. 'But are you sure there'll be room for me?'

'Of course there will,' said Rosie. 'It was Julia's idea that I should ask you. She's heard all about you. And you'll be able to stay with me in South Ken. There's bags of room, if you don't mind sharing my bed settee, that is?'

The two girls giggled together excitedly. It would be just like old times, Patsy thought, when they had crept into one another's beds to share secrets. She was glad that the former unease between herself and Rosie now seemed to have disappeared. A separation had done them both good.

Jenny, however, didn't seem too thrilled at the idea at first.

'I was hoping you'd come home, Patsy,' she said, 'seeing that you've a long weekend from college. Your dad and I are thinking of buying a television set. It would have been nice if we could have all watched it together.'

But before long there had been a change of plan. Annie Carter, in Blackpool, had also decided to buy a television set for the great occasion and as there were several vacancies at 'Pleasant View' for the beginning of June – most people, no doubt, more interested in watching the Coronation than in going on holiday – Jenny and Tom and Victor had been invited to spend a few days there.

'But I think we'll still buy a television,' Jenny told the girls. 'It will be nice for your dad and Victor to watch their sports programmes. And Mrs Jones next door says they have some really good plays on sometimes. Now, you'll look after Patsy, won't you, Rosie, when she goes down to London? Make sure you meet her at King's Cross. I don't want her getting lost on those tubes.'

'Stop fussing, Mum,' Patsy had said, a trifle irritably. 'I'm a big girl now.'

Rosie smiled disarmingly. 'Don't worry, Mum. I'll look after my little sister.'

Patsy pulled a face at her, then they both grinned. They would have a great time. It was all going to be wonderful.

Jenny's eyes softened as she looked at them. 'I hope you'll have a lovely time,' she said. 'Just think . . . you'll actually see the Queen.'

Neither had Patsy had time recently to think much about Neil Emmerson. Something quite unconnected with him had happened which had given her food for thought.

There had been an empty chair at the breakfast table when the students returned after the Easter Break.

'Where's Brenda?' asked Patsy, looking at the other girls, especially at Gwen and Marjorie who were special friends of hers. 'Is she ill?'

The two of them exchanged glances and Gwen started to answer. 'No, not exactly . . .'

But Jocelyn Reynolds spoke at the same time. 'It seems that the charms of the handsome Jeremy have proved irresistible,' she said, a faintly sardonic smile playing round her lips.

'What d'you mean?' said Patsy, then suddenly light dawned. 'You mean she's . . . ?'

Gwen and Marjorie both spoke at once.

'She's getting married,' said Gwen.

'She's preggers,' said Marjorie.

'Oh dear,' said Patsy, quite at a loss for words.

Jocelyn raised her eyebrows. 'It does happen, you know,' she said.

Gwen told her the tale later, how Brenda had written to her during the holiday, explaining that she had discovered she was having a baby and that she and Jeremy, the RAF flying officer, would be getting married in a few weeks' time.

Patsy suddenly felt scared. She knew that if such a thing were to happen to her – heaven forbid! – then Neil Emmerson would most definitely not marry her. Brenda and Jeremy had been engaged, she had been wearing his ring for ages, whereas she and Neil . . . Patsy shuddered to think how very nearly she had allowed herself to be tempted by his suggestion that she should go to his bedroom. She had thought about it a lot during the Easter holiday and, in spite of Rosie's insistence that she shouldn't, Patsy had still been unsure. Now, suddenly, in the face of this piece of news, the very idea was abhorrent to her. If something was to go wrong – and it could, quite easily – the shame and disgrace would be too much for her parents to bear. The thought of her mother's reaction filled Patsy with horror.

The next time Neil asked to make love to her she refused, and when he persisted she still refused. And so he had turned his attentions elsewhere. Patsy had seen him in the company of a few different girls. She realised now that she and Neil had never really been 'a couple'. Neil, she thought, would never want to belong to anyone.

Once School Practice started she found herself thinking about him less and less. She was too preoccupied to think of much else but her lessons for the next day. And as for Ronnie, he was many miles away.

She pushed a few clothes into a small hold-all on the morning of Monday, 1 June, and at the same time pushed firmly to the back of her mind all thoughts of Miss Fletcher and Jubilee Lane school. She was going to London, to see the Coronation, and it was going to be wonderful.

Even before she arrived at King's Cross she could see signs of the forthcoming celebration in the narrow streets that surrounded the station. Buntings and flags were draped from rooftops and lamp-posts and a lot of the houses had photos of the Queen and the Duke of Edinburgh in the windows. Patsy felt a surge of excitement as she pulled her bag off the luggage rack and went out into the corridor. She stepped off the train feeling bemused. What a crowd of people; far more than she had encountered at Castleburn or even at Leeford, although Blackpool at the height of the season would be comparable. But, of course, this was London, the capital, upon which the eyes of all the world were focused at the moment, and Patsy felt thrilled to be a part of it.

And there was Rosie at the barrier, waving frantically. She flung her arms round Patsy and took her bag from her, then, before you could say 'Jack Robinson', she had whisked her away through barriers and down escalators and along what seemed like miles of corridors on to the tube. Patsy was full of admiration for the way her sister was shepherding her around, as though she had lived here all her life.

'Gosh! I don't know how you do it,' exclaimed Patsy, flopping down gratefully on a seat in the rattling tube train. 'I'd be lost, I'm sure. I'd never find my way around. I'd be ending up at Blackfriars when I should be at Bayswater or something,' she added, looking with interest at the tube map above her head.

''Course you wouldn't,' Rosie replied. 'It's easy when you know how. Anyway, it wouldn't matter on this line. You'd just go round and round in a circle. But I felt just like you when I first came down here. Like a real country bumpkin. But it's amazing how soon you get used to it. I feel as though I've lived in London all my life.'

'And would you like to stay here?' asked Patsy. 'D'you think you'll get a job here when you've finished your course?'

'I don't know,' said Rosie. Her eyes narrowed thoughtfully and she gave a little smile. 'I might do . . . It all depends.'

Patsy could read her sister's mind. 'How's Jeff?' she asked now. 'Will I be seeing him while I'm down here? I'm dying to meet him.'

'No . . . no, I don't think you will,' answered Rosie. Her smile had just as quickly vanished and there was a sharp edge to her voice. 'He's watching the Coronation at home.

Well, at his parents' home, in Bermondsey. They've bought a television set 'specially for the occasion.' Patsy smiled to herself, thinking how many times she had heard that remark over the last few weeks. 'They wanted Jeff to be with them, of course,' Rosie went on. 'They'd be disappointed if he wasn't there. They like to make a family occasion of things like that, apparently.' She shrugged. 'That is, if Jeff condescends to watch at all. He's not much of a Royalist.'

Patsy looked at her keenly. She sensed, somehow, that there was something not quite right, but Rosie's smile when she looked at her again was as bright as ever, though there was a touch of defiance in her clear blue eyes.

'Never mind about Jeff,' said Rosie now. 'I'm sure we can manage very well without fellows for a couple of days. I was sorry about Neil – poor you! – but I think you were right not to do what he wanted. He'd have dropped you afterwards, you know, Patsy, like a hot brick.'

'So what? He's dropped me now, hasn't he?' she replied with a rueful smile.

'Yes, but you wouldn't have felt right about it if you'd given in to him,' said Rosie assertively. Patsy wondered how her sister could be so free and easy with her advice. It was quite obvious what she and Jeff were up to, with Rosie's flat in Kensington at their disposal and no one to check up on her. Patsy only hoped that the same thing that had happened to Brenda didn't happen to Rosie. 'Anyway, never mind about the fellows now,' said her sister again. 'We're going to have a great time, kid.'

The Coronation festivities were in evidence in South Kensington too, though rather more decorous here than in the streets near King's Cross. But it was later that evening, when Rosie and Patsy went down to the West End, that the full extent of the celebrations hit them.

Even Rosie, who now considered herself something of a Londoner, was amazed at the crowds that were already, the day before the celebration, thronging the streets. The only way to get into the centre of London was by tube as the roads encircling the Coronation route had, by 4 pm on 1 June, been closed and sealed off.

The whole of London was a riot of colour, predominantly red, white and blue, on flags, streamers and bunting which festooned every street and hung from every building and lamp-post. But there were other brilliant colours, too – crimson, orange, bright pink, royal purple and gold – in the thousands of fresh flowers that were blooming everywhere, in flower beds and in the crown-shaped baskets that decorated the walls of many of the public buildings. Patsy and Rosie were mesmerised, dazzled beyond belief at the brilliance of it all, as they walked along the streets where, tomorrow, the long procession would wend its way. Rosie, of course, was interested in the window displays, both in the small shops and in the large department stores. They had all 'set their stall out' as never before, and Rosie was particularly impressed by the life-size figure of the Queen on horseback in Selfridge's window, and in Liberty's marvellous display of the period costume of the various kings and queens since 1400.

The crowds near Buckingham Palace had to be seen to be believed. Already, along the length of the Mall, there was evidence of people camping out, preparing themselves for the long night ahead with sleeping bags, blankets, cushions, Thermos flasks, and bags and boxes full of provisions. It was cold, too, more like a March evening than June, and Patsy looked up anxiously at the sky.

'I do hope it doesn't rain,' she said to Rosie. 'Those poor people – wouldn't it be awful if it rained? They're going to be cold, even if it keeps fine. I tell you what, Rosie, I'm glad we've got our seats booked. I wouldn't like to be camping out.'

Rosie squeezed her arm. 'Don't be such an old misery. Of course it won't rain. The sky's lovely and clear. It couldn't rain on Coronation Day. But I'm glad we're sure of a good view. Ooh, Patsy, isn't it all exciting?'

She was still thinking about the people camping out. 'Rosie,' she said thoughtfully. 'I wonder what they'll do if they want to spend a penny? It's an awful long time to wait, isn't it?'

Rosie hooted with laughter. 'Trust you to think of that! They'll just have to go, that's all. Take it in turns and get somebody to save their places, I suppose. There's lots of public lavs around and they've brought in some portable ones as well. Look, there's one there. Anyway, don't start worrying your head about that. I expect they'll manage. Come on, let's get on the tube and get ourselves home. Big day tomorrow, kid.'

Patsy was awake by six o'clock, having slept surprisingly well in the comfortable bed settee next to her sister. She had thought she would be too excited to sleep, but it had been a long, tiring day. She woke as the light of a grey dawn crept in through the skylight above their heads and stared around for a moment, bemused, wondering where she was. Then she remembered. She was in London with Rosie. She'd come to see the Coronation. The words of a nursery rhyme suddenly flashed into her mind: '. . . I've been up to London to look at the Queen', and she almost laughed out loud for sheer excitement.

Rosie was still sleeping, so Patsy decided to surprise her with a cup of tea, if she could manage the antiquated gas stove. No, she reminded herself, coffee not tea. Rosie preferred coffee now, and she, Patsy, had been drinking more of it since she was away from home. Somewhat timorously she struck a match and lit the gas, which flared up with a sudden burst of blue flame. She spooned the coffee into the mugs and gave the stained table top a cursory wipe with a dishcloth, reflecting that Rosie's domestic arrangements were little better than those in the staffroom at Jubilee Lane. Still, it wasn't fair to criticise. It couldn't be easy for Rosie, looking after herself and working at that cafe, as well as doing her art course. She, Patsy, was positively pampered when you compared her with her sister.

She drew back the thin curtains that covered the small front windows overlooking the square. 'Oh no!' she muttered to herself as she glanced out, for it was raining, a thin nasty drizzle, the sort that soaked you through more quickly than a short sharp shower. Those poor people sleeping out, she thought again.

'It's raining,' she told Rosie, as she handed her the steaming mug of coffee.

'Oh heck, no!' said Rosie, sitting up and running her fingers through her short black hair, till it stood out in spikes like a porcupine. 'You've brought the northern weather with you, kid,' she grinned. 'Why didn't you leave it where it belonged? Never mind, I expect it'll clear up. You know what Mum always says. "Rain before seven, fine before eleven." Anyway, we'll have a smashing day, won't we, whatever it does?'

They switched on the wireless soon afterwards and were thrilled to hear the cheering news that Edmund Hillary and Sherpa Tenzing had reached the summit of Everest. The first amazing event in a day which was to be packed full of sights and impressions and surprises.

'There's no rush for us to get to Julia's shop,' Rosie

told Patsy. 'We won't be seeing the procession till the afternoon. It doesn't go along Oxford Street on the way to the Abbey. It's the returning processions we'll be seeing.'

'We'd better not waste too much time though,' Patsy reminded her. 'We'll have to push our way through the crowds, and I daresay the tubes will be busy. Now, what about lunch? Are we taking sandwiches with us?'

'Good idea,' said Rosie, who obviously hadn't given the matter much thought. 'If I've got anything in, that is. I'm not the most organised of people, you know.'

'You're not kidding!' laughed Patsy. 'It's a good job Mum isn't here. She'd have a fit.'

Breakfast had been a doorstep of bread spread with strawberry jam, and with the remainder of the loaf Patsy made corned beef sandwiches – luckily there was a tin in the cupboard – while Rosie had a wash. Then it was Patsy's turn in the Edwardian bathroom with the claw-footed cast iron bath, tarnished brass taps and flower-patterned lavatory. This house had obviously once belonged to a well-to-do family, Patsy thought, but the bathroom had, like the rest of the rooms, seen better days. She gave the bath a good scouring with Vim, but the marks on the chipped enamel were of long duration and could not be budged. No, she thought again, it's certainly a good job that Mum can't see this.

The crowds on Oxford Street were dense when they arrived there at mid-morning, although there were still several hours to go before the people would catch their first glimpse of the procession. They all seemed cheerful and in a holiday mood in spite of the rain – it had rained intermittently all morning and showed no sign of stopping – huddled beneath blankets and umbrellas and listening to the commentary which was being broadcast over the loud speakers.

'This is it,' said Rosie, stopping by a small shop, the window of which was gaily festooned with red, white and blue streamers garlanding the display of sweets, chocolates and tobacco. She rang the bell and Julia, a merry-faced girl with hair of a startling ginger, such as Patsy's had once been, ushered them through the empty shop, along a dark passageway and up two flights of dark stairs to the stock room above.

The room was a sea of faces, more than a dozen, and Patsy was never, all day, to sort them all out. Indeed, there was little time for introductions and they were deemed unnecessary as everyone was too busy watching and listening. Julia's mother and father were there, of course, and a couple of their friends, and the rest seemed to be friends of Julia's from the art school. They were sitting in a circle, on bentwood chairs round a couple of card tables, drinking tea – Julia's mother spent much of the day brewing tea – listening to the wireless. As yet there was nothing to see from the window but the crowds . . . and the rain.

The service broadcast from the Abbey was extremely moving and everyone was silent while it was taking place. Patsy found herself touched by it all, from Parry's jubilant anthem, 'I was Glad', which began the ceremony, through all the hymns, prayers and responses, right to the final Te Deum. Several people, Patsy noticed, were mouthing the words of the Lord's Prayer, as she was, when it came to that part of the service. And throughout it all was the unmistakable voice of Richard Dimbleby, making it all come alive.

They ate their sandwiches – everyone, it seemed, had brought their own picnic – and drank another cup of tea when the service came to an end. Then they arranged their chairs in rows by the window ready for the spectacle they were all awaiting. It was after three o'clock in the afternoon when the head of the processions, consisting of servicemen from the Colonial contingents, reached Oxford Street. And, from then on, it was just one thrilling, unbelievable extravaganza of pomp and pageantry as one glorious scene quickly followed another.

Looking back on it afterwards, Patsy couldn't decide which part she had loved the most, it had all been so wonderful. The Colonial and Commonwealth troops with their multi-coloured uniforms and flashing bayonets; the Canadian Mounties on their beautifully groomed horses, all the same lustrous dark brown; the Yeoman of the Guard and the Lifeguards, a brilliant splash of colour on that dreary grey day.

'Whoever's that?' they shouted in amazement, as they saw a huge black woman in an open carriage, oblivious to the rain, joyously waving both arms to the crowd. She was in the carriage procession of Colonial rulers, and Patsy quickly consulted her programme.

'It's Queen Salote of Tonga,' she said to Rosie, sitting beside her. 'And that's the Sultan of Kelatan in the carriage with her. But she's completely overshadowing him, isn't she?'

Then they all played at 'spotting the famous', as figures, familiar to them only from newspapers and newsreels, drove past their window. There was Pandit Nehru, in his distinctive white headgear; Sir Winston Churchill – and what a cheer he got, they could hear the roar soaring upwards from the excited crowd in the street. And then the 'Royals' – the Kents and the Gloucesters, and the Queen Mother and Princess Margaret.

Then the moment they had all been waiting for – the Queen's procession – and, at the very end, the Queen herself with the Duke of Edinburgh beside her, seated up high in the golden coach so that they could be seen quite clearly. Unbelievably there was at that moment a break in the clouds and a flash of sunshine glinted on the golden coach and on the gleaming harness of the grey horses.

Patsy felt a lump come into her throat, as she was sure that everyone in the room – everyone in the crowd – must have done at their first glimpse of the Queen. She looked beautiful and radiant, but so tiny, with that huge crown on her head and the Orb and Sceptre in her hands. Patsy reflected that she was, indeed, a small person and almost too frail, it seemed, to bear the huge weight of responsibility that was hers, just as her body looked too frail to bear the weight of the crown. Rosie told Patsy later that she had read somewhere that, as soon as the ceremony was over, the Queen had changed her crown for a different one that was lighter in weight, and that the coach had been fitted with special racks for the Orb and Sceptre so that she could appear to be holding them when, in reality, she wasn't actually bearing their weight. Patsy admired the Queen tremendously, and felt all her patriotic fervour rising anew, as many thousands must have done that day, along with her joy and wonder that she had been a part of it all.

'No, Mum, you stay there,' Julia said to her mother when, after the procession had passed, the woman got up to make yet another cup of tea. 'I'll go and make it. Come and help me, Patsy?'

She agreed readily. She liked the look of Julia, Rosie's friend, and would be glad to get to know her a little better. Rosie was deep in conversation with Alan, another of the art students, who, judging from his expression, was not impervious to Rosie's charms. Patsy followed Julia into the small cubby-hole behind the stockroom, where there was a gas stove and a tiny cupboard with crockery and the items required to make a cup of tea or a quick snack.

'I've been waiting for a chance to talk to you, Patsy,' said Julia in a low voice as they set the cups and saucers on a tray. 'I'm worried about Rosie, you see. I've found out something that I think she ought to know . . . that I ought to tell her. But I think it might be better coming from you. You're her sister – she's so fond of you – and you know her so much better than the rest of us do.'

'What is it, Julia?' asked Patsy. She felt puzzled; Rosie seemed perfectly all right, on top of the world, in fact.

'It's Jeff Burroni,' said Julia. 'You know, the tutor she's friendly with. He's . . . he's married.'

'Good grief!' Patsy had never expected this bombshell, and what a shock it was! Not half as much of a shock as it would be to Rosie, though. 'How do you know? Are you sure?'

'Quite sure, worse luck. And I know because one of the girls that I'm friendly with comes from Bermondsey. Marion – my friend – doesn't come into contact with Jeff. We're all in different groups, you see, and he doesn't take her group. But it's true. Marion lives quite near Jeff's mother. He's got a child as well, a little girl.'

'Good grief!' said Patsy again. 'But . . . but this is awful. And Rosie has no idea?'

'It seems not. Apparently Jeff and his wife are not very happy, but that's beside the point. I still think he's been unfair to Rosie. He should have told her.'

'I'm amazed,' said Patsy slowly. She shook her head disbelievingly. 'Rosie's such a sensible girl, you know. Very astute. I wouldn't have thought anyone could fool her. Oh dear! This will put a damper on the day when she finds out. I dread to think how she'll react.'

'She's got stars in her eyes, Patsy,' said Julia. She grinned ruefully. 'When you're gazing up at the stars, you don't bother to look at the pavement. You don't see the damn' great holes in the road, do you?'

'No . . . I suppose not. What do you think of him, this Jeff Burroni? Apart from the fact that he's married, I mean. Do you like him?'

'He's a charmer all right. Quite good-looking – expressive eyes and a dazzling smile. A lot of the girls fall for him, but he can be ruthless. And there's a self-centred streak in him. I've always thought so, even before I knew all this.'

'Rosie doesn't seem to have noticed,' said Patsy. 'I've heard nothing but Jeff, Jeff, Jeff, ever since she met him. Her letters are full of him. I've hardly heard her mention anyone else, any friends at college or at work. She's told me a bit about you . . .'

'Rosie hasn't made many friends,' said Julia. 'I like her. I think she's a great girl, and I suppose she's more friendly with me than with any of the other girls. Of course with living on her own, and then working at Lyon's, she hasn't had a chance to mix very much outside of college. And she's spent such a lot of time with Jeff. We didn't know about it at first. They kept it very quiet.'

'Hardly surprising,' Patsy remarked.

'But we all know about Rosie and Jeff now, and I'm afraid she's going to get hurt if someone blurts it out to her about him being married. A lot of people know that as well, now.'

'She's going to get hurt anyway . . .'

'Yes, she is. That's why I thought it might be better if you told her, Patsy. I'm sorry to pass the buck like this, but none of us is as close to her as you are.'

Patsy sighed. 'All right, I'll try. But it isn't going to be easy. And you say she hasn't many other friends? What about Alan there? He seems to like Rosie.'

'Yes . . . he does. Everyone likes Rosie. But she has eyes for no one but Jeff. I'd be so grateful, Patsy, if you could break it to her . . . gently.'

'I'll do my best,' said Patsy, suddenly feeling that all the gladness had gone from the day, leaving her as cheerless as the grey rain-filled clouds that still filled the sky. 'Come on. We'd better take this tea in. They'll be wondering what on earth we're doing.'

Patsy decided not to break the awful news to Rosie – and she still wasn't quite sure how she was going to broach the subject – until they were back in the flat in South Kensington. They left the Oxford Street shop in the late afternoon, just in time to see the RAF fly past in the grey clouds above them. Then, as Rosie seemed to want to do so, they walked in the direction of Buckingham Palace. The crowds were still thick, though moving now, and all, it seemed, in the same direction as themselves, towards the palace. Later that evening the Queen, with the rest of the Royal Family, would appear on the balcony. The pavements were inches deep in garbage – newspapers, red, white and blue flags with the colours running into one another, cartons, empty bottles. The street cleaners would have an awful job, Patsy thought, trying to clear that lot. They passed a troop of Royal Marines returning to their dismissal point, still marching smartly, but looking very dejected by now with the blanco from their helmets running down their smart navy blue jackets.

'Poor chaps,' remarked Rosie. 'What a day!'

Patsy wasn't sorry when her sister suggested that they should head for home. The crowds seemed to be worsening rather than thinning out and once or twice Patsy had experienced a moment of panic as the pressure of people around her became almost unbearable.

'Are you OK, kid?' Rosie looked at her in concern. 'You're a bit pale, and you've hardly said a word since we left Julia's.'

Patsy tried to smile. 'Fine, thanks. It's just the crowds. Even Blackpool's Golden Mile is nothing compared to this, is it? I'm cold too.'

'So am I,' agreed Rosie. 'We'll get off home,' she decided. 'Never mind the palace. We wouldn't be able to get near anyway. We'll go and cook ourselves some scrambled eggs. That do for you? I told you I'm not much of a cook.'

It was cosy in Rosie's flat with the gas-fire hissing and the glow from the red-shaded lamp; it was dusk much earlier that evening. Patsy stretched her bare toes towards the comforting warmth of the fire. She had soon thawed out, but it would take ages for the people who had camped out for twenty-four hours to do so, she reflected. She was still cold inside, though, frantically thinking how she could break the dreadful news to Rosie.

She began tentatively. 'It's a pity Jeff couldn't have been with you today, Rosie. You said he was with his . . . his family?'

'Yes . . . It doesn't matter. I'll be seeing him again tomorrow.' Rosie's lectures started again in the morning – they had had only the one day off for the Coronation – but as she had no lectures till eleven o'clock she had planned to see Patsy safely to the station. 'I'm sorry you didn't meet him, kid, but I daresay you'll be coming down again, won't you? It's been great though, hasn't it, just the two of us? Quite like old times.'

'Yes, great,' echoed Patsy bleakly. 'Rosie . . .' she tried again. 'Don't you sometimes think it's strange that you've never met Jeff's family? His mother and father, that you've never been to his home?'

Rosie shrugged. 'No, not really. Why should I? Bermondsey's a long way out, and this place is so near college. I expect I will meet them, when the time's right.'

'Rosie.' Patsy took a deep breath. 'Have you never thought that he might be . . . married?'

'Married? Of course he's not married.' Rosie's blue eyes stared in surprise at her sister. 'What the hell are you talking about?'

Oh crikey! thought Patsy. This was every bit as awful as she had anticipated. Worse, in fact, and now Rosie was getting angry. 'I just thought it was strange,' she went on, 'that he's never taken you to meet his family, after all this time. As though he had something to hide.'

'Well, he hasn't,' Rosie snapped. 'Oh, I know what your game is,' she continued. She nodded meaningfully. 'You're jealous. That's what it is. You lost Ronnie Sykes, and now you've gone and lost that Neil . . . whatever his name was. And you can't bear me to have a boyfriend when you haven't got one. You were always like that, weren't you? Dead jealous. It was just the same in Castleburn, at the Youth Club.'

'I wasn't!' Patsy cried. 'I'm not jealous. It's not that at all. I was just trying to break it to you gently. Listen, Rosie . . .' She spoke more quietly now, forcing herself to look into Rosie's vivid blue eyes which were gleaming with animosity. 'Jeff is married. Julia told me. She asked me to . . . to tell you.'

'I don't believe you. You've made it all up.' Rosie's voice was cutting and her eyes still blazed with hostility, but there was a flicker of something else there as well now – fear. 'How can he be married? D'you really think I wouldn't have known? You're pathetic, Patsy.'

'Rosie . . . Rosie, it's true.' Patsy was almost crying. 'He *is* married. He's got a child, a little girl. Surely you don't think I would make up a thing like that? You've got to believe me!'

Rosie looked at her in stunned silence for a few moments, the anger in her eyes gradually giving way to puzzlement and hurt. 'Tell me,' she whispered. 'What did Julia say?'

'Very little apart from that,' Patsy replied. 'But it's true. A lot of them know about it.'

'Oh, they do, do they? They're been laughing at me, have they?'

'No, of course they haven't. They're sorry . . . that he didn't tell you. They think he's been unfair to you. They don't want you to be hurt.'

'Hurt? I'm not hurt.' Rosie jumped to her feet and clenched her fists as she stalked up and down the room. 'I'm blazing mad, that's what I am. It'll take more than Jeff Burroni to hurt me. Just wait till I get my hands on him tomorrow.'

'Listen, Rosie. It might not be as bad as you think. I'm sure he wouldn't have got friendly with you if he'd got on well with his wife. Perhaps . . . perhaps he means to get a divorce. People do.'

'Shut up, Patsy! Shut up! Divorce? Whatever are you talking about?' Rosie stood still, staring wildly at her sister. 'D'you really think I'd have . . . gone with him if I'd known he had a wife and child? And d'you really think I'd even consider marrying him after he's played the fool with me like this?'

'But if they're not happy together, Rosie . . . And you do love him, don't you?'

'I thought I did. Yes . . . I did love him. I do love him. But . . . it's the child, Patsy,' Rosie went on, her voice bleak. She flopped down on to the bed settee. 'I remember what it's like, not having a father. I never had one, not till I had Tom, and I know how awful it can be for a kid. All the other kids pestering about why you haven't got one. You went on about it, Patsy, when I first met you.'

'I don't remember.'

'Well, I do. Kids that haven't a dad remember all sorts of things. And I wouldn't want to be responsible for that, taking a child's father away from her.'

'It's happening a lot more now than it used to,' said Patsy evenly. 'More people getting divorced.'

'Just think what it 'ud do to Mum, though,' said Rosie. 'You know how narrow-minded she is about things like that. No . . . Jeff Burroni's made his bed and he'll have to lie on it as far as I'm concerned. With . . . what did you say her name was?'

'I've no idea. Julia didn't say.'

'Well, with whatever her name is. And he'll not make a fool of me any longer, I can tell you.'

Patsy was surprised at how well her sister seemed to be taking the news, after her initial anger and disbelief had subsided, but she guessed that Rosie was hurting far more inside than she was letting on. She had always been a tough little customer, refusing to resort to tears when she fell down in the playground, and when she had been in trouble at school or at home she had always blinked hard and thrust her firm chin out defiantly, just as she was doing now. Even when her real mother had been killed, Patsy couldn't remember her crying. She was obviously sensitive, though. She had reacted so perceptively to the feelings of Jeff's little girl. Patsy felt sorry for Rosie and she wanted to make it up to her in some way. After all, she had been the one to tell her the devastating news.

Patsy spoke the next words impulsively. 'Listen, Rosie. Why don't you come up to Yorkshire for a day or two? There's a dance at college in a couple of weeks' time, on the Saturday night. And it'll be my birthday on the Sunday as well. We could have a real good time together. You don't have to work every weekend, do you?'

'No . . . I could always ask for a weekend off. There's always somebody that'll fill in. Yes. Do you know, I think I would like that, Patsy. It's perhaps what I need – now – to get away from here for a change.' Rosie smiled at her sister, but her eyes had lost a lot of their sparkle. 'Where would I stay though? You're not allowed visitors in your rooms, are you?'

'No, but there are a few places near college that do bed and breakfast. They're quite cheap, and students often get their friends in there. I could get you fixed up.'

'Yes, thanks.' Rosie nodded. 'And thanks for asking me. It'll be nice to meet some new people, all those friends of yours that you've told me about. Will it be a posh do, this dance? Evening dress and all that?'

'No, nothing like that. Very informal, just a summer dance. I'm so glad you've said you'll come, Rosie.'

'It'll be great, kid,' she replied, but her eyes still held that awful lost, forlorn look. 'And . . . thanks for breaking it to me about Jeff. I know it couldn't have been easy for you.' Rosie shook her head in a bewildered manner. 'I still can't believe it. I keep thinking I'll wake up . . . And I'm sorry I was mad at you.'

'It's all right. I don't blame you. Anyone 'ud have been mad.'

The two girls smiled at one another, the best of friends – loving sisters again.

Chapter 15

Jenny and Tom walked hand in hand along Blackpool beach. Just as though they were newly married, Jenny thought to herself. She couldn't recall that they had been on the sands very much at all since those faraway days, at least not on their own. Jenny had always been too busy working in the boarding house to savour the delights of the sea-side, and after they moved to Castleburn their visits to Blackpool had always been with the family. Now the girls were both away from home, and Victor, on this Coronation night, was enjoying himself with some new friends he had met at his gran's. Possibly he, too, was on the beach to watch the firework display, but he hadn't seemed keen to accompany his parents and Jenny, indulgently, hadn't insisted. She was finding that it was a pleasant change to spend some time just with Tom.

'I wonder what the girls are doing?' she remarked now.

'I expect they're having a whale of a time,' Tom replied. 'It was a wonderful chance for them to see the procession. I'm glad you didn't insist on Patsy coming home, Jenny.'

'I can't very well insist any more, can I? She's a grown-up young woman now. She pleases herself. Funny about Ronnie Sykes, wasn't it? She hasn't told me much about it, but it all seems to have fizzled out. And now he's in

Germany. Still, I suppose it was all for the best. I never thought he was right for her.'

'You've got to leave 'em to get on with it, love. I've told you before. Anyway, never mind about the lasses now. They'll be living it up in London, no doubt.' Tom squeezed her hand. 'We're having a smashing time, aren't we, Jen? Glad we came?'

She turned to smile at her husband. 'Yes, I'm really glad, Tom. It's been a grand day, hasn't it? It's cold though. More like November than June.'

'It's stayed fine most of the day here, though. Pity it couldn't have done the same in London,' he remarked. 'Those poor folks. They'll have had a soaking, sure enough.'

'I hope the girls managed to keep dry. Still, they'd be inside most of the day, wouldn't they?'

'I've told you, love. Stop worrying about them. You can bet your life they're not worrying about us and what we're doing. They'll have had a grand time. Come on, let's have a last look at the bonfire before we go back.'

It had been a memorable day at Annie Carter's boarding house too. Annie and Ada had put themselves out no end to make sure that the visitors and the Bradshaw family, staying there for a few days, enjoyed themselves. Annie had so far stuck to the time honoured Blackpool boarding house tradition of three substantial meals a day: cooked breakfast, mid-day dinner – it was always called dinner and not lunch in this part of the country – and high tea. Today, however, they had had a snack lunch at mid-day so that the viewing arrangements would not be disturbed and so that Annie and Ada would not miss too much of the proceedings. Their main meal, prepared when the proceedings finally came to an end, had been at six o'clock.

Annie's culinary arrangements today had been superb, as always. There had been mounds of sandwiches – tinned salmon, boiled ham, and egg and cress – passed round at lunchtime during the viewing of the Coronation ceremony, followed by Annie's feather-light sponge cakes, decorated today in red, white and blue icing. Each guest was provided with a special plate with a hollow at the end where you could place your cup. These items were being sold in a lot of the stores now for the new pastime of television watching which was taking hold of the nation.

And the nation was certainly watching television today. The visitors at 'Pleasant View' sat in the darkened lounge with the chairs arranged in rows, gazing at the nine-inch set which Annie had ordered from the Co-op a month ago and which had been delivered only last week. There must have been a couple of dozen people altogether, with the visitors, the Bradshaws, the girls who helped in the boarding house, and one or two neighbours from the smaller houses round the corner. Annie was always an hospitable soul and she was in her element today, bustling about making endless pots of tea for the guests and making sure they had plenty to eat.

'Sit down, Mother,' Jenny had admonished her once or twice. 'You're going to miss it, dashing about like that. We'll all help to clear away later.'

But you couldn't tell Annie. It was hard work that had kept her going, she always maintained, and she intended to go on working till the day she died. She was certainly showing no signs of slowing up, Jenny reflected. Annie was turned seventy now, but looked very little different than she had during the war years when she had looked after a houseful of RAF recruits. Possibly she had looked older than her years then – full-bosomed and matronly, with iron-grey hair and thick-lensed spectacles behind which her shrewd eyes missed nothing – which was why she appeared to have aged very little now. There had been no further signs of the illness she had suffered at the end of the war, the near heart attack that had almost prevented Jenny and her family from moving to Yorkshire. Jenny knew that it had been caused by stress. Her mother had, understandably, been upset by Violet's departure for America, and the grim war years, too, had taken their toll.

As they did of all of us, Jenny thought now, remembering a certain young man whom she didn't allow herself to think of very often. She shook her head as if to free her mind of distracting thoughts. It was amazing how the mind could go off at a tangent like that, triggered off, no doubt, by her return to 'Pleasant View' with all its poignant memories, and, possibly, by the sight of the RAF squadrons marching in the Coronation procession. Jenny forced herself to concentrate on the ceremony.

It was all so thrilling, and she thought it seemed like a miracle, though she knew it was only one of the wonders of modern science, to be watching the procession and the ceremony as it was actually taking place. She loved it all: the pomp and the pageantry and the splendour, and then the more moving parts of the ceremony; Prince Philip swearing allegiance to his Queen who was also his wife, and the Queen in a simple white dress for the anointing part of the service which took place behind a screen. The only thing missing was the colour, although the black and white television screen couldn't detract from the flashing jewels, especially those in the Queen's tiara as she was driven to the Abbey. Patsy and Rosie would be seeing the colour, though, and they would be able to tell them all about it when they came home again.

Victor and the two friends he had made, lads of roughly the same age, were growing restless by mid-afternoon.

'Come on,' said Victor, as the returning procession started. 'Let's go on the prom. We've seen all this before. It's only the same old thing again.'

But they were all back by six o'clock for the celebration meal that Annie and Ada had prepared. Roast chicken – it was never an 'occasion' to Annie if there wasn't a chicken – with all the trimmings, followed by a huge trifle decorated with hundreds and thousands in an EIIR design. And a Coronation cake, complete with gold crown and a tiny model of the state coach.

Most of the visitors were wearing something of red, white and blue – a red blouse, or a blue and white spotted dress, or a red waistcoat – and the two little girls among the guests had red, white and blue ribbons in their hair. Jenny was proud of the dress she had made for the occasion. It was of soft flowing cotton in cherry red, with a wide skirt, crisp white collar and a nipped in waist accentuated by a broad navy belt. She knew that she looked nice in it. Tom's appreciative glance had told her so.

As a fitting end to the day, there was a firework display and bonfire on Central Beach opposite the Tower. Jenny and Tom exclaimed with the rest of the crowd as the Roman candles, golden fountains and silver stars cascaded in the darkening, still cloudy sky. Jenny couldn't remember when she had felt so contented. Her little job at Fothergill's antique shop was working out very well and she was looking forward to returning there in a couple of days' time. She was meeting different people and developing new interests – the world of antiques was quite fascinating – and had decided that she would stop worrying about Patsy and Rosie; Patsy, in particular, though it was difficult.

They took a last look at the bonfire, still blazing

brightly, fanned by the stiff breeze, and Jenny leaned her head companionably against Tom's shoulder. 'It's been a lovely day,' she said quietly.

'It's not over yet,' Tom whispered in her ear, and as she turned to look at him she saw, to her surprise, a roguish gleam in his eyes and a flicker of desire.

She smiled. 'Come on, let's go home.'

Rosie waved cheerily as she saw Patsy standing at the barrier of Leeford City Station. She recalled a similar occasion, only a few weeks ago, when the roles had been reversed and it had been her, Rosie, meeting Patsy on her visit to London to see the Coronation. The visit that had ended with the discovery of Jeff's perfidy . . .

His penitence and protestations that he really had intended to tell her – soon – and that he'd thought he was acting for the best, had cut no ice with Rosie. She was adamant that she would not continue their relationship, that she would not even see him again, save when she was forced to do so, at lectures. She still cared for him – feelings such as she had held for Jeff couldn't easily be stifled – but she was determined that she must now continue her life without him.

'But Daphne and I don't get on,' he had insisted. 'It's just a sham, it's meaningless. Besides, she's being unfaithful to me. I know she is.'

Rosie had almost laughed, in spite of feeling so wretched, at the irony of Jeff's remark. She realised then that, in Jeff's eyes, there was one rule for men and an entirely different one for women, even in these days of shifting attitudes and the gradual move to a more liberal view of marriage – and the means of ending it if it didn't work out. Jeff, irrationally, was angry because Daphne had cheated on him.

And Rosie had seen the flicker of uncertainty – of a guarded affection – in his eyes when he had spoken, briefly, of the little girl, Marilyn. She had known then, beyond all doubt, that she had to be free of Jeff, no matter what anguish it might cause her, and however difficult it might prove to be seeing him at college day after day.

Which was why she had decided to come to Leeford to see Patsy. She needed a complete break away from London, away from Jeff, from the Lyon's teashop, and from her bed-sit which now seemed to have become a claustrophobic, slightly sordid place. As if for the first time, she had noticed the faded wallpaper, the threadbare carpets, the greasy gas stove, the general air of seediness. She couldn't wait to see the back of the place.

'Hiya, kid. Lovely to see you.' Rosie hugged her sister. 'You're looking great. Not so tired as you did when you came to London.'

'No, School Practice has just finished, that's why,' Patsy laughed. 'What a relief. Gosh, I can't tell you how glad I am that I'll never have to see that Miss Fletcher again, not as long as I live.'

'Made it hard for you, did she, after that incident at school dinners?'

'Not really. Not as much as you might imagine, but I think that was thanks to Mr Thomson. She completely ignored me for the rest of the time, but I was aware of her.' Patsy shuddered. 'Heaven help the poor kids – and the teachers too – who get her as a head. She keeps applying for Infant headships . . . Anyway, never mind about her. I got a good report, thanks mainly to Miss Kennedy. And now there's only three weeks till the end of term.'

'You'll be having exams though?'

'Yes, next week. But they're not all that dreadful, or so I've heard. They pay more attention to the essays we hand in month by month. The main exams are next summer, of course, the finals. I'll have to do well in those to qualify. What about you?' Patsy looked at her sister as they came out of the station into the brightness and bustle of City Square. 'Have you end of term exams as well?'

'Yes, next week, like you,' answered Rosie casually. 'But it's the work we've done all year that counts the most. Look – never mind exams. I want to forget exams . . . and everything. I've come to enjoy myself. OK?'

'OK,' Patsy answered happily. 'I'm dying to show you around and introduce you to everybody. They've heard all about you.'

'Oh dear.' Rosie grinned ruefully. 'I hope I come up to expectations.' She put down her travel bag as they reached the tram stop and looked up at the sky. It was blue and cloudless and, as it was Saturday afternoon and the mills were closed, free from the grey smoke which often obscured the sun. 'Smashing weather you're having up in the frozen north. Real birthday weather. Nineteen tomorrow, kid.'

'Yes . . . It'll be the first time I've been away from home on my birthday.'

'There has to be a first time for everything.' Rosie squeezed her sister's arm as she saw the pensive look cross her face. 'What are you planning to do tomorrow? Anything special?'

'No, I don't think so,' said Patsy. 'Sunday's a bit of a non-day at college. No lectures or anything. We just read and talk, or go for walks. It was the day I used to feel homesick at first, till I met Ronnie . . . I used to see him on a Sunday.' Patsy's eyes clouded over momentarily. 'But I'm footloose and fancy free now.' She gave a little laugh which Rosie couldn't help thinking sounded forced. 'No man in my life. I'm glad I gave Neil the shove, like you told me to.'

'I don't think I actually said that.'

'No, but you said not to give in to him . . . and I didn't. So he soon cooled off after that.'

'Never mind, kid. It didn't sound as though he was right for you.'

'No, I'm sure he wasn't,' said Patsy brightly. Too brightly her sister thought, but Patsy's next words seemed to imply that she really was well and truly over the man in question. 'Do you know, I've hardly given Neil a thought until just now. I haven't seen much of him, what with School Practice and everything. Been too busy. I haven't a clue what he's up to, and I care even less.'

'He'll be at the dance, though, tonight?'

'Oh, I expect so,' said Patsy airily. 'Neil Emmerson's not going to miss a chance to flaunt his good looks, have all the girls swooning.'

'Wow! That's a bit scathing.'

'Well, that's what he's like. Kath warned me, but I wouldn't take any notice at first. You'll like Kath, Rosie. She's great.'

'I'm sure I will.' Rosie smiled at her sister. 'And, Patsy, I'm footloose and fancy free as well. Nobody at all. No . . . Jeff.'

'No?' Patsy raised her eyebrows.

'No. N – O, NO,' said Rosie emphatically. She shook her head. 'And I don't want to talk about him. I don't even want to think about him. OK?'

'OK.' Patsy nodded. 'Look, here's the tram.' She picked up her sister's bag and led the way aboard the orange vehicle.

Rosie was no stranger to Leeford. She had often been there on shopping trips with her mother and Patsy as it was the nearest big city to Castleburn, but she had never been far from the city centre and the shops, never as far out as Woodley Bank where the college was situated. She was finding it strangely comforting to be back in the north again amongst so much that was familiar. She had not seen those particular mill chimneys before, nor those particular rows of terraced houses, nor, further out of the city, those greystone villas, but they were nevertheless part of a recognisable landscape that was well-known and well-loved and which, Rosie was now discovering with a pang of nostalgia, she'd missed far more than she had realised.

It had been so exciting, so thrilling to move down to London, to be part of the vibrant, fast-moving scene. She had thought that she would want to stay there for ever. But that was before she had found out about Jeff... Rosie blinked rapidly, forcing her eyes back to the view of suburban semis and rows of shops outside the window of the tram, and her mind back to the present and Patsy's college that she was now going to see for the first time. As she had just told her sister, she wasn't even going to think about Jeff Burroni.

They got off the tram and walked up Sycamore Avenue towards the college gates at the top.

'This is where you're staying tonight,' said Patsy, stopping at a semi-detached house halfway up the avenue. It was similar to the others in the row, a solid, greystone building with a well-tended lawn and a laburnum tree in full bloom by the gate, and there was a small notice in the window which read 'Bed and Breakfast'. 'A few of the houses round here take in guests,' Patsy explained, 'and somebody recommended Mrs Oldfield to me. You should be nice and comfy here. Shall we just pop in and leave your bag, then we'll go up to Calder? Tea's informal on a Saturday – a help-yourself sort of thing – so there'll be plenty of room for one more.'

Rosie was quietly amused at the way Patsy was shepherding her around. Usually the boot had been on the other foot, with Rosie taking the lead, but Patsy seemed to be thrilled to bits today to be able to entertain her sister. She introduced her to Mrs Oldfield, the comfortable middle-aged widow who did bed and breakfast 'mainly for a bit of company', as she explained to the girls. Then, with obvious pride, Patsy took her sister into Calder Hall where, at tea-time, Rosie met the friends she had heard so much about.

Rosie was impressed by the friendliness and camaraderie that abounded at Leeford Training College; something, she realised now, that she had been missing at the art school in Kensington. Rosie didn't find it difficult to make friends, but in London she hadn't done so. There was Julia, of course, and Alan who, Rosie suspected, would like to be more than a friend. But she certainly wasn't part of a happy, matey crowd, as Patsy seemed to be. It was because she lived alone in a bed-sit, Rosie thought now – many of the students did – and not in a hall of residence, and because she spent a lot of her time working at Lyon's. But Rosie knew that the main reason she had failed to make many friends was because of Jeff. He had filled her heart and her mind and had taken up most of her time. Now she was nearing the end of her first year, and whereas many of the students were part of a clique, an intimate circle, she, Rosie, was an outsider. And it was all her own fault.

Rosie suddenly felt lonely, something she hadn't felt since . . . she couldn't remember when. But these girls, these friends of Patsy's at Calder Hall, were doing all they could to make her feel welcome. Rosie made up her mind that she was going to enjoy herself this weekend. She was going to laugh and be happy and have a whale of a time.

'Happy birthday, love.' Rosie put an arm round her sister and kissed her cheek when they were alone again in Patsy's room. She reached into the depths of her shabby shoulder bag which accompanied her everywhere. 'Here, you'd better have this now. You might want to wear them tonight.'

'Gosh! Thanks, Rosie.' Patsy's cheeks glowed with excitement, and Rosie remembered how her sister had always loved birthdays. 'I shouldn't open it till tomorrow really, but I can't wait.' She tore off the wrapping paper. 'Gosh!' she said again, as she took out two packets of Kayser Bondor nylons. 'These must be the sheerest I've ever seen. Yes, I'll certainly wear them tonight. And perfume too. Lovely. Oh, it is kind of you, Rosie.'

Patsy sniffed appreciatively at the June perfume by Saville, then propped up the birthday card, a reproduction of a Monet cornfield, on the bookshelf where there were already a few others. 'These came this morning,' she said. 'From Mum and Dad and Victor, and Gran in Blackpool. And one came from Auntie Vi in Vermont the other day. There was lipstick from her as well, and a postal order from Gran. And Mum's made the dress I'm wearing tonight, and she's knitted me a cardigan.' Patsy was bubbling over with pleasure. It was a long time since Rosie had seen her so elated. 'I expect there'll be a few more cards tomorrow from the girls.'

'You remember one another's birthdays, do you?' asked Rosie. 'Give presents and all that?'

'Yes, just little ones,' said Patsy. 'I'm the last in our crowd. I was always one of the youngest in the class, if you remember, having a summer birthday. Kath's is in

September, same as yours. She must be just the same age as you, Rosie.'

Rosie reflected that there was no one at the college in London who even knew when her birthday was – except Jeff, and he didn't count any more – and she felt a pang of loneliness again. Birthdays were special – your very own day, when everyone should make a fuss of you. But it was more than likely that her own would pass by unnoticed, at least by her friends in London.

'I'd better be going now, hadn't I?' said Rosie. 'So that I can get ready for tonight. Shall I come and call for you here, when I'm ready?'

'Yes, about half-past seven,' said Patsy. 'Oh, Rosie, isn't it all exciting? We're going to have a lovely time, I know we are.'

Rosie looked at herself appraisingly in the full-length mirror in the bedroom, wondering if she might be a little overdressed for what Patsy had insisted was an informal occasion. She pursed her lips and turned this way and that, watching the wide stand-away skirt, held in position by two stiff petticoats, swaying alluringly. No, she decided firmly, it was not too dressy and she was going to wear it. She could play it down by not wearing elbow-length gloves, which would have been essential at a more formal occasion, and by wearing just the minimum of jewellery; pearl ear studs would suffice. She had designed and made the dress herself, with a little help from Julia, for the end of term dance at the art school. That was before she and Jeff had split up; now it was doubtful if she would even be going to the dance. But she was going to wear the dress. She had burned the midnight oil on several occasions finishing it and it would be a shame for it to go to waste.

It was of organza, in a vivid cerise pink, ballerina-length, with a wide skirt and sleekly fitting midriff which showed off her slim waist to perfection. The halter neckline draped softly over her bust, and high-heeled white sandals with ankle straps completed the ensemble. Rosie couldn't help thinking that she looked very nice. Smashing, in fact – there was no point in false modesty. What a pity it was . . . No, firmly she pushed the intrusive thought away. Now was no time to be thinking about Jeff.

She picked up her white woolly stole – not one that her mother had knitted for her this time, but a garment she had bought in one of her more affluent moments from a posh shop in Kensington – and put it over her arm. She would probably need it later if the evening became chilly, although there was no sign of it doing so yet. She couldn't walk up to college like this though. Even someone as unselfconscious as Rosie felt a little conspicuous in all that finery. She put on her chunky knit cardigan, covering her bare arms and shoulders. It spoiled the effect, but she could leave it in Patsy's room before they went across to the dance.

Patsy gasped with surprise when she caught sight of Rosie in the stunning pink dress. It was at that moment, she thought later, that she felt the first stab of apprehension; it was at that moment that things started to go wrong.

'Gosh!' she said, as Rosie divested herself of her unsuitable cardigan and draped a fluffy white stole becomingly round her shoulders. 'You look . . . nice. Super!'

Something in Patsy's tone must have alerted Rosie, because she looked sharply back at her sister. 'What's the matter? Do you think it looks too much? Too dressed up?'

'No, of course it doesn't. It's super . . . super,' said Patsy again. 'It was just a surprise, that's all, that bright pink colour. But I did tell you it was just an informal dance, didn't I? No evening dress or anything like that.'

'So you think it's too dressy then?' Rosie was not smiling now and her eyes looked a trifle wary. They had lost some of their radiance, and if it hadn't been Rosie – confident, self-assured Rosie – Patsy would have thought that her sister looked a little worried.

'No, don't be silly. I've told you, it's great. I was just amazed that you could have made such a gorgeous dress yourself,' Patsy went on, desperately trying to make amends. 'You did make it, didn't you? And designed it as well, I bet?'

'Yes, with a bit of help from Julia.' Rosie sounded somewhat mollified now, to Patsy's relief; she didn't want the evening to get off to a bad start. 'I was determined to wear it,' Rosie went on, 'after all the effort I'd put into it.'

'I should jolly well think so too.' Patsy's voice sounded, to her own ears, rather strained. 'I'd be dead proud of myself if I'd made a dress like that. But I'm hopeless at sewing. Well, you know that, don't you?'

'That's the dress that Mum made for you, is it?' Rosie asked now. Patsy wasn't sure if she had imagined it, but she felt that Rosie's tone was slightly critical. 'It's . . . nice,' her sister continued. 'Nice and summery.'

And simple and childish. Go on, why don't you say it? thought Patsy to herself. Until Rosie had walked into the room, looking absolutely gorgeous, she, Patsy, had been reasonably satisfied with the dress that Mum had made for her birthday. It was a sun-dress, made from a McCall's pattern, with wide shoulder straps and patch pockets and a detachable button-on bolero. The apple green cotton with yellow and white squiggles was, as Rosie said, summery-looking and crisp and clean. It was, Patsy had supposed, ideal for a summer dance. But now, by the side of Rosie, she felt like a gauche schoolgirl next to a glamorous film star.

But she tried to smile brightly. 'Yes, good old Mum,' she said. 'She gave it me when I went home for half-term. And she made this cardigan to go with it.' She pointed to a yellow garment on the bed, obviously hand knitted and, to Patsy's eyes, now looking ridiculously homely when compared with the sophisticated stole that her sister was wearing. 'But I don't think I'll need it tonight, do you? Not with having the bolero.'

'No, I wouldn't wear it if I were you,' agreed Rosie, almost too quickly. 'Cardigans are all right, I suppose, for casual wear, but not when you're dressed up. They take away all the style from what you're wearing.'

If there's any style there to start with, thought Patsy resentfully, eyeing her now unsatisfactory image in the mirror. With a brave display of indifference she picked up her comb and fluffed out her hair, noting that at least that looked presentable. She had washed it last night with a special Amami shampoo which had high-lighted the red-gold tones, and she knew that the slightly longer length, curling into the nape of her neck, suited her. Rosie's hair, she thought now, looked like a ragamuffin's; she was still sporting the short urchin style with which she had surprised them at Christmas.

Patsy nonchalantly picked up her Tangee lipstick and outlined her lips again, although she had already done them twice, in the peachy-orange shade. She knew that she was stalling for time, although there was no reason why she should feel nervous tonight. It wasn't as if she was going amongst people she didn't know. There would only be the students there tonight, together with the guests they had invited. Like Rosie. She knew though, if she were honest with herself, that she was nervous at the thought of seeing Neil again. What she had told Rosie earlier in the day was not entirely true. It was true that she was no longer 'going out' with him, but it wasn't true to say that she no longer gave him a second thought. She still thought about him a lot and felt that, given a little encouragement, he might just be interested in her again. He had stopped her in the corridor only yesterday and asked her if she was going to the dance, and had begged her to save a few dances for him. She knew she hadn't imagined the gleam in his eyes; she had seen the self-same look there before, many times.

'Come on then,' she said casually. 'We'd better be off. I said we'd meet Kath and Gwen and Marjorie in the foyer.'

But as they walked across to the Main Block where the dance was to be held it was Rosie who walked with Kath, while Patsy tagged along at the back with the two second years. It isn't fair, she's my friend, Patsy thought disconsolately, as she watched Kath and Rosie talking and laughing together. And she's my sister. But she didn't really know which of them she was vexed with. Or, come to think of it, why she should be vexed at all . . .

She should have known, Patsy thought afterwards; she should have guessed what would happen. Her first twinge of apprehension when she had set eyes on Rosie in the pink dress had been intuitive . . .

Neil didn't appear till about nine o'clock when the evening was well under way. Patsy had tried not to be continually looking over her shoulder, and when he finally did arrive on the scene she was dancing with Brian Lightfoot, an intense, bespectacled young man she had met at the gramophone society. Neil, she had to admit, did come to seek her out, and he did dance with her – just once – but there was no way of avoiding it: she had to introduce him to Rosie.

Patsy fiddled with her glass of lager and lime – there

was, for once, a licence for drinks to be served that night – running her fingers up and down the ice-cold tankard, helplessly watching the scene that was being played out in front of her and aware of the misery deep inside her. It was just like it had been in Castleburn, at the Youth Club and at the church socials, and even as far back as Blackpool, at the Junior School. She, Patsy, was a spectator, on the outside looking in, at Rosie, the centre of an admiring throng. Seated round the table were Kath and Roger, a man Kath was quite friendly with, off and on; Gwen and Marjorie; Edna and her boyfriend Bernard Hargreaves; and Rosie . . . and Neil.

He was leaning back nonchalantly in his chair, but his eyes were fixed on Rosie. Everyone's eyes, it seemed to Patsy, were fixed on her, but Neil's in particular. He had forgotten all about Patsy. But who wouldn't forget about me, she thought bitterly, boring, insignificant little Patsy Bradshaw, in the face of such vivacity and wit? Rosie was holding back her head, laughing with what appeared to be genuine amusement at a remark of Neil's, and her eyes were as blue as cornflowers. They were always bluer than blue when she was excited, as she obviously was now. Yes, Neil had completely forgotten about Patsy, but she was very much aware of him, electrically, vibrantly so. She looked at his long legs in their immaculate dark grey trousers, his well-shaped hands, pianist's hands, one of them closing over Rosie's as he leaned forward now, emphasising a point, his green eyes flashing with interest, desire . . .

Patsy turned away, unable to look any more. She had really believed at one time that she was over him. She had told Kath that she was, and Rosie too, but it wasn't true. She still wanted him; she couldn't in honesty say that she loved him, but if he were to ask her, she would go with him willingly, eagerly. But now . . . now he had been captivated by Rosie.

A feeling that was almost hatred engulfed Patsy as she stared down into the yellowy-green depths of her glass. Why couldn't she look like that, striking and vivacious, the sort of girl who turned every head? And why couldn't she act like that, confident and amusing and radiant? Rosie seemed to be at home wherever she went, perfectly at ease with whoever she met. Just look at her now, laughing and joking as though she hadn't a care in the world, and she was supposed to be heartbroken about that Jeff Burroni. Well, she couldn't have thought all that much about him from the way she was behaving now. She'd soon put him out of her mind. Why, oh why, had she been such a fool as to invite Rosie here? She might have guessed what would happen. All Patsy's old feelings of insecurity and self-doubt returned as she watched her sister with her friends. Yes, *her* friends, but no one would think so now. They were all being charmed by Rosie.

Patsy sat there, silent and miserable, feeling stupid and like a fish out of water. But no one seemed to notice. When Brian Lightfoot came over to ask her to dance again she could have hugged him. Brian would never be interested in Patsy, not in 'that way', just as she would never be interested in him. He had a girl friend – Patsy had seen her photo, and she was just as intense-looking and serious as Brian himself – at a college in the Midlands, but she had been unable to get away this weekend. Patsy and Brian got on well on the odd occasions that they met, and she was certainly glad of his company tonight. When they had danced he joined the crowd at the table and stayed with them for the rest of the evening.

Patsy hardly spoke to her sister again that night, and if Brian was surprised at Patsy's sudden interest in him and his stories of his home and family, he showed no sign of it. And Patsy appeared not to notice, or at least not to care, when, at the end of the evening, after the last waltz, Rosie was seen to walk away from the Main Hall and out of the building with Neil Emmerson. His arm was round her shoulders and she was smiling up at him.

Patsy walked back to Calder Hall with the rest of the crowd, joining in with their conversation and laughter, but feeling detached, as though she were watching herself in a slow-motion film. She said goodnight cheerfully to Brian, who had insisted on seeing her home, then walked into the hall a few steps behind Gwen and Marjorie. She counted the stone steps in her head, automatically, deliberately, to shut out all coherent thought, 27, 28, 29, 30 . . . 'Goodnight, Marjorie. Goodnight, Gwen . . . See you in the morning . . .'

What a relief it was to be on her own, to stumble into bed, to let the tears flow freely. Patsy wasn't sure why she was crying. It wasn't as if she loved Neil – she knew she didn't – but she felt betrayed, and, though she knew it was a stupid thought and that she was wallowing in self-pity, friendless and alone. Eventually her sobs subsided and she began to feel calmer. Bleary-eyed, she looked at the luminous dial of her bedside clock. It was only then that she remembered that today was her birthday. It was 1 am on 21 June and Patsy was nineteen years old.

Chapter 16

'What the hell do you think you were playing at, Rosie? How could you? If I hadn't seen it with my own eyes I would never have believed it.' Patsy hadn't really intended to start on at her sister the minute that Rosie walked through the door, but it was the sight of her face, so cheerful and unconcerned, as though nothing had happened, that made Patsy feel angry again. 'Walking off with Neil Emmerson like that, arms round one another, all lovey-dovey. I just couldn't believe it!'

'Hey, hang on a minute.' Rosie closed the door of the study bedroom behind her and sat down on the bed. 'I'm old enough to look after myself, you know. I don't need you telling me what I can do and what I can't. And I'm quite capable of coping with fellows like Neil Emmerson. So you don't need to start behaving like a mother hen all of a sudden.' Rosie smiled placatingly at her sister, her head on one side. 'It's nice of you to be so concerned about me, kid, but there's no need, honestly. I know what I'm doing.'

For a moment Patsy was so taken aback she couldn't speak. She opened her mouth, but the words just wouldn't come. How dare Rosie smile at her like that, and how dare she so deliberately misunderstand her? Did Rosie really think that she was upset because her sister might have been led astray? Was Rosie so stupid, so blind, that she couldn't see how badly she had hurt her sister, and why? When the words finally came, almost spewed out from a face that was ashen and spoken in a voice that was low with rage, there could be no mistaking the meaning now behind Patsy's outburst.

'You know what you're doing? I should bloody well think you *do* know what you're doing! You're pinching my boyfriend, that's what you're doing. And not content with that, you're pinching . . .'

'Hey, hang on a minute,' said Rosie for the second time, but this time her voice was indignant. 'Your boyfriend? *Your* boyfriend, for goodness' sake? What the hell are you talking about? Neil isn't your boyfriend. You finished with him, ages ago. You told me so. You said you couldn't care less. You said . . .'

'Never mind what I said! You took him away from me. You couldn't wait to get your hands on him. And it's not the first time either. You used to do it at home, at the Youth Club, at church. You always took the boys I liked. And you'd have done it with Ronnie Sykes, too, if he'd looked at you twice. I saw you making eyes at him when he called for me at New Year. But he didn't look at you, did he? He wanted me. And Neil wanted me too, until you came along.'

'Patsy, stop it! You're being childish and ridiculous. And you've got it all wrong. I didn't want Ronnie, and I don't want Neil either. For goodness' sake, grow up!'

'Don't you dare call me ridiculous! I know what you want. I know only too well what you want . . .' Patsy could feel the rage bubbling up inside her. She felt as though she would explode with it and she no longer seemed to have any control over the words she was speaking. 'You want anything in trousers. You always have, ever since you were a little kid. You wanted my dad, didn't you? You were always smarming all over him, climbing on his knee and kissing him. It made me sick. You're just like your mother. She was a . . . a street woman, that's what she was. And if you don't watch out, you'll end up just like her. You're a trollop, Rosie White!'

Patsy didn't know whether the use of Rosie's previous surname – the one she had had before she was adopted – was deliberate or not. The minute she had uttered it she realised what she had said, but it was too late then to retract it and, besides, everything she had said was true. Her sister had behaved shamefully at the dance.

Rosie had gone very quiet, alarmingly so, and Patsy began to feel frightened by the silence in the room and of the effect that her words might be having. She hadn't meant to go so far, to say quite so much . . . When Rosie spoke her voice was cold and her eyes were opaque blue pools, without a trace of their former brilliance.

'That's a childish thing to say, Patsy. If you knew what it meant you wouldn't say it. But you don't know what it means. You don't know anything about anything, do you? Because you're childish. Neil says you are, and I agree with him. I'm not surprised he got fed up with you . . . And you know nothing at all about my mother, so shut up about her!'

'I do know, so there!' Patsy knew as soon as she spoke that she sounded childish – the word that Rosie had already used, several times, about her – but she went on blindly, heedlessly. 'I do know about your mother, because I used to listen to my mum and gran talking . . . when she used to come to Blackpool to see you. And I know she used to . . . to entertain men.'

'Oh, yes, you always were a little snoop, weren't you? Ears flapping, listening to other people's conversations. I remember your gran saying, "Little pigs have big ears." And you had, hadn't you? Your ears were so big it's a wonder you didn't take off. You were a real nosy little tell-tale. And you haven't changed much now!'

'Well, it's better than being man mad, chasing after all the lads . . .' Patsy suddenly stopped shouting and burst into tears. The worst of her anger was subsiding now, leaving her feeling miserable and guilty.

Rosie gave a deep sigh. 'Oh, Patsy, what on earth are we doing?' she said wearily. 'Saying all these awful things and trying to hurt one another. Whatever's the matter with us? We never used to be like this.' Rosie sounded regretful, but she didn't come and put her arm round her sister, as she would have done at one time. The two girls looked cautiously at one another, Rosie standing up now by the side of the bed, Patsy opposite her, like sparring partners in a wrestling match. They both gave remorseful smiles.

'I'm sorry,' said Patsy quietly.

'I'm sorry, too,' said Rosie. 'I only came to wish you a happy birthday. Oh, Patsy, don't let's quarrel. We mustn't spoil your birthday.'

'I was mad at you,' said Patsy, still with a trace of her former petulance. 'I do like Neil, it's no use pretending that I don't, and he won't look at me now. Men never look at me when you're around. And now you've said he thinks I'm childish.'

'Oh, Patsy, for heaven's sake don't start all that again. He might not have used exactly that word. He said you were innocent . . . naive . . . and he knows I'm not, you see.'

No, I'll bet you're not, thought Patsy. I bet you let him do all sorts of things. I bet you went all the way with him. She was like a child with a wobbly tooth, niggling away at the soreness; she couldn't let the matter rest. 'You let him make love to you, didn't you?' she said now, in a quiet voice, staring down at the faded green carpet and not at her sister. 'Did you go to his room, or did you go in the woods?'

'No, I did not!' said Rosie indignantly. 'What d'you take me for? Oh, yes, I know perfectly well what you take me for, don't I? You've already told me. I'm a trollop. In other words, a prostitute. That's what it means, in case you didn't know.' Rosie gave an exasperated sigh. 'Oh, for God's sake, Patsy, we've got to stop all this. I don't want Neil Emmerson, honestly, and I didn't mean to hurt you. I didn't think you were bothered about him any more. You told me you weren't. Listen . . . he just walked me back to Mrs Oldfield's and kissed me goodnight, just once. I like him and I can understand why you fancied him. He's good company, and he's very good-looking. But he's certainly not the right fellow for you, Patsy, not in a month of Sundays. You must know that.'

'Thanks for the advice, I'm sure,' Patsy said huffily. She badly wanted to make up the quarrel with her sister, but was still smarting from the hurt that Rosie had caused her.

Rosie pretended not to notice her sarcastic reply. 'Now, what are you doing for your birthday?' she asked. 'I'm here all day, you know. I'm not going back to London till tomorrow morning. Shall we go out somewhere?'

'A few of us have planned to go to Temple Newsham,' said Patsy coolly. 'Kath and Gwen and Marjorie and me. We were talking about it at breakfast time.'

'Temple Newsham? What's that?'

'It's a Jacobean house, what they call a stately home, a few miles away. There are some nice grounds, I believe, and the house is open to the public. You can come with us if you like,' Patsy added grudgingly. Then her resentment flared up again and she couldn't help sticking the knife in the wound. 'I thought you might be otherwise occupied, though. Going out with Neil Emmerson . . .'

'As a matter of fact, he did ask me to go out with him today.' Rosie's blue eyes stared boldly at her sister. 'But I said I wasn't sure what I was doing, with its being your birthday.'

'Oh, don't bother about me. You just go and do whatever you like.' Patsy shrugged. 'I'll be perfectly all right. I've got all my own friends here.'

'All right then, I will!' Rosie's pointed chin stuck out aggressively and there was a stubborn gleam in her eyes. She jumped to her feet. 'I jolly well will! I'll go and find Neil now. Kirkstall Hall, isn't it?' Patsy, staring back at her sullenly, gave a brief nod. 'See you later, then, Patsy.' Rosie turned and flounced towards the door. 'Enjoy yourself.'

Patsy didn't reply 'You enjoy yourself too'. Neither did she say 'Drop dead', which was what she felt like saying. She said coldly, 'Don't forget your cardigan, Rosie. You left it last night.'

The day had started off so well, with cards from the girls on the table and a couple of little presents, too; a small framed print of a Peter Scott landscape from Kath and some Pond's Angel Face make-up from Gwen. Patsy had felt better after a night's sleep – surprisingly, she had slept quite well – and had woken up determined that she would not let Rosie's disloyalty spoil her birthday. She was well aware of her tendency to over-dramatise, to imagine the worst, and things hadn't seemed half so bad in the clear light of morning. Until Rosie had walked in with that smug, self-satisfied smile on her face. Then Patsy had seen red again. Well, she was going to have a nice day, she decided, in spite of Rosie. Her sister could go and do what the hell she liked.

The girls decided to forgo their mid-day meal at college and take a packed lunch with them. They were allowed into the kitchen on such occasions to prepare sandwiches and help themselves to the slab cake that was always available.

'Where's Rosie?' asked Kath, as she buttered the slices of bread that Patsy had cut. 'Isn't she coming with us?'

'She's other fish to fry,' said Patsy curtly. 'Neil Emmerson, in other words.'

'Oh . . . Oh, I see,' said Kath, with a sidelong glance at her friend. 'That's a bit much, isn't it, when it's your birthday? I thought she'd come to spend the weekend with you. Don't you mind?'

Patsy gave a slight shake of her head. 'Don't know. She can do what she likes, I suppose. I'm not my sister's keeper, as they say.' Then she added, more honestly, 'We've had a row, Kath, about Neil. It was my fault as much as hers – well, it was mostly my fault. I said some awful things. And now she's flounced off to spend the day with him.'

'Oh heck! What a mess.' Kath gave her friend a sympathetic glance. 'I could see you were a bit upset last night. But he's not worth it, love, honest he's not. And I thought you were over Neil Emmerson anyway. You said you were.'

'I thought I was . . . but obviously I wasn't,' replied Patsy. 'What d'you think about Rosie, Kath?'

'I like her. I think she's a great girl. Good fun, and I'm sure she thinks the world of you, in spite of . . . you know. I'm sorry you've had a row about it. She's a flirt, though,' Kath added, smiling. 'I can see that.'

'That's what I told her. Well, much worse than that,' said Patsy quietly. 'She's always been one for the lads.'

'I should imagine that's the worst you can say about her,' Kath remarked. 'She's a good sort, and you'd better make it up with her before she goes back to London. You will, won't you, kid?'

'Of course . . . if I can,' said Patsy. 'Anyway, it's not going to spoil our day.'

The weather was fine and warm, a perfect June day, and Patsy wore the new yellow cardigan that her mother had made over her Hungarian-style blouse and dirndl skirt. Temple Newsham was only a half-hour bus ride away, a Tudor and Jacobean house set in vast parklands landscaped by Capability Brown.

'Lord Darnley was born here,' Patsy told her friends, as they ate their lunch in the shade of one of the lovely groves of trees. 'You know, he was one of the husbands of Mary, Queen of Scots. And he was the father of James I of England – James VI of Scotland, of course.'

'You certainly know your history,' Gwen remarked. 'It's wasted on an Infant teacher, though.'

'Don't start that again,' said Patsy, laughing. 'You Junior and Secondary teachers seem to think we do nothing but sing nursery rhymes and play with sand. My interest in history has nothing to do with teaching. I got interested when I worked in the antique shop. It's fascinating.' Patsy felt herself warming to her subject. 'Seeing all the furniture and china from different periods. That was when I started reading up about the characters in history and all that. I'd never cared much for it at school. They made it all so boring, didn't they? Who the heck's bothered about Pitt's foreign policy, or the Unification of Germany, for goodness' sake? But when you visit places like this, it makes it all come to life.'

Patsy was enjoying the day far more than she had thought she would, after her row with Rosie. It was being amongst so much that was beautiful and precious and old, she supposed. It made you forget the trivial little worries of today.

Kath seemed impressed by her friend's ability to discern whether a china figure was Dresden or Chelsea or Rockingham, to recognise an Adam fireplace or a Chippendale chair. 'You're quite an expert,' she said admiringly. 'And you'll be back amongst it all in a few weeks' time, won't you? Aren't you working at Mr Fothergill's for the holiday?'

'I was going to,' said Patsy, ruefully, 'until my mother pinched my job. I told you, didn't I, that she was working there? I was flabbergasted, I can tell you, when I heard about it.'

'She's only part-time though, isn't she? Surely there'll be room for both of you?'

'I doubt it,' replied Patsy. 'Come to think of it, even if my mum hadn't been there I doubt if Mr Fothergill would have wanted me there all the time. I daresay I can get a job somewhere though. Woolie's, perhaps, or in one of the cafes. Castleburn's getting quite busy in the summer now, and they take on seasonal staff. Not so busy as Blackpool though. You can always get work there . . .'

Patsy stopped speaking as an idea struck her. That's what she would do. She would go to Blackpool for the summer holiday and work in the boarding house. Gran would be delighted to have her at 'Pleasant View'; she'd always got on so well with Gran. Even if she made up the quarrel with Rosie – as she must try to do – she felt that she didn't want to spend the whole of the summer vacation, about eight weeks in all, in the company of her sister. It would be too claustrophobic with both of them in the same house, sharing the same bedroom. It was strange, she had never felt like that before . . .

Rosie returned from her day out with Neil – they had been to Ilkley – somewhat subdued. She spent the evening with Patsy and some of her friends from Calder Hall in the lounge, chatting and listening to records.

'I'm sorry, kid,' Rosie had said earlier as she entered Patsy's bedroom, less exuberantly than she had done that morning. 'No hard feelings?'

'No . . . none at all,' replied Patsy airily. 'Why should there be? Have you had a good day?'

'Yes, thank you. Have you?'

'Yes, lovely, thank you.'

'We're still friends, aren't we? I want us to be friends, Patsy.'

'Of course we are. Why shouldn't we be?'

Everything was fine . . . on the surface. But Patsy didn't see her sister next morning to say goodbye. She had a lecture at nine o'clock and Rosie was catching an early train back to London.

Jeff called on Rosie again that evening. She had a feeling that it was him as soon as she heard the knock. It was the third time he had come unexpectedly, pestering her, although she had told him she didn't want to see him. She was tempted not to answer, but she did finally open the door.

He stepped inside without waiting for an invitation. 'Rosie . . . I must talk to you.'

'There's no point in talking, Jeff. We've said it all. I've heard it all before.'

'But Daphne's seeing the fellow across the landing. I know she is. Twice lately when I've come home she's been . . .'

'I don't want to know, Jeff. It's none of my business.'

'But it is, Rosie. I love you . . . Listen, I've been thinking. If I get a private detective I can catch her out. I can get evidence.'

'Do whatever you like, Jeff,' said Rosie wearily, 'but, I've told you, it's none of my business. Now, will you please go?'

She almost capitulated when she saw the look of bewilderment in his deep brown eyes – Jeff was usually so self-assured – but she hardened her heart. She couldn't forget how he had deceived her for so long by not telling her about his wife, just as he had also deceived Daphne. And now he was making it all sound so sordid – detectives, evidence, the fellow across the landing . . . And that was just what she, Rosie, was, she thought bitterly; she was the girl in the bed-sit.

When he had gone Rosie stared around the room thinking again how squalid it all seemed to her now. She decided that once the term ended, in a fortnight's time, she would not be coming back here. She wasn't quite sure what she would do; she only knew that she couldn't wait to get back home to Castleburn. Then, she might be able to come to some decision, to sort out the mess and muddle that her mind was in at the moment.

Patsy's words had affected Rosie deeply, and she couldn't stop thinking about them. She had known that her sister was being peevish and spiteful – uncharacteristically so, but then, Rosie supposed, she did have cause – but there was a good deal of truth, nevertheless, in Patsy's outburst. Rosie was a flirt, she did enjoy the company of men, and she was doing so more and more as she got older. She was, in fact, a good deal like her mother – her real mother, Daisy White.

Rosie had sensed immediately that Neil Emmerson was interested in her and knew now, to her shame, that she had gone out of her way to encourage him. Even though she had also known, in spite of Patsy's protestations that she no longer cared, that her sister was still keen on him. It had seemed to be fun at the time, a good laugh, to see Neil hanging on her every word and to know, when he walked her home after the dance, that he was simply longing to make love to her. She had scotched that idea though – that would have been going a bit far with someone she had only just met – just as she had resisted his amorous advances the next day on the hills above Ilkley. She had been tempted though. And now she had hurt Patsy and knew that, though they might pretend otherwise, relations between the two of them were still very strained.

Rosie hadn't wanted to spend Sunday afternoon in the company of a crowd of girls, trailing round a stately home, and it hadn't taken much persuasion for her to abandon the idea and go off with Neil. That had been much more fun. Men were more fun than women, she had always thought so. But Jeff had been more than good fun . . . She had loved Jeff. She knew that she loved him still. And she knew that the real reason she had gone so willingly with Neil was because she was trying to forget Jeff Burroni . . . and she couldn't.

Rosie flung herself on the divan and gazed up at the ceiling, at the crack that resembled the map of Italy and at the sky in the rectangle of skylight, still blue at nine o'clock in the evening. Oh God, what a mess it all was! But she had only two more weeks to endure at college and here, in this lonely flat; she had already packed in her job at Lyon's because of pressure of work. Then she could say goodbye to it all. It was ironic how it had all turned sour on her – the excitement of having a place of her own, the thrill of living in the big city, the varied aspects of the course that had so enthralled her at first. And all because of a man.

She was still not sure, two weeks later, when she bundled all her belongings into two bulging suitcases – so heavy she could hardly lift them – what she had in mind. If she were to abandon her course after only one year her mother and father would be so disappointed. And rightly so too. They had done all they could, especially Jenny, to ensure that she had had her own way in coming to London. She had already given up her flat so would need somewhere else to live, always supposing that she came back to London. She could hardly, in all fairness, descend on Joan and Bernard Carstairs in Finchley again. She already felt guilty that she had seen so little of them since the course got under way and she had found her own flat. And – most importantly – if she gave up her training partway through she would not be able to get such a good job, or to pursue her dream of eventually going into textile design. Her head was reeling with it all. And it was all because of Jeff Burroni, damn him to hell and back!

But the main thing now was to get home to Castleburn. Rosie picked up the antiquated phone on the landing, for what she knew would be the last time, and rang for a taxi to take her to the station.

Rosie was relieved to be home a couple of days before Patsy. It was a breathing space before what she felt might be an awkward meeting. She said nothing to her mother about giving up her flat or, obviously, about abandoning her training. Or about the end of her love affair. Jenny had never known, anyway, how serious it was, still believing it to have been a friendship with one of the college tutors, a prestige thing which had impressed her when she had first heard of it. It was strange, then, that her mother didn't ask her about it, or pass any comment about the vast amount of luggage that Rosie had brought home. But Jenny had her own interests these days and was therefore no longer so obsessed with the doings of her family. Three mornings a week she dashed off to Mr Fothergill's antique shop, looking bright and attractive and much younger, Rosie thought, in her pretty summer dresses. She took a turn, too, on the market stall on an occasional Saturday, she had told Rosie, obviously thrilled to bits at the whole venture.

Jenny put down her breakfast cup with a loud clatter and turned a startled look on Rosie when she heard what the girl was saying. Rosie had chosen her moment well. It was the morning after she had returned home and she and her mother were enjoying a leisurely second cup of coffee. Victor had gone to school – they had not yet broken up – and Tom had gone to work, and it was a morning when Jenny was not at the shop.

'I want you to tell me about my natural mother,' Rosie had said, looking directly at Jenny. 'About Daisy White.'

'Good gracious, Rosie! Whatever for?' Jenny looked alarmed out of all proportion; surely it wasn't such an unusual request? 'You haven't mentioned her for years. Whatever's made you think about her, all of a sudden?'

'Just because I haven't mentioned her, it doesn't mean that I don't think about her,' replied Rosie evenly. Then, seeing Jenny's anxious, almost hurt, expression she added, 'Look . . . you're my mum. You have been for years and years, but it wouldn't be natural if I didn't think about her – about Daisy White – sometimes.'

'But – why now, Rosie?'

'Oh, it was just something that came into my mind,' Rosie replied casually. Not for the world would she reveal to Jenny what Patsy had said in a moment of anger, how the two of them had quarrelled. 'I want to know, Mum. Tell me, was she a prostitute?'

Jenny's mouth dropped open with shock and she didn't

reply. But that was all the answer that Rosie needed.

'She was, wasn't she? I think I've always known that she was. I remember, you see, the men coming to our house, all the "uncles" I had.'

'Rosie . . . Rosie love, don't start upsetting yourself.' Jenny had found her voice at last. 'I met your . . . your mother a few times during the war. She was a lovely person – she really was – very pretty and jolly. And very kind, too. Try not to condemn her too harshly. Times were hard, Rosie. She was all on her own with you. She had you to support.'

'So she did . . . entertain men?'

'I don't know, Rosie. I don't honestly know.' Jenny sighed. 'She was in Liverpool, and we were in Blackpool. I don't know what went on. How could I?'

'But you guessed, didn't you? You were able to draw your own conclusions. You must have done.'

'Only from the little bits you had told me yourself, love. About you having no daddy and about your mum working at the pub. You know how kiddies chatter, and you were always a little chatter-box.' Jenny looked at her fondly. 'Don't go torturing yourself, Rosie. It's no use. It's all so long ago. She was a good mother in her own way, I'm sure. And now you've got us – me and your dad.'

'And what about my father? My real one, I mean,' said Rosie. 'Did you never know? When you adopted me, did they never tell you?'

'No . . . it was all pretty straightforward. Your mother had been killed in the air-raid, and there was never any mention of your father. We never knew who he was.'

'No,' said Rosie slowly. 'Neither did I. I never knew him.'

'Now don't worry any more about it, love.' Jenny looked at her pleadingly. 'Promise me you won't. Tom's your father now, isn't he? And he loves you just as much as he loves the others . . . like I do,' she added quietly.

'All right, Mum,' said Rosie. 'I won't worry about it. I promise. I just wondered, that's all. It was something that I just happened to think about.'

Jenny looked at her levelly for a few seconds, then changed the subject. 'And what are you going to do for the holidays? You'll be finding a little job, I suppose?' Her voice still sounded strained. 'A few of the cafes have vacancies, I see. Or have you had enough of that, working at Lyon's?'

'No, I don't think so. It's what I'm used to. I might try Pickersgill's in the square, see if they want any waitresses. I'll find something, Mum.'

Rosie was taken on later that day at Pickersgill's, the cafe in the Market Square, an 'olde-worlde' place, very different from Lyon's, which specialised in home-made cakes and pastries, elegantly served on flowered china and crisp white tablecloths. Rosie's stint at Lyon's stood her in good stead and they were pleased to employ her for a few hours a day for the next few weeks.

She had promised Jenny that she wouldn't worry about what had happened in the past, about her mother's dubious goings-on and her unknown father, but it didn't stop her from thinking. Patsy's words had been the catalyst, planting the germ of the idea in her mind, and now she couldn't rid herself of it. She feared, as her sister had taunted her, that she was like her mother. She liked men; she enjoyed their company, basked in their admiration, and couldn't help leading them on when she saw their appreciative glances. But she had, so far, only given herself wholly in love to one man. Surely, she asked herself, she couldn't be the brazen tart that her sister had made her out to be?

Maybe, though, her interest in men had been precipitated by her lack of a father. Patsy was right in saying that she had made a fuss of Tom. It had been wonderful, after so long without one, to have a dad to run to, to climb on his knee and feel his strong arms around her. Although Tom, cautious and reticent, had not been the most affectionate of fathers. Rosie brooded about her real father. Who was he, where was he, had she inherited any of his characteristics? Environment, she knew, played a large part in a child's make-up and she had been with Tom and Jenny a long time now. But heredity, too, must count for something. Rosie already suspected, to her chagrin, that she might be more than a little like her mother. She wondered if she was also like her father?

She thought about this unknown person a lot over the next few weeks as she waited at the tables, serving teas and coffees, sandwiches and ice-cream sundaes and fancy cakes. At home in the evenings she looked at Tom, reading his newspaper and smoking his pipe, and at Jenny, busy with her sewing or knitting. And Rosie sometimes felt, for the first time since she had known them, that she wasn't sure that she belonged. Part of her did, but part of her was elsewhere. But where?

Chapter 17

'What do you mean, Patsy, you're going to Blackpool for the holiday? You've only just come home.' Jenny frowned slightly at her daughter and her voice was a shade resentful. 'We see little enough of you as it is. I should've thought you'd have been glad to have a few weeks at home.'

'I've got to have a job for the holidays, Mum. You know as well as I do that the money will be useful.'

'We're not exactly penniless, Patsy.' Jenny sounded aggrieved. 'Your dad and I can manage to support you. We've been doing so for the last nineteen years and I'm sure we can do it for another year, until you start working properly. Until you become a teacher,' she added with that smug edge to her voice and the self-satisfied smile which so annoyed her daughter. Though why exactly it should annoy her so much Patsy wasn't sure.

'Well, I want a job, apart from the money,' Patsy persisted. 'Nearly all students work now, during the holidays, and I can't stick around here all summer kicking my heels. I'd be bored to tears.'

'I thought you'd some work to do, some compositions to write.'

'Essays, Mum. They call them essays. And theses – those are the very long ones. Yes, I've some work to do on my thesis on Thomas Hardy, but it doesn't have to be handed in till next spring; there's plenty of time. And I can study just as well in Blackpool as I could here. There's a very good reference library there.'

'I thought the idea was to work at the boarding house.' Jenny scoured the inside of the milk pan with more force than was necessary, not looking at Patsy. 'If you're going to spend your time studying, you might just as well stay here.'

'I won't be working all the time, will I?' replied Patsy, a trifle irritably. It was always the same. When she had been at home with her mother for more than a few hours they started niggling at one another. She had come home only yesterday and already, washing up the breakfast pots, the two of them were at it again, hammer and tongs. 'I should imagine Grandma will give me some time off. Well, I know she will. We've arranged that I shall work mornings and meal-times, and the rest of the time I'll be free. And she's paying me the same rate as she pays the other girls who work there.'

'Hmmm . . . you've got it all cut and dried between you, haven't you?' Jenny's mouth closed in a thin line and she nodded at her daughter with more than a touch of pique. 'And I've only just heard about it. I must say, I think you've been deceitful, Patsy, not telling me about it before. And my mother, too. Making all these plans behind my back.'

'Well, that's a bit rich, Mum, coming from you.' Patsy glared indignantly at her mother. 'What about you, pinching my job as soon as my back was turned?'

'Oh, don't be so melodramatic, Patsy! Of course I didn't pinch your job. What nonsense you talk.'

'Well, what do you call it then? I'd have been working at Mr Fothergill's this summer if you hadn't gone and stolen a march on me. I couldn't believe it when you wrote and told me.'

'But I did tell you, didn't I, Patsy? You knew about it nearly as soon as I did. Anyway, it's only three mornings a week. Mr Fothergill doesn't need somebody there all the time, so I hardly think it would have done for you this holiday. But you could find a job in Castleburn quite easily without going tearing off to Blackpool. There's Woolworth's, and there's quite a few cafes, like that one that Rosie's working at. I don't see why you can't stay here.'

Patsy shrugged. 'Nearly all the jobs'll have gone by now. Rosie started work a couple of days ago, didn't she? And the schools break up soon. I daresay a lot of the jobs'll have been bagged in advance by the sixth formers.'

'And what's gone wrong between you and Rosie, anyway?' Jenny looked shrewdly at her daughter. 'You've hardly said two words to one another since you came home. I should've thought the pair of you would want to spend your holidays together, seeing that you're apart so much. What's up?'

'There's nothing up.' Patsy looked apprehensively at her mother. 'Why? What did Rosie say? Did she say there was something wrong?'

'No . . . she didn't,' Jenny replied slowly. 'Not about you and her, at any rate. I just thought you seemed quiet with one another, that's all.'

'I daresay it's because we've both got new friends now, Mum,' Patsy replied casually. 'It takes a bit of getting used to, being together again.' She smiled at her mother, feeling relieved that Rosie hadn't blabbed about their quarrel and the awful things that she, Patsy, had said. She was sorry, now, about the way she had gone on at Rosie, but she hadn't broached the subject since she came home. It seemed wiser to let sleeping dogs lie. 'I'm sorry I didn't tell you about Blackpool,' she went on. 'I really didn't think you'd mind. And I'm not going for a couple of weeks yet. Not until just before August Bank Holiday, so it'll give me some time at home. I'll be able to do some work first, and look up a few of my old school friends.'

'How's Gwen?' asked Jenny, her good humour obviously restored. 'Your college mother. Will you be seeing her at all?'

'Yes, I expect I will, occasionally,' Patsy replied. 'She's got a job in a village just outside York, so she'll be living at home. She wasn't nearly so snooty, Mum, once I got to know her. I got on very well with her.'

'Hmm . . . She looked down her nose at us though, me and your dad,' said Jenny tightly. 'She thought she was it, did that one, but perhaps it was just an act she put on. I'm glad you managed to get on with her, Patsy. It takes all sorts to make a world, as the saying goes. You say Gwen's got a job near home? That's nice for her. What about you, love? Have you thought what you'll do, when you become a teacher?' Again, the slightly smug smile, but Patsy decided that she mustn't let it annoy her this time. 'D'you think you'll try to get a job here, in Castleburn?'

Patsy, to her surprise, didn't know how to answer her mother. It seemed ridiculous, but she had given very little thought to what would happen after she qualified; whether she would teach in her own town, or try to find a post – and somewhere to live – elsewhere. The main thing had been to get through the course, the three teaching practices and the exams, to become a teacher, to please her mother . . . She had barely considered what would happen afterwards.

'I might, Mum,' she answered now. 'There are some

good schools in Castleburn and round about. But it's early days yet. They don't start talking about jobs until next spring. That's when the adverts start coming in for vacant posts. There's plenty of time.'

'It would be nice if you could live at home,' said Jenny musingly, smiling at her daughter. 'And cheaper for you as well, instead of living in digs. And you'll find you're tired at first, I daresay, settling into a new job. Yes, it would be much better if you could get a job in Castleburn and live at home.'

Patsy felt a stab of foreboding, both at the thought of living at home again – she was just getting used to her freedom – and at the thought of becoming a real teacher. School Practice, what you might call playing at it, was all very well, but as for the real thing . . . Patsy often trembled at the very idea of it. And her mother seemed to have got it all worked out. She would get a job in Castleburn, she would live at home . . . Patsy was damned if she was going to have her life mapped out for her in this way, but she bit her tongue and smiled disarmingly enough at her mother. They had done quite enough bickering for one day.

'Let's leave it for the moment, shall we, Mum?' she said. 'I daresay things'll work out. You were talking about Gwen, my college mother. Well, I've got a college daughter now, believe it or not. She lives in Blackpool, so that's another reason I wanted to go there this summer, so I can meet her.'

'Well, fancy that,' said Jenny. 'You a mother already. A college mother, I mean,' she laughed, 'not a real one. I don't want any grandchildren yet, thank you very much. What's she called? And whereabouts does she live in Blackpool?'

'She's called Hilary Schofield, and she lives at Layton,

not all that far from Gran's, so I'll be able to go and see her. Like Gwen came to see me. You don't feel quite so strange when you arrive at college if you know somebody who's there already.'

'Yes, it's a good idea, love.' Jenny wiped her hands on a towel and smoothed down her apron. 'Now, what are you going to do today? I should get out into the nice sunshine, if I were you. Get some roses back into your cheeks. You're looking a bit peaky, Patsy. All that poring over books, I daresay. Off you go now and get some fresh air.'

As though I'm a child being sent out to play with her skipping rope, thought Patsy, as she combed her hair and draped her yellow cardigan over her shoulders. But it was just Mum's way, to treat her as though she was still a little girl. She had always done so, and it seemed impossible for her to get out of the habit now. It was maddening, though, that she didn't treat Rosie in the same way. Mum and Rosie always seemed to be such good friends, more like sisters than mother and daughter. Patsy felt a pang of resentment, then of guilt, as she remembered the awful things she had said to Rosie about her real mother. She decided she would call into Pickersgill's cafe later that morning and have a cup of coffee, exchange a few words with Rosie and prove there was no ill will between them. Patsy made up her mind, too, that she would be more tolerant towards her mother and make a determined effort not to rile her. And now there was, as Mum had said, the nice sunshine to enjoy and the heady freedom of the first day of the holiday.

Castleburn was becoming a thriving little tourist centre, often referred to on railway posters and in guide books as 'The Gateway to the Dales'. On a summer's day, such as today, the narrow streets of the market town were busy more with visitors than with residents. Women in cotton frocks and cardigans and low-heeled sandals, and men in open-neck shirts and flannels. And, of course, the hikers; men and women of all ages and shapes and sizes, but all clad in windjammers, thick socks and heavy-soled boots, with bulging rucksacks slung across their shoulders.

A few shops in the town now sold hiking equipment and clothing: heavy-knit sweaters, boots and pure wool socks, maps and guide books, as well as ropes and ice-axes, although the nearest mountains were quite a long way north, in the Lake District. Then there were the souvenir shops which sold all manner of odds and ends, emblazoned with 'A Present from Castleburn'; tea towels, mugs, ashtrays, vases; revolving racks of postcards, too, and framed prints of scenic views of the river, castle, Cistercian Abbey and market square.

Patsy wandered contentedly along, looking into the windows of the shops that edged two sides of the square. On the other two sides were the fourteenth-century castle which gave the town its name, and the parish church of All Saints with its square Norman tower, which Patsy and Rosie had attended until they went away to college. The cobbled market square was rapidly filling up with cars – there was no market today – some of red and blue, even yellow, Patsy noticed with interest, as well as the more conventional black. Interesting shapes, too, although Patsy had no idea of their make; to her they were just cars. Her father, like many men of his generation, had never owned a car and never learned to drive, so Patsy had grown up largely in ignorance of this form of transport. She and Rosie, and Victor too, had had bikes – they were still there in the shed in the back garden, but pretty well discarded now as far as the girls were concerned – otherwise they had used buses and trains for longer journeys. Patsy could count on the fingers of one hand the times she had travelled in a car, apart from the odd taxi to and from the station.

The shops, to Patsy's eyes, now appeared somewhat old-fashioned, compared with the more stylish displays she was used to seeing in the windows of the stores in Leeford. Cotton dresses of indeterminate style and colour hanging limply from full-busted dummies; outmoded shoes with cuban heels and high fronts; lisle stockings, lock-knit underslips and knickers, and pink corsets, stiffly boned with dozens of hooks and eyes. Patsy suppressed a smile, trying to imagine herself – or anyone of her acquaintance, for that matter – wearing such garments. Grandma in Blackpool, maybe?

Her steps took her, as she had known all along they would, to Fothergill's antique shop. This was not one of the mornings that her mother was working there; if it had been Patsy felt that she would have given the place a wide berth. She stared wistfully at the display in the window, silver, brassware, glass and china, which was pretty much the same as it had been when she worked there. Antique shops didn't change their displays as regularly as did the more modern establishments, but there were one or two differences. A collection of Coronation souvenirs for the present Queen, for instance – up-to-the-minute pieces, these, certainly not antiques – right at the front of the window.

Patsy peered through the door, between the notices for church jumble sales, amateur dramatic performances and village fetes, into the dark interior of the shop. It was empty, Mr Fothergill, no doubt, busy at the back. Patsy couldn't resist pushing open the door, delighted to hear the familiar ping of the bell as she stepped over the threshold.

'Patsy, my dear, I'm delighted to see you. Delighted.' Eustace Fothergill beamed at her through his thick-lensed spectacles as he rocked back and forth on his tiny feet. 'Home from college, are you? Your mother was telling me how she was looking forward to having you home.'

'Yes, but not for long, Mr Fothergill,' Patsy replied. 'I'm going to Blackpool soon to work in my gran's boarding house.'

'Blackpool, eh?' Mr Fothergill raised his eyebrows. 'You'll have a rare old time there, I shouldn't wonder. Up the Tower and along the Golden Mile. Yes, you'll have a rare old time.'

Patsy smiled. 'I'm going to work, not to hit the high spots. I've got to earn some money, you know.'

'Yes, of course. Work . . . I'm sorry I couldn't fit you in here, my dear, but I don't need another assistant now, as you know. It's a pity though. A real pity. You had this job at your finger tips. You did that, at your finger tips. You were getting to be a real expert at the business by the time you went off to college. But it's a schoolteacher you're going to be, isn't it, my dear? And your mum's so proud of you. She is that.'

Patsy didn't answer. She just looked longingly at the familiar surroundings: the glowing patina of the rosewood chiffonier at the back of the shop; the rows of warming pans, horse-brasses and toasting forks; the clocks – large and small, wooden and gilt and marble – ticking away quietly in a corner.

'These are a new venture, aren't they?' she said after a moment or two, pointing to some Coronation mugs, similar to the ones in the window, depicting the newly crowned Queen. 'Not antiques though, are they? They were only made this year.'

'You sound as though you disapprove, my dear,' said Mr Fothergill. His glasses had slid to the end of his nose and his short-sighted eyes were peering at her over the top of them. He was still smiling though. 'No, you're quite right, Patsy. Quite right.' He pushed his spectacles back with his forefinger. 'They're new pieces, but quite beautiful some of them, I think. Just look at the gilding on that one and the lovely portrait of the Queen. And that one with the flowers of the realm – roses, daffodils, thistles, shamrocks . . . quite beautiful.

'And this business is mainly about making money, when all's said and done. Every business is, my dear. We've all got to find ways of earning an extra bit of brass. So I wasn't going to turn up my nose at the idea when the traveller asked me if I was interested in stocking them, even though it's primarily an antique shop. And they've gone very well, I must admit. Very well indeed.'

Patsy nodded, carefully picking up one of the more sturdy-looking pieces, a white jam-pot in the shape of a plump cushion with a purple crown on the top. She turned it over in her hands. 'Wedgwood? Yes, I thought it was. It has the look of their pottery about it.'

'You know your onions all right, young woman,' said Mr Fothergill, beaming at her. 'I always said you did. Yes, you know your onions.'

'You think it's a good idea then?' Patsy went on. 'Combining the old with the new? It works all right, does it?'

'It seems to,' replied Mr Fothergill. 'As a matter of fact, this was an idea of your mother's, stocking the Coronation ware. The traveller called when I was out and it was Jenny who persuaded me that it might be a good idea. And she was right, I must admit.'

Patsy bit the inside of her lip, feeling a trifle peeved that her mother was making her presence felt here, in what had once been Patsy's domain. But she smiled pleasantly enough at Mr Fothergill. 'Good,' she said brightly. 'Mum says she enjoys working here.'

'She seems to, Patsy. She's a great help to me when I have to go out to auctions and suchlike.' Mr Fothergill rocked on his feet, leaning closer. 'She's almost as good as you. Almost . . . but not quite.' He nodded confidentially, lowering his voice. 'She's not got your flair with the lovely old pieces, arranging them nicely and all that. But don't tell her I told you so.' He lifted an admonitory finger. 'Don't tell her. That's between you and me. She's settled in very nicely has Jenny, and I'm very grateful to her, stepping into your shoes as you might say. Besides, you've got more important things to do, haven't you, my dear? We'll all be bowing and scraping to you when you're headmistress of Moor Lane Primary School.' He laughed and shook his head, looking at her fondly.

Patsy smiled back at him, feeling suddenly gratified, not at his remark about her being a headmistress – heaven forbid! – but at his favourable comparison of her abilities with those of her mother.

The bell on the door rang as a middle-aged woman, a prospective customer, walked in, and Patsy knew she mustn't hinder Mr Fothergill. As he told her, he had a living to make.

She said her goodbyes and stepped out of the dimness of the shop into a pool of brilliant sunshine. She blinked at the brightness, feeling the warmth of the sun on her bare arms and legs. It was a glorious day, a day for putting an end to discord. She made her way through the parked cars to the other side of the market square, to Pickersgill's cafe.

Rosie, wearing a pink and white flowered frilly apron – very 'un-Rosie-like' – over her own black skirt and white blouse, came over to her table in the corner.

'Good morning, Madam. What can I do for you?' She stood with her tiny pencil poised over her pad, smiling at her sister. But her eyes were wary; there was still a vestige of unease between them.

Patsy smiled back uncertainly. 'A cup of coffee, please, my dear,' she said, inclining her head and speaking in mock-refined tones. Then, more normally, 'That's if you think I can afford it. Or does it cost an arm and a leg in this place?'

'I think you might just about manage it,' said Rosie evenly. 'But it's a pot here, not a cup. A pot of coffee. I'll be with you in a minute.'

'It's a bit different from Gino's,' Patsy remarked a few moments later as Rosie returned with her order on a polished wooden tray: a small silver pot of coffee, a minute jug of cream and a china cup and saucer patterned with pink roses. She looked at the oak-panelled walls, the crisp white tablecloths and little vases of fresh flowers – sweet peas, carnations and pinks – on every table. She laughed, a trifle embarrassed, as Rosie placed the china in front of her. 'Different from Lyon's, too, isn't it, Rosie?'

'You could say that.' Rosie nodded, off-handedly, her sister thought. 'Look, kid, I can't stand here chatting, much as I'd like to.' She didn't sound as though she would like to at all. 'Some of us have work to do. I'll see you later.'

The coffee was delicious and the surroundings, though they were what Patsy would term posh, intimate and friendly. But Patsy felt deflated as she paid for her order at the cash desk at the counter – the shop also sold a variety of cakes to take out, and expensive chocolates – and walked out once more into the sunshine. Rosie hadn't come across to talk to her again, but she was, Patsy had to admit, busy with customers elsewhere in the cafe.

There was an uneasy truce between the sisters, but things were still far from right and Patsy knew that, for the moment, she could do no more. She was relieved more than ever now that she had decided to spend most of her summer holiday in Blackpool. The time for her departure couldn't come soon enough.

The weather was set fair at the start of the Bank Holiday weekend, when Patsy alighted from the train at Blackpool North Station, with the promise of more sunshine to come. The station was a hive of activity already on this Friday afternoon, although it was on the following day that the hordes of visitors would arrive. Saturday was traditionally 'change-over' day, with one lot of visitors departing and another lot arriving, with Bank Holiday weekend, the first weekend in August, the busiest of all.

When she was away from the seaside Patsy forgot, by and large, about Blackpool; its crowds, its bustle and noise, its flamboyance and friendliness . . . its uniqueness. But the moment she walked out of the station a wave of nostalgia engulfed her and the memories came flooding back. There were so many remembrances of the place, mostly connected with her childhood and the war-time years. She remembered when Blackpool had been a sea of airforce blue, a houseful of the recruits billeted at her grandma's. But the war had by no means curtailed all the childhood pleasures. There had been outings to the beach, paddling and making sand castles; rides on the back of the wooden elephant at the Boating Pool at North Shore; trips to Fairyland on Central Beach, and – occasionally – to the Pleasure Beach. Yes, there were so many happy memories, all tied up with Grandma and Auntie Violet, Auntie Ada and Uncle Fred, Ronnie and Raymond Sykes . . . and Rosie. Always there had been Rosie.

It wasn't very far from North Station to Annie Carter's boarding house, just a ten-minute walk along Dickson Road and then round the corner, but much too far to walk with a heavy suitcase. Patsy stood on the forecourt of the station waiting her turn for a taxi and reading the posters on the station wall. Harry Secombe and Eve Boswell were appearing at the Opera House, and Arthur Askey and his daughter Anthea and Thora Hird at the Grand Theatre, in a farcical play called *The Love Match*. It was Blackpool's proud boast that they had the best seasonal shows of any seaside resort and were able to attract many of the big stars.

Dickson Road, as Patsy rode along in the taxi, was busy with holidaymakers returning from the sands. Perspiring, red-faced fathers with open-necked shirts and white pumps, mothers in sun-dresses, many with red shoulders and angry red vees at the neck, and children carrying buckets and dragging metal spades along the pavement. Brightly coloured beach balls and towels, straw hats and sunglasses and fishing nets hung in shop doorways, and on the pavement outside visitors pored over racks of post-cards depicting fat women and tiny hen-pecked husbands.

It was great to see Gran again, so little changed from how she had looked at New Year – Patsy hadn't seen her since then – and Aunt Ada too. They were both taking a well-deserved 'five minutes' when Patsy arrived, cups of tea balanced on their laps, as they sat in the kitchen, the living room of the house, one room where visitors were not welcomed. Gran's bunions, making a pronounced bulge in her old black shoes, were obviously 'giving her jip', as she would say. Patsy could tell by the way she winced when she got up to give her granddaughter a hug and a kiss on the cheek. Patsy thought how hard it must be for a woman of Gran's age – seventyish – standing for long hours at the kitchen stove and sink. But Annie Carter always maintained she would work until they had to carry her out, and her family knew there was no point in arguing with her. And Aunt Ada had been a godsend to the boarding house since she had gone into partnership with Annie after the war.

'I was just taking the weight off me old feet for a minute or two,' said Annie, collapsing gratefully once more into the shabby fireside chair. 'The teas are all ready, and they'll all be traipsing back in ten minutes or so.'

Patsy had glimpsed through the dining-room window, as she waited for one of the young helpers to answer her knock, evidence of high tea awaiting the visitors. Plates of boiled ham, thickly cut, with salad and beetroot at the side, were already laid on the tables, as was the custom when it was a cold meal. In the centre of each table was a three-tiered stand with plates of bread and butter, scones, and homemade cakes – Annie's special iced sponges, maids of honour and Eccles cakes.

'Now, tell us all your news. How's your mam and dad and Victor? And how are you going on at that there college? Enjoying it, are you?' Annie's eyes were shrewd as she listened to Patsy's cautious answer that she was enjoying it very much. Gran, she knew, was not a great believer in 'all that book learning for girls'. But Patsy didn't tell her gran how she really felt about the place. To be truthful her feelings were still ambivalent; she knew it was a relief to be away from it for a few weeks.

Gran, she noticed, hadn't enquired about Rosie. Though she had never said so openly, the girl was not a great favourite with Annie Carter. Patsy recalled her grandma saying years ago to her mother that Rosie had 'too much off for a young 'un'. That had been one of the occasions when she, Patsy, shouldn't have been listening, she remembered with a twinge of guilt. It was Aunt Ada who asked about Rosie and it was obvious that she at least was very fond of her adoptive niece.

'It 'ud be nice for the pair of you to see one another again, wouldn't it?' said Aunt Ada. 'You were always such good pals.' Patsy smiled and nodded her agreement without actually answering. 'Has she still got that young man of hers, down in London? That teacher fellow?'

'You know about him then, do you?' said Patsy guardedly.

'Yes, she was telling me about him at New Year. She seemed proper smitten with him.'

'No . . . I'm afraid it's all over between Rosie and Jeff,' said Patsy. 'She isn't seeing him now.'

'Oh, deary me! She will be upset, won't she? Whatever's gone wrong?'

'I really don't know, Auntie Ada,' said Patsy evenly. 'I just know that they're not friendly any more. And – yes – she was rather upset.' Patsy knew that she must keep quiet about the reason for the rift between her sister and Jeff. Rosie had accused her, when they had had that awful row, of being a sneak, a 'nosy little tell-tale'. Patsy felt herself going all hot at the shameful remembrance of this and she certainly didn't want to give Rosie any more reason to condemn her.

'Do you want me to help with the teas?' she asked now, changing the subject. 'I can clear away when they've finished, help to wash up, anything you like.'

'No, tomorrow'll do, lass,' said Annie. 'Just get settled in today, then you can start your chores tomorrow. It'll be all hands on deck then, I can tell you, ready for t'big weekend.'

Patsy smiled happily to herself as she put her clothes in the old oak wardrobe in the attic bedroom and arranged her make-up and brush and comb on the shabby dressing-table. This room, more of a lumber room than a bedroom, with piles of boxes in a corner and mattresses standing on their ends against the wall, was not deemed suitable for visitors. But Patsy was very glad to be here. She stood on tiptoe to see if she could catch a glimpse of the sea from the tiny window. No, all that was visible from here were grey slated roof tops and chimneys, and concrete backyards with washing lines and dustbins and lean-to sheds. The sea, though, was only five minutes' walk away and she would go there just as soon as she had had a cup of tea and something to eat.

Patsy crossed the tramtrack by the Carlton Hotel and walked across to the promenade railings. Here, at this part of North Shore, was the famous three-tier promenade. This, where Patsy was standing, was the upper promenade, where the gleaming tramtrack led all the way to Fleetwood in the north and Squire's Gate in the south. Below were the colonnades, with pillars reminiscent of a Greek temple, and below that the lower prom, where the waves oftentimes came cascading over the sea wall, drenching everything and everyone in their wake.

Although Patsy had been born here and was what they proudly termed in this area 'sand-grown', she had never got over her thrill at her first sight of the Irish Sea after months of being away from it. The sea was calm tonight, a gleaming stretch of iridescent turquoise, flecked here and there with silver and rosy pink where the setting sun cast its rays. The big orange ball of the sun was low in the sky now, gradually sinking towards the horizon where, on a very clear day, you could sometimes catch a glimpse of the Isle of Man. The glory of its sunsets, Patsy thought, must surely be one of the most striking features of Blackpool. The sky was deep blue after a perfect summer day, shot with orange and vermilion, with golden-tipped clouds like dark mysterious mountains.

Patsy found herself recalling her visit to the prom on New Year's Eve. Then she had stood with Ronnie near to North Pier, listening to the church bells welcoming in 1953 and feeling sad because she had known that, before long, the two of them must part. Now her friendship with Ronnie Sykes was a thing of the past. She had been devastated at first when they had parted and she still thought about him from time to time but a lot had happened since then and he was no longer at the forefront of her mind.

He was in her thoughts that evening though as she walked south towards North Pier, nearing the spot where they had seen in the New Year together. She thought at first that she was seeing things when she caught sight of the figure coming towards her. That tousled, mid-brown hair, rugged face and firm jawline – surely she must have conjured up the image because thoughts of him were in her mind? But as he drew closer she could see that he was real enough.

They both stood stock still, staring at one another, a look of incredulous delight on both their faces. Then Patsy noticed that this young man was slimmer, less robust, and over his left eyebrow there was a very faint blemish, which had been the only way, when they were children, of distinguishing one twin from the other.

'Patsy . . .'

'Raymond . . .' They both spoke together.

'How lovely to see you,' she said, because although she had in the beginning mistaken him for Ronnie it was, all the same, lovely to see his twin brother. 'Whatever are you doing here?'

Raymond laughed. 'I live here . . . remember? It's you that's the visitor, not me.'

He explained that he had been working late at the solicitor's office where he was employed and had decided to have a breath of fresh air before returning home, and Patsy explained that she was in Blackpool for the next few weeks, working at her gran's. They leaned against the promenade railings chatting like old friends, which was, of course, what they were. She had known Raymond, as she had known his brother, since she was a little girl.

'So you had a row with our Ronnie then?' he asked. 'It's all over between you?'

'Sort of,' said Patsy. 'More of a misunderstanding really. I thought he hadn't written . . . but he had. But I never got the letter. Then I started seeing somebody else, so – yes – it's all over.'

'He's seeing somebody else, too,' said Raymond.

'What?' gasped Patsy, in surprise. 'Who? What d'you mean?'

'Our Ronnie. He's got a girlfriend in Germany. One of the local girls. Ingrid, she's called. His letters are full of her.'

'Oh . . . I see.' Patsy couldn't understand why she should feel so shocked. After all, she had gone out with Neil, hadn't she? Pretty nearly broken her heart over him as well. She tried to smile. 'I didn't know. But then I wouldn't, would I?'

'Not that he writes home all that much,' Raymond continued. 'Our kid's not much of a letter writer, but he always mentions this Ingrid. She's a nurse at the local hospital.'

'Oh . . . I see,' said Patsy again.

'You're not bothered, are you?'

'No, why should I be?' She grinned at him, trying to hide the hurt in her voice.

'That's good.' Raymond grinned back and she thought how much like his brother he was. The same grey eyes, clear and candid, but more serious. 'Come on. Let's go and have a coffee,' he said. 'It's getting a bit chilly.'

They crossed the tramtrack by the Tower and found a coffee bar near to Central Station. Patsy wasn't surprised when Raymond asked if he could see her again.

She saw a lot of him over the next few weeks and her first impression of Raymond – that he was more serious-minded than his brother – proved to be correct. When he was younger he had been the same happy-go-lucky clown that his brother had been; she guessed it might be his illness that had made him more introspective, although he seemed to be fully recovered now from his bout of tuberculosis. He was, in fact, as far as temperament was concerned, a lot like Patsy herself. Their taste in films was similar and they enjoyed together *The Quiet Man*, and *The Cruel Sea*, and Charlie Chaplin's latest and very different film, *Limelight*.

Raymond said that he didn't care much for seasonal shows – too frivolous for his liking, he maintained – but he agreed to accompany Patsy to a Sunday evening concert at the Palace Variety Theatre, by the Luton Girls' Choir. Patsy had heard their record of 'Count Your Blessings' many times on *Family Favourites*, and was delighted to be able to see them in the flesh. Ronnie, she felt sure, would not have been so amenable to listening to a choir of fresh-faced girls with crystal clear voices singing old-fashioned, sentimental – what he would have termed soppy – songs. As her mother was fond of saying, it took all sorts to make a world. Ronnie Sykes was one sort, but his twin brother Raymond was quite a different sort altogether. The sort though, Patsy couldn't help thinking, of whom her mother, this time, might approve . . .

Blackpool was agog that summer with a local murder which had hit the national headlines. Earlier that year the nation had been horrified by the series of murders in Rillington Place, by an insignificant little man called John Christie. And in Blackpool, Louisa Merrifield, a forty-eight-year-old housekeeper, had murdered her employer with rat poison and was sentenced to death at Manchester Assizes. Raymond, working in a solicitor's office, knew much of the inside story but, obviously well-trained, wouldn't divulge any details. But, like Patsy, he was appalled at hearing of the holidaymakers from 'Pleasant View' who took bus trips up Devonshire Road to stare at the bungalow where the deed had been committed.

'Ghouls, that's what they are, Patsy,' he declared. 'There's a macabre side to human nature that I can't understand at times.'

And Patsy told him that her college daughter, Hilary, whom she had met recently, had seen Alfred Merrifield, the husband of the condemned woman, walking round Marks and Spencer as though he hadn't a care in the world. Hilary was working there for the season and reported that he frequently came into the shop, a dapper little man in his seventies, in a light suit and straw hat, seeming totally unconcerned that his wife was to be hanged on 18 September.

'Yes, he was released on the order of the Attorney General,' said Raymond. 'It appears that they could find no evidence against him. Forget about it, Patsy. It's morbid. Now, how much longer will you be here? You'll stay to see the Lights switched on, won't you?'

It had been a happy summer. Patsy had enjoyed the work at the boarding house; she had got on well with her daughter Hilary, an uncomplicated girl who was looking forward to her training; and an added bonus had been the agreeable and unexpected company of Raymond Sykes. She decided to stay and see the Lights switched on, on 9 September, then spend a few days in Castleburn before returning to college the following week.

As might be expected in this Coronation year, the Illuminations had a distinctly Royal flavour with tableaux of Merrie England and Queen Victoria on the cliffs at Bispham. The whole vista had been televised a few days previously, with the inimitable Richard Dimbleby, in an illuminated tram, providing the commentary. And now, on 9 September, an evening of black cloud and gale force winds, Patsy stood with Raymond amongst the crowds in Talbot Square, watching George Formby perform the 'switching on' ceremony. But before George appeared, Stan Mortensen, the popular and now famous footballer from Blackpool Football Club, led the community singing.

'We want Morty. We want Morty,' yelled the crowd, impatient to see their hero who had scored a hat-trick earlier that year in the FA match against Bolton and, together with Stanley Matthews, saved the day and won the coveted cup for Blackpool. The cheers when he appeared must have been heard, Patsy felt sure, as far away as Central Pier. Cheers which were repeated when, finally, George Formby appeared with his wide toothy grin and ukelele.

'It's turned out nice again,' he quipped, as the crowd roared their approval. Then they all joined in with him to sing 'I'm Twenty-one Today', because this was the twenty-first birthday of Blackpool's famous Illuminations.

When the crowd had dispersed Patsy strolled with Raymond on the middle promenade, near to the spot where, nine months earlier, she had stood with Ronnie. And there, for the first time – he was much more circumspect than his brother – Raymond drew her into the shadow of the colonnades and kissed her. His mouth was cold against her cheek, and then, a moment later, tender and inviting as he kissed her on the lips, lingeringly and fervently. Patsy felt herself responding to his embrace and enjoying it. She liked Raymond, she liked him a lot, and knew that he was, in many ways, a perfect complement to her. But she didn't experience the longing she had known when his brother had kissed her. Raymond didn't attempt to take their lovemaking any further. He kissed her a few times then walked her home.

'So this is goodbye then, Patsy?' he said, stopping by the gate of 'Pleasant View'. Occasionally he had come in for a cup of tea, but it was late now and Annie Carter would be preparing for bed. He had only ever come in, Patsy thought in amusement, when they had had a chaperone. No, Raymond was not like his brother . . . He looked at her quizzically. 'Will you write to me, Patsy? I'd like you to, please.'

'Yes, I'll write, Raymond,' she replied easily. 'When I have time. It will be a busy year for me. Final School Practice and exams and all that.'

His glance was appraising. 'You'll find time if you want to write, Patsy,' he said. He stooped and kissed her cheek briefly. ''Bye. It's been lovely having you here.'

'Goodbye, Raymond,' she replied. But she didn't feel the same sense of loss or loneliness as he walked away that she used to feel when she said goodbye to Ronnie.

Patsy called the next evening at the house in Raikes Parade to say goodbye to Aunt Ada. She gasped when her aunt led her into the small living room at the back of the house. There, seated by the fire in an easy chair, opposite Uncle Fred, was Rosie.

'Whatever are you doing here?' Patsy asked, only

realising afterwards how ungracious she sounded.

'Well, that's a fine greeting to your sister, I must say,' said Aunt Ada, but Patsy was relieved to see that her aunt was smiling. 'Anybody 'ud think you weren't pleased to see the lass.'

'Of course I am,' Patsy faltered. 'Of course I'm pleased. But it was such a surprise. I thought you were in Castleburn, Rosie. I didn't know . . .'

Rosie grinned secretively. 'I've a lot to tell you, Patsy,' she said. 'Such a lot.' Then she turned to Aunt Ada and a conspiratorial glance passed between the two of them, a glance that Patsy didn't altogether care for. 'Shall we tell her, Auntie?'

'Aye, I reckon we'd better let her in on it,' said Aunt Ada. 'Sit yourself down, Patsy. Rosie's got some news for you . . .'

Chapter 18

Jenny had not been totally surprised when Rosie told her what she intended to do. The girl had seemed odd – preoccupied and distant – for much of the holiday, unlike her usual cheerful, happy self, and even though she had promised her mother that she would not brood, Jenny felt that she knew what was troubling her adopted daughter.

'Oh, goodness, Tom! I wonder what's going to happen?' said Jenny now, for the umpteenth time. 'D'you think anything'll come of it? D'you think she'll be able to find out about . . . anything?'

It was the first week in September, and there had been a damp, chilly start to the month that would mark the end of summer and the start of autumn. Jenny usually loved autumn, a time of flickering firelight and curtains drawn early against the dusk, misty mornings, and glorious flaming colours in the woods and hedgerows. But this year she felt as though the end of summer was also bringing to an end a part of her life that had been filled with such happiness.

Rosie had brought her such joy, ever since she had first come to her as a little girl, at a time when Jenny had been experiencing heartache and loneliness and uncertainty. She had come to love the girl as much as she loved her own daughter and son; Rosie, indeed, in many ways was much easier to get along with than either Patsy or Victor. Now she feared that she was going to lose her, although Tom assured her time and again that it would not be so.

'Jenny . . . Jenny love, stop fretting,' he said now. 'I've told you, we'll never lose our Rosie, whatever happens. She's part of the family. D'you really think she'd want nothing more to do with us, even if . . .' He leaned forward, staring intently at his wife in the opposite fireside chair. 'Even if she found her real father? If you ask me, I think it's strange she's never thought about it before, a lively inquiring girl like Rosie.'

'But . . . don't you mind, Tom? Don't you feel hurt?'

'Aye, I reckon I do, a bit, if I'm honest,' he said. 'I've always done my best for her, but she's bound to be curious, Jenny. Just put yourself in her shoes. Wouldn't you be?'

Jenny nodded. 'I suppose I might. But I always thought she was so happy with us, Tom. She always seemed to be. She's such an uncomplicated sort of girl, friendly and easy-going. You wouldn't think that anything 'ud bother her like this seems to have done. If it had been our Patsy now, she's a different kettle of fish altogether. She's a deep one at times, is Patsy. I don't always know what's going on in that mind of hers.'

'Yes, I reckon our Patsy's a lot like me,' said Tom thoughtfully. 'Maybe that's why I find it hard to talk to her sometimes. It can be hard with your own . . .' He stared pensively into the fire. 'Rosie, though . . . She's been like a ray of sunshine, hasn't she, ever since she came to us?'

'She has. She certainly has.' Jenny's eyes filled up with tears. Tom had expressed her own feelings so exactly; it wasn't like him to be so poetic in his speech. 'And that's why I can't bear to think of losing her, Tom.'

'You'll not lose her, love,' he said quietly, 'no more than you'd lose any lass who goes to live away from home. And she'll get married in time; both of 'em will. You can't have 'em tied to your apron strings all their life. You know, Jenny . . .' Tom paused, looking at her steadily. 'I've never said this to you before, but don't you think you might possibly have made too much of the lass – Rosie, I mean – shown too much – well, favouritism?'

'I haven't, Tom,' replied Jenny hotly. 'How can you say that? I love them all the same, Patsy and Victor . . . and Rosie. What's made you say that? It's an awful thing to say.'

Tom smiled, a trifle sadly. 'I've seen a look in our Patsy's eyes, once or twice, as though she might be a bit – you know – jealous like. Happen we should both try a bit harder to show her that we think as much of her as we do of Rosie.'

'Patsy's harder to get on with, I must admit,' replied Jenny. 'She can be difficult at times. Yes, maybe you're right, Tom. I must admit I've always been able to talk to Rosie much more easily . . . and look where it's got me.' She spread her hands wide in a gesture of defeat. 'Still, I suppose all families have their ups and downs, and things have gone pretty easily for us most of the time, haven't they, since we moved to Castleburn? You've got to take the rough with the smooth . . . D'you think she'll find him though, Tom?' Jenny couldn't let the matter rest.

'There you go again.' He gave a little laugh. 'Stop worriting, Jenny. I daresay we'll hear from our Rosie in a day or two. She'll happen be writing to us from Liverpool. That's where she's gone, isn't it?'

'For a start, yes,' said Jenny flatly. 'She's gone to see Jean Williams, to see if the woman can give her any lead about who her . . . her father might be. You won't remember Mrs Williams, Tom. She's the mother of Ben, the evacuee who stayed with Eileen Sykes during the war. She lived in the same street as Rosie's . . . as Daisy White.'

'It's a long time ago, Jenny,' said Tom. 'Twenty years since Rosie was born. And there was never any talk of him when she was a child, was there?'

'It seems not,' replied Jenny. 'Like you say, Tom, it's a long time.' She smiled brightly at him. 'So what are we worrying about, eh?' But her smile didn't reach her eyes, and it certainly didn't reach her mind, which was filled with foreboding.

By the beginning of September Rosie had known that the uncertainty was driving her mad, and that she must do something, even if she was doomed to failure and disappointment, to put an end to the doubt and confusion in her mind. She had nearly three weeks' holiday left before she was due to return to the art school – something she had hardly given a thought to all summer – time enough, surely, to carry out her quest. She gave in her notice at the cafe and made her plans. It had been painful for her to see the hurt look on Mum's face – she had known that Mum wouldn't fully understand – when she told her. Dad had seemed much more resigned, his grey eyes kind and thoughtful, though possibly a shade sad, as he had said, 'You must do whatever you think best, lass, but don't forget that this is your home, with me and your mum.' As if she could ever forget, for one moment, Tom and Jenny and all they had meant to her for so long. But she had to know . . .

Jean Williams looked uncertainly at first at the girl standing on her doorstep. 'Good morning,' she said. 'Can I help you?' Her eyebrows were raised questioningly and there was no glimmer of recognition in her eyes.

Until Rosie spoke. 'Don't you remember me, Auntie Jean?' That was what she had called her when she and Ben had played together as children. And when they had boarded the train as evacuees it had been Auntie Jean who had been there to see them off. 'It's Rosie.'

'Rosie! Of course!' The older woman beamed as she recognised her. 'Well, what a surprise. And after all this time. It must be – what? – eight or nine years since I saw you. It was when I came to Blackpool to see our Ben towards the end of the war. I wouldn't have known you – well, I didn't at first, did I? But now I look at you I can see it's Rosie all right. Come on in, love. Don't stand on the doorstep.'

Jean Williams had always been one of the most house-proud of the women in that street of terraced houses, and it seemed as though she was still the same. And this was the first stroke of luck, finding that the family was still living in the same place, near the Liverpool docks, after all that time. The door opened straight off the street, and the steps and the flags outside were newly washed. Inside the house there was evidence of freshly decorated walls, and when Rosie was shown into the front room she noted, with some surprise, the modern coffee table and three-piece suite with spindly legs, and the geometric pattern of the curtains. Jean Williams was obviously keeping abreast of the times.

'We decided to stay here and do the place up, instead of moving,' Jean told her over a cup of tea. 'Bert's earning good money at the docks, but we were used to living here. And it's plenty big enough for us. Ben's away, of course, in the RAF.'

'I was going to ask about him,' said Rosie. 'I was forgetting. He'll be doing his National Service, won't he?'

'Yes, he's stationed in the Midlands. He was home last

weekend. It's a pity you've missed him.'

Rosie nodded, thinking that she must get round to the real reason for her visit. 'I'm certainly glad that you decided to stay here, and that I've been able to find you,' she said. 'I wondered if you might be able to help me . . . I'm looking for my father.'

'Your father?' Jean was quite obviously – and understandably – astonished. 'But you never had . . . you never knew your father.'

'No.' Rosie smiled wistfully. 'I never knew him. That's why I want to find him . . . now. You were going to say, weren't you, that I never had a father? I know what you mean – I never had one officially – but there must have been someone who fathered me. And I wondered if you might have any idea . . . who it was?'

Rosie thought how little changed Jean Williams looked. Small and neat with the same deep brown eyes that Ben had had. They were looking at her now in concern. She didn't answer Rosie's question directly. 'I knew your mother quite well,' she said softly. 'Daisy had a hard time.'

'I know about my mother,' Rosie answered flatly, staring fixedly at the cup in her lap. 'At least, I've guessed about her, from what I remember. What she did for a living . . . her gentlemen callers. You don't need to be afraid of upsetting me, Auntie Jean.'

'Daisy had a hard time,' Jean repeated. 'She was married very young, but he died . . .'

'He died?' Rosie's cup rattled in the saucer as she stared at Jean in alarm. She steadied it with a hand that was trembling slightly. 'My father's dead then? I never knew she was a widow. She never said.'

'No . . . no, that was before,' Jean went on to explain. 'Daisy was only seventeen when she came to live in this street – with Norman White. She was married to him, but he wasn't your father. Norman was a docker, like a lot of the fellows round here, but he wasn't a strong sort of a chap at all. Anyroad, like I was saying, he died of the 'flu – must have been the early thirties – and Daisy was left on her own. She did a lot of jobs to make ends meet, then she started working at the pub across the road. That was when she started . . . well, she had a few gentlemen friends, Rosie love, to put it kindly. That's all they were at first, just friends. But one thing led to another, and I can't say that anybody really blamed her.'

'But my father,' said Rosie quietly. 'You must have had some idea?'

'Well, of course we had. Or we thought we had. We all knew that Daisy was very friendly with Archie at the time. We always supposed that it might be him. But we never knew for certain.'

'Archie?' said Rosie, wondering at the unfamiliar name, one she had certainly never heard mentioned in her childhood. 'And what happened to him, this Archie?'

'Archie Thoroughgood,' said Jean. 'He had the pawnshop on the row next to the pub. Your mother was going around with him for quite a while. We all thought she'd end up marrying him, but he upped and went, it must have been – let me see – early in 1933. I can remember because it was the year I had my miscarriage.'

'And the year I was born,' said Rosie. She nodded thoughtfully. 'So he disappeared when he knew . . .'

'Oh no, nothing like that, love,' said Jean. 'I'm sure Archie never knew that Daisy was pregnant. I've told you he was called Archie Thoroughgood, and that's what he was, Rosie. A thoroughly good sort of chap. We all of us thought so, round here. Like I say, he had the pawnshop, and there's many a family in this neighbourhood who had reason to be grateful to him. He'd always be willing to stretch a point with folks who were down on their luck. No, I reckon he left because Daisy had him on a string, as you might say. She was a flighty little madam, I have to admit, and she'd one or two fellows on the go. I think Archie was hurt and a bit jealous at her goings-on – you couldn't blame him. Anyroad, he upped and left and we've never seen hair nor hide of him since.'

'And where did he go? Do you know?'

'I've heard tell that it was Preston way. I think he had some relatives there, but I'm not certain. Joe at the pub might be able to tell you – you remember Joe Latham, the landlord? He's still there, although he's getting on for retiring age now. I think he kept in touch with Archie for a while. But it's a long time ago, Rosie love.' Jean Williams sighed. 'A very long time.'

'Twenty years,' she replied. 'Perhaps not all that long, not when you compare it with a lifetime. You say Mr Latham's still at the pub, so maybe this . . . Archie has stayed in the same place as well? And you think it's possible he might be my father? You said that she – my mother – had a few others though, at the same time. Might there not be some . . . doubt?'

Jean looked at Rosie steadily, her brown eyes appraising her. 'I think it's more than likely that it was Archie Thoroughgood,' she said quietly. 'I always thought so, and now that I look at you . . .' She didn't finish the sentence.

'But why did my mother not want to marry him?' asked Rosie. 'You said she was having a struggle to make ends meet, and then with a baby – with me, I mean – on the way . . . ?'

'Who knows?' Jean shook her head. 'Daisy was always a law unto herself. She liked having a good time. And Archie was a lot older than she was. He'll be well into his sixties now, if he's still . . . if he's still in Preston.'

Rosie knew that Jean had been going to say 'if he's still alive'. But he must be, thought Rosie. He *had* to be, and she was going to find him.

'Come on, Rosie,' said Jean suddenly. 'If you've finished your tea we'll go across and have a word with Joe Latham. The pub'll be just about closing now for the afternoon. He'll be surprised, I don't doubt, but if anybody can help you it'll be Joe.'

Rosie hadn't seen much of the inside of The Jolly Roger as a child, but she had spent many long summer evenings on the pavement outside, playing hopscotch and skipping, or cricket sometimes with the lads, while her mother was inside serving pints. She remembered catching a glimpse of Daisy now and again when the door swung back; she recalled the noise and hilarity, the smoky air and the smell of beer, and Daisy's red lips and platinum blonde hair and tinkling laughter. Sometimes, when her mother was working, she had spent the night with Auntie Nellie – a surrogate aunt, of course, as Daisy had had few relatives of her own. Rosie remembered a granddad, a gentle kindly man whom they had used to visit when she was a tiny girl. He had lived on the other side of the river – Birkenhead, she supposed – but he had died before the war started. And Nellie Cartwright had now 'passed on', Jean told her, as had quite a few of the older folk in the street.

Rosie imagined that The Jolly Roger had changed little since her childhood and was still, by and large, a male preserve with few concessions or niceties for the woman who dared to enter its portals.

'Well, well, well! Little Rosie White!' Joe Latham, red-faced and corpulent – the typical landlord, in fact, as he had always been – remembered Rosie well enough once Jean had introduced her. 'Fancy that, after all this time.'

'Rosie Bradshaw now,' she corrected him. 'Jenny and

Tom adopted me during the war.'

'Aye, I remember summat o' the sort,' Joe said, leaning on the bar and observing her closely. 'But from what I can see of you, you're a chip off the old block, all right.' He nodded meaningfully at Jean. 'She is, isn't she?'

Jean's eyes were wary as she nodded briefly back at him. 'Rosie's come to see if you can help her. To see if you can tell her anything about Archie . . . Archie Thoroughgood.'

Rosie had noticed the glances that had passed between Jean and Joe. She knew that she resembled her mother very little, at least as far as looks were concerned, so they could mean only one thing. She came straight to the point. 'Yes . . . I believe he might be my father.'

'Good God! After all this time.' Joe Latham took a huge white handkerchief out of his apron pocket and mopped at his face. He was perspiring heavily. 'I always said Daisy should've told him, but she was dead against it. I had a dickens of a row with her at the time, but she made me swear I'd never let on to Archie. And I never did. And he never asked about Daisy, not once, so I never told him about the nipper. About you, I should say, Rosie.'

'Mrs Williams says he went to live in Preston?' Rosie looked enquiringly at Joe.

'Aye, so he did. Back in 'thirty-three, that 'ud be. But I haven't the foggiest where he is now. He might still be there, who knows?' He spread his hands expansively.

'You lost touch with him then?' Rosie felt a flicker of disappointment. She had thought things were going so well.

'Aye, you know how it is. We sent Christmas cards for a year or two, and the wife used to drop him a line now and again. She was very fond of Archie, my Alice. She passed away a couple of years back, did Alice.'

'I'm sorry to hear that, Mr Latham,' said Rosie. She was sorry because she remembered Alice Latham, a plump, jolly woman who used to give her a handful of those tiny scented sweets called floral gums. But she was also sorry because Alice Latham was a link with the past and she was no longer here; nor was Nellie Cartwright, although neither of them would have been what you could call old. Would the person she was seeking also have 'passed on', Rosie wondered?

'Anyroad, like I was saying,' Joe went on, 'we lost touch. The last we heard was when Archie dropped us a line telling us he was getting wed. That 'ud be a few years before the war, I reckon. I never said anything to Daisy. There didn't seem to be much point.'

'Married?' Rosie felt bemused. This was something she hadn't thought about, although she wasn't sure why. She might have a whole lot of relatives somewhere that she knew nothing of. Half brothers and sisters . . .

'Yes, he was getting wed, and that was the last we heard of him,' said Joe. 'I never thought he would. He'd had a wife once, but she died young. That was before he took up with Daisy. He must've been well turned forty when he took the plunge the second time. He was a cautious sort of chap . . .'

'Would you have his address, Joe?' Jean Williams cut short his reminiscences. 'That's what Rosie really wants. I know he may not be there now, but it's worth a try.'

'Aye, I suppose so.' Joe scratched his bald head. 'Come through to t' back and I'll see if I can find the wife's old address book.' He did, eventually, at the bottom of a sideboard drawer. He thumbed through the pages to the Ts. 'Let's see . . . Taylor, Thomson, Tomlinson . . . There it is. Thoroughgood. Twenty-one, Ribbleton Street. I think he said it was somewhere at the bottom end of

Fishergate, where the smaller shops are. I did tell you it was an antique shop, didn't I?'

'No, you didn't say.'

'Oh aye, he went into the same line of business in Preston. It was a pawnshop he had here first, then he branched off into antiques. At least that's what he was doing fifteen years back, but whether he's still there remains to be seen. Anyroad, there's one thing in your favour, lass. It's an uncommon name.'

But there was no longer anyone called Thoroughgood at the address in Ribbleton Street, nor was it an antique shop any longer. Number 21 was a newsagent's and tobacconist's, the sort of shop that sold a bit of everything, including milk and bread and the commodities that housewives tended to run out of. Rosie gathered from her enquiries that it had changed hands fairly frequently and as the present owners had been there only six months they were unable to be of much help. Neither were the inhabitants of the shops on either side, a gloomy ironmonger's whose merchandise looked as though it had been there since pre-war days, and a greengrocer's whose stock seemed to consist of limp lettuces and cabbages and wizened or over-ripe fruit. Not a very prepossessing neighbourhood, and Rosie felt somewhat relieved that her father – if this Archie Thoroughgood was, indeed, her father – was no longer living there.

Once again it was the landlord of the pub on the corner, The Rising Sun, who was able to be of the most assistance.

'Archie Thoroughgood? Aye, I remember him well enough,' he told Rosie. 'Him and his wife, Mavis. They've been gone a good few years though now.' Rosie's heart sank, wondering how many times she was to hear this before her search was over, if it ever was to be. 'They were here all through the war. Mavis looked after the shop, such as it was – there wasn't much call for stuff like that while the war was on.'

'Antiques, you mean?' asked Rosie.

'Aye, the antique trade was practically dead, but she went in for second-hand clothes and pots and pans, all that sort o' thing, did Mavis. And Archie did his bit at the munitions factory, same as me. That's how I got to know him really. We were both a bit long in the tooth for war service.'

'And have you any idea where he is now?' Reminiscences were all very well, but not really of much practical help to Rosie.

'I was just coming to that.' The landlord of The Rising Sun was obviously not a man to be rushed. 'Mavis's health was none too good after the war, so that was when they decided to move. They'd heard tell of a little business – an antique shop again – at the seaside, and they thought it 'ud be just the job, what with Mavis and her bronchitis.'

'At the seaside? Do you remember where?' Rosie hardly dared to ask.

'Of course I do. It was Blackpool. I'm not likely to forget that, am I? You don't forget when somebody tells you they're going to live in Blackpool.'

'Blackpool? But that's incredible! That's where I used to live.' Rosie was amazed to think that her father might be in the town that she herself had once known as home. 'You don't know whereabouts in Blackpool?'

'Hang on a minute.' The landlord rubbed his chin thoughtfully. 'It wasn't Blackpool exactly. It was that little place just outside, just along the coast.'

'St Annes?'

'No . . . T'other way.'

'Fleetwood?'

'No, not as far as that. It was that suburb of Blackpool, where they have some big posh hotels. Now, what do they call it?'

'Bispham,' said Rosie. 'Was it Bispham?'

'Aye, that's it. Bispham.' The landlord nodded emphatically. 'But that's all I can tell you, lassie. We were never what you might call close, Archie and me, and we haven't kept in touch. I don't know the street or 'owt like that. And he might have moved on by now.' He looked at Rosie more closely. 'A relative of his, are you? You have a look of him. Same eyes and same dark hair, although he was going grey before he left.'

'Yes . . . he's a relation,' said Rosie. 'Just a distant one. But I'd like to look him up if he's still there. Thank you so much for all your help.'

She walked briskly along the length of Fishergate to the railway station and caught, by the skin of her teeth, a mid-afternoon Blackpool-bound train. She decided that when she arrived at the resort she would find some 'digs' at a small boarding house. She didn't feel like going into involved explanations at 'Pleasant View' about her reasons for being in Blackpool. Besides, Annie Carter's place would probably be full up in readiness for the Lights; they were to be switched on, Rosie remembered now, the following day. Also, she knew that Patsy would still be there, working at her grandmother's. Rosie found that she didn't want to think about Patsy; there was still so much that rankled. And though she knew that she would be very welcome at Aunt Ada's, Rosie decided that, for the moment, it would be as well to play her cards close to her chest.

She leaned back in her corner seat watching the flat countryside of the Fylde flash past the window. This

Blackpool-bound train was unusually quiet – there was only one other person in the carriage – because most of the holidaymakers were, no doubt, already there, eagerly awaiting the dazzling spectacle, the next evening, of the greatest free show on earth. After the stop at Kirkham station there was a series of gentle undulating hills, and then, suddenly, there on the skyline like a child's Meccano toy was Blackpool Tower. The first sight of it was always a thrill; Rosie recalled how she and Patsy and Victor would sit with their eyes glued to the window when they came on their visits from Yorkshire, waiting to see who would be the first to spot the familiar landmark. It was always Victor who won the game, really because his sisters allowed him to do so; at twelve years of age they had been getting rather old for such childish pastimes.

The train pulled into North Station with a squeal of brakes and a hiss of steam and Rosie pulled her overnight bag off the luggage rack and opened the door. She had travelled light, not being sure how long her search would take her, or how many trains she might have to lift her luggage on and off before she was through. Jean Williams had insisted on her staying the previous night in Liverpool, and Rosie hadn't had the heart to refuse. Jean had been so kind and helpful, putting Rosie's feet firmly on the first rung of the ladder. She hoped that the climb wouldn't be too long or too hard. But here she was in Blackpool – dear old Blackpool; she had always loved the place – and she had an uncanny feeling, one that she hardly dared to give much credence to, that here she might well be lucky.

Fortified by a gargantuan breakfast the following morning – bacon and egg, sausage, mushrooms, tomatoes, and that Lancashire delicacy, black pudding – Rosie set off once more on her quest. She had a knot of tangled nerves in the pit of her stomach, part excitement, part apprehension and part, she thought, indigestion. It was ages since she had tucked into a meal such as that and she knew that she would have to walk it off. It would be far better, also, to conduct her search on foot rather than by tram or bus.

She had found digs in North Shore in the Gynn Square area, which was not too near to 'Pleasant View'. She hadn't wanted to risk, at this stage, bumping into her grandmother. She had booked in for two nights, hoping that by tomorrow . . . But Rosie found that she didn't dare to voice her hopes too openly, not even in her own mind.

She walked briskly along the promenade, northwards towards Bispham, through the sunken gardens, bright with marigolds, begonias and sea-pinks – only the most hardy of flowers would survive in the keen Blackpool breezes – and on to the cliffs. These were man-made cliffs, constructed from clay and huge boulders of rock, and it was here, teetering on the edge, that the entertainment place known as Uncle Tom's Cabin, had stood in times past. It had closed in 1907, due to serious cliff erosion, and now a hotel of the same name stood on the other side of the tramtrack.

At the foot of the cliffs was the Boating Pool where, Rosie recalled, she had spent many happy hours with Jenny . . . and Patsy. She leaned against the railings now, looking down on the striped awning of the ice-cream stall, the wooden animals on the automated ride and the gaily coloured paddle-boats. It was very little changed since the days when she and Patsy had visited it as children. It was not doing much trade today, though; the children, no doubt, would have returned to school. Besides, it was decidedly chilly; there was a strong northerly breeze and a touch of rain in the air, building up to what the local people called 'real Lights weather'.

Rosie pulled up the hood of her windjammer and went on walking, behind the vast tableaux erected on the cliffs which tonight would be illuminated and displayed in their full glory. She crossed the tramtrack again at the junction of Red Bank Road, because she knew that it was here that her search must begin. The road led all the way from the prom to Bispham village, although this would be the first time she had walked the full length of it. There were quite a few shops here and, with a bit of luck, she might find one bearing the name of Thoroughgood. She crossed her fingers tightly in the depths of her pocket, then, knowing how foolish that was, she released them again. What would be, would be.

There were the usual shops catering for visitors, selling postcards and buckets and spades, as well as the shops that the residents used; newsagents, dress shops, an ironmonger's and a greengrocer's, a small jeweller's, and a large cafe where late-season holidaymakers were huddled round Formica-topped tables sheltering from the inclement weather. But there was no antique shop or anything resembling one. The shops petered out as Rosie walked east, away from the sea, giving way to rows of residential houses, Victorian and Edwardian and some of more modern construction. Bispham village itself was a little further on, beyond the main road, and surely it would be here, if anywhere, that she would find the person she was seeking.

Bispham had, until fairly recently, been an old-world village with white-walled thatched cottages edging All Hallows Road, leading down to the church of the same name. Rosie had often heard Annie Carter refer to the place, telling her visitors that they must be sure to take a bus ride along Devonshire Road to the 'old village'. Much had changed by now and many of the lovely old cottages had been demolished, but there was still a great deal of charm attached to the place. Ivy Cottage was still there; it was here that countless Blackpool visitors, over the years, had come for tea and cakes, regarding the outing as a trip to the 'country'. Opposite was a row of thatched cottages and it was near to there, in a row of shops set back from the road, that Rosie found what she had been looking for.

She gave a gasp of astonishment when she saw the name over the door and blinked in disbelief. She hadn't even needed to enquire, and she hadn't, strangely enough, at that moment, really been thinking about her quest. She had been staring around, intrigued by the quaint old buildings, so different from the blatant modern image that Blackpool liked to present. But there it was above the shop, A and M Thoroughgood, in letters that were, however, somewhat faded and worse for wear.

For the moment Rosie's courage failed her and she spent a moment or two staring in at the window, trying to still her turbulent thoughts. Like the sign above the door, the display in the window looked as though it had seen better days. There was the usual accumulation that one saw in an antique shop, or what might more accurately be called a junk shop. Plates and jugs, old pictures, tarnished brassware, bottles, clocks and barometers and, in the centre, a Victorian hand-sewing machine, but all looking as though they could do with a good dust and sort-out. Rosie could see at the back of the shop a man in a brown overall. He was looking enquiringly in her direction; perhaps it wasn't every day that he had young women such as Rosie looking into his window. The shop certainly didn't inspire one to linger for long.

Rosie felt her heart contract with something like fear. Now that the moment had come, whatever was she to say? Excuse me, but I think you might be my father? Don't be such a fool, she said to herself. It might not even be him. It might be just an assistant, or the Thoroughgoods might have moved on ages ago. The sign needed painting; perhaps it also needed changing. But standing here on the pavement wasn't going to get her anywhere. Rosie took a deep breath and pushed open the door.

As soon as she entered the shop and looked more closely at the man who was standing there, Rosie knew that her search was at an end. It was not so much the dark hair, now almost entirely grey, or the blue eyes, but an underlying resemblance that told Rosie that this man must be her father. He looked across at her from the other side of the mahogany table that served as a counter, his eyes curious, and Rosie could see a likeness to the face that often stared back at her from the mirror. The same confident, challenging glance.

'Good morning,' said Rosie, smiling at him. 'I'm sorry to trouble you, but . . .' She stopped. No, that wasn't right at all. She wasn't sorry, why on earth should she be? She began again. 'I rather think that you might be . . . that you and I might be related.'

The man continued to look at her, the slightly curious glance giving way to one of interest and – almost – of recognition. But still he didn't speak.

'You are Mr Thoroughgood, aren't you?' asked Rosie, a trifle discomposed.

'Yes . . . yes, I am. Archie Thoroughgood. But I wasn't aware that I had any relatives, certainly not any young ones. Some distant cousins, maybe. But I can see that . . .' He put his head on one side, in a way that Rosie had often seen herself do. 'Yes, I can certainly see . . . You'd better come upstairs, my dear, and tell me all about it.

Just a minute.' He walked across to the door and pushed a bolt into position, then he turned the sign so that it read Closed instead of Open. 'Now we won't be disturbed.'

'Oh dear.' Rosie felt guilty. 'It's not a good idea to keep trade away, is it?'

Archie Thoroughgood laughed. 'There'll not be much trade on a day like this. Proper miserable it's turned out to be. Real Lights weather. Anyway, it's half-day closing today.' He consulted his watch. 'I'd be closing in an hour or so.'

The living quarters above the shop had the same dilapidated appearance as the shop itself; not exactly dirty, just dusty and in need of what Jenny would call 'a woman's touch'. Rosie wondered where Mrs Thoroughgood was.

'Now, my dear, sit down and tell me all about it.' Archie Thoroughgood gestured towards a large three-piece suite with a brown and orange rectangular design, and Rosie sat down thankfully on one of the chairs, still not sure how to begin.

'My name's Rosie Bradshaw,' she said, 'and I live in Castleburn, in Yorkshire. But I've not always been called Bradshaw. I was adopted, you see, during the war, after my mother was killed in an air-raid. My mother lived in Liverpool.' She hesitated, looking away from the man who was regarding her so intently. She looked down at the brown and orange patterned rug as she said, in a quiet voice: 'She was called Daisy White.'

'Daisy White?' Rosie looked up again at the man in the chair opposite her. He had spoken her name as though he couldn't believe what he was saying. He had turned pale too, although he hadn't had much colour to start with. 'But I never knew that Daisy had a child . . .' He leaned forward, his hands hanging limply between his knees. 'Tell me, my dear, how old are you?'

'I'm nearly twenty,' answered Rosie, still very quietly. 'I'll be twenty later this month.'

'September . . . And I left Liverpool in . . .' He sat bolt upright in the chair, concentrating hard, then suddenly he slumped back against the cushions. 'Oh, my God! It could be . . .' His face was ashen now and he had closed his eyes. Rosie feared that he might have fainted.

She was filled with remorse as she quickly got up from her chair and went over to him. 'Mr Thoroughgood.' She took hold of his hand. 'I'm so sorry. I shouldn't have told you like that. I've given you a shock. Oh dear, I was trying to break it to you gently, but there didn't seem to be any other way . . .'

'It's all right, my dear.' He opened his eyes and nodded gently at her. 'I'm all right, really I am. It was just – like you said – a bit of a shock. And I haven't been too well lately. I was in hospital earlier this year . . . but we won't go into all that now.' He looked at her steadily, and Rosie was relieved to see a trace of colour now returning to his cheeks. 'Yes, I can see there was no other way of telling me. You couldn't wrap it up.'

'I could have written,' she said, still full of self-reproach at the way she had blurted out the devastating news. 'But I didn't know your address, not until just now. I'd found out that you might be in Bispham, and when I discovered the shop, well, I was so surprised that I just . . . came in. I realise now that I should have gone away and then written to you. It wouldn't have been so much of a shock, that way.'

'No . . . no, you mustn't reproach yourself. I'm glad you came in. And it must have taken some courage, too.' Archie Thoroughgood seemed fully recovered now. But he was still staring at her in some disbelief. 'I can't quite take it in though. Have I got it right? You're trying to tell me that I'm your . . .'

'Yes, I think so.' Rosie smiled at him. 'I rather think that I'm your daughter.'

He leaned back in the chair, still shaking his head as he murmured, 'Incredible . . . I just can't take it in.'

'Mr Thoroughgood.' Rosie leaned over him. 'Let me get you something. A cup of tea or coffee? Or would you like some brandy? I've given you a shock. I feel dreadful.'

He smiled at her. 'I'd love a cup of tea. And I usually make myself a sandwich or something about this time. I'm not much of a hand in the kitchen, but I've had to fend for myself since Mavis went.'

'Your wife?' Rosie asked. She had been wondering about Mrs Thoroughgood, but hadn't liked to ask.

'Yes.' Archie's eyes were sad. 'My wife died a couple of years ago. Make us a cup of tea, there's a good lass, then I can tell you all about myself. And I reckon you've a thing or two to tell me, haven't you?'

He was remarkably easy to talk to, this new father of Rosie's. She knew it would be an exaggeration to say that she felt as though she had known him all her life, but she thought that after a few meetings it might well be so.

'You're taking a great deal on trust,' she told him. 'I might be an imposter. Haven't you thought of that?'

'Not you.' He looked at her keenly. 'It's like looking at myself in the mirror. Not now, of course – I'm knocking on a bit now. I'll be sixty-five in a few months, retiring age – but like I was thirty or forty years back. Anyway, I daresay you've got documents and all that, haven't you? From when you were adopted?'

'Yes, I expect my mother – Jenny – has,' she told him. 'I've never really bothered much about it, till recently.'

She had filled him in, as they ate their snack lunches of cheese sandwiches and shop bought cake she had found in a tin, about her life in war-time Blackpool, then later in Castleburn.

'So you would be leaving Blackpool just as we arrived?' said Archie Thoroughgood. 'Back in 'forty-five. And we never knew. What I can't get over, though, is Daisy not saying anything. That was wrong, that was real wicked of her, I think, not to say anything. I'd have married her. Look at all the grief she's caused. And then the poor lass was killed . . .'

'You might not have been happy with her,' said Rosie gently, 'so perhaps it's all worked out for the best. You were happy with your Mavis, weren't you?'

'Yes, I was,' Archie agreed. 'Very happy. And you had a good home with the Bradshaws, from what you say. So maybe you're right. Things have worked out. But I'm glad you've come now, Rosie, real glad.'

He told her how he had often been lonely since his wife had died, although he had tried hard to keep the business going. Most of the income from the shop, she gathered, came from the sale of second-hand books, and he also ran a small lending library. It was certainly not an antique business like Mr Fothergill's in Castleburn, but Archie Thoroughgood seemed to make enough to live on, together with the bit, he told her, that he and Mavis had saved over the years.

'I have a woman in to clean for me once a week,' he said. 'The rest of the time I tend to let the dust accumulate. I've never been much of a one for housework.'

'Like my father,' said Rosie, only realising, after she had spoken, the irony of her words. She smiled at him then, a trifle apologetically. 'I'm not sure what to call you,' she said.

'What about Archie?' he said, grinning. 'That's what everyone else calls me and I reckon it'll do as well as anything. You can't very well call me Dad, can you? You've got one of those, and I'm sure he's a grand one as well, isn't he?'

'Yes.' Rosie nodded thoughtfully. 'Tom and Jenny, they've both been grand. But I'm glad I've found you as well . . . Archie.'

It was the middle of the afternoon when she left, with a promise that she would come and see him again. Soon. As soon as she had sorted herself out. For Rosie knew now that she would not be returning to London. She had told Archie about her art course; she had also given him the impression that it was only for a year, and that she was now through with it. An idea had been forming in Rosie's mind throughout the last few days, while she had been in Liverpool and Preston, and here, in Blackpool, it had finally come to fruition. Rosie now knew what she was going to do . . .

Patsy stared at her sister in surprise when she'd heard the whole story, in the small living room at Aunt Ada's. 'Good gracious! You've soon got things worked out, haven't you? You say you're finishing your art course here, in Blackpool?'

'Yes, there's a very good art school in Palatine Road. I've been to see them today, and they say it's all right for me to transfer. Only if I'm resident in Blackpool, of course. Which I am.' She turned to grin at Aunt Ada. 'I'll be lodging here, thanks to Aunt Ada and Uncle Fred. It's only a ten-minute walk from the college.'

'You certainly haven't let the grass grow under your feet,' Patsy remarked in amazement. 'Mum and Dad know all about this, do they? And about this . . . Archie

Thoroughgood as well? They're going to be surprised, and that's putting it mildly.'

'No . . . they don't know yet,' replied Rosie slowly. 'I'm going home on Saturday, and I shall break it to them then.'

'I'm going home tomorrow,' said Patsy.

'Then keep this buttoned, little sister,' said Rosie, putting a finger on her lips. She was smiling but Patsy was aware of the warning note in her voice.

'Don't worry,' said Patsy nonchalantly. 'I shan't say a word.'

Chapter 19

'So what you're trying to tell us, Rosie, is that you're going to live in Blackpool because of this . . . Archie fellow.' Jenny's greenish-brown eyes, usually so alive and glowing with warmth, were blank, like dull pebbles.

Rosie was filled with anguish as she looked at her mother. She had known it would be difficult to explain to both of them; she had felt that Jenny, in particular, would find it all hard to understand, but this was dreadful. And it wasn't like her mother was making out at all. That wasn't the real reason for her deciding to complete her art course in Blackpool and go to live at Aunt Ada's, but she was having a devil of a job to convince her of it.

It was Saturday evening and the three of them, Tom, Jenny and Rosie, were sitting round the fireside. Patsy, wisely, had gone to visit a school friend and Victor was up in his room doing his homework; he had recently started at the Grammar School. The atmosphere had been decidedly strained since Rosie had arrived home earlier that day and she was not surprised that her brother and sister had decided to absent themselves. At least Patsy had had the sense not to spill the beans; on the other hand, it might have made it a little easier if her parents had been forewarned of her plans. It seemed as though they were not even trying to understand, at least Jenny wasn't.

'No, Mum, it isn't like that at all,' said Rosie now. 'That's not why I'm going to Blackpool. I know it may seem like it, but it's just a coincidence. I'd almost made up my mind to transfer to the college there before I met . . . Archie Thoroughgood. And then I went to talk things over with Aunt Ada.'

'Oh yes, talk it over with Ada, that's right,' said Jenny bitterly. 'You'd rather discuss things with my cousin, I suppose, than with me. And what's our Ada ever done for you, I'd like to know?'

Rosie bit her lip, realising that – again – she had said the wrong thing. 'We only talked about me going to live there – to lodge there – Mum. It seemed a sensible thing to do. She's bags of room in that house, and it's only a few minutes' walk from the college.'

'It beats me why you want to go changing horses in mid-stream,' said Jenny. 'I can't understand you, Rosie. You were full of it last year, the art school and going down to London. We even arranged for you to go and live at Joan's, so that you could have your own way. And now you're throwing it all up.'

'I'm not, Mum. I'm just transferring. They say it's all right for me to do that. I just have to prove that I'm resident in the area. I've told them I've a few relations living in Blackpool, and that that's where I'll be living. Anyway, my course would be changing, wherever I was. It's my year for specialising, for the finals for the NDD. I'm concentrating on Textile Design, and I can do that just as well in Blackpool.'

'Never mind all your fancy talk, Rosie,' Jenny snapped. 'You know very well your dad and I don't know what you're on about. I'm blessed if I can understand you at all these days.' Jenny pressed her lips together in a thin line and picked up her knitting from the bag beside her chair. Defiantly she tucked the ball of grey wool – for a school jumper for Victor – down by the side of her, then her needles started to click furiously as they always did when she was distressed.

Rosie sighed, but she was determined that her mother was going to listen to her. 'Mum, put that blasted knitting down and listen to me,' she said sharply. 'It isn't like you think at all.'

Jenny didn't tell her to 'watch her language', as she might have done. She put her knitting in her lap and stared frostily at her daughter. 'I'm listening, Rosie,' she said.

'Eh dear, I don't know!' Tom sighed from the other side of the fire. He had said very little throughout Rosie's long and involved explanation, only interrupting now and again with an odd regretful word or two, and shaking his head bemusedly.

'I can't go back to London,' Rosie went on. 'The way things have turned out, it's impossible.' Jenny raised her eyebrows enquiringly and Tom continued to look puzzled. 'I wasn't going to tell you about it, but I think you'd better know . . .' Rosie knew that by telling them about her affair with Jeff – about some of it, at least – she might defuse the situation and give her mother something else of import to think about, instead of dwelling on the emotive issue of her natural father.

'You remember me telling you about Jeff?' she continued. 'The lecturer I was friendly with?'

Jenny nodded. 'Yes, I remember,' she said flatly.

'Well . . . it didn't work out, Mum. I'd got very fond of him, and then I found out that he . . . well, he was married.' Rosie didn't need to assume the pathos in her voice; it was always there when she spoke about Jeff, but she did exaggerate it a little.

'Oh dear! That's dreadful.' Rosie's words must have had the desired effect, or at least were beginning to have, because Jenny's expression was now more sympathetic than angry. 'And you had no idea that he was married?'

'No, none at all. I found out by chance – someone at college knew his family. There's always someone who knows, of course. Jeff admitted it – he had to, didn't he? He said they weren't happy, he and his wife – the usual tale, you know, Mum. But I knew I couldn't go on seeing him, especially this next year. I'd have to see a lot more of him, because he's the tutor in design – that's the subject I'm specialising in. So I decided that I had to leave . . .'

Jenny had gone very quiet, staring down at her hands folded in her lap.

'I know that it's hard for you to understand, Mum,' Rosie went on. 'Things are a lot different now than they were when you were my age. But I don't approve of taking a man away from his wife, any more than you would. I made it quite clear to Jeff that it was all over. And I can't go back to London.'

Jenny looked up then. 'I don't know why you should think I don't understand, Rosie,' she said quietly. 'Things haven't changed all that much. And I probably understand much more than you give me credit for.' Her eyes were shrewd and a trifle sad as she looked at her daughter. 'I'm sorry it didn't work out for you, but you're only young, love. You'll find somebody else. And I'm sure you did the right thing . . . giving him up.'

'I don't know, it's a rum do, all of it,' said Tom again, looking first at his wife, then at his daughter. 'But there's one thing to be said for it, Jenny. Haven't you realised? Our Rosie'll be a good deal nearer home if she's living in Blackpool.'

'Of course I will, Dad,' said Rosie, smiling at him gratefully. 'And I'll be able to pop over and see you every couple of weeks or so. I couldn't do that when I was in London.'

'And you'll be seeing this . . . Archie as well, I suppose?' said Jenny, with a trace of her former coolness.

'Now and again, Mum,' said Rosie, as casually as she could. 'It's the least I can do, isn't it? I gave the poor fellow an awful shock. But you mustn't worry about it. It doesn't alter the way I feel about you. Both of you.' She smiled uncertainly at her mother, then at her father. 'It's just something I had to do. And now I've done it, I feel tons better.'

'All right, love.' Tom nodded gravely, but he looked much more composed. 'You've told us all about it, and I reckon that's the end of it now. Your mum and I'll get used to it, won't we, Jenny? It was a bit of a shock to us at first, like it must have been to this Archie, but we'll survive. And you won't go far wrong at our Ada's, that's for sure. You'll have a good home there.'

'This is her home, Tom,' Jenny reminded him. 'She's only lodging at Ada's. You'll be paying her something, won't you, Rosie? Although I've got to admit our Ada's not short of a bob or two.'

'She says she won't take much, Mum. But of course I'll give her something, to pay for gas and electric and all that. And I daresay I shall get a little job in Blackpool, at a cafe or something, like I did in London.'

'Mmm, I suppose so.' Jenny still looked somewhat deflated. 'But you'll concentrate on your work, won't you, Rosie? On your drawing and painting. You'll want some good results to get a job next year, same as our Patsy will.'

'Don't worry, Mum. I'll work hard,' she replied. 'And I shall have no distractions in Blackpool,' she added with a cheeky smile.

She was glad when her mother seemed to respond. 'Yes, fellows can be a devil of a distraction,' said Jenny, a glint of warmth showing in her eyes for the first time that evening. 'You'd be well advised to steer clear of them, Rosie. Just get on with your work, there's a good girl.'

'When we leave this blinking college,
Oh, how happy we shall be . . .'

Patsy joined in with the singing of the college songs outside the bedroom doors of the first-year students, recalling how exactly a year ago she had lain in her bed listening to the same songs. Now, earlier that day, returning to college had been almost like coming home. It had been great to greet old friends again – Kath, Shirley and Edna – and to meet a whole new set of college daughters.

'Oh, how happy we shall be . . .' The words repeated themselves over and over in Patsy's head as she lay in bed half an hour later. The song seemed to suggest that the students would be glad to leave college, to put behind them the rigid routine as they embarked on life in the world outside. But Patsy somehow could not see herself in front of a class of children, day after day, year after year . . .

Teaching was only 'chalk and talk'. Patsy had learned, with difficulty, to chalk on a blackboard and could now write, more or less, in a straight line. But as far as the talk was concerned, Patsy wondered if she would ever be able to do it. She had listened admiringly and enviously to teachers who were able to hold a class in the palm of their hand, talking, talking endlessly, with scarcely a sign of inattentiveness from the children. And yet, when you assessed what they had actually said, what did it amount to? Very little. Teachers certainly needed to be born with 'the gift of the gab', a gift that Patsy knew she didn't possess. When she was confronted with a class she was always afraid of drying up, except in story lessons, of course. She loved those, but you couldn't be telling stories all the time.

The reports on her two School Practices had been surprisingly good, so Patsy knew she might be exaggerating her own inadequacies. 'And it'll be much easier when you have a class of your own,' she had frequently been assured. But Patsy doubted it. At all events, next summer, when she must seriously think about getting a job, was a long time off. In the meantime she was determined to work hard, and had made up her mind that this year there would be no distractions. No Ronnie, no Neil – he was now far away in the south of England – no men at all in fact. There was only Raymond Sykes in Blackpool, whom she had promised to write to now and again. But it was surprising how very seldom Raymond came into her thoughts.

'Old Fletcher's leaving at Christmas. Did you know, Patsy?' Peter Fennimore asked over the tea table, his mouth full of baked beans.

'Don't be so rude, Peter,' his mother rebuked him. 'It's Miss Fletcher to you. And don't speak with your mouth full.'

'Sorry, Mum,' said Peter. But he didn't look at all sorry as he grinned at Patsy, his big brown eyes alight with pleasure at the news he was imparting. And with admiration, too; Patsy knew that she had an admirer, and always would have, in young Peter Fennimore.

Barbara Fennimore had called in again at Jubilee Lane School, after the dinner-time débâcle, repeating her invitation for Patsy to come to tea. She had been pleased to do so. It was a pleasant change to be in a real home again after life in a hall of residence and she found that she got on famously with Barbara. She felt, however, that it wouldn't be wise to overdo things or to presume on the young woman's friendship, so limited her visits to about once every three weeks or so. Peter was overjoyed whenever his beloved Miss Bradshaw appeared, and he had been even more thrilled when she insisted that he should call her Patsy. 'We're not in school now, Peter,' she had assured him, 'and, anyway, I'm not a real teacher, you know . . . not yet.'

'But did you know, Patsy?' he persisted now. He hadn't needed a second invitation to use her Christian name and did so now with alacrity. 'Did you know that she – Miss Fletcher – was leaving?'

'No, I didn't, Peter,' Patsy replied. 'I know she kept applying for jobs – for headships. She's got one now, has she?'

'Yes, at Spring Gardens, I believe,' Barbara joined in. 'She's been trying for one for ages, or so I've heard. It's that new estate on the outskirts, Bradford way. I can't say I'm all that interested, though. I'm just glad that she's leaving. She's caused a lot of trouble in her time,' she added quietly. 'Now, Patsy, some apple pie and cream?'

'Yes, please,' she said eagerly. She reflected on Barbara's words. Miss Fletcher had certainly caused trouble – heaven help the poor children and teachers at her new school – but the woman had, indirectly, been the cause of this new friendship of Patsy's. She looked across fondly at Peter, and at his younger brother and sister, Timothy and Dawn. She loved children when they were in small groups like this, but it was children en masse, thirty or forty faces staring at her fixedly, that she found so unnerving. And how headteachers coped, with hundreds of youngsters facing them each day, as they did in morning assembly, she couldn't imagine. She pushed the thought away and concentrated on her apple pie. Barbara was a good cook, every bit as good as Mum.

'Now, Rosie, how's it going? Tell me all your news.' Archie Thoroughgood leaned forward eagerly, his eyes fixed on the girl who had come to mean so much to him over the last couple of months. 'You've been over to Castleburn, have you, to see your mum and dad? How are they? Glad to see you, I daresay?'

'Yes, I was there last weekend, Archie,' Rosie told him. 'Patsy was there as well because it was half-term, so it was a nice family get-together.' She stopped then, not wanting to say too much about families. It could be hurtful to Archie, although she was touched by the way he always asked about her parents and the genuine interest he showed in them.

He was a dear man, and Rosie never ceased to be thankful for whatever it was that had driven her to find him. Providence, maybe? It had all stemmed, she recalled, from that awful row with Patsy, but perhaps that had been providential too. She had fallen into the habit of seeing him once a week, on Wednesday afternoon, which was half-day closing at the shop and also an afternoon on which she had no lectures. They chatted and had tea together, then watched television – a recent acquisition for Archie – or had a game of cards. It was a happy, companionable time for both of them and Rosie found herself taking great pleasure in this relationship which was unlike any that she had known before.

She could talk with him on all manner of subjects. He showed great enthusiasm for her course and for her interest in textile design, and in what she told him of the lectures she attended on the history of art. This, she discovered, was Archie's consuming passion, a knowledge acquired over the years and fostered by his dealings in the antique business. He had had little formal education, having left school at fourteen, but he had taught himself by visiting art galleries and by poring over books of paintings, when he couldn't see the real thing. Rosie realised now whence had come her own talent for art. Archie, too, was artistic – he could do lightning sketches, mostly of a humorous nature – but it was a talent that had not been developed. Had it been, she was sure he could have become a successful artist.

He was not, however, like a father and never did she think of him as such. Tom was her dad, dear ordinary old Tom whom Archie never failed to ask about. Archie was more like a favourite uncle – he was, in fact, old enough to be Rosie's grandfather – but, chiefly, he was a very good friend, a companion with whom she always seemed to be on exactly the same wavelength.

It was November and now, with the end of the Lights, business was tailing off, Archie told her.

'I shouldn't have thought you would get many holidaymakers up here,' Rosie remarked. 'It's a fair stretch from the promenade.'

'Oh, you'd be surprised. A lot of visitors stay in the Red Bank Road area, and they have a walk up here to look at the old church.' All Hallows, the parish church of Bispham, was an attractive, stone-built church, the third one known to have existed on the site. There had been worshippers there since the twelfth century, but now the main attraction was the pretty lych-gate, a popular site for photographs on a summer's day. 'And then they wander over here to see what I've got to offer,' Archie went on. 'It's mostly the books that interest them, I must admit. I do a good trade in books.'

Rosie guessed that without the sale of second-hand books and the lending library, the shop would be hard-pressed to keep going at all. Archie, she gathered, had allowed things to deteriorate since the death of his wife and, more especially, since his own recent illness. He had been reluctant to talk about that and she wasn't sure what the trouble was. He seemed to have recovered now, though he never had much colour. His greyish pallor sometimes alarmed Rosie, but he assured her that he was all right and that he had always been pale.

One Wednesday afternoon the pair of them had set to and given the shop a real good going-over. Rosie had sorted out a few of the best bits and pieces she could find – a couple of flowered tureens, a chromium-plated teaset, and some flat-back Staffordshire figures – and had tried to make a more attractive display at the window. She hadn't pressed the matter too much, however, realising that Archie's interest in this side of the business seemed to have waned. She got the impression that he was loath to display his most appealing merchandise too openly for fear that someone should buy it! The best pieces, indeed, were tucked away at the back of the shop and many of them were in the living quarters.

The living room was a mixture of styles, depicting the personality and choice of both Archie and his late wife. The furnishings couldn't be called modern; they were more in the style of the twenties and thirties, the mode which was now beginning to be known as Art Deco. The lines of the furniture were simple and geometric. There was a plain, functional dining suite, with a sideboard in highly polished sycamore, over which hung a bevelled edged mirror in the shape of a tulip with pale yellow petals. A lamp similar to one in Rosie's home in Castleburn stood in the centre of the sideboard, a gilded female form with amber glass wings; the Butterfly Girl, Archie had called her, when he saw Rosie admiring it. This had been chosen by Mavis, he said, as had the furnishings.

Archie's taste tended more towards a decorative, ornate style. A pair of china figures, a shepherd and shepherdess, stood on either side of the tiled fireplace. Rosie guessed they might be Rockingham, although she was not sure; Patsy, she thought, would have known. And a pair of tall blue vases with gilded handles, painted with pastoral scenes, stood on either side of the naked lady lamp. A strange conglomeration of styles, but Rosie had to admit that the rooms had character and she was beginning to feel very much at home there.

'So tell me about college,' said Archie that November evening, when they had finished their meal. 'Still enjoying it, are you? And which painter are you discussing now?'

Gainsborough, she told him, not one of her favourites – Rosie leaned more towards the Impressionists – but it turned out that Archie was an admirer of his work and, as always, they had an interesting discussion.

'And what about the social life?' he asked. 'You get out and about, I hope, as well as going to lectures. You can't keep your nose to the grindstone all the time, a pretty girl like you.'

'There are plenty of places I can go if I want to,' Rosie told him. 'We're spoiled for choice in Blackpool, aren't we? I go to the pictures occasionally, with some of the other students, and I went to the Winter Gardens once, on a Saturday night.'

'And what about the college? Do they have social functions there?'

'Yes, there are all sorts of societies, and they have college hops now and again. And there's a holiday to Switzerland soon after Christmas. I'm working hard though. It won't be all that long till the finals and I've a lot of work to get through.'

Rosie had thrown herself wholeheartedly into her studies since starting at the Blackpool college. Her room at Aunt Ada's was now adorned with the evidence of her labours – sketches and ideas, experimentations in the use of colour, all connected with textile design – as her flat in Kensington had once been. As she had told Archie, she had been out occasionally with friends from college, but most of the time she was working, either at her college projects or, three evenings a week, at a coffee bar in town. Work was the only antidote for intrusive, pointless thoughts. Because Rosie still found herself thinking about Jeff . . .

'Don't work too hard,' Archie told her gently now. 'Take time for leisure as well. What were you saying about a holiday in Switzerland? Are you thinking of going?'

Rosie shook her head. 'I can't afford it, Archie. Although I suppose it's quite reasonable, all things considered. Celia, one of the girls in my group, was trying to persuade me to go, but I told her it's out of the question. There's all the clothes I'd need as well, you see.'

'Why?'

'What d'you mean, why?'

'Why is it out of the question?'

'I've told you, Archie, I can't afford it.' Rosie smiled wrily. 'Celia's father's a doctor, not a bricklayer like mine. And she doesn't have to do a part-time job either to eke out her grant.' Rosie stopped, realising that she might sound envious. And she wasn't, not at all. 'Don't think I'm criticising my dad,' she went on. 'In fact, if I were to mention it, I know very well what Mum and Dad would say. They'd say, "You go, Rosie. We'll manage it somehow." So I'm not going to tell them about it.'

'It's a skiing trip, I suppose?'

'Yes, skiing and skating and sledging. A bit of everything. They're going to a camp in the Bernese Oberland.'

'And you're going with them.'

Rosie looked at Archie in surprise. He had spoken so decisively. 'You're going with them, Rosie lass, because I'm going to make sure you do. I'm going to treat you.'

'No! Oh no . . . you can't!' She was horrified at the suggestion. It must seem to Archie as though she had been hinting. 'Oh no, Archie, I didn't mean . . . Please don't think I was trying to suggest . . . It never entered my head.'

'No, I know it hadn't, Rosie.' Archie's voice was gentle. 'I think I know you well enough by now to realise what sort of a girl you are. And you're certainly not a grasping one.'

'But I couldn't let you . . . It wouldn't be right.'

'Please, Rosie. It would mean such a lot to me. It would give me so much pleasure.' Archie's eyes were glowing with a quiet joy and Rosie knew that she hadn't the heart to say no again.

She smiled at him gratefully and very fondly. 'You're very kind, and I must admit I would like to go. But what about Mum and Dad? They'll be very hurt if they find out.'

'Don't tell them, Rosie. I'm not suggesting you should deceive them, but there's no real reason for them to know, is there? Let them think you're paying for it yourself. You've saved up a bit from your job at the coffee bar, surely?'

'Yes, a little. It's not costing me nearly as much at Aunt Ada's as it did in London. In fact I'd started saving up for the holiday, just in case, then I realised I wouldn't have nearly enough.'

'Well, you have now.' Archie's eyes were bluer than Rosie had ever seen them, shining with happiness. 'Just be sure you send me a postcard of those snow-covered mountains. It's a place I've always wanted to visit, but I've never managed it.'

'I'll do more than that.' Rosie laughed. 'I'll bring you a cuckoo clock!' Impulsively she went over to him and kissed his cheek, something she had never done before. 'And thank you so much, so very much . . .' Her voice tailed off with the emotion that seemed to be choking her. 'I don't know what else to say . . . to thank you.'

'Then say no more. Just sit down and tell me all about it. When are you going, and what d'you think you'll need?'

Archie stared thoughtfully into the dying embers of the fire after Rosie had gone. Rosie, his daughter . . . He still couldn't fully grasp the idea, even though more than two months had elapsed since she had surprised him with the stupendous news. She had insisted, later, on showing him evidence to bear out her story; her birth certificate with the name of Daisy White as the only parent, and her adoption papers. Not that he had needed any corroborative evidence; it was there when he looked in the mirror and, more particularly, at old snapshots of himself. And it was there, too, in his heart. She was all that he could have wished for in a daughter; as well as being very lovely she was kind and amusing and vivacious. Strong-willed, too, he guessed, and resolute, but there had been no ulterior motive in her mind, he felt certain, when she had mentioned the holiday. Rosie, he knew, was much more of a giver than a taker, and in the short time that he had known her she had already given him so much joy.

He regretted so much the wasted years; if only he had known, if only Daisy had told him. But he realised the futility of 'if only'. The important thing was the here and now. Rosie had sought him out at last, and she had found him. She had found him in time . . . For that he would never cease to be thankful. As Rosie had suggested to him soon after they met, it was more than likely that he and Daisy would not have been happy together. It had been, he recalled, chiefly a physical thing, but out of their union, blessedly, had come Rosie. And if he had married Daisy White he would never have found Mavis, his dear Mavis. Yes, maybe things had worked out in the best possible way. Archie had never been a religious man, certainly not a church-goer, but now he found himself clinging to the idea of a Divine Providence. Why else should this lovely girl have come to find him? Now, when he felt there was so little time left. The doctors had said very little after his spell in hospital earlier that year. They had done what they called an exploratory operation and after ten days had pronounced him fit to go home. They had never told him the results of their findings. But Archie had a good idea.

'A penny for them, Rosie.' She looked up from her seat in the corner of the barn-like room where the dance was being held. She had, she knew, been miles away from the Bernese Oberland, back in England, or, more precisely, in South Kensington.

'Oh, hello there, Dave.' She smiled at the man as he sat down on the empty stool beside her. 'I was wool-gathering.'

'I could see that. Feeling homesick, were you? You were looking very pensive.' Dave's blue eyes, which reminded Rosie quite a lot of Archie's, were concerned. 'Why aren't you dancing? You shouldn't be sitting here on your own, you know.'

'No, I'm not really homesick, and I have been dancing,'

Rosie replied, in answer to both questions. 'I'm just sitting this one out, and that's when I started . . . thinking.'

Dave Whorton was a lecturer at the art school in Blackpool, one of the two who had come with the group on the holiday to Switzerland. He lectured on the history of art, making the various painters and their works come alive in the students' minds. It wasn't just his eyes that reminded her of Archie. He was like him in a lot of ways, not so much in looks but in his eager way of talking and in his enthusiasm for his subject which came over in a quiet, yet compelling, manner. Rosie couldn't help but compare this lecturer with Jeff. He too had taught enthusiastically, but in a much more flamboyant, often aggressive, way. Dave was older than Jeff – Rosie guessed he would be in his mid-thirties – and she also guessed that he was a little attracted to her . . . possibly more than a little. Rosie liked him too, but he was a tutor and she was wary of tutors.

It had been Jeff who was occupying her thoughts when Dave came over to her. Jeff had written to her twice, not at Aunt Ada's, as he didn't know her address, but at the college in Blackpool, and the letters had been passed on to her. He had been astounded and dismayed, he wrote, when he found that she had disappeared so suddenly to Blackpool. He still loved her, he was still having problems with Daphne, he still wanted a divorce . . . Rosie had strengthened her resolve and hadn't replied to his letter. The second one, which had arrived just before Christmas, was in a similar vein. He also told her that he had bought a small car and that he intended driving up to Blackpool soon to make her see reason.

Rosie had imagined that if she refused to answer his letters he would be forced to give in graciously. But then, she realised, Jeff had never been one to admit defeat. He was stubborn, pig-headed in fact, not the sort of man to take no for an answer. She had told him no, many times, but it seemed that it was still not enough. Now Rosie was finding herself vacillating, an unusual state of affairs for a normally decisive girl, wondering how much longer she would be able to hold out against his persistence. Should she reply to his letter and tell him to keep away, that nothing would make her change her mind? Or should she agree to see him? And, if she did, how would she feel after several months away from him? Rosie's mind was in a turmoil and when she departed for Switzerland at the end of December the problem had still not been resolved.

'I was thinking about my family, back home,' she told Dave now. It was partly true; they had been in her mind as well, but recently thoughts of Jeff had seemed to be paramount again, just when she had begun to think she might be getting over him. 'It's the first time I've been abroad,' Rosie continued, 'and the fuss my mother made you'd've thought I was travelling to the North Pole, not just across to Europe.'

'I daresay it seemed like that to your parents,' Dave remarked. 'People haven't been in the habit of taking holidays abroad, until very recently. I don't suppose either of them has ever been across the Channel, have they?'

'My dad has,' said Rosie, 'but it was during the war so it doesn't really count.'

'Like me,' said Dave. 'I served in Europe. I was part of the carry-on at Dunkirk . . . Anyway, never mind about all that. It's ancient history now, thank goodness.' He leaned forward, looking at her earnestly across the pine-wood table. 'Are you enjoying your holiday, Rosie? I hope you are.'

She smiled. 'How could I help but enjoy it? It's all so different from anything I've done before. It's a wonderful experience.'

It was not, however, what you could call a luxurious holiday. Their accommodation in the little village, high in the Bernese Oberland, was in wooden chalets. There were eight students in each dormitory, which was heated by an antiquated stove, stoked up each morning and evening with pine logs. Their meals were taken in a similar chalet, a much larger one, with wooden beams holding up the roof and an uncarpeted wooden floor. The whole camp, in fact – for that was what it was, a holiday camp for students – was constructed of wood. The distinctive aromatic smell of pinewood was in Rosie's nostrils now, as it had been since the first day, together with the scent of Continental cigarettes, coffee and minestrone soup. This dish was served up at nearly every meal, thin and watery with noodles floating on the surface, a far cry from the thick brown stews that Rosie was accustomed to in Lancashire and Yorkshire.

The journey, too, had been anything but luxurious. An overnight train from Blackpool to London, then to Dover, a decidedly choppy crossing to Ostend, then another overnight journey across Europe. They had snatched what little rest they could in the crowded compartments, and some of the more agile – and lighter in weight – had slept, or endeavoured to do so, on the luggage racks.

It had been worth it, however, for the first glimpse of the Swiss mountains. On either side of the track rose the massive peaks, the sparkling whiteness of the snow pink-tinged with the rising sun. Deep dark pine forests and tiny alpine houses clung to the slopes, and little red mountain trains climbed to almost impossible heights.

After a day or two, however, Rosie had found that the magnificence of these mountains was also very oppressive. She began to feel hemmed in and to compare the craggy peaks, in her mind, with the familiar hills and vales of Yorkshire. She tried to explain her feelings to Dave

Whorton now, as he asked her what she thought of the scenery.

'Impressive, of course,' she said. 'Who could fail to be impressed? But, seeing it all with an artist's eye, possibly a wee bit . . . chocolate-boxish, don't you think so?'

Dave laughed. 'Cadbury's and Rowntree's have certainly made use of them, I must admit. And they must have featured on thousands of calendars and Christmas cards.'

'And apart from that,' Rosie went on, 'they're not the hills of home, are they? Yes, Dave, I suppose I was feeling a little homesick when you came over, thinking about the friendly old hills where I live.'

'Hills?' said Dave, sounding surprised. 'There are no hills in Blackpool, luv.'

'Yorkshire.' She smiled at him. 'My home's in Yorkshire, although we used to live in Blackpool, and I'm living there again now, until I've finished my course.'

'And then?' Dave looked at her with interest.

Rosie gave a slight shrug. 'Who knows? It depends on where I get a job, and what sort of job. It depends on . . . all sorts of things. What about you, Dave?' she asked now, deciding to change the subject away from herself. 'What does your wife think about you being away for a fortnight? Didn't she want to come with you?' Rosie had no idea, in fact, whether Dave was married or not, but it was a reasonable assumption with a man of his age. Besides, it would be as well to find out.

She was unprepared for his reaction. 'My wife?' His eyes, which had looked so alive and interested – in her, she had thought – became blank as he stared at her in bewilderment.

'I'm sorry, Dave,' she replied. 'I assumed you were married. You're . . . not?'

He shook his head, not answering for several seconds. When he looked at her again his eyes were sad. 'No . . . not now. My wife – Helen – died eighteen months ago. A brain tumour. It was very sudden.'

'Oh, Dave, I'm so sorry. I'd no idea. Whatever must you think of me? I feel dreadful . . .'

'Don't feel dreadful, Rosie. Don't worry about it. I'm so used to people skirting round the subject, never referring to it – trying to be tactful, I suppose. It just gave me a start hearing you mention her.' He leaned across the table and patted her hand. 'Think no more about it. Drink up your lager, then we'll have a dance, shall we?'

Dave was a pleasant companion, quiet and unassuming – very different from Jeff, Rosie couldn't help thinking – and they spent many enjoyable hours together over the next week, though usually in the company of several others. They continued their skiing lessons on the nursery slopes, most of them becoming proficient only when it was time to return home, they skated on the frozen lake, they danced in the evenings to a gramophone or to a piano accordion played by one of the local men. And on the last afternoon they took a sleigh ride to the next village, travelling through narrow lanes banked high with snow, a dazzling white tunnel all around them, on sledges drawn by pairs of husky dogs. Rosie felt that her cheeks were glowing as red as the scarf and mittens she wore – a Christmas present from Mum – and she knew that this holiday had done her good. Tomorrow, though, she must return home.

She was aware of Dave's growing interest in her, though she had tried not to give him any encouragement. On the last evening he walked back with her to her chalet and, very gently, he took hold of her shoulders and kissed her softly on the lips.

'I've enjoyed your company, Rosie,' he said. 'When we get back home, would you . . . could I . . . see you again?'

She shook her head. 'I don't think so, Dave. I don't think it would be a good idea. I've enjoyed your company too – very much – but let's leave it at that, shall we?' Rosie was wary of getting too friendly with a tutor again.

There was a pained expression in his eyes, just for a moment, and Rosie felt regretful. But she hadn't encouraged him, she hadn't . . . She knew, to her chagrin, the effect she sometimes had on men – hadn't Patsy told her so, in no uncertain terms? – and so, for that reason, she had been very careful not to do anything to ensnare this very nice man who had already had so much sadness in his life.

She was relieved when he smiled at her again. 'Very well then, Rosie. As you wish. We'll leave things as they are. Thank you for a lovely holiday.' He nodded at her, then walked away.

Rosie sighed. She liked Dave, he was a real gentleman in the true sense of the word, gentle and kind and considerate, very much like Archie . . . She wasn't sure why she had refused to see him again; it wouldn't have done any harm. But there was still the problem of Jeff Burroni to be settled. She must decide what she was going to do about Jeff.

Chapter 20

'Whatever is the matter with those two girls of ours?' asked Jenny, one evening in January. Earlier that day both Patsy and Rosie had returned to their respective colleges, Rosie having come home to Castleburn for a day or two after her holiday in Switzerland. 'When they're together the atmosphere is so tense you could cut it with a knife.'

Tom looked up from his newspaper in surprise. 'Our Patsy and Rosie? I haven't noticed anything. What d'you mean, Jenny? They seem all right to me, the pair of them.'

'Of course they're not all right!' she snapped. 'But I might have known you wouldn't notice. You never see anything unless it jumps up and hits you in the face. You've always got your head buried in a newspaper, or else in those blessed football pools. You don't even notice me these days, Tom. You never said anything about that dress I made for myself at Christmas, nor about the new cake I made the other day.' Jenny pouted. 'I don't know why I bother sometimes.'

'Aw, come on, love. Don't be like that.' Tom put his paper down and looked placatingly at his wife. 'You always look nice, but I can't be telling you all the time, can I? And you bake so many lovely cakes that I'm blessed I know whether it's a new one or not.'

'Never mind the soft soap, Tom.' Jenny smiled in spite

of herself. 'I'm worried about the girls, I am really. You must be blind if you haven't noticed.'

Tom frowned. 'They were both a bit quiet, I'll grant you that, the last time they were home. But we didn't see all that much of our Rosie, did we? She was off to Switzerland a few days after Christmas. And then we were at your mother's for the New Year, like we always are. Happen our Patsy's a bit jealous like, d'you think, with Rosie going off abroad? They've always done things together before.'

'I don't think it's that, Tom. Patsy's not the sort of girl to be jealous, not about something like that, though I think she's a bit envious at times of Rosie's personality. She's such a lively one, is Rosie, and Patsy's so quiet. At least she was till she went off to college. That seems to have brought her out a bit. No, I don't think it was Switzerland. They were funny with one another before that, going back to last summer.'

'That was a rum do, that Swiss trip,' said Tom. 'We never got to the bottom of it, did we? I find it hard to believe that the lass could pay for it all by herself. D'you reckon our Ada had a hand in it? I know she's very fond of Rosie.'

'No, I don't think so, Tom.' Jenny raised her eyebrows. 'Don't tell me that's something else you haven't twigged? I think it was Archie Thoroughgood who paid for it.'

'No! Whatever makes you think that, Jenny? Why, the lass hardly knows him.'

'I think she knows him quite well by now, Tom,' said Jenny calmly. She found, to her surprise, that she could be quite unemotional about the situation now. As Rosie had promised, finding her real father had made no difference at all to the girl's feelings for her adoptive parents. But Jenny suspected that she went to see Archie Thoroughgood at his home in Bispham far more frequently than she let on. 'The girl's living in Blackpool, you know, and it wouldn't be natural if she didn't see him from time to time. He sounds a nice chap, from what our Rosie says. Anyway, it was just an idea I had, that he might have financed the trip.'

'Aye, perhaps he did. But none of it has made any difference to us, has it, Jen?' said Tom, echoing her own thoughts. 'She's still the same old Rosie. And we were able to chip in with a bit of spending money for her, weren't we?'

'Yes, it's worked out all right, in spite of my misgivings,' said Jenny. 'And her living at our Ada's seems to have been a good idea too. I must admit I'm much happier about her up here in the north than I was when she was living in London . . . You say she's still the same old Rosie, but she's not, you know, Tom. She's much quieter. She might be the same with us, thank God, but like I've told you, it's her and Patsy that I'm worried about. They're . . . odd. I can't put my finger on it.'

'I expect they've both made new friends, that's all,' said Tom. 'You can't expect them to be as close as they were. Patsy's forever on about that Kath – the Geordie lass – and Rosie has had all sorts of new experiences. Including that teacher chap that she was telling us about. I daresay she's quiet because of that. She seemed proper cut up about it.'

'Yes, the fellow that was married,' said Jenny thoughtfully. 'I'm glad she had the sense to get away from that. Perhaps it's as you say, Tom, they've both made new friends . . . Our Patsy didn't seem to be right smitten with Raymond, the other Sykes twin, did she? Not like she was with his brother. As far as I know she only saw him the once when we were in Blackpool. Still, it's perhaps just as well.'

Tom laughed. 'She's only to go out with young Len and she'll have been through the whole family.'

'Tom! What a thing to say! Our Patsy's not like that.'

'I'm only joking, love. I don't know what you've got against the Sykes family though, Jenny. That Raymond seemed a real nice sort of lad when he called at your mother's.'

'Yes, he was all right,' Jenny replied off-handedly. 'I preferred him to his brother, at any rate. But our Patsy's a lot of studying to do yet; she's no time to be fooling about with lads. Just think, Tom, we'll have a teacher in the family before long. Won't that be grand?' Jenny beamed with gratification. 'Especially if she gets a job here, in Castleburn.'

'Don't count your chickens, Jenny,' said Tom, a warning note in his voice. 'I've tried to tell you before, you can't plan their lives for them. And there's a lot of water to flow under the bridge before then.'

Jenny felt a stab of premonition and was glad when Tom changed the subject.

'I'm sorry if I seem preoccupied, Jenny,' he went on. 'Not noticing things and all that. To tell you the truth, love, I've been feeling tired lately. There have been fellows off at work with this 'flu epidemic, and we're hard pushed to get those houses finished over Newbury way. I've been doing a bit of everything lately as well as being the foreman.'

'Don't overdo it, Tom. You're supposed to be the gaffer, aren't you?'

'Aye, I daresay, but I can't expect the lads to do extra when I won't do it myself. I'm sorry if I seem as though I'm not noticing you, Jenny. We'll have a night out soon, I promise, to the pictures or happen to the theatre in

Leeds or somewhere. We'll just wait till the weather's a bit more settled.'

We're always waiting for something, Jenny mused. Tom had made promises before. They would always do this or that, when the winter was over, when he had a bit more time, when the girls left home, when Victor was settled at the Grammar School . . . He might just as well say 'when we retire', thought Jenny, a trifle resentfully. They went on from day to day, living the same humdrum existence; work, mealtimes and bed, work, mealtimes and bed. And there was little excitement to be had in bed these days, Tom always seemed so tired. Most evenings he fell asleep listening to the radio, or watching the nine-inch television set that they had bought, like many other people, at the time of the Coronation last year. Jenny couldn't remember the last time they had been out together . . . Yes, it had been last June – Coronation Day – when they had gone to the bonfire in Blackpool. Tom always perked up when he was away from home, she recalled.

But he really must be tired out, she thought more solicitously. He had always been a conscientious man, taking himself and his job of work very seriously, always willing to 'go the extra mile'. He had put in long hours at the building site recently. It was dark early, of course, but he had done extra shifts, often working Saturday mornings. He drew the line at Saturday afternoon, though, if he could. Nothing had to interfere with football! So perhaps it wasn't fair to blame him if their life was less than exciting.

Jenny had always craved excitement, as a young girl, as a young married woman . . . Now, in her early forties, she sometimes felt that life was passing her by. That was why she had been so glad of the job at Mr Fothergill's and why, now, she found herself looking forward, possibly more than she should, to the visits of Ralph Bailey, the traveller in fancy goods.

Jeff was waiting when Rosie came out of the college building one afternoon in mid-February. He wound down the window of the little red Austin car and shouted to her.

'Hi there, Rosie. Remember me?'

She gave a start when she saw him. Though it had been at the back of her mind that he might turn up out of the blue, as he had promised, it was still a shock. She had prevaricated for so long, not replying to his letters, that she had been beginning to think that he had finally given up on the idea of her going back to him. She went over to the car noting, with a familiar leap of her heart, his raised eyebrows, the half-amused, half-tender gleam in his deep brown eyes, and the faintly sardonic smile pulling at the corners of his mouth. He looked just the same as ever and she knew, too, that her feelings for him at that moment were, regrettably, just the same as well.

'Good heavens, Jeff, whatever are you doing here?' Rosie was determined not to let her feelings show. 'You might have let me know you were coming.'

'What difference would it have made? I have told you anyway. I told you I'd turn up if you continued with this ridiculous nonsense.' He flung open the door of the passenger seat. 'Get in,' he said brusquely.

Rosie gritted her teeth as she climbed into the car. She was damned if she was going to be spoken to like that, but, she reminded herself, Jeff had driven a long way to see her, foolhardy though it may be . . . and it had been churlish of her not to reply to his letters.

'Why aren't you at college?' she asked. 'Is it half term?'

'I'm not there, that's all,' he answered tersely. 'As far

as they're concerned I have a sore throat. I'll be back in a day or two . . . I had to see you, Rosie.' He turned towards her, grasping her hands. 'I've tried to forget about you, really I have, but I can't. Come back to me, please come back. I'll leave Daphne . . . and Marilyn. We'll get a flat somewhere. I'll be able to divorce her soon anyway. Things are just the same between her and me . . .'

Rosie pushed his hands away. 'Stop it, Jeff. You're talking nonsense. Anyway, I've told you, time and time again, I won't let you get a divorce on my account. I can't do it, Jeff.' She sighed. 'Look, I'm terribly sorry, but we've been through all this before.'

'There must be some way, Rosie.' Jeff's eyes were pleading and he looked more of a 'little boy lost' than she had ever seen him.

She relented somewhat then, knowing that she still cared for him a lot. 'Come to my place then, and we'll have a chat, but I can't promise you that it'll be any different. Where are you staying, by the way?'

'I've booked into a boarding house on Hornby Road, not far from here, just for tonight. But I can always cancel it. I was hoping that I might . . . You did say that I was to come to your place . . .'

'You must be joking!' Rosie replied. 'You know I'm living at my aunt's. She'd have a fit. You can come home with me and I'll make you a meal, but that's all.'

'I didn't know where you were living,' replied Jeff sulkily. 'How should I know? You've told me nothing. I only found out – in a roundabout way, I might add – that you'd transferred to this one-eyed place.' He waved his hand dismissively in the direction of the college building.

Rosie felt her hackles rise. 'It's a very good college, I'll have you know. Every bit as good as the one where you are. And I'm working hard here and I don't want any distractions.' She sighed again. Jeff was making her so angry, but he had come such a long way to see her. 'Come on, drive me home,' she said more calmly. 'It's only a few streets away. I'll direct you.'

Aunt Ada and Uncle Fred were both out. Fred was engaged on one of the part-time decorating jobs that he did during the winter, and Ada was round at 'Pleasant View', helping Annie to 'bottom' the bedrooms in preparation for the spring visitors. Rosie cooked bacon and eggs for Jeff, then they talked. She didn't invite him up to her room. She was not sure when Aunt Ada would be back. Besides, Rosie was afraid of her feelings. She knew that she still cared for Jeff, and if he were to touch her she would find it impossible not to give in to him.

But as they covered the same old ground – Daphne and Marilyn, Jeff's Catholic upbringing, Rosie's unfinished course – she began to realise more and more that he was looking at this whole situation as a battle that he must at all costs win. Jeff wasn't used to being beaten, he was used to getting his own way. Possibly his capitulation, when he had been forced to marry his pregnant girlfriend, had been the only time he had failed to do so. Rosie was sure – almost sure – that when he said he loved her he meant it, but was it possible that he loved himself and his own desires more? Rosie began to see, for the first time, that she and Jeff were very much alike, too much so for them to be happy together for long. Self-willed, determined, single-minded . . . but Rosie hoped that she wasn't also self-seeking, as she was beginning now to fear that Jeff might be.

Rosie was relieved that he had gone before her aunt and uncle returned. He got the message eventually, but she could tell from the belligerent glint in his eyes that he was determined finally to be the victor. He stood up from the dining table, where they had been conducting their futile argument, with such force that his chair toppled backwards and fell to the floor.

'Very well, Rosie. I'll trouble you no more. Don't bother to see me out.' He snatched his duffel-coat from the back of a chair and stormed out into the darkness.

She heard the sound of the car engine coming to life, then its roar as Jeff zoomed away down the street. He drives too fast, she thought, and it's a hell of a long way back to London.

When the phone call came two days later with news of an accident, her thoughts flew immediately to Jeff.

'No, Ralph, I can't. I'm sorry, but . . . no.' Jenny smiled at Ralph Bailey across the counter of Fothergill's antique shop. He was a personable man in his mid-forties, a couple of years older than Jenny, with crinkly greying hair and greyish-blue eyes which twinkled merrily from behind horn-rimmed spectacles. She had first met him when he had called with samples of Coronation ware, some of which she had persuaded Eustace Fothergill to buy. Since then Ralph had called regularly with other lines – china vases, figures and ashtrays – several of which they had ordered from him to sell in the shop as a change from the antique articles.

Jenny knew that he admired her. Why else did he so often arrange his visits to coincide with the times when he knew Eustace would be out? Jenny was now in charge of this modern side of the business and Ralph was always most helpful in advising her as to which lines would be good sellers. She felt herself sparkle in his presence, something she hadn't experienced for many a long day in her relationship with Tom. She had, she supposed, flirted with him in a mild way, laughing at his witticisms and smiling coyly, blushing a little, at his flattery. What woman wouldn't? she asked herself. There was no harm in it.

But she drew the line now at his suggestion that she should go out to dinner with him the following evening. Ralph was married – and quite happily too, she surmised – although she knew little of his wife and family. His home was in Leeford, some fifty miles away. No doubt he thought he would be on safe ground so far away from home. Or maybe, as Jenny suspected, she was just one of several attractive, slightly bored, women whom he met on his travels? At all events any philandering with him, apart from a laugh and a joke across the counter, was definitely out of the question.

'No?' He raised a sardonic eyebrow. 'You've wounded me, Jenny. You've cut me to the quick.' He put his hand over his heart in an exaggerated gesture.

'You'll get over it, Ralph,' she said, laughing, as he packed his samples away in his case and prepared to leave the shop.

Jenny was so thankful two days later that she had said no. Not that for one moment she had seriously considered going out with Ralph, but, had she agreed, she would always have looked upon what happened afterwards as some kind of dreadful retribution.

It was mid-day when the policeman called at the house. Jenny was shocked to see the sombre-faced young man on the doorstep.

'Yes?' she said fearfully, her hand going to her throat and her thoughts going immediately to Victor, Patsy, Rosie . . . in that order. The mothering instinct, she supposed, which was why she didn't automatically think of her husband. It was only a split second before the policeman spoke; it was incredible the number of random thoughts that could race through one's mind in such a short time.

'Mrs Bradshaw?'

'Yes . . .'

'I'm afraid there's been an accident. It's your husband. They've taken him to the Infirmary.'

'Tom? Oh no . . . he's not . . . ?'

'He's unconscious, Mrs Bradshaw. He fell from some scaffolding. They seem to think he had a dizzy spell. You'd better get there as soon as you can. I'll run you there in the car, if you can come now?'

'Yes . . . yes, of course I can.'

Tom was in intensive care, tubes attached to various parts of his body and a machine monitoring his frail heartbeat. She stood at his bedside for several moments, too stunned even to cry. She took hold of his hand, noting the particles of cement beneath the finger nails; he had no doubt been doing a job he could quite easily have delegated, she thought dispassionately. She felt too numb to feel bitterness or any recrimination. Her thought processes seemed to be frozen, except for one over-riding desire.

'He will get better, won't he?' she said to the nurse at her side.

'We hope so, Mrs Bradshaw. We're doing all we can,' said the girl kindly. 'Now, is there anyone you would like to ring? Members of your family?'

'Oh, yes . . . my daughters,' said Jenny. It was the first time she had thought of them since hearing of Tom's accident. 'I'll have to let them know. And my son – he'll be coming home from school soon. He'll wonder where I am.'

She managed, somehow, to contact all of them without breaking down. It is amazing what strength we are given, she thought afterwards, to cope in a crisis. Mrs Jones, her next-door neighbour who had a phone, was to intercept Victor on his way home and give him his tea and explain that his dad had had 'a little accident'. There was no point in alarming the lad unduly.

To Patsy and Rosie she spoke the truth. They were to come as soon as they could; their father was dangerously ill. Besides, Jenny knew that she needed them, both of them, as she had never needed them before.

It was much later that evening when the girls arrived at the hospital, Patsy first, then Rosie about an hour afterwards. And as Jenny watched them fling their arms around one another at Tom's bedside, Patsy weeping a little against Rosie's shoulder, she wondered why she had thought they were at variance. Whatever it was that had been wrong between them, all sign of discord had vanished now.

'You'd better go home,' the doctor told the three of them gently. 'Get some rest. If there's any . . . change, we'll let you know. You can leave a phone number?'

'Yes,' said Jenny numbly. 'Mrs Jones's, my next-door neighbour.'

'He will get better, won't he?' Patsy whispered to Rosie in the darkness of their bedroom. 'I don't think I could bear it, Rosie, if he . . . if he didn't get better.'

'Of course he will,' Rosie said, with more confidence than she was feeling. 'This always happens when someone has a fall. He'll be all right. I'm sure he will.'

'Rosie . . .' Patsy spoke again after a few moments. 'I'm sorry. I'm so terribly sorry about all those awful things I said to you. It's been worrying me for ages, but I couldn't say anything . . . till now.'

'Forget it, kid.' Rosie's voice was filled with emotion. 'I'm sorry, too. We've been a couple of idiots, haven't we? I'm sorry I pinched Neil Emmerson off you like that. I did, you know; it was dead mean of me. And I didn't want him. I was just upset about Jeff.'

'Yes . . . I know you must have been,' said Patsy slowly. 'And I'm sorry that I was the one who had to tell you about him. That was when things started to go wrong between us, wasn't it?'

'Yes . . . I suppose it was. But they're all right now, aren't they, Patsy?'

'Of course they are,' Patsy replied warmly.

'And we won't ever fall out again?'

'Of course we won't.' The silence was emotional and Patsy tried to lighten it. 'How's your love life, by the way? Any new man on the horizon?'

'No . . . not really. One of the fellows at college asked me out – he's a tutor actually, which is probably why I said no.' Rosie gave a bitter laugh. 'Once bitten, twice shy.'

'You thought he might be married?'

'No . . . I know he's not married.'

Rosie thought for a moment, regretfully, of the man to whom she had said no and who had taken her at her word. She saw Dave Whorton several times a week and he was always most friendly and courteous towards her, but he hadn't asked her again if she would go out with him. Rosie was sorry now that she had refused him that first time in Switzerland. She liked Dave very much, seeing in him many qualities – kindness, integrity, dependability – that she admired. But she had been obsessed with thoughts of Jeff at the time. That blasted Jeff . . .

'D'you know, Patsy?' she said now. 'When Mum rang and told me there'd been an accident I immediately thought of Jeff. Wasn't that awful? It was only afterwards that I realised that Mum couldn't possibly know anything about Jeff.'

'Why did you think about him?'

'He came to see me the other day, drove all the way from London. I sent him packing – for the last time, I hope. And he zoomed off in the car like a bat out of hell. I was sure he'd have an accident. That's why I thought . . .'

'I'm glad you sent him away, Rosie. It wouldn't be any good, you know.' Rosie smiled to herself at her sister's knowledgeable tone of voice. 'And I'm sure he's got back to London all in one piece. He sounds as though he can take good care of himself.'

'Yes. . . . he's a survivor. Like me, I suppose.'

'Let's hope Dad's a survivor, too,' said Patsy quietly. 'Oh, Rosie, you don't think . . . ?' On impulse she got out of bed and tiptoed across to her sister's bed. 'You don't think he'll . . . ?'

'No, of course not.' Rosie moved up closer to the wall. 'Come on, kid. Get in with me for a few minutes. It's bloomin' cold in this room, isn't it? Like it always was.'

The two girls huddled together, talking in whispers.

'We used to do this when we were kids, didn't we?'

'Yes, and Mum got mad with us.'

Rosie went on to tell her sister about Archie; she hadn't mentioned him much, things being as they were between the pair of them, but now they found they had such a lot to catch up on.

'So you've two dads now,' Patsy commented. 'D'you think of him as a dad?'

'No, not at all. Tom's my dad. But Archie's great; he's like a special friend. You'll have to come and meet him, Patsy.'

'I will, one day. When Dad . . .' Patsy hesitated for a moment before she went on, 'Rosie, d'you still say your prayers?'

'Mmm . . . now and again. I don't go to church, but I

do pray. I know it sounds awful, but I pray when there's something I want.'

'I think we all do that,' said Patsy. 'D'you think it does any good?'

'It depends what you ask for. D'you remember that little rhyme that Granny Bradshaw used to say sometimes?

' "Sometimes He says yes, sometimes He says no, Sometimes, "Do it by yourself, you don't need me, you know . . ." '

'Yes, I remember,' said Patsy, joining in with the rest of the verse.

' "But whether He says yes, or whether He says no, We know God always answers prayer, because He loves us so." '

'I think God said no to me about Jeff Burroni,' said Rosie wrily.

'But about Dad. He wouldn't say no . . . surely?'

'It's worth a try, Patsy,' said Rosie gently. 'Go on, back to your own bed, and we'll try to get some sleep.'

In the quiet darkness both girls closed their eyes tightly.

Jenny prayed too, in the solitude of All Saints church. She knelt on the worn hassock, laying her head on her arms on the high-backed pew in front of her. It was a good while since she had been to a service here and she felt little desire to come to one now, but she knew that she wanted to be alone with the God that she believed in even though she seldom entered His house. She had chosen a time when she knew she would not be disturbed. It was mid-day and the busy women parishioners who cleaned the silver and arranged the flowers would, no doubt, be occupied elsewhere with their own lunch preparations.

She loved this old Norman church with its musty smell, high oak pews and stone altar. She was always aware of an aura here, the lingering presence of countless generations of worshippers who had knelt there, in praise or thanksgiving, or in supplication, as she was kneeling now.

'Please, God, let him get better,' she prayed simply, an almost wordless prayer, her thoughts all centred around her husband, still unconscious this day after the accident, in his hospital bed. She found it difficult to form the words in her mind, but she knew that God, who knew the secrets of all hearts, would hear . . . and would answer.

Her thoughts drifted for a few moments to her children. To Rosie, calm and confident, taking charge of the situation, organising them all. She and Patsy seemed as close as ever again, thank God. She thought about Patsy, her brown eyes frightened and worried – with concern for her father, of course, but Jenny knew that there was something else troubling her daughter, something to do with college. Her final School Practice was coming up soon, the one that was crucial to her becoming a teacher. But Patsy refused to discuss it. Jenny knew that she had been on what they called a preliminary visit to the school, but when she had come home for half-term, only a few days before, she had declined to say anything about it. Her face wore a closed look and Jenny knew that there was something of significance on her mind. Jenny had wondered, for the very first time, if she had been right in encouraging the girl to become a teacher . . .

Jenny thought of Victor, too – his brown eyes, so like Patsy's, perplexed and, for once, the cheerful grin absent from his face. The girls were still home on compassionate leave from their colleges, until such time as their father recovered. As he must, he must . . . Jenny's thoughts returned to Tom, so pale and helpless in the high white bed. She would be going there again soon, to sit at his side, to hold his hand, to will him to get better. She knew that she could never have had a kinder, more gentle husband, for all his taciturn manner and lack of sparkle and gaiety. Over the last eight years, the time they had lived in Yorkshire since the end of the war, she had come to appreciate his worth. Her occasional spurts of defiance against him and the unexciting life they led were of short duration. She knew that she loved Tom deeply and couldn't imagine life without him. Ralph Bailey was a nobody, worthless and insignificant, compared with Tom. What a mercy it was that she hadn't succumbed to his charms . . .

Jenny remembered a time when she had fallen victim to the charms of another man, a much more sterling character, however, than she knew Ralph Bailey to be. And how she had knelt in this very church, asking for guidance. It had been in the dark days in the middle of the war, when it had seemed, for a time, that things were going badly for Britain. The vicar, she recalled, had come to chat with her and had given her some spiritual advice.

Jenny knew that she wouldn't welcome the presence of the vicar today, a different one now, a fussy, self-important man whom she didn't particularly care for. She knew that it was no use her bargaining with God, promising that she would come back to church, if only . . . God, she believed, was not a person to be bargained with. He was too wise, too powerful to place much reliance in our petty promises and resolutions to do better. Promises that are so readily broken. He knew how often His children failed Him, but God, she believed, could make Tom well again . . . if only He would. Jenny closed her eyes again.

It was later that afternoon that Tom opened his eyes to see his wife sitting at his bedside.

'Hello . . . Jenny.' His voice was just a whisper and he

was still very poorly, taking little interest in where he was or why he was there. His head was swathed in bandages and there was still a tube attached to his arm; but he had spoken to her and Jenny's heart was full of joy and gratitude . . . and hope. Her husband would get well again, he would make a full recovery. He must get better . . . he must.

It was two days later that the doctors pronounced that Tom was off the danger list. He would not die, as they had feared he might – it had been touch and go – but his spine had been injured in the accident and it was believed that he would not walk again. For the rest of his life, they told Jenny, he would be confined to a wheelchair.

Chapter 21

The preliminary visits to the schools for the final School Practice had taken place at the beginning of February, and Patsy had been delighted, at first, on finding that this time she and Kath had been allocated to the same school. It was at Spring Hill, a new housing estate to the south of the city, one of several that had sprung up in Leeford since the war ended. The students had been allowed to choose the age group they would teach for this, their final attempt before the 'real thing', and Patsy had opted for a class of six- to seven-year-olds, 'top class' Infants.

'I believe it's a lovely school,' Jane, one of the girls from Derwent Hall, remarked as they sat on the top deck of the bus that February morning, on their way to Spring Hill. 'Cloakrooms attached to all the classrooms, and verandas outside the french windows. And a separate dining hall, too. So many schools have to use the main hall, don't they?'

'Yes, and then the smell of cabbage lingers all afternoon,' said Sheila, the fourth member of the little group.

'It sounds something like the school I was at for my first School Practice,' said Patsy. 'Parklands. That was a school on a new housing estate as well, with all mod cons.'

'And did you like it?' asked Sheila. 'I'm looking forward to teaching in a new building. My last two schools have been real grotty old places.'

'Yes, it was all right,' said Patsy. 'I liked it well enough, I suppose. As well as you can like any School Practice. But not as much as my last place. You mentioned old buildings, Sheila. Well, Jubilee Lane, where I was last time, was a real antiquated place. Smelly lavs in the yard and high iron railings and windows that wouldn't open. God, it was awful! You'd have thought it was ready for demolition. But it was such a happy school, much happier than Parklands. I realised then that it isn't really the building that counts.'

'No, it's the kids . . . and the headteacher,' Kath remarked. 'It wasn't all plain sailing, though, at Jubilee Lane, was it, Patsy? You had a devil of a time with that Miss Fletcher.'

'Fletcher?' said Jane. 'That's the name of the head at the place we're going to.' She pulled a piece of paper from her bag. 'Miss E. Fletcher. Spring Hill Infant School. This is the letter she sent, confirming the dates and all that. D'you suppose it's the same one?'

'Good grief, I don't know,' replied Patsy in a tiny voice. She had gone cold; she could feel the goose pimples rising on her arms and legs. 'No . . . it can't be the same one. That wasn't the school she went to. It was Spring . . .' Oh, my God! she thought. Supposing Barbara Fennimore had been mistaken? The name was nearly the same. 'It was Spring Gardens, that's on the other side of town. It must be another Miss Fletcher.'

'I expect you're right, Patsy,' said Kath consolingly. 'They know the names of the students they're having. It's hardly likely that Miss Fletcher – the one from Jubilee Lane – would agree to take you again. Not when she knows you . . . it wouldn't be fair.'

But Patsy felt sick, and by the time they had walked from the bus stop, through the streets of identical box-like houses, to the new single-storey building, she was sure that her worst fears were to be realised. The school was surrounded by well-tended lawns and flower beds which, in the summer, would be gay with flowering shrubs and roses. The plate glass windows gleamed, and through them could be seen low modern tables and chairs, and walls covered with brightly coloured pictures and charts. Patsy thought back to their earlier conversation, that it was not the building that constituted the happiness of a school. It was the children . . . and the head.

It was, of course, the same Miss Fletcher, as Patsy had known it would be. Her steely blue eyes rested on each of them in turn as she ushered them into her study, lingering a fraction longer on Patsy as she said, 'I have, of course, met Miss Bradshaw before.' Apart from that she said no more to Patsy than she did to the others.

Patsy's heart sank even further when she met her class teacher. Miss Nichols was a small mousy woman who, Patsy learnt, had been at college with Miss Fletcher, and from the woman's conversation she gathered that the two of them were bosom friends. Miss Nichols didn't appear to have the same drive as her friend – the reason, no doubt, why Miss Fletcher was a head and she wasn't – but Patsy felt sure that she would be a 'yes woman', the sort of teacher who was continually toadying to those in authority. A 'bum wiper', she'd heard such a teacher referred to by Mr Bateson, the joker of the staff at Jubilee Lane. Patsy had been amused at the expression at the time, but she wasn't laughing now, not one little bit.

She discussed her schemes of work with Miss Nichols. She had decided on an animal project, this theme to be introduced into the various subjects wherever possible, and the class teacher seemed quite agreeable. At least she made no adverse comments. Neither did she give the slightest hint that she knew of Patsy's former altercation with her friend. But Patsy felt sure that the woman did know . . .

'What on earth are you worrying about?' said Kath, on the way back to college. 'Miss Fletcher must be prepared to overlook what happened before or else she would have refused to have you, surely?' Not quite the same argument that Kath had put forward earlier, Patsy noticed, but she knew that her friend was, as ever, trying to be kind. 'It won't be too bad, I'm sure. It's a lovely school.'

'I don't like it, Kath. It's going to be awful. I know it is.'

'If you adopt that attitude then it probably will be. Come on, Patsy, this isn't like you. You're not usually afraid of facing up to things. It'll be all right, you'll see.'

'I'm afraid of this,' said Patsy. 'I don't think I can go there, to that place. I'm going to see Miss Pritchard about it.'

'This is highly irregular, Miss Bradshaw,' said Miss Pritchard, the resident tutor at Calder Hall and also Patsy's Education tutor, when she put her case to her. 'You say you want to change schools because of Miss Fletcher?'

'If I can, Miss Pritchard,' Patsy replied. 'We had a . . . a misunderstanding on my last School Practice, and I feel that we might not get on very well.'

Patsy knew that her words sounded feeble, and Miss Pritchard said pretty much the same as Kath had said; that if Miss Fletcher was willing to live and let live, as she so obviously was, then Patsy must be prepared to do the same. When she started her final School Practice at Spring Hill towards the end of February it couldn't have been in much worse circumstances.

'You really will have to go and see the doctor about those headaches,' Kath had said the previous week. 'You can't start teaching feeling like that.'

'I always get headaches,' replied Patsy listlessly. 'It's just tension, and it's not to be wondered at, is it? What with Dad and School Practice next week, and now this smallpox scare.'

There had been an outbreak of smallpox in Leeford – a child at one of the city schools, in fact, had died – and all the students who were going on teaching practice had had to be vaccinated. Patsy hadn't fared too badly as she had been vaccinated as a baby, and her 'booster' dose had given her little trouble, but some of her colleagues had had very sore arms.

'You're not worried about that, are you?' asked Kath. 'The smallpox epidemic seems to be at an end now. There haven't been any new cases for quite a while. They wouldn't let us go, you know, if there was any danger.'

'No, it's not that particularly,' said Patsy. 'It's just . . . everything. I feel really low, Kath, mostly about Dad of course. I can't believe this has happened to him and that he'll never walk again.'

'He might. Doctors can be wrong and it's early days yet. Try to look on the bright side, Patsy.'

'I am trying. I am, really. But Mum's so upset I couldn't tell her anything about School Practice and Miss Fletcher. I didn't want to worry her, and it's been getting on my mind. I'm dreading it, Kath.'

'Go to the doctor, love.'

The doctor gave her some stronger pills than the aspirin she had been in the habit of taking and told her to try to stop worrying. That was easier said than done.

Miss Nichols' class of six- to seven-year-olds – thirty-eight of them – were somewhat boisterous, but then, Patsy asked herself, which children were not? The first day didn't go too badly, with Miss Nichols still in charge and Patsy acquainting herself with the children and taking small groups to help them with their maths and reading. But outside of their respective classrooms the four students, Patsy, Kath, Jane and Sheila, were made to feel very much the unwanted guests. Patsy remembered anew, that first playtime, what she had always known: Miss Fletcher didn't like students, and now that she had a school of her own, was obviously going to treat them with the contempt she thought they deserved.

'I thought you four would be happier in here than in the staffroom,' she said to them, as she pushed open the door of a bare cheerless room which was normally used, when doctors and dentists visited the school, as the medical room. 'I know you will have certain things to discuss,' she said frostily, an arch little smile barely curving her lips. 'And the staff, too, like their privacy,' she added. 'You can make yourselves a cup of tea but be sure to wash up afterwards. And the bell goes in fifteen minutes, prompt.'

The four girls stared round at the bleak surroundings; at the high bed in the corner, covered with a stiff white sheet and a grey army blanket, reminding Patsy too forcibly of the one her father had occupied recently; at the weighing scales and the clinical-looking sink and the four uncomfortable wooden chairs; at the fawn-coloured walls with not a trace of adornment and the dingy brown curtains at the window.

'Have you ever felt you're not wanted?' said Jane. 'My God, Patsy. What was that you said about it being the head who makes a school? I only hope the rest of the staff aren't like her. She's enough to turn the milk sour, that woman.'

'Never mind,' said Kath. 'At least there's a kettle and a teapot. She's even left us some milk. Now, isn't that generous? We can make a cup of tea. That's if the old so-

and-so hasn't turned the milk sour, like you said, Jane.'

It was the next day, when she was left in charge of the class for the first time, that Patsy's troubles really started. She had been determined, in spite of feeling sick at heart and depressed at the whole venture, to be well prepared and had worked hard in getting everything ready for her class well in advance.

She decided to rearrange the room, placing the children into five animal groups. They could compete against each other for team points, awarded for satisfactory work and good behaviour, an incentive to them, she hoped, and a way of bringing the animal theme into every aspect of the curriculum. Lions, bears, wolves, giraffes and monkeys; those were the five groups. Miss Nichols, the class teacher, could have warned Patsy in advance that monkeys would not be a very wise choice, but Miss Nichols had scurried away to the staffroom at the first opportunity, leaving her student to the mercies of a room full of wild animals. Besides, Patsy's choice of groups had been largely dictated by the number of pictures she could procure of each species, to paste on the cover of the books she had given them.

Patsy had been unprepared for the inventiveness of children's minds when presented with a chance like this, or for the cunning wiles they will use to take advantage of a less than confident teacher, or for the way they will gang together – even the normally most timid or most friendly of them – when led on by an undisputed leader of the pack. There were two such leaders in this class. Patsy had noticed them even on her preliminary visits. Dennis was a thin, pasty-faced boy with a scowl and a belligerent manner whose dark hair was cut short, barely one inch in length, all over his head. His sparring partner was Gareth, a large blond boy, almost as tall as Patsy herself, with pale blue eyes and a face which would, she thought, as the years advanced, become coarse and lecherous; she had already seen him sneaking a crafty look up the girls' skirts when they sat cross-legged on the floor.

It was these two, Dennis and Gareth, who were the instigators of what followed when the animal books were distributed. From one corner of the room lions roared, 'Grrr . . . grrr . . .', while in the opposite corner the wolves threw back their heads and howled. 'Ya-oow . . . ya-oow . . .' Not to be outdone, the bears grunted and the giraffes, those very silent creatures, contented themselves with waving their arms above their heads in the semblance of a long neck, nodding and bowing to one another. And as for the monkeys, led by Dennis, their creativity knew no bounds. They ran round the table, they jumped on the chairs, they scratched beneath their armpits.

'Stop this noise! Stop it at once!' Patsy stood in front of the class and yelled, something you were told you must never do. You should try to control an unruly class by some means other than shouting, the Education lecturer had told them; you should endeavour to attract their attention by switching on a light, for example, or by opening a window.

Patsy stood there and yelled. After a few moments there was a return to some kind of discipline, not perfect by any means, but at least Patsy could now hear herself speak. 'That was disgraceful behaviour,' she admonished them. 'Just make sure it doesn't happen again.'

Dennis and Gareth didn't retaliate. They merely grinned at one another. Even the most hardened criminals know when the time has come to lie low for a while; there will always be another opportunity. The rest of the day passed without any return to conspicuously bad behaviour, but Patsy was shaken and knew that already she was failing to give of her best. Besides, all that day she was waiting for and dreading the visit of Miss Fletcher to the classroom. It was the headteacher's job to keep an eye on all the students and see how they were coping with a class. Patsy knew that a visitation from Miss Fletcher was inevitable.

She came towards the end of the afternoon when Patsy was halfway through reading the story of 'The Cat That Walked by Himself'. For once the class was quiet, seemingly engrossed in the tale of the creature who refused to be tamed or submit to the will of man. But they turned as one at the sound of the door opening and then closing, more loudly than was necessary.

'Now take no notice of me,' said Miss Fletcher. 'Just listen to Miss Bradshaw's story, and I'll sit here and listen as well.'

She picked up one of the two normal sized teacher's chairs and carried it across the room, seating herself in full view of the children, not inconspicuously at the back as tutors usually did. She had, as Patsy was sure she had intended to, interrupted the flow of the story and put Patsy off her stride. She prided herself on her dramatic reading, but now, with Miss Fletcher's steely blue eyes upon her, felt that her rendering of the story was less than convincing. She faltered through to the end.

' " . . . Then he goes out to the Wet Wild Woods or up the Wet Wild Trees or on the Wet Wild Roofs, waving his wild tail and walking his wild lone." That's the end of the story, children,' said Patsy with a inward sigh of relief. 'Did you enjoy it?'

'Yes, Miss Bradshaw,' came the chorus of sing-song voices.

'Good, then we'll have another animal story tomorrow.' She looked enquiringly in the direction of Miss Fletcher who hadn't spoken and was still sitting there motionless.

'Carry on, Miss Bradshaw. You're in charge,' said Miss Fletcher, in the tone of voice that implied that the girl was anything but. 'Carry on and dismiss the class. The bell will be going soon, then I'd like a word with you.'

Patsy was aware of the woman's piercing glance as she told the children to put their chairs on their tables. They did this with the forceful bangs that invariably followed such a request and she saw the headteacher wince. Their hometime prayer, 'Lord, keep us safe this night . . .' was recited in a way that was anything but reverent and Patsy felt her heart sink lower and lower as the class filed out into the cloakroom. She helped them with lost coats and gloves, then returned to the classroom where her adversary – for that was how she thought of the woman – was waiting for her.

Miss Fletcher didn't invite Patsy to sit down, but the girl did so, perching on the edge of one of the children's tables opposite to the headmistress. Her legs were feeling wobbly and she could feel another headache just starting.

'Miss Bradshaw, am I correct in thinking that it is a directive of your college that you should tell the stories and not read them?' Miss Fletcher looked unsmilingly at her, the sinews of her scrawny neck taut as she tilted her chin in the girl's direction.

'Yes . . . yes, I suppose so,' Patsy began. 'It all depends . . .'

'Then why did you not do so? Why did you read that story instead of telling it . . . as you have been instructed to do?'

'I was going to say, Miss Fletcher, that it all depends on the story,' Patsy went on bravely. 'I felt that these stories – the "Just So" stories – would be better read. I don't think we should try to improve upon the words of Rudyard Kipling.'

'What you really mean is that you couldn't be bothered to learn the story,' said Miss Fletcher. 'Too lazy, perhaps?'

'No, that's not true,' Patsy retorted. 'It's not that at all.'

'I think it is.' Miss Fletcher gave a curt nod. 'And I'm telling you that I want you to tell these stories, not read them. I shall come in again tomorrow afternoon to make sure that you do just that.'

'It's not fair, Kath. It's just not fair,' Patsy cried when they reached the haven, albeit a comparative one, of the hall of residence. She flung her bag of books to the floor and sat down heavily on the bed. 'She's got it in for me all right. I told you she would have. I don't know how I'm going to carry on there, day after day, with that woman breathing down my neck. And I've got such a blinding headache.'

'Just get your feet up for ten minutes and I'll make you a cup of tea,' said Kath, looking at her friend with concern. 'And take two of those tablets the doctor gave you.'

'I keep taking them,' said Patsy a few minutes later, swallowing two of the oval-shaped pills with the welcome drink that Kath had made her. 'They're supposed to be stronger than aspirin, but they don't seem to be doing me much good. Oh God, what on earth am I going to do, Kath?'

'Just show her she can't get the better of you,' said her friend. 'Rotten old cow!'

It was the first time Patsy had ever heard her friend use an expression like that and she gave a weak smile. 'Yes, she is, isn't she? I'll try, Kath. I will, really, but it isn't going to be easy.'

That was a vast understatement and Patsy found her troubles increasing day by day. She never really managed to get to grips with the class, worried as she was by her father's state of health – he was, her mum had said, becoming very depressed – her recurrent headaches and, above all, the attitude of Miss Fletcher. Always, it seemed, she would appear when the class was at its worst and Patsy was trying to quell the noise by shouting above it, something Miss Fletcher made clear by her critical frown that she disapproved of most strongly.

It was not only from Miss Fletcher that Patsy received criticism. Miss Osborne, the tutor for the practice and the Physical Education lecturer at college, found a great deal with which to find fault. PE was not Patsy's forte – it had never been, since she was a child – but she had tried valiantly to make her PE lessons interesting, obeying all the dictums that the tutor had passed on to them. Why was it then, Patsy wondered, when she had prepared it all so carefully, that her lessons invariably developed into a 'free for all', with the children chasing wildly around the hall, hurling beanbags at one another or trying to lasso one another with ropes? And why was it that Miss Osborne always seemed to appear when the uproar was at its height?

Patsy struggled on bravely, even attempting to teach a few simple songs, though her piano playing was less than proficient. Very courageously she distributed a selection of percussion instruments – triangles, cymbals, drums and tambourines – and launched into a somewhat faltering rendition of 'Aiken Drum'. It was at the moment that the cymbals were clashing and the drums were booming so loudly that Patsy could scarcely hear herself, and Dennis was wearing his tambourine on his head like a saucy straw boater, that Miss Osborne appeared in the doorway. Patsy might have known that it would be so. Nothing, just nothing, had gone right for her this practice.

'I'm sorry about that, really I am,' Barbara Fennimore

had said, when Patsy told her that the dreaded Miss Fletcher was at Spring Hill and not at Spring Gardens as she had thought. 'There are so many of these new estates being built that you tend to forget which is which. I felt sure she was at Spring Gardens . . . But then, I must admit, I was so glad to see the back of her that I didn't take a great deal of notice as to where she was going. Oh dear, Patsy, how awful for you. She's giving you a hard time, is she?'

Patsy nodded bleakly. 'It's partly my own fault. I can't seem to get to grips with it, Barbara. The kids are little monsters. I just feel I can't cope with it. And I have tried. I've tried so hard. I'm just not cut out for it.'

'Of course you are,' said Barbara. 'Your other two practices have been OK, haven't they?'

'Not so bad.'

'Well then, everyone has to have one bad practice out of the three. It always happens. Anyway, it'll be different when you start teaching properly, when you have your own class . . .'

Patsy had heard that so many times, and now she heard it again with a sinking heart. She didn't want to be a teacher; she knew very definitely now that she didn't. But she also knew that she couldn't possibly tell her mother that, not now, with all the worry about Dad. It would break her heart. Patsy looked across the room at Barbara's three children, Peter, Timothy and Dawn, happily watching Muffin the Mule on television. If children were all like these three everything would be fine. They were angelic kids all right; not too much so – they each had a little spark of spirit and individuality – but they were adorable, loving children and Patsy had grown so fond of them. Especially Peter, of course.

Barbara was concerned about him at the moment, so

Patsy didn't want to worry the young mother too much with her own troubles. Peter had been off school for a week with the recurrent asthma that always made him so poorly. He was getting over it now, but he was still very pale with dark shadows beneath his eyes. Patsy smiled at him fondly as he turned round suddenly and grinned at her.

'Yes, I daresay I'll be all right,' she said now to her friend, trying to conceal the deep-seated misery and fear at the heart of her. 'I'll have to be, won't I? As my mum would say, "It'll all come out in the wash." ' But Patsy feared that this time it wouldn't.

'Miss Bradshaw is hopeless, of course,' said Elsie Fletcher to Miss Osborne, when they had their final discussion about the students. 'She'll never make a teacher. She can't control a class. Miss Nichols or myself have had to sit in to nearly all her lessons to make sure there wasn't a riot. And you can't call that teaching, not when there's someone else in the room, someone that the children know is in control of the situation.'

'I can't help feeling that the girl has tried, though,' said Miss Osborne, wanting to give her, if possible, the benefit of the doubt. The college didn't like turning out failures; it was bad for their image. 'Her lesson notes are well prepared and she has some very good ideas.'

'It's no use having good ideas if you can't carry them out,' Miss Fletcher scoffed. 'And Miss Bradshaw obviously can't.'

'I think we should try to be lenient,' said Miss Osborne. 'I believe she has been having some problems lately. Her father has been very ill; it's sure to have affected her work.'

'Then it shouldn't,' retorted Miss Fletcher. 'A teacher should be single-minded. She should learn to put personal problems behind her when she's in the classroom.'

'But Miss Bradshaw is only a student. She's still learning . . .'

'Then she doesn't seem to have learned very much during her two years at college. Not about controlling a class, at any rate. She has an unfortunate manner too. She can be very insolent. I had a disagreement with her on her last School Practice and she was extremely rude to me.'

'Yes, of course. You've met Miss Bradshaw before, haven't you?' Miss Osborne was thoughtful for a moment. 'But it's this practice we're considering, Miss Fletcher, not the last one. You mustn't let it prejudice your judgment.'

'I've told you, that girl will never make a teacher,' snapped Miss Fletcher. 'Not in a thousand years.'

Miss Osborne sighed. 'I must admit that I'm inclined to agree with you . . . But we must give her another chance.'

Elsie Fletcher had never forgiven the girl who had stood up to her so boldly at Jubilee Lane, trying to put her in the wrong – she, Elsie Fletcher, who was never wrong – in front of the dinner ladies and children. She had sensed in this auburn-haired girl a spark of determination as strong as her own. She knew, too, that the girl had a feeling for the children, a warmth and compassion, that she had never had in all her twenty-five years of teaching. Elsie Fletcher was in the wrong job and she knew it. She didn't like children, but she was determined to get to the top in the career that she had stumbled into.

It had seemed providential when she had found out that the Bradshaw girl was being sent to Spring Hill for her final School Practice. No one was ever allowed to get the better of Elsie Fletcher, and it still rankled that Mr Thomson, the head of Jubilee Lane, had taken the girl's part so readily over that business with that wretched child and his dinner. When she discovered, as she soon did after a few visits to the classroom, that Patsy Bradshaw was making a hash of this School Practice, she felt vindicated. And when she told Miss Osborne that the girl would never make a teacher the words were not spoken entirely out of spite. Instinctively, she knew them to be true.

Chapter 22

It came as no surprise to Patsy to learn, just before she went home for the Easter holidays, that she had failed her final School Practice. But Miss Pritchard, her Education tutor, informed her that she was going to be given another chance. She was to do another three weeks at an entirely different school when they returned after the Easter break.

'Bloody hell! That's all I need.' Patsy flopped down on the bed and looked at her friend, agonised. 'I'd rather they'd just failed me and thrown me out. Told me I was no good at all. I can't do it, Kath. I just can't stand it.'

'Of course you can. You were just unlucky getting Miss Fletcher. It'll be better next time, you'll see. And you've a fortnight's holiday now. Just go home and forget all about it.'

'A fat chance of that, with all the work I have to do,' moaned Patsy. 'And whatever am I going to say to Mum? She'll be furious . . .'

Surprisingly, Jenny was very understanding about Patsy's failure.

'Never mind, dear,' was all she said. 'It was a bad time for you, with your dad being ill. It'll be all right next time.'

Jenny was sympathetic and smiled consolingly at her daughter, but her eyes were sad, as they had been ever since Tom had had the accident. Patsy gathered that her mother had too many other things on her mind at the moment to be unduly concerned about her daughter's career. Tom was finding it hard to adjust to his life in a wheelchair, confined to the downstairs rooms. The house was full of builders – from the firm where Tom had been employed – and joiners and plumbers, making the necessary alterations. The front room, rarely used, was being converted into a bedroom for Tom and Jenny, and a 'glory hole' under the stairs made into a small washroom and toilet. They had also had a phone installed. There were pulleys and handles and rails, and slopes instead of steps, all made for the convenience of a wheelchair, and Patsy felt sick at heart and more depressed than ever when she looked at them.

The Bradshaw family hadn't been over to Blackpool this year as they usually did in the late spring, because of Tom's accident and the alterations to the house. Rosie, of course, was living in Blackpool now, most of the time, but was back in Castleburn for two weeks' holiday from the art school. Patsy hadn't heard from Raymond Sykes recently. Their letter writing had dwindled to about once a month and she rarely thought about him. In one of his letters he had mentioned that Ronnie was now demobbed and was living at home again, working at his former job of joiner and shop-fitter. Patsy wondered, idly, if he still had his German girlfriend, if she would ever see him again . . . but without a great deal of enthusiasm. The melancholy that had threatened to engulf her when she heard about her failed practice had been alleviated slightly by her return to Castleburn, but not entirely so. She couldn't talk about her problems, not even to Rosie to whom she was now as close as ever, and dreaded the return to college – to three weeks' teaching, to final exams, to a pile of essays and projects still to be completed. And never, it seemed, was she free from a headache.

As they were unable to visit Blackpool, Annie Carter came on a rare visit to Yorkshire. She had always been fond of her son-in-law and had been shocked to hear of his accident. When she came, just before the girls were due to return to college, it was the second time she had made the journey by train. Ada and Fred, too, had driven across in their Morris Minor, but once the season started, as it would in a few weeks' time, there would be little opportunity for days off.

'It's a pity we don't all live nearer to one another,' Annie remarked. 'It's a nuisance with me and our Ada and Fred in Blackpool, and you lot on t'other side of the Pennines. Families need one another at times like this, and I won't be able to keep popping over here, not once the visitors start arriving. And it won't be as easy for you to come to us either, our Jenny . . . not now.'

Jenny was glad that her mother had stopped speaking when she did. She didn't want her going on about Tom's accident and the great changes it was bound to make to all their lives. Her mother could be so tactless at times, although Tom knew her well enough to take everything she said with a pinch of salt; he had, Jenny was glad to see, cheered up considerably during Annie's short visit. He had always got on well with his mother-in-law, who had usually tended to take his side and not Jenny's in any family disagreements.

'I don't know so much about that, Ma,' he said now. 'I don't see why we won't be able to come over to Blackpool, like we always did. 'Specially since Jenny's learning to drive.'

'Are you, our Jenny?' Her mother looked at her in amazement. 'You never told me. I'm surprised you're able to find the time.'

'I've only had a couple of lessons, Mother. It was our Rosie's idea. She's been taking lessons in Blackpool, and she persuaded me that it might be a good thing. I've plenty of time really. I've not been working at Mr Fothergill's, not since Tom had his accident. The district nurse pops in to see him a few times a week, and she said it would be better for all of us if I got out as much as I could.'

'So you're thinking of buying a car then, are you?' Annie sniffed. 'I shouldn't have thought you could afford it.'

'Oh, we're not short of a bit of brass, Ma.' Tom grinned at Annie and winked. 'I've always been thrifty. I'm a Yorkshireman born and bred, tha knows,' he added in an exaggerated accent. 'And there'll be compensation for this lot.' He patted at his lower limbs beneath the tartan rug. 'Mind you, I'd rather have the use of me legs and not the money, but that's the way it goes.'

Jenny was pleased to see her husband so cheerful, but she knew that, just as suddenly, his mood was liable to change and that the next day he might well be in the depths of despair.

'And you say Rosie's learning to drive an' all?' said Annie. 'I never knew that. I daresay our Ada knows, but she's never let on. Her and young Rosie are as thick as thieves at times. She won't be able to afford a car just yet, surely?'

'Probably not, Mother. But it'll be handy for her to learn.' And I expect she'll soon be driving Ada and Fred's car, Jenny thought to herself, but didn't voice her thought.

'Aye, she always did have big ideas, that 'un,' remarked Annie, in Rosie's absence. Rosie, Patsy and Victor were all out together that evening on a visit to the cinema, a treat for Victor before his sisters returned to college. 'And what's she going to do with herself when she finishes at that art school?' asked Annie. 'Is she going to get a job in Blackpool?'

'I've no idea, Mother,' said Jenny. 'I don't think she knows either.'

'Aye, well, I suppose time'll tell,' remarked Annie. Her eyes seemed to be focused on Tom's wheelchair. 'I tell you what, our Jenny,' she went on. 'It's a darned sight flatter in Blackpool than it is here. I'm proper puffed with climbing up and down these blessed hills.' She put her hand on her chest, breathing hard. 'It wouldn't do me heart much good if I lived here, and that's a fact.' But Jenny didn't think that Annie was really thinking about herself.

Jenny lay awake for ages that night, the thoughts racing round and round in her mind. Her mother's query as to what Rosie was going to do when she finished college had started her thinking. What a state of flux they seemed to be in at the moment. Both Rosie's and Patsy's future was uncertain, and now Patsy had gone and failed her School Practice. Still, the girl could hardly be blamed for that. And as for herself and Tom, there were times when Jenny felt afraid to look too far ahead. She was overjoyed, of course, that he was still alive, but the future was certainly not going to be easy. They had moved here, to Castleburn, eight years ago because they felt they were ready for a change. Tom had been hankering to return to Yorkshire and his family. Now his mother was dead and they saw very little of his brothers and sisters. Jenny wondered if it was time for another change, but she didn't want to be the one to make the suggestion. As her mother had said, time would tell. She closed her eyes and endeavoured, once more, to go to sleep. But she was still awake, as she often was, when the grey light of dawn peeped through the curtains.

'Those designs of yours are good, you know, Rosie. Damned good, in fact,' said Clive Morrison, Rosie's tutor in design, as they sat together over coffee one morning soon after the Easter break. 'Is that what you want to do eventually, become a textile designer?'

'Yes, I'd like to . . . eventually.' She smiled. 'That's the operative word, isn't it, Clive? Eventually. I know there are a lot of students with the same idea. I'm only one among many.'

'You should have faith in yourself, Rosie. Believe that you can do it . . . and you will.'

'Oh, I do, I do. I know my designs are good.' There was no point in denying the talent that she knew she possessed. 'But I happen to be a realist as well. I know I'll have to get another job in the meantime, to keep the wolf from the door. I'm hoping there might be a job as a window dresser at one of the big stores when I've finished here.'

'In Blackpool?'

'Yes,' said Rosie, with no hesitation. She had settled down in Blackpool so well, so much better than she had anticipated, and now she had no desire to go back to Yorkshire . . . or to London. Dad's accident had complicated matters a little, but once she had learned to drive she would be more mobile. 'Yes, there are quite a few big stores here. I'll have to wait and see if anything comes up.'

'You really should try and do something with those designs of yours though,' Clive went on. 'You have a quite exceptional talent.'

Clive was the second tutor in design to take an interest in Rosie, but she knew that, unlike Jeff Burroni, he was interested only in her work and subsequent career. He was an unexceptional-looking man, fiftyish, with thinning hair and mild grey eyes, but an exceptional artist and tutor, and if he said that Rosie's work was good she knew that it undoubtedly was.

'I particularly like those floral designs you do,' he continued. 'So bold and original. As a matter of fact, I have a friend who owns a mill near Garstang – just a small, family-run business – and I have a feeling that he might be interested in your sort of work. I know he's trying to branch out and get away from the old, stereotyped patterns. What do you think, Rosie? Would you lend me one or two to show him? Mind you, I'm not promising anything . . .'

'Would I?' Her blue eyes opened wide. 'What do you think, Clive? Of course I'll lend them to you. I'm over the moon about it. I'll bring them tomorrow.'

'The sunflower one, of course,' said Clive. 'That one's superb. And the roses design. I know they're part of your portfolio, aren't they, for the NDD? But if we can get a manufacturer interested in the meantime, it will be all to the good. Don't build your hopes up too much though. It's just an idea I had, but it's worth a try.'

'And if you don't try, you never get anywhere, do you?' said Rosie. 'Thanks ever so much, Clive. It's really good of you to suggest it.'

Rosie's floral designs bore little resemblance to the dainty flower patterns – nosegays of forget-me-nots, unobtrusive daisies or delicate sprigs of heather – that had been printed on cotton for many years. Her designs, on the contrary, were eye-catching and bold, almost brash in their conception. They could be very well summed up by the word that was being used more and more in description of anything modern or up-to-date: contemporary.

It seemed to Rosie that nearly every modern home or building that one entered nowadays had the same curtains hanging at the windows: a fabric by David Whitehead with a design of rectangles and circles in bold colours, orange, black, yellow and green. Rosie had been influenced, as had many designers, by this innovative approach, but had concentrated on flowers rather than geometric shapes. Her sunflowers were reminiscent of Van Gogh's, over-large and simply executed, linked by flowing black lines following the curve of the petals. Her roses, too, were overblown, and she had combined colours, pink, red and orange, which at one time no one would ever have considered putting together. But Rosie had confidence in them and in herself. She presented these two, and a couple of others, one of foxgloves and another of autumn leaves, to Clive the next morning, then she metaphorically crossed her fingers and waited.

When Patsy returned to college after the Easter break to start her last term at CLTC, she was in a predicament that she had vowed, at the beginning of her training, that she would never allow herself to get into. The work had piled up alarmingly and she couldn't, for the life of her, see how she was going to get through it all. Always, throughout her first year, she had been conscientious, finishing and handing in essays on time, completing projects and making sure she had done enough 'swotting' to get her through the end of year exams. Now, at the beginning of May, she found herself with an unfinished Education thesis, another uncompleted one on Thomas Hardy for her English course, a shorter essay on Keats to be handed in next week, plus all the revision she knew she must do before final exams started in the middle of June. And, to crown it all, in a fortnight's time she was due to begin her extra School Practice.

She would have thought, at one time, that it was impossible to get into such a situation, but she knew it was due more to force of circumstances than to her own lack of planning and foresight. There had been Dad's accident, of course, which had entailed her being at home for several days; days when, if she had been at college, she would have been working. And then that disastrous practice at Spring Hill for which she had worked so hard, night after night, in the confines of her room – planning projects, drawing pictures, learning stories by heart – and all, in the end, to no avail.

Patsy felt tears of frustration spring to her eyes, as they frequently did these days. Impatiently she brushed them away; she certainly had no time to be sitting around weeping in her PS period. She would work hard, she decided, for the next hour, then go to the phone box in the grounds and ring her friend, Barbara. She was due for a visit there and Barbara and the three children would go a long way towards cheering her up.

Barbara Fennimore, however, on the other end of the line, sounded distracted.

'Oh . . . hello, Patsy. How nice to hear from you.' But her voice didn't have its usual cheerful timbre.

'I was wondering if I could come round and see you all?' Patsy went on. 'One day this week, perhaps?'

There was a pause before Barbara answered, 'I think it would better if you leave it for the moment, Patsy . . .'

'There's something wrong, isn't there, Barbara? You sound worried.'

'Yes . . . I am worried. It's Peter . . . he's not well again.'

'Oh dear. You've had the doctor, have you?'

'Yes, earlier today. He just said to keep him in bed. He's very hot and can't get his breath. The doctor thought it was another attack of asthma. It seemed like it, but I'm afraid he's getting worse. He's complaining of a sore throat and a headache . . . and now there's a rash appearing on his face and arms.'

'Oh, goodness!' Patsy's problems were forgotten for the

moment at the thought of poor little Peter lying ill in bed. And a rash and a sore throat – that sounded ominous. 'Don't you think you'd better call the doctor again?'

'We've just rung him. Colin rang only ten minutes ago. We're waiting for him now. In fact, when you rang I thought it might be some message . . .'

'I'll ring off now, Barbara, and leave you in peace. I'll be in touch with you tomorrow to see how he is. Try not to worry. I'm sure he'll be all right. He's had asthma before.' Patsy tried to force some confidence into her voice, but she had a good idea what Barbara was worrying about. A rash on his face and arms . . . Patsy went cold at the thought.

When she rang again the next day, Patsy's worst fears were confirmed. Peter had smallpox and had been taken into Leeford Sanatorium. 'We can't even see him, except through a window,' his distraught mother told Patsy.

'Oh, Barbara . . . I'm so terribly sorry.' To say she was sorry was not enough, not nearly enough, but Patsy couldn't find words to express the sympathy she was feeling for Barbara and Colin. 'There's no point in me visiting him, then?'

'None at all. Just . . . just say your prayers for him, Patsy.' Barbara's voice broke. 'And for the other two, Timothy and Dawn . . . They'd been playing with him.'

'Of course I will. I'll think about all of you.' Patsy could hardly speak for the lump in her throat and the tears rolling down her cheeks. She pushed open the door of the phone box and blindly made her way back to Calder Hall.

Patsy didn't ring Barbara again, but made a daily enquiry at the Sanatorium, only to be told, each time, that there had been 'no change'. When she rang on the fourth day there was a pause before the voice at the other end enquired, 'Who is that speaking? Are you a relative?'

'No, just a close friend,' Patsy answered. 'Peter used to be in . . . in my class. I was his teacher.'

'I'm very sorry,' said the impersonal voice. 'Peter died early this morning.'

'You're in no fit state to go to the funeral this afternoon,' said Kath to her friend one morning a few days later. 'You've been complaining of a headache for the last three days, and you look far from well. And you've eaten hardly any breakfast. Get back into bed, Patsy, and stay there for the rest of the day. I'll tell Matron.'

'No, I can't.' Patsy shook her head irritably. 'It's not surprising if I look ill, is it?' Her voice sounded petulant. 'You'd look ill if you'd had all that I've had to put up with. First Dad, and then that damned School Practice, and now Peter . . .'

'I know, love, I know.' Kath put a consoling arm round her friend. 'And you've been awfully brave. I know I couldn't have coped with it all any better than you have done. But I think you need a rest. A complete day in bed. You're due at Burnsall Road on Monday, aren't you? You want to be fit for that.'

Patsy shook her head, bemused. 'I'm not fit for anything, Kath. Certainly not for another School Practice. But I've got to go to Peter's funeral. I'd never forgive myself if I didn't. You know I've asked for time off from lectures . . . I'm sorry I snapped at you, love. I know I'm irritable lately. I've such a lot on my mind.' Patsy put both hands to her temples, pressing at the dull ache starting again in her head and closed her eyes tightly. 'I've got to go, Kath.'

'Then I'm coming with you. I'm certainly not letting you go on your own.'

'What about your lectures?'

'Be hanged to the lectures! It'll be the first time that I've skipped any in two years, and if they want to know why, I'll tell them the truth.'

'Thanks, Kath.' Patsy smiled sadly. 'I don't know what I'd do without you.'

The two young women stood at the back of the crowd of mourners, a little away from the family and close friends who were grouped round the open grave, that ominous gaping hole in the ground. The last funeral Patsy had attended – the only one, in fact, that she had ever attended – had been that of her Granny Bradshaw. She had been sad that day, of course, at the death of her beloved grandmother and friend, but she had known that Gran had had a long life, a good and satisfying one, too. There had been rejoicing as well as sadness at the thought that the old lady had gone to meet her Lord and Saviour whom she had loved and served so faithfully.

This death of a child, though, was something that Patsy was finding very hard to accept; but not nearly so hard, she was sure, as his parents must be finding it. Barbara had seemed to bear up surprisingly well during the church service, supported by the arm of her husband round her all the time. They both looked very pale and small – Barbara dressed completely in black and Colin in a dark grey suit – and appeared abstracted, as though their minds were elsewhere. Patsy hadn't spoken to Barbara since Peter's death, but had written to her and had found out from Jubilee Lane school when and where the funeral was to be held. She couldn't let Peter go without saying her own personal goodbye to him. He had been one of the few children who had brought any joy at all into her limited experience of teaching. She knew how much she would miss him, but if she was feeling grief-stricken and bereft – and unbelieving – then how, she wondered, must his parents be feeling? The death of a child must surely be the worst tragedy of all to face. It was contrary to the natural order of things; one expected, eventually, to lose one's parents – and how near she had come to losing Dad, Patsy thought – but a child, how could one ever face up to it? Would it help at all, Patsy mused, that Barbara and Colin had two more children, or that Peter had always been a frail child and that they might, therefore, have been somewhat prepared for his early demise?

Patsy had been unable to join in the singing of the hymns: 'Jesu, Lover of my soul' – the one they had sung at her gran's funeral – or the heart-rending Victorian hymn, 'There's a Friend for Little Children'.

'. . . A rest from every turmoil,
From sin and sorrow free,
Where every little pilgrim
Shall rest eternally.'

But what comfort was that, when Peter was only eight years old, loving and cherished, with, one would have supposed, a whole lifetime ahead of him? Patsy tried to fight back the tears, but failed. She saw them drop on to the page of her open hymn book, then, at the same moment, felt Kath's arm clinging tightly to her own. She half-turned to meet her friend's compassionate glance. Whatever would she do without Kath?

In the churchyard the sun shone brightly from a sky of cloudless blue. The mourners blinked when they filed out of the gloomy greystone church into its brilliance. How dare the sun shine on such a day? thought Patsy, bathing everyone in its life, giving warmth and radiance, when at the heart of several of those present there must be blackness and despair and a fear as to how on earth they were going to carry on, to face the morrow. The fear was in Patsy's own heart, and not solely because of Peter's death. There was so much else that was troubling her. The dappled sunlight filtered through the branches of the sycamore trees in their late-spring foliage; on to the headstones of mottled marble and soot-grimed stone; on to the bowed heads of the mourners; on to the rows and rows of floral tributes, carnations, early roses, pinks and sweet williams fashioned into wreaths and sprays, one in the shape of a football – the game that Peter had tried so manfully to play – another in the form of a teddy bear.

As the tiny coffin was lowered into the ground and Patsy heard the clods of earth fall on to the lid she felt she could bear it no longer. She hid her head against Kath's shoulder and wept.

'Come on, love. It's all over,' said her friend gently, a few moments later. 'Let's go and sit on that seat for a little while, shall we, before we get the tram back?'

Patsy nodded bleakly. She felt dazed, caring little about what she was to do in the next few minutes, or hours, or days . . .

'Now, you're sure you're feeling better?' Kath asked later that evening. 'Has your headache gone?'

'For the moment, yes,' answered Patsy. 'It eased off after I'd had my tea.'

'I told you that you needed something to eat,' said Kath. She looked solicitously at her friend, her grey eyes grave. 'Now, you will have an early night, won't you? Never mind about your work tonight. There's always tomorrow, and I'm sure if you explain how you've been feeling the tutors won't mind if you're a bit late handing in your theses. They know you've had a lot on your plate, lately.'

'Work . . . what does it matter? What does anything matter, Kath? I'm past caring.' Patsy's voice was apathetic and her eyes were blank pools of nothingness.

Kath look at her sharply. 'You're tired, love. You'll feel better about things in the morning.'

'Yes . . . I'm tired, Kath. Very . . . tired. I'll have an early night, like you said.' Patsy put her arm round her friend then and kissed her cheek, something she had never done before. 'Thanks, Kath . . . for everything.'

'Don't mention it, kid.' Kath smiled. 'See you in the morning.'

'Yes . . . see you,' echoed Patsy as her friend closed the bedroom door behind her.

Patsy wanted to be on her own, completely on her own. At the moment she didn't even want Kath. Her headache had not gone, as she had told her friend. It was always with her now, a throbbing in her temples, sometimes faint and bearable, at other times like red hot needles searing into her brain. It was coming on again now, increasing in intensity, bringing in its wake thoughts and images and worries that she wanted, so badly, to black out. Dad, a prisoner in his wheelchair . . . Peter's coffin being lowered mercilessly into the ground . . . Miss Fletcher's pale blue eyes, venomous with dislike . . . Neil Emmerson walking away from her, his arm round Rosie . . . Teaching practice, unfinished theses, Keats, Thomas Hardy . . . They were all spinning round and round in Patsy's mind like whirling dervishes. She wanted oblivion, a respite from her chaotic thoughts. She stood in the middle of the bedroom, her head in her hands. Stop, stop, stop, she shouted to the shifting images inside her head. Stop, for God's sake, stop . . .

She glanced at her bedside clock. 8.30, right in the middle of the Private Study period. But Patsy knew that she couldn't study tonight. She doubted if she could ever study again. Blindly, hardly knowing what she was doing, she picked up a beaker and crept along to the washroom to fill it from the tap. She was still hardly aware of her actions when, back in the silence and solitude of her bedroom, she unscrewed the cap of her bottle of pills and tipped out the contents on to her hand. There were about twenty of the small oval tablets left. Hazily, Patsy stared at them; she had taken six already today – or was it more? – and the pain in her head was still there. All Patsy wanted was relief from the unbearable pain, and peace and quiet. She got up and walked across to the door and turned the key in the lock.

Kath wasn't sure why, at 10.30 that night, she felt a compulsion to go and see if her friend was all right. It was no doubt a silly thing to do, she thought, as she crept along the corridor. Patsy would more than likely be asleep and would curse Kath if she woke her up. But she was worried; Patsy had seemed so strange . . . She was even more worried when she tried the handle of the door and found that it was locked. Patsy never locked herself in at night. Some students did and some didn't. Patsy always said it made her feel as though she was in prison, even though the key was on her side of the door.

Kath knocked gently. 'Patsy . . . Patsy, are you all right?'

There was no answer.

Kath knocked again, louder this time. So loudly, in fact, that the neighbouring door opened and Hilary Schofield, Patsy's college daughter, came out. 'What is going on?' she asked, a trifle irritably.

Kath could see from the girl's attire of pyjamas and dressing gown, and the curlers in her hair, that Hilary had been preparing for bed. 'Sorry,' she whispered. 'I didn't mean to disturb you. I'm worried about Patsy. Her bedroom door's locked. She never locks it as a rule . . . and she's not been well, you know.'

Hilary looked concerned. 'No, I know she's been under a lot of strain. But you don't think . . . ?'

'I don't know what I think,' said Kath, 'but I'm worried.' She knocked again. 'Patsy, Patsy . . . open the door.'

'Look,' she went on, when there was still no reply. 'I'm going down to fetch Matron. She has a master key. She'll be able to get in.'

'I'll come with you,' said Hilary. 'But I expect she'll think we're making a fuss about nothing.'

Miss Macallister was indeed not pleased to be disturbed as she was preparing for bed, but she listened gravely to what the girls told her. 'Yes . . . yes, I do understand,' she said. 'Miss Bradshaw has not been herself for some time. I did have a word with her, but she insisted she was all right.'

Kath and Hilary heard the key on the inside of the door fall with a heavy clunk as Miss Macallister inserted the master key. Then she pushed open the door. Before she switched on the light they could see, in the dim light filtering through the thin curtains, that Patsy was lying on the bed fully clothed, on top of the counterpane. When Kath, panic-stricken, turned on the light, they saw with mounting horror the beaker on Patsy's bedside table, the empty pill bottle at its side and their friend's white, death-like face and motionless form.

'Oh no . . . My God, no!' Kath rushed forward and seized her friend's hand, feeling desperately for a pulse. 'She's not . . . She can't be . . .' She turned to Miss Macallister, staring at her pleadingly. 'Tell me she isn't . . .'

'I don't know, Miss Merriman. Step back a minute, please.' Matron's tone was curt, but Kath knew she didn't mean to be unkind. She took a step back while Matron placed her hand on Patsy's forehead. 'We'd better get an ambulance right away,' she said, not looking at the terrified girls. 'There's no time to lose.'

'She isn't . . . ?' Kath faltered again.

'I don't know, Miss Merriman,' said Matron, for the second time. She shook her head and hurried away while Kath and Hilary cowered together in Patsy's doorway, too frightened even to speak.

It wasn't long before the ambulance men arrived and carried Patsy's inert form out to the waiting vehicle.

Kath held her head in her hands and wept. 'Oh, Patsy, why? Why did you do it?'

Chapter 23

'This is all your fault, our Jenny.' Annie Carter's breathing was laboured, not with the Yorkshire hills this time – she had just taken a taxi from the station – but with concern for her beloved granddaughter. 'I knew right from the start that the lass wasn't happy at that there college.'

'Don't start on at me, Mother, the minute you set foot through the door.' Jenny glared at her mother, then gave a heartfelt sigh. 'Don't you think I've already been through it all, time and time again? Reproaching myself, wondering where I've gone wrong . . .'

'She should never have gone there in the first place.' Annie flopped down in the armchair, her legs stuck stiffly out in front of her as she took the weight off her bunioned feet. 'She wasn't happy, I tell you. Anyone with half an eye could see that.'

'She always seemed happy enough, Mother. She had some nice friends there. That Gwen who was her college mother. And Kath Merriman's a lovely girl. She came here once and I was so glad our Patsy had such a nice friend.'

'She couldn't have been happy to try and do what she did, poor lamb.' Annie produced a large handkerchief from the depths of her capacious black bag and dabbed at her eyes behind the thick-lensed spectacles. 'When I think of what might have happened . . .'

Jenny interrupted swiftly. 'Well, it didn't, Mother, thank God. And we don't know that Patsy did try to . . . We don't know why she did it. She doesn't even know herself. They said at the hospital that she was under severe strain, that she was more poorly with those damned headaches than any of us realised.'

'And she was unhappy, Jenny,' said Tom softly. He had been sitting quietly and taking it all in, but speaking little, as was his way. 'She's been unhappy about me. I know that, and then that little lad died. Poor lass . . . she's had an awful lot to put up with just lately, not just with the teaching. So you mustn't go blaming yourself, Jenny love. 'It's not your fault.' He looked meaningfully at his mother-in-law. 'No one's saying it is.'

'No . . . no, I'm not really blaming you, our Jenny,' said Annie gruffly. 'I'm sorry if I spoke out of turn, but I've been that upset about it all. I couldn't rest till I came over to see you all.'

'We've all been upset, Mother,' said Jenny quietly.

'I thought right from the start, though, that the lass wasn't cut out to be a teacher,' Annie went on, determined to press her point. 'You can't fit a square peg into a round hole, and it strikes me that that's what they've been trying to do at that college. Making a teacher out of Patsy when she's not right for it. She's too quiet to be a teacher.'

'I don't think that being quiet has very much to do with it, Gran,' Rosie remarked. She, too, had said very little since Annie came in. 'Lots of teachers are quiet people. It's possibly the quiet ones that make some of the best teachers. But you're quite right in saying that Patsy wasn't cut out for it. Her heart wasn't in it – it never has been – and I should imagine that if you don't really want to do it, then teaching can be one of the worst jobs in the world.' She smiled at Annie, who nodded briefly and smiled back at her. Rosie and the older woman were in agreement for once.

'Well, she doesn't need to do it now, does she?' said Jenny flatly. 'She's not going back to college, and it seemed to be a load off her mind straightaway when she knew that. I'm not afraid of admitting when I'm wrong.' She stared at the three of them, Annie, Tom and Rosie, in turn. 'And I know now that I was wrong in persuading her to train to be a teacher . . . I just wanted her to have all the chances I never had,' she added quietly, half to herself.

'Nobody's blaming you, lass,' said Tom again. They looked at one another and smiled, a look of deep understanding and, on Jenny's part, of gratitude.

The last couple of days had been traumatic for all of them. The phone call had come late at night from the hospital, telling them that Patsy had taken an overdose of pills, although by that time, thankfully, they had been able to bring her round. Jenny had dashed over to Leeford the next day to see her daughter and now, the following day, Saturday, Annie had come over post haste from Blackpool. She would be going with Jenny later that day to see her granddaughter. Rosie, too, was in Yorkshire for the weekend although she had to return in time for lectures on Monday. Victor was out playing cricket; he knew his sister was ill, but they had told him very few details.

Patsy had been quiet and subdued when Jenny visited her and had said little about what had happened, or why. And Jenny, wisely for once, hadn't pressed her.

'All that work, Mum. And the teaching . . . I just felt I'd never get through,' was the only clue she gave, but from the listless tone of her voice it sounded as though she didn't much care either.

'Don't worry, love. You won't have to.' Jenny patted her hand, lying on the stark white hospital sheet. 'You're not going back there. That's all settled.'

It had been amazing, Jenny thought, how the weight immediately seemed to fall from her daughter's shoulders, and how she smiled – really smiled, with her eyes as well as her lips – for the first time since her mother had entered the ward. 'Oh, Mum, do you really mean it? I haven't to finish my course? I haven't to do my School Practice?'

'No, none of it, dear. Just concentrate on getting well, that's all we want, your dad and me.'

The doctor had warned Jenny that it would be unwise for Patsy to continue with her teaching course. She had been on the verge of a breakdown and he saw her overdose as a cry for help, although the girl herself may not have known this. At all events, she was in good hands now and a few days' nursing could only be beneficial. She would be coming home to Castleburn some time next week and Mr Jones from next-door had offered to run Jenny over in the car to collect her.

'And she'll need looking after,' Jenny said now to her mother and Tom and Rosie. She was determined to make amends for the dreadful guilt that she was feeling about her daughter's unhappiness. She had had no idea that the girl was so miserable, that her aversion to the career that her mother had unwittingly coerced her into had been so great. 'She'll not go short of anything here. She'll have the best care and attention. I daresay it'll take her a while to get over all she's been through. Yes, I shall make sure I look after our Patsy when she comes home.'

'Mum . . .' Rosie was looking keenly at her mother. 'If you don't mind me saying so, I don't think that that's what Patsy needs at all.'

'Whatever are you talking about, Rosie?' Jenny's voice was sharp. 'Please trust me to know what's best for my own daughter.'

'Yes . . . yes, I know you mean well,' Rosie said placatingly. 'Of course you want to do your best for Patsy. But I don't think it would be wise to fuss over her too much, to make her think she's an invalid. She's not. She's been ill, I know, but it's in her mind, not her body. She needs time now to sort herself out. To . . . find herself, I suppose. She's been forcing herself into a mould that's all wrong for her these last two years. You've admitted that, haven't you, Mum? Now she'll have to decide – by herself – what it is she really wants to do.'

'The lass is right, you know, Jenny,' said Annie, looking approvingly at Rosie. 'She's just about put her finger on it. Leave our Patsy alone. Let her decide for herself . . . for a change,' she added quietly.

Jenny nodded. 'Yes . . . yes, I know you're right. And what Patsy'll want, you can be sure, is to go back and work in the antique shop.'

'And is it such a bad idea, if it's what she wants?' said Tom gently.

'Never mind about her finding a job, not just yet,' said Annie. 'From all accounts she's been working like a slave at that damned college. Nearly driven herself barmy with it all. I never did approve of all that book learning, especially for a girl. It strikes me that what our Patsy'll really need is a holiday. Let her come over to Blackpool for a few weeks and have a complete rest. She can think about getting a job later on.'

'Yes, that's a good idea, Mother,' said Jenny. 'I'd like her with me though, just for a little while.' Her eyes suddenly filled up with tears and Annie nodded understandingly.

'Aye, of course you will. I know that. But Patsy's always liked the seaside. She's sand-grown, don't forget, and the Blackpool breezes'll be better for her than any tonic.

Anyroad, we'll see what she thinks of the idea this afternoon. She can come over to "Pleasant View" whenever she's ready.'

'Or she could stay at Aunt Ada's with me, Gran,' suggested Rosie. 'There's twin beds in my room.'

'Oh aye, I keep forgetting you're there an' all now,' said Annie. 'Well, the lass can please herself where she stays. But she's always been happy with me,' she added, a touch defiantly. 'And I shan't have her working like she did last year, if that's what you're thinking. She'll be a visitor this time, good and proper.'

Tom grinned. 'How are they managing without you, Ma, this weekend? It's change-over day, isn't it? And you're not there to supervise.'

'I don't suppose the place'll collapse,' said Annie drily. 'Ada and Fred can manage well enough, with the two lasses we've got in to help. We're not full up yet – it's only the middle of May – but it'll be getting hectic in a week or two, round about Whit week. Anyroad, it makes no difference how busy we are. Family comes first and I had to get myself over here when I heard about Patsy.

'My goodness,' she continued. 'We've had some upsets one way and another just lately. Let's hope there's no more of 'em. They always say troubles come in threes, don't they?'

'Then we've had our three, Gran,' Rosie broke in quickly. 'At least Patsy has. There was Dad, and then that poor little lad, Peter, and then Patsy's . . . accident. There won't be any more catastrophes,' she added firmly, her glance saying quite clearly that her gran hadn't to go anticipating any.

'I certainly hope not,' said Annie. 'I seem to have done nothing just lately but traipse over here. Not that I mind, of course, but I told you before, our Jenny, we should all be living a bit nearer to one another.'

Jenny looked across at Tom and he nodded meaningfully at her. But he also motioned to her by a shushing movement with his lips that now was not the time to discuss their plans. It was several hours later that he brought the subject up, as they both lay wide awake, as they often still were at midnight, in their big double bed.

'I've been thinking,' he began, a remark that prefaced many of Tom's more serious discussions. 'What your mother said about us all living nearer to one another makes senses, doesn't it? How would you feel about moving back to Blackpool?'

Jenny smiled in the semi-darkness, then she felt for Tom's hand where it lay on top of the counterpane. 'I think it would be a grand idea,' she said. 'But it has to be what you want, Tom. I don't want to feel that you're suggesting it just to please me.'

'I'm not. I really think it would be for the best. Your ma's not getting any younger and – like she keeps telling us – there's not so many hills in Blackpool. It 'ud be easier to negotiate that damned wheelchair on the flatter ground.'

Jenny noticed the hint of bitterness in his voice and she squeezed his hand before she adroitly latched on to his earlier remark about her mother's age. 'Yes, I've felt for quite a while that it would be better if we lived nearer to Mother. She's no spring chicken now, although she'll never admit it. Like she says, she'll never leave that kitchen till they carry her out feet first. It's up to me, I suppose, to keep an eye on her. Our Violet can't do much, over in Vermont. It's funny though, when you come to think of it,' Jenny added thoughtfully. 'One of the main reasons for me wanting to come and live in Yorkshire was to get away from Mother.'

'Circumstances alter cases, Jenny,' replied Tom. 'I reckon you and your ma had seen more than enough of one another at that time. Working together all through the war, and for years before that as well, you got on one another's nerves. It would be different now. You're independent of her now, love. You've been free of her for the last eight years.'

'She still tries to boss me though,' said Jenny, 'if she gets half a chance. You heard what she said about our Patsy. Blaming me like that . . .'

'I don't think she meant to be unkind, love. She was very upset. She thinks the world of Patsy; always has.'

'And so do I, Tom,' said Jenny quietly. 'I know I haven't always shown it. We've been like cat and dog sometimes, me and our Patsy, but if anything had happened to her . . . Oh, Tom.' Jenny's voice broke. 'If it had, I just wouldn't have been able to bear it.'

'Hush, love. Hush.' Tom threw his arm round his wife and stroked her shoulder. 'It doesn't do to dwell on what might have happened. Just thank God that it didn't. The lass is all right. At least she soon will be, once she gets out of hospital.'

'History repeats itself, Tom,' said Jenny reflectively. 'I've thought so many a time. When me and our Patsy have been going at it hammer and tongs I've thought to myself, it's just like my mother and me all over again. Mother tried to dominate me and – I knew all the time I shouldn't have been doing it – I tried to dominate Patsy. And I'm sorry now. I should have let her go her own way. If she hadn't gone to that college . . .'

'I've told you, Jenny, it's useless to say if. It'll all sort itself out, you'll see.'

'And I tried to interfere when she was friendly with Ronnie Sykes,' Jenny went on as though Tom hadn't spoken. 'And that all broke up, didn't it?'

'That wasn't your fault,' said Tom decidedly. 'The pair of them had a quarrel, ages afterwards. It was nothing to do with you, Jenny.'

'No, perhaps not . . . Anyway, she may be able to see him if she goes to Blackpool.'

'Just leave it, Jenny,' said Tom patiently. 'Let it all sort itself out. Anyroad, it's the other twin she's friendly with now, isn't it?' Jenny felt, rather than saw, Tom's grin.

'Oh, yes . . . Raymond. I forgot. D'you think she'll want to move to Blackpool with us, Tom? You've all been going on at me about letting Patsy go her own way. We'll have to let her make up her own mind. She might not be terribly keen on leaving Yorkshire. She's made friends here . . .'

'I think you'll find that she'll want to be where Rosie is,' said Tom. 'Those two are the best of friends again now, aren't they? Anyroad, I don't think Rosie'll want to leave Blackpool now, do you? She seems very settled there, especially with that window dresser's job coming up when she leaves college.'

'Yes, and then there's Archie,' said Jenny.

'Yes, there's him,' agreed Tom. There was a few seconds' silence before he spoke again. 'At any rate, Jenny, I can tell you one thing. We won't be living round the corner from your mother this time. I've no objection to living in Blackpool . . .'

'What d'you mean, you've no objection? It was you who suggested it, wasn't it?'

'Aye, well, maybe it was. Like I say, I don't mind living there, but it'll have to be far enough away this time, not just round the corner from "Pleasant View", like we were before. Near enough, but far enough, if you know what I mean.'

'We'll go over then soon, shall we, Tom, and do a spot of house-hunting? We could go on the train, perhaps, the same time as Patsy goes to stay with my mother. I could easily manage your wheelchair on the train.'

'No, that's not a good idea,' he said. 'You know what we've said about letting the lass be independent. We don't want her to think we're following her around. Let's just sit on it for a while, Jenny, and keep it to ourselves. There's all summer ahead of us. But we'll go, I promise you. We'll definitely go.'

Jenny knew that Tom would be making the move primarily for her benefit, just as, when they moved to Castleburn eight years ago, Jenny had done it mainly because she had known it was what her husband desired. Such, she thought, was the basis of a good marriage – an equal share of giving and taking – and, all told, the two of them hadn't fared too badly during their twenty-two years together. Jenny closed her eyes and that night slept more peacefully than she had done since Tom's accident.

Patsy's meeting with Rosie was far more emotional and, therefore, far more beneficial to Patsy than her meeting with her mother and gran had been. Jenny and Annie had decided to let Rosie visit Leeford hospital on her own on the Sunday, knowing that the girls would want some time alone together. And Jenny was taking to heart the advice of all her family to let Patsy find her own feet.

Patsy's tears fell freely and uncontrollably when she saw her sister at her bedside, and when Rosie put her arms round her she clung to her and gave vent to the emotion she hadn't felt able to express in front of her mother and grandmother.

'Hush . . . hush, love.' Rosie disengaged herself and reached in her shoulder bag for a tissue. Gently she wiped her sister's eyes and cheeks. 'Don't make all that noise. The nurses'll be turning me out. They'll think I'm upsetting you.'

Patsy glanced round half-fearfully. 'They're not here at the moment. But they're all very kind . . . Oh, Rosie, I'm so glad to see you. It was all so awful – college and School Practice and Dad . . . and then Peter – and I couldn't tell Mum about it and you weren't there. I didn't know what I was going to do. I felt as though I was going mad.'

Rosie sat down on the chair beside the bed. 'Don't think about it, Patsy. It's all over now. Not unless you want to think about it. Does it help . . . to talk?'

'I don't know.' She shook her head. 'I think it might help . . . I'd got into such a mess and a muddle that I didn't know what I was doing. And those headaches . . . I couldn't describe how awful they'd become.'

'And they've gone now, have they?'

'Yes, completely. When I woke up after . . . when I woke up, my headache had gone. And now that Mum has told me that I don't need to go back to college my mind feels much clearer. I don't think I'll be troubled with them again, not such severe ones anyway.'

'That's good. That's very good. Was it so awful, Patsy, at college? It must have been dreadful for you, being there day after day and hating it so much. And you never said . . .'

'I didn't hate it, Rosie. I liked college, but it was what had to come at the end of it all – teaching – that I couldn't face. I knew it wasn't for me. But I didn't dare tell Mum . . . she wanted it so badly and I was trying to please her. I daresay she'll be mad with me when she gets over the shock of it all.'

'I don't think so, Patsy,' said Rosie quietly. 'In fact, I know she won't be mad at you. Mum realises now that you made a wrong decision in going to college.'

'You mean *she* did.'

'Well . . . whatever. She knows it wasn't right for you. She just wants you to get well again now, before you decide what it is you really want to do.'

Patsy was silent for a moment. Then, 'I suppose I'll go back to Mr Fothergill's,' she said. 'Mum doesn't seem to want to go back to work there, since Dad had his accident.'

Rosie nodded. 'That's just a few half days a week, isn't it? Still, I suppose it would do for the time being and you always enjoyed working there. There's no rush though, is there, for you to get a job? You need a holiday first. Gran was suggesting that you went to Blackpool to stay with her.'

'Yes, she was very insistent that I should go, and Mum was, too. And I will, of course, in a week or two. That job at Mr Fothergill's,' Patsy went on musingly. 'I've a feeling there could be a full-time job there soon, and I know he'd offer it to me if I wanted it. He was hinting, the last time I called in, that part-time help wasn't enough. He's getting older, and the business has expanded quite a lot recently.'

'That's great, kid!' said Rosie eagerly. 'Just what you need. It couldn't be better.' She looked at her sister's serious face. 'What's the matter? You don't seem very keen on the idea.'

'I'm not. Oh heck! This sounds awful, Rosie, but it would mean living at home again. With Mum fussing all over me. I know what's going to happen the minute I leave here. She'll try to smother me, try to tell me what to do . . .'

'I don't think so, Patsy,' said Rosie again. 'I think you'll find she's changed.' She took hold of her sister's hand.

'Anyway, we shouldn't be talking about jobs, should we? Never mind about work; just concentrate on getting well again.'

'You know what I mean though, don't you?' Patsy persisted. 'About living at home again. I don't think I could do it now, after I've had my freedom for two years – well, comparative freedom. College wasn't all bad. It's helped me to stand on my own feet. You couldn't go back to living at home, could you, Rosie, not now?'

'No . . . it's great at Aunt Ada's. Just like having my own flat.'

'And you've a job lined up in Blackpool when you finish at college, haven't you? So there's no chance of you going back to Yorkshire.'

'Yes, it was a stroke of luck getting that window dresser's job at Hill's store,' said Rosie. 'They want me to start straightaway, as soon as I finish at the end of June.'

'Smashing!' Patsy smiled at her sister. 'That's great, isn't it? Are you looking forward to it?'

Rosie could see that Patsy was genuinely pleased for her. They had always, before they started being at loggerheads, rejoiced in one another's good fortune and Rosie was happy that their relationship was now back on its former footing. She could see, though, that her sister was tired – she was very pale, with dark shadows beneath her eyes – and still worried about many things. Even though she insisted that those wretched headaches had disappeared and though the burden of college and the threat of an unwanted teaching career had been lifted, she still looked anxious, her future, as yet, very uncertain.

Now, Rosie decided, was not the time to tell her sister her other piece of news, that her floral textile designs had been accepted by the mill near Garstang and were to be reproduced – in limited quantities at first – in the next month or two. Rosie now had two jobs in the offing, while all Patsy had at the moment was an abandoned teaching course and, quite possibly, a sense of failure.

'Yes, I'm looking forward to the job at Hill's,' Rosie answered brightly, not adding, as she often thought to herself, that it would be just a stop-gap until she saw how her other venture progressed. 'It will be a real challenge. I used to be very impressed by the window displays in Harrod's, when I lived in South Kensington. It'll be good to introduce some new ideas up in Blackpool. Contemporary, they call them now.'

'So you intend to make Blackpool sit up and take notice?' Patsy grinned. 'Rosie Bradshaw's window displays'll be the talk of the town, I can see.'

'Oh, I don't think Blackpool does too badly anyway,' Rosie remarked. 'The town's motto is "Progress", you know, and they certainly try to live up to it. But I shall try to add a bit of sparkle to Bank Hey Street.'

'And I'm sure you'll succeed,' said Patsy. She was silent for a moment, then her next words echoed Rosie's fears. 'You know . . . I can't help feeling I'm a hopeless failure. Two years at college, and what have I got to show for it? Nothing . . . nothing at all. And what a waste of the rate payers' money too . . .'

Rosie laughed. 'You sound just like Gran. I shouldn't worry too much about that if I were you. It's far better for you to decide now that it isn't for you than to find you hated your first teaching post. And there's an awful lot of wastage in the teaching profession anyway; girls teaching for a year or two then leaving as soon as they start a family. It's happening all the time.'

'At least they've achieved something,' said Patsy flatly, 'which is more than I've done.'

'Rubbish!' said Rosie. 'Look at all the good things

you've got from college. Your independence, and all those nice friends. I was very impressed with your friends, Patsy, especially Kath.'

'Yes, Kath,' said Patsy quietly. 'I shall miss her a lot. She called in to see me yesterday, with Hilary, but they couldn't stay long because Mum and Gran were here. It's strange to think I won't be seeing Kath every day. I'll hardly see her at all now.'

'Of course you will. Didn't you tell me she's getting a teaching post in Leeford, that she's decided to stay here instead of going back up north?' Patsy nodded. 'Then you'll see a lot of her, you can be sure. Friendships like that don't disappear overnight. Try to look on the bright side, Patsy. Think positive! And you'll achieve what you want in the end, I know you will.'

'There was Ronnie Sykes, too,' said Patsy thoughtfully.

'Hmmm?' Rosie looked at her enquiringly. 'What about him?'

'That was something good that came out of college . . . then I went and lost him.'

'Then you found his brother instead, didn't you? Make up your mind, Patsy Bradshaw. Proper little flirt you are and no mistake.'

The sisters grinned at one another, both remembering that that was the very accusation Patsy had once levelled at Rosie. But that awful time was now behind them, thank goodness.

Patsy squeezed her sister's hand. 'You've done me good, Rosie. You don't know how much. I feel tons better now . . . about everything.'

'And we'll have a great time when you come to Blackpool,' said Rosie, kissing her sister on the cheek. She could see the nurse hovering in the background, hinting that it was near the end of visiting time. 'Just get well quickly, and don't worry about anything. You know what Mum would say, "It'll all come out in the wash." '

'Yes, of course it will. Thanks for coming, Rosie. See you soon.'

'Yes, see you, kid. And remember what I've said; chin up and don't worry about a thing.'

'No . . . I'll try not to.' Patsy leaned back against the propped up pillows and watched her sister walk confidently from the ward, her cherry red accordion-pleated skirt swinging gently from her hips and her glossy black hair – now long again, in a page-boy style – bobbing round her shoulders. Rosie had done her a power of good, with her commonsense, no-nonsense approach to everything.

Rosie was a great tonic, and Patsy was relieved that her former jealousy of her sister had now vanished completely. Nevertheless, she couldn't help making comparisons. There was Rosie, striding fearlessly towards the future, to a new career and with, no doubt, some brilliant results at the end of her art course. She sighed and reached for the magazines that Rosie had brought her, this week's copies of *Woman* and *Woman's Own*. She had promised that she wouldn't worry and was determined that she wasn't going to do so. She turned to Mary Grant's problem page; that should help her to get her own worries into perspective.

Annie Carter came in the kitchen of 'Pleasant View' beaming. 'Someone to see you, Patsy.'

She looked up from the book she was reading, one of the latest Agatha Christies to which she had treated herself to bring away on holiday, and smiled with pleasure when she saw the familiar figure behind her grandmother. Tall and fairly slim, dressed in a familiar sports jacket and grey flannels he had been wearing when she last saw him, his mid-brown hair tousled as usual, and his grey eyes warm and smiling. How nice of Raymond to come and see her, and so quickly too; she had only arrived earlier that day. She pushed aside the faint flicker of disappointment that it was Raymond and not his twin brother.

Then her heart gave a massive leap and her mouth dropped open in a gasp of surprise as he walked towards her. She uncurled her legs from beneath her and sprang to her feet, the paperback book falling to the hearthrug. 'Ronnie . . . Ronnie!' she cried, going towards him with her arms outstretched. Of course it was Ronnie! Raymond's eyes, though kind and warm, had never been quite so twinkly and smiley, nor his firm jaw quite so pugnacious.

Ronnie put his arms right round her, enveloping her in a bearlike hug. 'Hiya, Ginger,' he said softly, tweaking at one of her auburn curls.

Patsy didn't speak for a moment, resting her cheek against the roughness of his tweed jacket, smelling the faint aroma of after-shave and cigarettes that she remembered so well. It had been a long time, a very long time . . .

Ronnie didn't attempt to kiss her, but just held her closely for a few moments. She leaned back from him, looking up into his face. She had no need to look to see whether or not there was a birthmark above his left eyebrow. This, without any doubt, was Ronnie.

'I think you've lost weight,' she said. 'You look different somehow . . . thinner.'

'All that square bashing in Germany, I daresay,' Ronnie laughed. 'And I've been working hard since I came back an' all. There are any amount of new shops opening in Blackpool and the Fylde, and yours truly seems to be fitting most of 'em. Well, the firm I work for, I should say.'

He stepped back from her now, holding her at arm's

length. 'Never mind about me. What about you? You've been a bit off colour, I hear? Feeling better now, are you?' His grey eyes were full of concern as he regarded her and Patsy, as she looked back at him, felt a warm glow inside her. How could she ever have imagined that she cared for Neil Emmerson? And Raymond, though a very estimable young man, was a pale shadow compared to his twin brother, at least in Patsy's view. She knew at that moment that she loved him, but she also knew that there were a few things to be sorted out.

'Yes, I'm feeling much better now, thanks,' she said. 'I was in hospital for a few days, about three weeks ago. Bad headaches . . . I've had to leave college. You know about that, do you?'

Ronnie nodded, his intense grey eyes never leaving her face. 'I know a little about it . . . I heard you'd been ill. But you'll soon get better in Blackpool, won't you?' He reached out and gently stroked her cheek with the tip of his finger, then down her neck and beneath the collar of her blouse. Patsy shivered with delight at his touch, but she glanced round apprehensively.

'Your gran's made herself scarce,' Ronnie whispered. 'Gone to make us a cup of tea, I expect.' He sat down on the shabby settee, pushing a pile of newspapers to one side. He patted the floral cretonne cushion next to him. 'Come on, sit down. We've a lot of catching up to do.'

'How did you know I was here?' Patsy asked. 'I only came a few hours ago.'

'Aha . . . a little bird told me.'

'Gran?'

'No . . . it was Rosie, as a matter of fact. I met her quite by accident, in Abingdon Street last week. She told me you were coming over very soon. So I rang your gran to see when you were arriving.'

'Gran never said . . . nor Rosie.'

'No, I wanted to surprise you.'

'You certainly did that.'

They looked at one another searchingly for a few seconds, then Ronnie leaned towards her. Patsy thought he was going to kiss her, but he drew back again. Now was not the time, not with Annie Carter coming in from the back kitchen with a laden tray. She put it on a small table to the side of them, then, just as quickly, scuttled out again. Patsy felt confident as they chatted together that there was all the time in the world . . .

Ronnie told her that Raymond was now going steady, it seemed, with a girl from the office. 'A real sobersides, like he is,' he added, laughing.

'That'll be why he hasn't written recently,' Patsy observed. 'You knew I went out with him last year, didn't you, when I was working here?'

Ronnie nodded briefly. 'He said so. But it wasn't important, was it?'

'No . . . no, not at all. He said you had a girlfriend too. Ingrid?'

'Not any more. She was just . . . well, we were "ships that pass in the night" you might say. No more than that.' He put his square brown hand over Patsy's delicate one, squeezing her fingers. 'I'm glad I've found you again, Patsy. I'm sorry we fell out.'

'It was my fault,' she said quickly. 'I was horrid to you.'

'And so was I. But I did write. I did try to make amends. Aunt Florrie said you never got the letter.'

'No, I didn't. Anyway, never mind about that now. It's all water under the bridge, as my gran would say.'

That lady bustled in. 'Now, you two, aren't you going to get some fresh air into your lungs? Patsy's already been down to look at the sea, haven't you, love? Try to keep her away! She's a real sand-grown 'un, is this one.' She smiled fondly at her granddaughter. 'But I'm sure she'd like to go again. Come back for supper later, if you want to. That's if you've no other plans?'

'Yes, thanks, Mrs Carter. We'd like that. Come on Patsy. Let's go, shall we?'

It was as though they had never been apart, Patsy thought, as they leaned companionably against the railings near to North Pier, watching the sun setting in a glory of orange and crimson and gold. That was after they had walked, for miles it had seemed, northwards towards the cliffs at Norbreck and back again, stopping for a coffee at a promenade cafe. Ronnie kissed her several times on the way back to her gran's, but gently, reverently almost displaying little of the former passion he had shown in those heated encounters at his Aunt Florrie's. But Patsy knew that there was plenty of time.

She saw a lot of Ronnie during her stay in Blackpool which amounted to almost three weeks. She insisted, however, that she must be back in Castleburn to celebrate her twentieth birthday on 21 June. She had been away for it last year and Mum always liked to make something of a family occasion of birthdays. Also, there was her job at Mr Fothergill's – he had offered her a full-time post, as she had anticipated – which she felt, in fairness to him, she should start as soon as possible.

She didn't see Ronnie every night. There was Rosie in Blackpool, too, and the two girls spent many happy hours together; at the cinema, drinking coffee in snack bars, or just talking, talking endlessly in Rosie's room at Aunt Ada's.

During the daytime, though, when Rosie was at college and Ronnie was working, Patsy spent much of her time walking in solitude along the limitless stretch of golden sand or, when the tide was in, along the cliffs at Bispham. It was quieter here, away from the hustle and bustle of Central Beach, and Patsy welcomed this time on her own, knowing that it was part of the healing process that was needed to restore her to full strength, both in body and mind. She loved the familiar sounds around her – the gentle splash of the waves, the cry of the wheeling seagulls, and the metallic jangle of the trams as they rattled along the line to Fleetwood – feeling that this seaside place was in her blood, that she was an integral part of it. Her home was in Castleburn now and she had thought that she loved it as much, if not more, than the place where she was born. But there was a sense of homecoming here, in Blackpool, as though this was where she truly belonged. And she was hopeful that some day she might live here again.

Gradually, over the three weeks, Patsy felt that she was getting back to normal. Her headaches had vanished and her mind was clearer than it had been for two years, now that the burden of college and all that it entailed had been lifted. She found that she was looking forward to her job at Mr Fothergill's, if not with ecstatic delight then with resignation and a quiet pleasure. It was with resignation, too, that she thought about the prospect – inevitable, it seemed – of living at home again. Mum certainly was now much less possessive and protective in her dealings with Patsy; they were, in fact, becoming quite good friends.

And, of course, now there was Ronnie. Patsy knew that very soon he would ask her to marry him. She knew that was what she wanted, and what he wanted too. Their frantic, rapturous embraces on the settee at his mother's had left her in no doubt about that. Ronnie's kisses had not remained chaste for very long, not after that first evening. She was somewhat disappointed, therefore, when he gave her her birthday present the night before she was due to go back to Castleburn. The gift-wrapped box was too large to be what she had half-hoped for. Patsy loved presents though, whatever they were, and eagerly she tore off the paper.

She enthused over the elegant bottle of Chanel No. 5 in its distinctive white box. 'Gosh! That's super. I've never had any of this before. Thanks, Ronnie. It must have cost a fortune.'

'Never mind what it cost,' he laughed. 'That's a real Yorkshire remark if ever there was one. The sooner you come and live in Blackpool, the better it'll be.'

A hint, surely, that one day she would? And you certainly didn't give perfume like that to someone you didn't care about an awful lot. Patsy pushed her disappointment firmly to the back of her mind, determined to enjoy their last evening together. They were going to the cinema to see *Genevieve*, now on the rounds again, and then to Auntie Eileen's for supper.

'See you soon, love,' said Ronnie, as he kissed her for the last time on the doorstep of 'Pleasant View'. 'Cheer up – it's not a million miles to Castleburn.' He frowned at her despondent face. 'I'll come over and see you. I'm sure your mother won't mind now, will she?' Patsy shook her head. 'And you'll be coming again before long, won't you?'

'Yes, I expect so,' she said, but not very animatedly. 'Thanks, Ronnie, for my birthday present . . . and for everything.'

'See you, love,' he said cheerily, as she turned her key in the lock. 'Don't forget me, will you?' He blew a kiss and strolled off down the road.

There was no chance of that, Patsy thought as she made her way somewhat dejectedly up the stairs to her attic room. She could never forget Ronnie. She only hoped she wasn't reading too much into his lighthearted remarks. Ronnie had always been such a clown.

'Thanks for looking after our Patsy so well,' Annie Carter had said to Ronnie one evening, as he waited in the kitchen for Patsy to come downstairs. 'You've done the lass a world of good. The roses are back in her cheeks and there's a sparkle in her eyes that certainly wasn't here when she first arrived, poor lamb.'

'You don't need to thank me, Mrs Carter,' he said. 'It's been a pleasure – much more than a pleasure. You must know what Patsy means to me . . . how much I care for her. We fell out, you know, and I tried to forget about her – I thought perhaps she wasn't the right girl for me – but now I've met her again I know that she is. I'm dreading the thought of her going back to Yorkshire. I wish she could stay here for ever.'

'I shouldn't rush things, lad, if I were you,' said Annie. 'Just give the lass a bit of time.' But Ronnie could see that, though Annie's words seemed to be discouraging, her glance was kindly and he felt that the older woman was sympathetic towards him.

'Why is that, Mrs Carter?' he asked. 'D'you think there might be some opposition? Mrs Bradshaw, perhaps? I sensed she wasn't too keen on the idea when I was friendly with Patsy before.'

'No, I don't think you'll have any problems with our Jenny now,' replied Annie. 'She only wants what's right for Patsy, after all the upset the poor girl's had. And I happen to think you're right for Patsy. But what I mean is . . . I don't want her to rush into anything before she's sure. Tell me to mind my own business, if you like. I know I'm an interfering old so-and-so.' Annie chuckled.

'I always have been. But our Patsy's vulnerable at the moment. She's had a rough time one way or another and she might cling to you like a life-line if you ask her to marry you right now. I take it that's what you have in mind?'

'Yes, of course,' said Ronnie quietly. 'I want to marry Patsy.'

'Well, if you'll take my advice you'll leave it, just a little while. I know she's fond of you. I'm sure she thinks she's in love with you. She probably is. But Patsy needs time to "find herself". Those were Rosie's words, and I think they're very true. She needs time to find out just what it is she wants from life – by herself – and she needs a bit of space around her. D'you see what I mean?'

'Yes, I think I do,' said Ronnie. 'I know we're only young, too. Patsy's not twenty till next week, is she? And I'll be twenty-one in September. I'd have to ask her mother and father anyway.'

'I'm sure Tom won't object, when it's the right time,' said Annie, 'nor Jenny either, now. And age has very little to do with it. Our Jenny was married when she was nineteen. But Patsy . . . like I say, she needs time to sort herself out.'

Ronnie nodded. 'Yes, it makes sense. I suppose I'm just scared I'll lose her when she goes back to Yorkshire, that she'll forget about me.'

'She'll not do that,' said Annie confidently. 'And if she did, well, it 'ud prove it wasn't right, wouldn't it? But I'm sure it is. Don't worry, lad. Just give her time.'

Which was why Ronnie didn't propose to Patsy, as he intended doing, before she returned to Castleburn. But he could sense her disappointment and that was a very good sign. He was quietly confident that, one day, when he asked her to marry him, Patsy would say yes.

Chapter 24

One of the highlights of Patsy's visit to Blackpool, apart from her reunion with Ronnie, had been her meeting with Rosie's real father, Archie Thoroughgood. She had felt some trepidation at the encounter, partly because she always felt nervous at meeting new people and partly because it was such an odd state of affairs, this long-lost father turning up – or, more correctly, having been turned up – after so many years. But she need not have feared. Archie was every bit as friendly and welcoming as Rosie had said he would be, and she discovered that what Rosie had said about him, that he was not at all like a father, was true as well. Rosie and Archie, despite the great difference in their ages, were more like very good pals.

Patsy could see that this relationship was entirely different from the one that Rosie had with Tom; there would be no danger of this man supplanting him in Rosie's affections. Patsy was surprised at how dispassionately she could view these family relationships now. At one time, she recalled, she had been envious of Rosie's easy friendship with her father. Now all jealousy was a thing of the past and she realised that Tom loved all his children, but in different ways because she and Rosie and Victor were all different personalities.

It was the Wednesday afternoon of Patsy's second week in Blackpool when she went with Rosie to the antique shop in Bispham to meet Archie.

'Don't expect it to be like Mr Fothergill's,' Rosie had told her. 'It's more of a junkshop really, mainly a second-hand bookshop and lending library, but Archie does all right with it. He certainly doesn't seem to go short of anything.'

Junkshop was the right word, thought Patsy, as she stared wide-eyed at the confusion and clutter around her. And that was after Rosie had said that she and Archie had had a go at tidying it up! It wasn't dirty, not by any means, just untidy and lacking in organisation, the way Mr Fothergill's had been before Patsy and, later, Jenny had had a hand in sorting it out. But this place was much worse than the antique shop in Castleburn had been.

Patsy's critical eye took in the stacks of books ranged on the shelves and piled up on the floor. Leatherette-bound copies of the classics and major poets, or some of them maybe genuine leather with gold lettering on the spines; book club editions of fairly recent novels with their distinctive paper covers, a different colour for each month; Penguin paperbacks – the orange and white-backed novels and the green and white mystery series; and many books with lurid covers – daring damsels bursting out of their bodices, cowboys in wild pursuit of Indians, and mutilated bodies lying in pools of blood, which had, no doubt, come from across the Atlantic. It was obvious, as Rosie had said, that this was the part of the shop that did the most business.

Patsy's eyes, those of a connoisseur, narrowed as she looked away from the books to the other half, the largely neglected part, of the shop. This was where confusion reigned, although there were some very good pieces of furniture, the patina of which could very easily be restored with loving care and an application of elbow grease as well as polish. There was a Victorian walnut dressing table with a swivel mirror, a couple of ornate Victorian whatnots, also in walnut, and a mahogany washstand with a colourful tiled splashback and marble top. Patsy thought the assortment of bamboo furniture – a small table, a writing desk and another rickety-looking whatnot – quite ghastly, but she found the oak settle with its linenfold decoration very appealing, even though she knew it to be a reproduction piece. Lovingly she ran her hand over the satin smooth, tawny wood. This was one piece that Archie seemed to have kept well polished.

He smiled at her, seeing her obvious interest. 'You have the eye of an expert, my dear, I can see that. Rosie was telling me that you have worked in an antique shop.'

'And I'm going back there soon,' Patsy replied. 'I'm hardly an expert though, Archie. I'm still learning. There's so much to learn, isn't there?' Her enthusiasm showed in her voice and he nodded in agreement.

'Indeed there is. I've been almost a lifetime in the business, one way and another, and I still don't know it all, not by a long chalk. Lately, of course, I've concentrated more on the books and this lot . . .' he waved his hand towards the collection of furniture and odds and ends pushed to one side of the shop, 'this side of the business has tended to be neglected. I don't suppose your place is much like this, is it, Patsy? Not so much of a shambles?'

'No, not much like it,' she agreed. Then, thinking her reply might sound somewhat rude, she went on to clarify her statement. 'I mean . . . we don't sell books, and Mr Fothergill has started stocking a few modern bits and pieces now. It started when my mum persuaded him to order the Coronation souvenirs. Now we've got modern vases and bowls and ash-trays – all that sort of thing – along with the older stuff. It seems to work quite well.'

She had said 'we' quite involuntarily, she noticed to her surprise, as though she was already working there. Well, she would be very soon, she thought resignedly, and perhaps it wouldn't be such a bad thing after all, even if it did mean living at home. She knew Mr Fothergill's shop well and loved it, and this trip to Archie's treasure-house – for that was how she saw it, though some of the treasures here were in need of some restoration – had confirmed in her her desire for old and beautiful objects.

She looked now at the brassware and copper objects – warming pans, toasting forks, horse brasses and candlesticks – displayed, or, more accurately, hidden away in a dark corner, all badly tarnished; at the silver objects, also lack-lustre, crowded into a display cabinet with odd cups and saucers, teapots and jugs. 'You do sell these things though, don't you, Archie, if anyone wants to buy them? You have some lovely pieces here.'

'Yes, of course I do.' He laughed. 'I'm a businessman when all's said and done, though not a very good one I must admit. My heart hasn't been in it the same since Mavis died. She was the one with the flair for selling these things. She used to tell me I was too much of a hoarder to make a fortune. I'm like a squirrel, you see, storing things away. But we didn't do too badly, thanks largely to Mavis. I get fond of things you see, Patsy, and then I don't want to part with 'em. Look at this lot.' He moved across to the oak settle that she had admired and flung back the lid. 'I bet you can't guess at what I've got hidden in here.'

Patsy and Rosie both gasped in astonishment as Archie drew out the hidden treasures, each one of them carefully wrapped in layers of newspaper. Cranberry glassware, millefiori paperweights, Art Nouveau vases and bowls and a few in Art Deco as well, lustreware jugs, Staffordshire figures and flatback ornaments . . . Not every piece, Patsy guessed, was of great value, though some must be 'worth a bob or two' as they said in Yorkshire, but all were beautiful in their own way and each had an intrinsic and aesthetic appeal. Archie stood them on the marble wash-stand and the dressing table as he unwrapped them one by one.

'There . . . lovely, aren't they?' he said, stepping back and admiring his treasures.

'Breathtaking,' said Patsy, almost at a loss for words.

'You're a dark horse, Archie,' said Rosie. 'I knew you had some stuff that you kept hidden, but I'd no idea you had all that lot stashed away.'

'Don't you think you should display it?' said Patsy tentatively. 'I know it's nothing to do with me, but all these things are too lovely never to see the light of day.'

'He's scared someone'll want to buy them, aren't you, Archie?' said Rosie laughing.

'Something like that,' he agreed. 'And there are a lot of memories tied up with those pieces. Mavis and I used to go scouring the markets and junkshops together and she always had an eye for a bargain. And I've not wanted to part with any of it since she died. I take a few pieces upstairs occasionally, into the living room where I can enjoy them. There's only me to see 'em though. At least there was till Rosie came along.' He smiled fondly at his daughter, then at Patsy.

'You're right though, Patsy. These things are too lovely to be hidden away. And I'm going to start right now.' Archie waved his hand expansively towards the array of objects. 'Now, you two, take your pick. I want you each to choose something for yourself. A little present from me. It's your birthday soon, I believe, young lady?' He looked at Patsy. 'And I don't need an excuse to give you a present, do I?' he said, smiling at Rosie. 'Come on now, what would you like?'

Both girls knew that Archie would be offended if they demurred and so they took him at his word. Patsy chose one of the beautiful millefiori paperweights and Rosie, not surprisingly, a more modern piece, a vase painted in primary colours in a bold Art Deco design.

'Good, that's that,' said Archie, rubbing his hands together. 'Now, let's get this hoard out of the way again, then we'll go and make ourselves some tea.'

Archie was thoughtful after the girls had gone. It wasn't just Patsy's rapt expression at the revelation of his treasure-trove or Rosie's incredulity that influenced his thinking. There was something that he had had on his mind for quite some time and today's meeting with those two lovely girls had convinced him that it was high time he did something about it. It was Rosie, of course, his beloved daughter, who was at the forefront of his thoughts as she had been since he had met her so miraculously nine months ago. But there was Patsy, too. He could see that she was a grand girl and so enraptured by beautiful objects; her enthusiasm positively glowed from her.

It was a few days later that he went to the surgery.

'How much longer do I have?' Archie looked uncompromisingly at the doctor at the other side of the desk. 'I want you to tell me, honestly. No beating about the bush.'

Dr Pearson looked back at his patient, his glance steady but kindly. He gave a tight smile. 'Hmmm . . . I know there's no point in trying to pull the wool over your eyes, is there, Archie?'

'None at all.'

'Well, to be quite honest, you've surprised me. I wouldn't have given much for your chances when you came out of hospital, and that's . . . what? Fifteen months or so ago?'

'Yes, thereabouts. A year last March it was.'

'Yes. Of course we didn't say much to you at the time. We didn't tell you . . .'

'No, you lot never do, do you?' said Archie grimly. 'But we always know, by what you don't say rather than by what you do.'

'Quite.' Dr Pearson nodded. 'And you go for your check-ups to the hospital, once a month now, isn't it? And they seem satisfied with you. You're as well as can be expected, better in fact. As I was saying, you've surprised me. It seems as though something has given you a new lease of life.'

'And I don't have to look very far to know what that is, Doctor. It's that daughter of mine, Rosie. I told you about her turning up out of the blue, didn't I? It was like a miracle. She gave me something to go on living for . . . but I know I won't live for ever. I was asking you, Doctor . . . how long?'

Dr Pearson hesitated. Then, 'A year,' he said. 'Possibly longer. That is if you do what I've been urging you to do and retire. You should have given up the shop long ago, of course. Yes, yes . . . I know it's given you an interest, but I think the time has come now.'

'I couldn't agree more,' said Archie. 'That's one of the things I came to tell you. I've decided to leave the shop. I've had my eye on a little bungalow, just off Red Bank Road. In fact I've made an offer for it and the agent's negotiating for me now. That's why I wanted to know.' He looked keenly at the doctor.

'This . . . condition of yours,' said Dr Pearson. He made

a steeple with his fingers. 'At the moment it seems to be . . . in abeyance, one might say. Static. You're taking the tablets, aren't you?'

'Yes, regularly.'

'Good, good. They seem to be doing the trick. But the surgeon has done all he can. You know that, don't you?'

Archie nodded.

'Well then, if you're sensible there's no reason why you shouldn't have . . . a little while longer, I can't say more than that. I take it you'll be living alone in this bungalow? That's all very well, provided there's someone to see to you now and again, to do the heavy cleaning and all that. You mustn't go over-exerting yourself, dragging furniture around or scrubbing floors. You've got to take it easy, Archie, much as it may go against the grain. And it's hard work moving house, settling in. Have you thought about that?'

'I've thought about it all,' Archie said, 'and, believe me, it couldn't be better. I've a woman who cleans for me at the shop – she's worth her weight in gold – and I know she'll continue to come in and "do" for me at the bungalow. It's only a stone's throw away from where she lives. And there's my daughter, Rosie.' Archie's eyes grew misty for a moment. 'I always see her on a Wednesday afternoon – half-day closing at the shop, you see – and I expect I'll carry on doing so when I move. She's got a job at a shop herself, you know. She's going to be one of the chief window dressers at Hill's. She's just finishing at art school.' Archie couldn't keep the pride out of his voice. 'So I shan't be lonely, I've no fear of that.

'And the bungalow's almost ready to move into. The couple who are moving out have left it in pretty good shape. Nicely decorated, and they're leaving the carpets and curtains, so there's not much for me to do. Only hire a removal van and get my furniture moved, and I've plenty of that.' Archie grinned.

'So it's all signed and sealed?'

'Should be in a couple of weeks, all being well.'

'You're a sensible man, Archie, and a brave one too. You'll just have to take a day at a time.'

'I know that's all I can do, Doctor.'

'Take a day at a time, and who knows? You may well amaze us all. We doctors are not infallible, and you have made a remarkable come-back already.'

'I'm grateful for whatever time I've got left,' Archie said simply. 'Now.' He leaned forward. 'Let me tell you what I intend to do about the shop . . .'

Rosie stepped back to admire the partially dressed window, knowing that she would get a better impression of it if she stepped outside into Bank Hey Street, to mingle with the shoppers and see it through their eyes. But she didn't think that would be quite the thing to do. She would have to rely on her judgment which she knew to be good, and when she went home at teatime she would be able to view the finished effect critically and, if necessary, make the final adjustments the next day.

This was her first big project for Hill's and she was determined that it was going to be stupendous. She had planned an all-American scene for one of the large windows, displaying the casual clothes that were being worn now on this side of the Atlantic as well. Square dancing for instance was now all the rage and had been since the time when the Queen – then Princess Elizabeth – had danced her way, three years ago, into the hearts of the North Americans, wearing a circular felt skirt. Rosie had begged some gigantic posters from a nearby travel agent's depicting the New York skyscrapers, the Rocky

Mountains, and one with nothing but a vast expanse of desert and a single cactus. These were pinned at the rear of the window, a background to the eye-catching clothes which would be the focal point of the display. That, Rosie knew, was the whole idea. The clothes, surrounded by all the trappings, had to say, quite simply, 'Come in and buy me.'

Simplicity and economy, she felt, were the essentials in good window dressing. Many stores filled their windows with too much clutter so that the shopper became confused. Rosie had chosen a full circular skirt with a stunning design of geometric shapes in vivid blues, greens and yellows, to be worn with a simple short-sleeved white blouse in the new Terylene fabric, finished off with a three-inch-wide blue belt. The other model was wearing a blue and white checked gingham dress, again with an incredibly wide skirt, held in position with two 'can-can' petticoats, the pale blue frills of nylon net peeping alluringly from below the skirt.

Now for the male attire, to be displayed at the other side of the window. Rosie picked up the fawn Dacron slacks and the gaily printed shirt – blue, to match the female clothes, with a bold design of moons and stars – and gently fingered the material. It had a half-silky, half-cottony feel to it; these new polyester fibres, often referred to as 'drip-dry', were such a boon to the busy housewife, she thought, and to bachelor fellows living alone.

It was at that moment that she became aware that someone was looking at her keenly from outside the window. She could just see the still figure at the periphery of her vision. She turned sharply and then raised her hand in greeting as she recognised David Whorton, the tutor she had been friendly with, briefly, in Switzerland. She beckoned to him to come inside the store and stepped out of the window, very conscious of her untidy hair and workaday attire. The loose-fitting smock, baggy cotton trousers and felt carpet slippers did nothing, Rosie knew, to enhance her appearance, but they were essential gear for a window dresser. Short skirts and tight blouses might give window gazers a view of something they weren't supposed to see when she was grovelling on all-fours, and fashionable shoes would be hard on the feet for all the standing she was forced to do. Anyway, she was a working girl now and Dave would have to take her as he found her.

'Hi there, Rosie.' His greeting was cheerful and when he smiled at her, creasing the laughter lines round his blue eyes, she thought again how much he reminded her of Archie. 'Someone told me you were working here, but even so, it was a surprise to see you slap bang in the middle of the window. Enjoying it, are you?'

'Yes, it's great, Dave. It's only my first week and this is my first big project on my own, but I'm sure it's going to be fantastic. I love it.'

'Good . . . good.' He looked at her steadily, not speaking for several seconds. 'It was only after college had finished . . . after you had left that I . . . What I'm trying to say, Rosie, is this. I asked you once if you would go out with me. For reasons of your own you said no. But now . . . well, I'm asking you again. Would you, Rosie? Would you come out with me?'

She smiled. 'Of course I will, Dave. I'd love to.' She raised her eyebrows. 'Where? When?'

'Tomorrow, perhaps? Is that too soon?'

'No, that's fine.'

'Now, let me see, where is it you live? Somewhere near Raikes Parade, isn't it? I know it isn't all that far from college.' She told him her address at Aunt Ada's. 'That's great. Shall I call for you then, about 7.30, and we'll take it from there?'

'Best bib and tucker, Dave?'

'No, nothing too elaborate. I thought we might have a drive into the country – Great Eccleston or Churchtown perhaps – and have a quiet drink and some supper. OK?'

'Very much so,' said Rosie. 'I shall look forward to it. Now, I really must get back to work.'

'Of course you must. The window's looking superb already. I can see Rosie Bradshaw's inimitable touch.'

'That's just what I like to hear.' Rosie laughed. 'See you tomorrow, Dave.'

That was the first surprising event in an amazing fortnight. It was during the next week, on their usual Wednesday afternoon together, that Archie told her the news that rendered her speechless, something that didn't often happen to the garrulous Rosie. It was only for a few moments, but she was, nevertheless, dumbstruck at first.

'But how . . . why . . . you can't!' she gasped.

'I jolly well can, you know, and I'm going to,' said Archie, nodding determinedly. 'I'm making all this lot over to you – the flat and the shop and all the contents. I own it, you know, it's not rented, and it's all in the solicitor's hands. All it needs now is your signature.'

'I'm overwhelmed . . . I can't believe it.' Rosie shook her head incredulously. 'To say thank you just isn't enough, not for all this. You shouldn't, Archie. You really shouldn't. You've only known me a little while. Not nearly long enough . . .'

'Quite long enough to know you very well, my dear,' said Archie, 'and to know that this is the way I want it, the way it's got to be.'

Rosie knew that he was resolute once he had made up his mind to something, as she herself was, but there were still so many queries; it was all so incredible.

'You say you're moving into a bungalow?' said Rosie.

'But . . . but can you afford to . . . I mean, without selling the shop? I know that sounds terribly nosey, but . . .'

'Yes, I can well afford it.' Archie smiled gently. 'I've told you more than once what a good businesswoman my Mavis was, and we didn't have any family or close relations, either of us. Not till now. So who else would I leave it to? Besides, there's something I think you should know, Rosie love.'

Her elation turned to sorrow, but again touched with disbelief, as Archie told her that he believed he hadn't long to live, that his condition was incurable.

'But . . . it can't be!' she cried. 'I know you'd been ill, before you met me, but you've looked so much better recently. It can't be so. Doctors aren't always right, you know.' She looked firmly at Archie, her chin tilted aggressively. 'Prove them wrong, Archie. Let them see you're not going to be beaten.'

He gave a quiet laugh though his blue eyes held a trace of sadness. 'I intend to have a damn' good try, don't you worry. Now . . . about this business. I know the shop isn't much in your line, and you've got your job at Hill's, haven't you? But I thought you might like to live in the flat – have a place of your own – and I'll tell you what ideas I had about the shop. Of course, it's entirely up to you. It'll be your business . . .'

Rosie listened in growing wonderment and approval as Archie talked.

'That's a marvellous idea,' she said when he paused. 'It would be up to Patsy though, we can't decide for her. But I'm sure she'd be thrilled at the idea. And there's plenty of room in the flat for both of us if she wanted to . . . Oh, Archie, you are a wonderful man.' Rosie got up from the settee and walked across the room to where he was sitting. She put her hands on his shoulders and, leaning forward, placed a kiss on his cheek. 'I can't believe this is all happening, and I'm sure Patsy won't be able to believe it either. It'll be like a dream come true for her.' But Rosie couldn't help noticing, with a stab of fear, that Archie's shoulders felt very bony and she knew that, though he looked in the best of health, he might possibly be losing weight. She gave an inward shudder as she sat down again.

'We'd better not jump the gun,' said Archie. 'Like you say, we can't make up Patsy's mind for her, but it was seeing the way she looked at those treasures of mine – enchanted with 'em, she was – that started me thinking. How you decide to sort it out would be up to you. Whether she would go into partnership, or be a manager for you . . .'

'I'll ring her up tonight,' said Rosie, 'and see if she can come over to Blackpool when she finishes work on Saturday. I'll tell her I've some news that's too important to discuss over the phone, or to write to her. I've got to see her. But I'm sure she'll be over the moon at the idea.'

Patsy stared in disbelief at Rosie, just as Rosie, a few days earlier, had stared disbelievingly at Archie. 'He's giving you the flat . . . and the shop . . . and you want me to run it? To manage it for you? But that's incredible, Rosie. I can't take it in. It's what I've always dreamed of, a shop of my own, but I never thought it would happen, at least not for years and years.'

'It'll be hard work though, kid. You've seen the state it's in. It's awfully run down and you might not want to bother with all those books. I didn't say all this to Archie, of course. It would have looked as though I was throwing it all back in his face, but you know what it's like.'

'Archie knows too, doesn't he?' said Patsy. 'He's the first to admit the place is a shambles, but there's potential there, Rosie. All those lovely pieces he had stored away, and there was some beautiful furniture at the back of the shop. And you say it's all to be yours?'

'Yes, apart from the stuff he needs to furnish his bungalow, mostly the things from upstairs. So we'll have to furnish our own flat, kid, that's if you'd like to come and live there with me?'

'You bet!' said Patsy. 'You've been OK here though, haven't you?' She glanced round Rosie's bedroom at Aunt Ada's, converted into more of a bed-sitting room, the way it had been in South Kensington. 'But it'll be nice to have your very own place – our own place, I should say. Won't it be great? But I'll have to pay you rent. It's your property.'

'Of course you won't! Not if you're managing the shop. I'd really like you to be a partner with me, Patsy.' Rosie frowned. 'Oh dear! I'm not really a businesswoman at all, there are all sorts of things I don't know about, but I'm sure we can get a solicitor or someone to sort it all out for us. That's if you're willing to give it a try?'

'Yes,' said Patsy, but she frowned too and bit her lip. 'I don't know though . . . I can't help thinking . . .'

'You're not absolutely sure? No, I can't say I blame you. It is a big undertaking and I know I've rushed you into it all. You know what I'm like. Sleep on it, Patsy, see how you feel in a day or two.'

'No, it isn't that,' she said. 'I am sure, very sure, that it's what I'd like to do. It would be a wonderful challenge. But it's you I'm thinking of, Rosie. It doesn't seem fair. It's your business – Archie's giving it to you, not me – even if we manage to come to some arrangement, and it seems as though you wouldn't be having any part in it.'

'I'd be living there, over the shop. And you know that antiques aren't really my line. I can see that they're beautiful, but they don't attract me particularly like they do you. I've never cared all that much for ancient things. You know me – I'm all for modern stuff.'

'Mmm . . . ancient and modern,' said Patsy thoughtfully.

'Anyway, I've got my job at Hill's, haven't I?' said Rosie. 'I'm determined to make a go of that. Then there are my designs that Campion's mill have taken.'

'Oh, yes – how are you going on with that?' asked Patsy.

'They've bought two designs to begin with,' said Rosie. 'The sunflower and the rose. They're going to have each of them printed in two colourways. My sunflower design was predominantly yellow, of course, but they're going to try a mainly orange pattern, too. And my red and pink roses are going to be printed in blue and purple as well.'

'Blue and purple roses?' said Patsy, grimacing. 'It sounds weird.'

'I know it does,' agreed Rosie, 'but it'll be stunning, believe me. The sample swatches should be ready soon for me to see. I can't wait!'

'It really thrills you, all this modern design, doesn't it?' said Patsy. 'Just like antiques thrill me. Like Gran says, it takes all sorts to make a world.'

'It's a good job we're not all alike,' replied Rosie, quoting another of Annie Carter's favourite sayings, and they both laughed.

Patsy fell silent, her forehead creased in a frown and her eyes staring unfocusedly across the room. 'Hey, you've gone into a brown study again,' said Rosie, waving a hand in front of her eyes. 'Come on, out with it. There's something bothering you, isn't there?'

Patsy nodded. 'I was thinking about what you were saying, that I'm all for the old things while you're all for the new. Listen, Rosie . . . it's just a vague idea I've got, but couldn't you have some part in the business as well, with your floral fabrics? Couldn't you sell some of them in the shop?'

'I don't see how,' said Rosie. 'It's only material and it's very modern. I don't see how you can sell material in an antique shop, especially with designs like mine on it. It's going from one extreme to the other.'

'And why not?' said Patsy, her brown eyes dancing excitedly. 'Why not have the two extremes? Rosie . . . just think about it. What will your material be made into eventually? Curtains, cushions?'

'Yes, that sort of thing,' agreed Rosie. 'They're furnishing fabrics. Possibly bedspreads as well, if people want exotic designs like that in their bedrooms.'

'Then why couldn't you have some of the material made into curtains?' said Patsy. 'And cushions and bedspreads, and we could sell them in the shop along with the furniture and china and everything? Oh Rosie, it would be fantastic!'

'Do you really think so?' she said slowly. 'Do you think it would work, mixing old and new?'

'Of course it would,' said Patsy eagerly. 'Old and new, ancient and modern. There, we've got a name for the shop already: Ancient and Modern.'

'Ancient and Modern?' Rosie's mouth turned down in a grimace. 'It sounds like a hymn book.'

Patsy laughed. 'Yes, I suppose it does. You're right. We want something like that, though. Old and new . . .' She frowned slightly. 'Let's think. I know. What about "Something Old, Something New"? How d'you like that?'

'That's great, kid,' said Rosie. She repeated the name thoughtfully. 'Something Old, Something New . . . Yes, it definitely has a ring to it. And it might just work, combining the antiques and the modern stuff.'

'Of course it will,' said Patsy again. Rosie thought that

it was a long time since she had seen her sister so animated, so bubbling over with enthusiasm. She was positively sparkling. 'It works at Mr Fothergill's, on a smaller scale though. People come in to buy an antique and they start looking at the modern pieces, or sometimes it happens the other way round. One complements the other, and I'm sure it would do so even more with furnishing fabrics. We could have curtains draped behind all that lovely furniture.' Patsy waved her hands in the air. 'That oak settle or the mahogany bookcase . . . all they need is a bit of spit and polish, and with your material showing them off . . .'

'Hold on, hold on.' Rosie laughed. 'Let's calm down a bit. We're trying to run before we can walk. The material's not even ready yet and the shop's certainly not suitable for what you have in mind. The way it is at the moment, you can hardly swing a cat round in it.'

'It could be extended though. If it was knocked through into that store room at the back there'd be bags of room. And I know a shopfitter, don't I?' Patsy's eyes shone with delight.

'Ronnie Sykes.'

'Who else?'

'And I think we know someone who would do some sewing for us,' said Rosie thoughtfully. 'Someone who's a dab hand at making curtains and cushions.'

'Mum?'

'Yes . . . Mum. The only problem is that she's in Castleburn and we'll be here, but I'm sure we could sort something out.'

'You'll be driving soon, won't you?' said Patsy. 'Once you've passed your test it'll all be plain sailing. Aunt Ada doesn't mind you using her car and you could easily nip over to Castleburn with the fabric.'

'Hey, steady on,' said Rosie laughing, putting a brake on her sister's fervour for the second time. All the same it was wonderful to see Patsy's enthusiasm, and to think that only a few weeks ago she had been in the depths of despair, feeling that life wasn't worth living. 'It's if I pass my test,' Rosie went on, crossing her fingers tightly. 'And we haven't even asked Mum yet, let alone the mill. I'd have to negotiate with them about buying some of the material back and having it made into furnishings. They own the copyright now for the designs, you see, because they've bought them off me. And I would want to use my own name on them if I could. Anyway, we'd have to go into it all thoroughly. Isn't it exciting though, Patsy? And what a brilliant idea of yours . . .'

They talked until midnight, agreeing that the first thing that Patsy must do was go home and talk it over with Tom and Jenny. Then she would come over to Blackpool again the following weekend when they could proceed a little further with their planning.

Chapter 25

'My goodness, Patsy. That's a tale and a half you're telling us,' said Tom, grinning, as she came to the end of her long story. It had been quite late on the Sunday evening when she returned home from Blackpool but her parents were still up. She had told them all about the antique shop; how Archie Thoroughgood was making it over to Rosie, and how she, Patsy, was going to manage it; how she was going to live in Blackpool in Rosie's flat; and, finally, that they wanted Jenny to do some sewing for them. 'You've fair taken the wind out of my sails. What do you say, Jenny?' Tom looked across at his wife. 'This lot needs some taking in, doesn't it? It's like one of them magazine stories you're always reading, a young girl inheriting a fortune an' all that.'

'It's not all happy news though, I'm afraid,' said Patsy. She went on to tell her mother and father about Archie's illness and how he might not have long to live.

'Oh dear! That's a bad do, it is that,' said Tom. 'Poor chap. I've never met him but he's been good to our Rosie and she seems fond of him. That's terrible.' He shook his head sadly. 'But at least he won't be ending his days all on his own, not now he's met Rosie. Perhaps it's all been for the best. Things have a way of working out . . .'

'Yes, it seems as though they have,' said Jenny quietly.

'It's amazing sometimes the way they do work out. I think we'd better tell Patsy our news now, hadn't we, Tom?'

'Yes, I reckon we had,' he said. Patsy noticed the way her mother and father exchanged secret smiles. 'Go on, Jenny. You tell her.'

'You say you intend living in Blackpool, Patsy?' asked Jenny. 'At this flat that Rosie's been given?'

'Yes, that's right,' she replied, feeling a momentary qualm. Surely Mum wasn't going to prove difficult about her living away from home again? 'I didn't think you would mind, and I've got to leave home sometime, you know.' Patsy tried not to sound aggressive. She had been getting on so well with her mother recently; it would be a pity to spoil things now. 'And if you're bothered about me giving up my job with Mr Fothergill, I don't think he'll mind. I sometimes think that he's doing me a favour anyway, taking me on full-time.'

'No, it's not that, Patsy. Not at all.' Jenny was smiling warmly. 'Your dad and I are really pleased for you, aren't we, Tom? And we hope this venture at the antique shop works out splendidly for you both, although there'll be a lot of planning to do. And of course I'd be delighted to do some sewing for you. It's just up my street. No . . . what we wanted to tell you was . . . that we're planning to go and live in Blackpool as well. Me and your dad and Victor. So that we can be near your gran and so that it'll be easier for your dad with his wheelchair. We've been thinking about it for some time, and now we've got a list of bungalows that an estate agent's found for us, and we're going over there next week to have a look at them.'

Patsy didn't know whether to feel glad or sorry. Indeed, she didn't know what to make of it at all. It almost seemed as though her parents were following her to Blackpool, unable, as ever, to leave her alone, but it couldn't be so, could it? They had already planned this before they knew about Rosie's news. 'You didn't say anything,' she said now, looking and sounding bewildered. 'I'd no idea you were thinking of moving from here.'

'We didn't quite know how to tell you, dear,' said her mother. 'You seemed so nicely settled at Mr Fothergill's again and we didn't know whether you'd like the idea of moving. We would have told you, of course. We were going to tell you tonight and then you got in first with your own news. Isn't it amazing, all of us deciding at the same time to go and live over there?'

'Yes . . . amazing,' repeated Patsy, dazedly.

'You don't sound all that thrilled at the idea,' said Tom.

'I am, Dad. Of course I am,' she replied. 'I'm just surprised, that's all. It's all happened so suddenly.'

'Don't worry, love,' said Tom, with just the hint of a wink at his daughter. 'We won't go interfering with what you and Rosie are doing, if that's what you're thinking. You'll have your place and we'll have ours, and that's the way it should be. If your mum wants to do a bit of sewing for you then I think that's a grand idea, but we'll all have our independence, don't worry about that.'

'I wasn't doing, Dad,' said Patsy. She decided she was being silly. Of course they weren't following her around; it was just a coincidence. Besides, she and Rosie, in their new venture, would need all the help they could get. She told them so now. 'In fact we'd be glad of your advice, Rosie and me. It's a big undertaking, I realise that. I know you won't be able to do as much, Dad, not now . . .' Patsy stopped speaking, knowing that Tom didn't like to be reminded of his disability.

But he didn't seem to be affronted. 'I can supervise, can't I?' he said. 'I can be the gaffer. I'm good at that.'

'As a matter of fact, we were thinking of getting Ronnie

Sykes's firm in to do the shopfitting,' said Patsy.

'What a splendid idea,' said Jenny, to Patsy's astonishment. Her mother certainly had changed her tune! 'But where's the money coming from? Have you thought of that? Archie's given Rosie the shop, but you can't expect him to pay for alterations as well.'

'No, we're not . . . I daresay we could get a bank loan,' said Patsy airily. Good gracious! There was so much she hadn't even considered. She was beginning to realise that she and Rosie would, indeed, need some help and guidance. 'We could, couldn't we?' she said, looking doubtfully at her parents. 'We'd be able to get a loan, wouldn't we?'

Jenny shook her head, but she was still smiling. 'Never mind about loans, Patsy,' she said. 'Your dad and I are not short of a bit of brass. Are we, Tom? We'll be only too willing to help you to get started. And if I'm going to be sewing for you, then I think we should be considering some sort of partnership anyway. We'll have to get a solicitor to sort out the details. Let's take a step at a time, shall we? But I'm so pleased you've found something you really want to do. It's fate, that's what it is. It's fate, the way things have worked out so well.'

And looking at Jenny's radiant face and satisfied smile, Patsy had to agree. Her dad's accident, college, Ronnie Sykes, Rosie, Archie . . . At one time they had all seemed to be separate parts of a great big muddle. Now, like a jigsaw puzzle, they were all coming together. There was one person they hadn't mentioned though.

'What about our Victor?' said Patsy now. 'What does he think about moving to Blackpool?'

'He doesn't know yet,' Jenny admitted. 'We're going to tell him tomorrow. And remember we haven't actually found a bungalow yet . . .'

'But we will,' said Tom confidently. 'I know we will. And don't worry about Victor. There's a good Grammar

School in Blackpool. And – more important – there's a good football team too! Victor'll be tickled pink to be able to watch Stanley Matthews nearly every week.'

'Here, what do you think of that?' Rosie pushed a small piece of paper towards Patsy. On it was a modernistic design of a red rose and the words in simple black letters, 'A Rosie White design'.

'I think it's great,' said Patsy. 'Rosie White though?' She looked questioningly at her sister. 'Why White?'

'I think it has a better ring to it than Bradshaw,' said Rosie, 'and it fits in with the design – you know, a red rose on a white background.'

Patsy put her head on one side and pursed her lips. 'Yes . . . I think you're right. And I'm sure Mum won't be offended. She might have been at one time, but she's been great lately. She and Dad both have. They're really keen about this venture of ours. What about Campion's mill, though? Have they agreed to let you use your own name?'

'Yes, it's OK so long as I use their name as well. It'll be on the selvedge of the material, but that won't show once it's made up. So I shall include "fabric by Campion" or something like that. And they say I can buy as much as I like from them at cost, so there's no problem there. And – wait for it! – this is the material.'

Like a conjuror pulling a rabbit from a hat Rosie produced from a bag at her side four short lengths of fabric; her sunflower design printed in bright shades of both yellow and orange and her rose design in pink and red and in blue and purple.

'Oh . . .' Patsy gazed in admiration. 'They're wonderful. And to think that you've actually designed these. You must be thrilled to bits, Rosie. When will the material be ready for sale?'

'In a few weeks, some time in August. In plenty of time

for us to have everything ready for the grand opening.'

Patsy was again spending the weekend in Blackpool. She had dashed over as soon as she had finished work at the antique shop on Saturday and would have to return home late on the Sunday, but she thought it was worth all the time and trouble involved. There was so much for the two of them to discuss. Besides – an added bonus – she would be able to see Ronnie as well.

By the time they rolled into bed after 1 am Patsy and Rosie had made many important decisions. The shop in Bispham village was to open on Monday 20 September, just before Rosie's twenty-first birthday. The shop was closed now and Archie was to move into his little bungalow the following Wednesday. Rosie was to help him with the removal on her half-day and also to organise the clearing of the shop so that the firm of shopfitters – Ronnie's firm – could move in as soon as they were able. The stuff from the shop was to be stored upstairs for the moment until such time as it could be sorted out.

'Phew! That'll be some job, I can tell you,' Rosie remarked. 'D'you think we'll be able to manage, kid, especially with you in Castleburn and me over here? Sometimes I wonder whatever we're taking on . . .'

'Don't worry,' said Patsy. 'We'll manage.' It was unusual for her to be the one who was calmly confident whilst her sister was getting in rather a flap, but that was the way Patsy felt. She was convinced that their enterprise was going to work out; not only that, it was going to be a tremendous success. 'I'm not going to leave all the donkey work to you,' she assured her sister. 'I'm finishing at Mr Fothergill's in a few weeks' time. He knows all about it and he's really thrilled for us. So I shall move to Blackpool then, and by that time Mum and Dad and Victor might be settled here as well.'

It hadn't taken Tom and Jenny long to find the bungalow they wanted, a well-maintained property near to the bowling green at Layton.

'Just the job,' Tom had said. 'Near the library, and I'll be able to go and watch the bowling matches. And it's near enough to Bispham an' all, where you and Rosie'll be. And to North Shore where your gran is. Couldn't be better.'

'It's fate, that's what it is, it's fate,' Jenny had said for the umpteenth time. 'I would never have believed that things could work out so well. The only thing we have to do now is sell this place.' But they already had a prospective buyer, a friend of a friend, so it seemed as though all was going smoothly at that end as well.

Rosie had decided to keep on with her window dressing job for the time being. She loved the work and felt that it would be unfair to the store to terminate her employment so soon. Besides, the money was important and they knew they would need every penny they could lay their hands on. Archie's original generosity had been overwhelming and Tom and Jenny had offered to pay for the shopfitting; all the same, it was a colossal undertaking for the two young women. Patsy was to manage the shop on her own at first, with Jenny coming in to lend a hand occasionally, while Rosie, with her natural flair for it and all the experience she was gaining at Hill's, would be in charge of the window dressing. Then, if the business came up to their hopes and expectations, Rosie would come and work there as well. As yet it was all still in the planning stage, but it was a stage they were both enjoying tremendously.

Patsy held up the rose-printed fabric, looking at it reflectively. 'This would look fabulous behind a display of cranberry glassware,' she said. 'The pinks and reds would set one another off perfectly.'

'Or what about this with some highly polished copper and brass?' said Rosie, picking up the orange sunflower material. 'With that oak settle you like so much, Patsy, in the centre. I can just see it . . .' She closed one eye thoughtfully. 'Now, what do you think of this idea . . . ?'

'I just can't believe you're coming to live in Blackpool again,' said Ronnie the next evening as they strolled hand in hand along the lower promenade. 'And so soon too. And the manageress of a shop as well . . . My goodness, I am keeping exalted company, aren't I? You won't be speaking to an ordinary bloke such as me before long.'

Patsy laughed. 'I think you know me a bit better than that, Ronnie. I shan't let it go to my head. And never mind the shop. You know what the best thing is about me coming to live here, don't you?' She gave him a sidelong glance. 'At least, I think it is.'

'Of course I do.' Ronnie stopped near to the sea wall and drew her into his arms. 'We can be together, Patsy, can't we?'

She nodded. 'Yes, we can be together.'

'For ever and ever . . .' said Ronnie.

He stooped to kiss her and she responded eagerly. There were holiday makers passing by, but Patsy and Ronnie were oblivious to them. Courting couples were often to be seen on this stretch of promenade and very little heed was paid to them. They leaned against the wall of grey concrete, their arms around each other. 'I was only teasing about the shop,' said Ronnie. 'I'm real glad for you and I know it'll be a terrific success. It's bound to be.'

'A lot of it depends on you,' said Patsy. 'We're relying on your firm, you know, to get in there as soon as you can. And to obey our instructions to the letter,' she added with mock severity.

'Yes, Ma'am,' said Ronnie, touching his forehead. 'We should be starting the week after next. That'll give us plenty of time, won't it? When are you thinking of opening?'

'September the twentieth,' said Patsy. 'Just before Rosie's twenty-first birthday. And it'll be your twenty-first as well, won't it, yours and Raymond's?'

'Yes, on the seventeenth,' Ronnie replied. 'I was wondering if you and I might have a special celebration then, love.' He turned suddenly to look at her. There was a few seconds' silence, then, 'Will you marry me, Patsy?' he said.

She gave a gasp of surprise. The question had been so abrupt, not what she had been expecting at all, not at that moment. 'Of course I will, Ronnie,' she said. 'But . . .'

'We'll get engaged then, shall we, on my twenty-first? I'll ask your mum and dad, make it all correct and above board. I could perhaps come over to Castleburn soon, eh? Your mother doesn't object to me now, does she?'

Patsy smiled. 'No, my mother doesn't object to you. But . . .' She noticed Ronnie's look of consternation and went on hurriedly: 'Yes, of course I'll marry you, Ronnie. I love you, you know that.' She took hold of his hand, idly playing with the brown, square-tipped fingers. 'I'd love to get engaged on your birthday. But – I hope you understand this, darling – I don't want to get married just yet. Give me time, Ronnie. I shall need time – to make a go of the shop, to get used to looking after myself, cooking and all that.' She laughed. 'I guess I'll have to do most of it. Rosie's not much good in the kitchen. I'll need time to adjust . . . be myself. Do you understand?'

Ronnie was silent for a moment, then he gave a smile of acquiescence. 'Yes, of course I understand, Patsy,' he said slowly. 'Just tell me again that you love me. That's all I want to know.'

'I love you, Ronnie.'

'And I love you, darling. So very, very much.'

As he kissed her again he thought of Annie Carter's words, that Patsy needed time to find herself. 'Don't rush her,' Annie had said. 'Give her time.' Ronnie had felt that he couldn't possibly go on waiting any longer; he loved Patsy so much and wanted to make sure of her. But he also knew that Patsy's words, 'not just yet', were possibly the biggest breakthrough she had made in finding herself. Patsy had to make a success of life on her own at first. She had already, poor girl, experienced failure and a false start in something that was entirely wrong for her. She was on the right road now and the best way Ronnie could help her, he knew, was by holding back until such time as she was ready to share her life with him. As he was confident that she would be, before very long. They were getting engaged, and that was the first step.

'Come on, love,' he said. 'We'd better be going back to pick up your bag from your gran's, then I'll see you to the station. These partings are hell, aren't they?'

'It won't be for long, darling,' Patsy replied happily. 'Only a few more weeks and I'll be here for good. Oh, Ronnie, I can't tell you how much I'm looking forward to it all.'

A much more confident Patsy, thought Ronnie, than the girl he had known in Leeford. She sounded as though she knew exactly where she was going and, what was more, that she was determined to get there.

The party that was held in Rosie and Patsy's flat on Thursday 23 September was to celebrate not only Rosie's twenty-first birthday but the launching of the shop, Something Old, Something New, which had opened its doors for the first time on Monday. It had caused more than a few curious glances before that though, as the shopfitters moved in and then as the two young women busied themselves making the window and the interior more eye-catching than they had been for years.

Above the door, in gilt lettering, was the newly painted sign, Something Old, Something New, and below it, in smaller letters, P. and R. Bradshaw. The window was a blaze of yellow and orange, tempered by the glowing wood of the furniture, its patina carefully restored with loving care. In the centre was Patsy's favourite oak settle with the orange sunflower material draped artistically behind it. On its lid was a row of copper lustre jugs and a bowl filled with orange and yellow marigolds from the garden of Tom and Jenny's new bungalow. To one side was a display of brightly burnished brassware and copper utensils – a huge warming pan, toasting forks, horse brasses, candlesticks, trivets and kettles – and at the other side a mahogany bookcase, the reddish-brown shelves filled with the most pleasing-looking books that the girls could find from the original store, their leather bindings and gilt lettering adding a touch of distinction. Patsy had chosen vases with tones of gold and orange to stand on top, and the acid yellow and ochre of the sunflower material set it all off to perfection.

Inside the shop Rosie's other design was prominent. A rose-patterned counterpane was draped casually over a brass bedstead and Patsy's favourite ruby and cranberry glassware was highlighted by the bold red and pink curtains which hung behind it. The blue and purple roses came into their own when displayed near a collection of willow pattern pottery and other oddments of blue and white, and a couple of blue and purple cushions adorned a bentwood rocking chair and an Edwardian two-seater settee. All told the effect from both inside and outside was pleasing and the girls were more than satisfied with the way things were going so far. There had been a steady trickle of both residents and holiday makers, many of them 'just looking', but others who were genuinely interested and willing to part with their money.

Patsy, as she looked round at their guests, couldn't recall ever feeling quite so happy or so sure of herself. It was not so much a party as a get-together of relations and close friends who meant a lot to her and Rosie and who had come to wish them well. There were Mum and Dad and Victor – there had been a lot of willing hands to assist Tom up the stairs to the flat – Aunt Ada and Uncle Fred, and Gran, who had insisted, as might be expected, on doing the catering. Those were all the relations, apart from Archie Thoroughgood who, Patsy was pleased to see, seemed to be getting on well with everyone. Then there were all the Sykes family, not only Ronnie but his two brothers and his mother and father as well, for an unexpected pleasure to everyone had been Jenny's decision to renew her friendship with Eileen Sykes. Kath Merriman was unable to be there, to Patsy's disappointment, because she was teaching in Leeford, but Hilary Schofield, Patsy's college daughter, who lived in Blackpool, was there. And the only other person was Dave Whorton, Rosie's young man. She had insisted that they were 'just good friends', but Patsy had a feeling from the way they looked at one another that they might soon be very much more.

Patsy hoped that her sister would be happy with him, just as happy as she was with Ronnie. The two of them were engaged now and Patsy was proudly sporting her ring, a cross-over design of a sapphire and two small diamonds. Their celebration, a few days ago, had been a very private one, just the two of them, but meaningful for all that. Patsy had no doubts about how much she loved Ronnie.

Archie, too, looked round contentedly. Yes, he knew he had made the right decision in handing all this over to Rosie, and not before time either, he thought. The niggling pain in his side had been much worse recently and he found that he tired very quickly. He was glad there were no stairs in his new home; it had exhausted him climbing up these steps here tonight, but he had hidden his discomfort well, determined to join in the celebration for Rosie's birthday and to wish the pair of them, Rosie and Patsy, every possible success in their new venture. They had worked wonders already with that shabby old shop of his and he was sure they would go from strength to strength; it was just unfortunate that he wouldn't be there to rejoice with them in their assured success.

But tonight was no time to be indulging in morbid thoughts. He pushed them away and went to mingle with the other guests, all unknown to him before tonight apart from Jenny. He had met her once when she had bobbed into the shop at the same time as he had to see how the work was progressing. A pretty, vivacious woman, he had thought – very much like Rosie, although he knew that didn't really make sense – her natural friendliness tempered somewhat that first time by her initial wariness of him. But Jenny had no such reservations tonight. She greeted him warmly and took him to meet her husband, a much quieter man than his wife with Patsy's colouring and features and with her air of reticence about him. Archie, however, had the knack of drawing people out of themselves. He had done it with Patsy and now he was able to do the same with her father. They were soon chatting like old friends.

'You and I have something in common, haven't we?'

said Tom. 'This lovely girl who's twenty-one today.'

Archie noted Tom's loving, and proprietory, glance at the dark-haired girl at the other side of the room and knew that this daughter of his, whom he had known so briefly, could not possibly have had a better father than she had had in Tom Bradshaw. And he was thankful. 'We have indeed,' he replied. 'You have three lovely children, haven't you, Tom? You're a lucky man.'

'I am that,' he answered. 'And I don't mind sharing one of 'em with you. I'd like you to know that. Now . . . it seems to me that one of us should propose a toast – to Rosie, and to the pair of 'em as well. I'm a diffident sort of chap – don't know as how I could talk in front of all these folk. What about you doing it, Archie?'

'I'd be delighted,' he replied.

So when Annie's sumptuous spread had been demolished, Archie asked everyone to raise their glasses of sherry and drink the health of the two young women. 'Tom has asked me to do this,' he began, 'and very privileged I am to be asked as well. As you may be aware, I haven't known Rosie all that long. I'm sure you all know the story so I'm not going to go into it all again now. Sufficient to say that during the year that I have known her, I have grown very very fond of her. No man anywhere could have a finer daughter, and I know Tom agrees with me there.' Tom nodded, looking somewhat embarrassed, and there were a few murmurs of 'Hear, hear,' and 'Yes, that's true.' 'And during the last few months it has been my very great pleasure to get to know Patsy as well,' Archie went on. 'She's a lovely lass, too. They're grand girls, both of them. And now, ladies and gentlemen, I'd like you to raise your glasses. First, to Rosie. A very happy birthday and many, many more of them.'

'Happy birthday, Rosie,' they all replied.

'And now . . . to Patsy and Rosie and to the continued success of their business.'

'Patsy and Rosie,' they all echoed.

Then the cake was cut. At Rosie's request it had been iced not as a birthday cake but with the words 'Patsy and Rosie, Something Old, Something New' and a design of yellow and orange sunflowers. This was Patsy's day just as much as hers, Rosie had declared.

'Tired, Archie?' she asked a little while later. 'You're looking a bit jaded. Are you feeling all right?'

'Perfectly all right,' he replied, smiling at her, though she could see that his blue eyes were weary and had lost much of their sparkle. 'Tired though, like you say. I think I'd better be making tracks for home.'

'Hang on a minute and I'll take you,' she said. 'Aunt Ada's car's outside and she won't mind.'

Rosie came back in a moment dangling the car keys. She had passed her test a couple of weeks before and now frequently borrowed the vehicle with Fred and Ada's delighted permission. If things went well she might soon be able to afford one of her own.

'Now, are you sure you'll be all right?' she asked as she stopped the car outside Archie's bungalow. 'Shall I come in with you and make a cup of tea?'

'No thanks. I'll be fine, love. Really I will. You get back and see to your guests. Don't worry about me. I'll be . . . fine.'

'OK then, if you're sure.' Rosie hesitated, looking at him in concern. Then she leaned over and kissed his cheek. 'It's been a wonderful evening,' she said. 'Goodnight, Archie. Thanks for everything. And . . . take care.'

'I will, lass. Don't worry. And you take care too. Goodbye, Rosie.'

Archie made a mug of tea and carried it into his

bedroom, a late night indulgence that he enjoyed. It had been a truly wonderful evening, meeting all those lovely friends of Rosie's and Patsy's; it was a pity he had felt so tired all the time, utterly exhausted, in fact. And the pain at one point had been almost more than he could bear. He never went anywhere without his pills though, and they had eased it somewhat. He swallowed two more of them now with his hot drink, then slid down between the sheets. A good night's sleep should see him right.

Archie closed his eyes for the last time.

When Rosie returned to the party, Patsy greeted her. 'Archie enjoyed himself, didn't he? You could see that. And wasn't it great the way he got on with Mum and Dad?'

'Yes, I'm really glad about that,' Rosie replied. 'Those two seem to be getting on famously as well, don't they?' She nodded in the direction of Dave Whorton and Ronnie Sykes who were deep in conversation.

'Yes, Ronnie gets on well with most people,' Patsy replied. 'And Dave's a super bloke, Rosie. D'you like him?'

'Of course I like him, you idiot!'

'No, you know what I mean, really like him? D'you think you might . . . ?'

'Fall in love with him? Yes, I might. There's plenty of time. But – yes – I might,' said Rosie slowly. 'But I've other things to think of at the moment. What about you and Ronnie? I know you're engaged to him, but you are quite sure, aren't you?'

'Oh, yes,' said Patsy confidently. 'I love Ronnie. There's no one else for me but him. But, like you, I've other things to think about just now. I want us to make a success of all this. I want Something Old, Something New to be the best antique shop for miles around.' Patsy's eyes shone with excitement.

'It will be, kid. It will be. There's no doubt about that. Come on, let's go and join the men, shall we?'

Arm in arm, the two girls walked across the room.